TROUBLE IN DOS BAYOU

TROUBLE IN DOS BAYOU

ELVIN C. BELL

iUniverse, Inc.
New York   Bloomington

iUniverse books may be ordered through booksellers or by contacting:

iUniverse
1663 Liberty Drive
Bloomington, IN 47403
www.iuniverse.com
1-800-Authors (1-800-288-4677)

Because of the dynamic nature of the Internet, any Web addresses or links contained in this book may have changed since publication and may no longer be valid. The views expressed in this work are solely those of the author and do not necessarily reflect the views of the publisher, and the publisher hereby disclaims any responsibility for them.

ISBN: 978-1-4401-4586-5 (sc)
ISBN: 978-1-4401-4584-1 (ebook)
ISBN: 978-1-4401-4585-8 (dj)

Library of Congress Control Number: 2009929214

Printed in the United States of America

iUniverse rev. date: 6/15/2009

IN MEMORY

This book is dedicated to my sister, Geneva, and to my brothers, Jimmie and Morley.

Their incredible journey through life took many twists and turns, and they amazed so many by their wit, wink and quick smile. Each had a blessed depth of humor that was deeper and wider than any mother lode.

The brilliant rays of sunshine from their smiles put neon to shame.

If God has a wallet, their pictures are in it.

In remembering them, I am reminded of the words of Franz Kafka:

"No one else could ever be admitted here, since this gate was made only for you. I am now going to shut it."

- - - - - -

This book is also dedicated, in fond memory, to the best friends (and late "in-laws") a guy could ever have; Howard "Pinky" Halstead and Henly "Oggie" Ogburn. They were two of the finest combat pilots the United States had during World War II, Korea and Viet Nam.

Pinky was the luckiest cribbage player I ever met, as well as being one of the luckiest pilots during the WW II Battle of the Bulge. His aircraft was the target for Germany's--and the world's-- first combat launch of a missile; a missile that zoomed past Pinky's cockpit. On his next flight during that historic battle, Pinky was the target for Germany's--and the world's-- introduction of a new aircraft; a jet fighter. The jet's first combat flight in the history of aviation missed gunning down Pinky's plane by mere feet.

Oggie may have been a tad luckier. During his WW II service as a B-17 pilot, Oggie was shot down three times during bombing missions over Germany. Each time he evaded capture, found his way back, and insisted on flying again. He did. He also refused a few Purple Hearts because the injuries, he said "Were too minor to get a hissy fit over."

Oggie was also the luckiest fishing partner I ever had. His favorite spot was about two hundred yards south of the Rocky Bayou Bridge, near his home in Niceville, Florida. We usually had our limit by the time we drained the coffee thermos and ate a box of doughnuts.

Fishing with Oggie, in his flat bottom boat, was a southern delight because each adventure started with a visit to the pastry shop where glazed doughnuts were the house specialty.

-Elvin

We are all here on earth to help others;
what on earth the others are here for,
I don't know.

--W. H. Auden

One of the problems . . .

The 268 disciples of Osama bin Laden gawked in amazement as they walked around the damp, odorous cave illuminated by torches and al-Qaida camera lights. The disciples were boisterous as they gestured and discussed how much wider, higher and deeper the cave was than any they had seen in Afghanistan.

Their host stood on the ledge in front of the cave. As he turned slowly and faced his guests, his hardened face displayed a forced smile that split the chiseled features of a seasoned, rugged, manipulative terrorist. He wore a battle dress uniform, a beret, jungle boots with large metal plates on the inside heels, and a double-holster ammo belt with 9-mm ivory-handled pistols.

He held a bullhorn in his beefy left hand and his right hand balanced a U.S.-made Stinger on his shoulder.

Carlos Santiago Dominguez, the largest arms dealer in the terrorist world, transformed his facial contortions into a compassionate persona as he looked at the large gathering of al-Qaida and Taliban customers assembled before him.

He raised the bullhorn to his mouth.

"To you, my brothers from our worldwide network, I thank you for accepting my humble invitation.

"Because of the violence we have created, the American President calls us terrorists. We engage in violence because it is only a reaction against an injustice.

"On behalf of Osama bin Laden and the Taliban Priests, I welcome you to Chile."

Shouts of approval erupted. Arms parted and reached skyward as praise to Allah evolved into a thunderous roar.

CHAPTER 1

As the old Boeing 727 taxied to its gate at Bogota International, Mayor Pro Tempore Carlos Santiago Dominguez, Jr., from Dos Bayou, Florida, impatiently unbuckled his belt, forced his bulky frame out of the first-class seat, and snapped open the overhead compartment. Mayor Dominguez, who was always in a hurry, glanced at other first class passengers, elbowed around them with his wardrobe bag and took his place in line to deplane.

It was a hard three-bounce landing caused by a strong cross wind, but Mayor Dominguez had experienced worse arrivals.

The noise from coach passengers in the rear of the aircraft caught his attention. The noise seemed to be much louder than he had heard on previous risky flights into BOG.

Mayor Dominguez turned and saw the aisle was crowded with anxious passengers. About half of them were crossing themselves, fingering beads and thanking the Blessed Mary for a safe landing.

Others bartered names and addresses of cocaine and marijuana dealers who sold their commodities at discount, and rented virgin children for siestas or long weekend respites.

"It is bad, my brother, very bad and it just gets worse."

Mayor Dominguez turned to his left, in the direction of the soft, clearly enunciated words.

1

"Are you not your brother's keeper?" she asked.

It was the nun. He had seen her in the boarding area at Quito International before the plane departed Ecuador for Colombia. She was seated two rows in front of him.

Mayor Dominguez spent a considerable amount of his time on the two-hour flight wondering how a Sister or her Order could afford a first-class seat.

It was the first time he had seen her face. She was exquisite with delicately shaped high cheekbones, narrow slits revealed alert, hazel eyes under lustrous dark eyebrows, and her lips puckered over both vowels and consonants. But what was so fascinatingly radiant about her was not the perfectly shaped pearl-write teeth, but the rich, creamy dark tan on such youthful skin.

Mayor Dominguez, who over the years had developed a heart as hard as a diamond, a stomach of iron and a tearless eye, heard himself say in a rare show of kindness, "Yes, Sister, the need is great but we are so few."

"You look American," the Sister said. "Can your country help us?"

By his own proud count, Mayor Dominguez had never donated a penny or a peso to charity in his life, except St. Mary's St. Vincent dePaul in the City of Dos Bayou, but those donations were based purely on political purposes—he controlled the catholic vote!

There was something enticing, mesmerizing and charming about the petite Sister, and her "damn the torpedoes, full speed ahead" attitude.

Dominguez reached into his pocket, withdrew his card wallet, opened it, and handed her a business card.

"For your convenience, Sister, one side is Spanish and the other side is English."

"How thoughtful of you, senor, to acknowledge our provisional status and remind us of it."

Mayor Dominguez bowed his head with a faint, embarrassed smile.

He knew what she meant. Her words were a clever substitute for a swift kick in the balls.

As she held the card and started to read, her long, smooth

fingers displayed squared-off manicured nails that glistened from coats of clear polish. As she finished reading, she tilted her head up and the hazel eyes blinked and widened. They turned from compassionate grief to expectation of fulfillment.

She turned the card over and read the English version.

"As you can see, Sister, I am part of an international organization, as well as a participant in a continental organization. Send me your needs and I will respond. I cannot promise miracles," he said shaking his head and forcing a smile, "but I will respond."

"You are President of the International Sister City Program, Senor?" the Sister asked as she placed the card in her handbag.

"No, Sister. I am President of the City of Dos Bayou, Florida International Sister City Program. I am a city councilman and mayor pro tempore. I serve the people of our mutual faith, Sister, and all the other people in my district who may not have any faith."

"Oh, Senor Mayor," the Sister said with the facial display of a humble servant, "and you are also the United States Delegate to the Organization of American States. I am unworthy to be in your presence, but so thankful to have met you. I shall surely send you a note in short time.

"Good day, you kind and generous servant of his Holiness."

She moved ahead of him and disappeared into the crowd.

Carlos Santiago Dominguez, Jr., an avid aficionado of Cuba's hand-rolled cigars, pulled some of his favorites out of a side pocket. He selected a Cohibas and lit it with a flaming Dunhill as he hurried through the mass of humanity in the terminal. Only a keen eye would notice the irregular gait in his left foot.

He exited through the side door where the taxis and buses were always lined up, tossed his bag through the open door of the first cab he came to, climbed in and handed the driver a note with some currency.

As the cab egressed the terminal, Dominguez saw the Sister entering the back seat of a black Lincoln Navigator. She was escorted by several men in three-piece suits. Each had a cell phone in his ear. The Lincoln Navigator was one of three black SUVs that pulled away in unison.

"A Sister with a beautiful tan and a manicure who has her own escorts and convoy," Dominguez whispered to himself. His face slowly wrinkled into concern as he took a deep drag on his Cohibas.

"How remarkable. How intriguing. How captivating." He took another long drag. "It will be interesting to discover what agency she works for, or directs."

The constant blare of the taxi's horn was a high decibel nuisance to everyone but cigar-puffing Mayor Dominguez. He was in a hurry and the driver had his orders.

The cabbie kept his foot on the gas pedal as he maneuvered around pedestrians on Avenida Caraeas, made a sharp, rubber-burning turn onto Carrera Septima, increased his speed to max throttle until he reached the intersection of Avenida Jimenez de Quezada where he slammed on the brakes, executed a 180-degree spin, pulled to a stop in front of an unpretentious apartment complex, ran around the taxi and opened the back door.

Heavy stogie smoke billowed from the vehicle.

"Bueno," the passenger said as he heaved himself out of the vehicle.

On his way from the taxi to his apartment, Mayor Dominguez had his wardrobe bag slung over his right shoulder, his coat was unbuttoned, his rakish cap covered most of his salt and pepper hair, and the Cohibas was jammed into the left side of his mouth. As his pace quickened, a cloud of thick, bluish stogie smoke trailed behind him.

Carlos Santiago Dominguez, Jr., climbed the familiar broken steps to his Bogota, Colombia apartment house, opened the door and tipped his cap to the desk clerk. With an unlit butt dangling from her lips, the clerk mumbled a greeting to her strange tenant who showed up a couple days every other month, but always paid his rent in advance.

The clerk's eyes followed the tenant as he walked through the pale yellow lobby. He walked by a few shabby tenants and a paper salesman chatting about the falsification of hand-rolled tobacco products, and the counterfeiting of high-quality cigars from Honduras and the Dominican Republic.

The tenant's steps scratched along the battered floor, past the toilet, then made quick, tapping sounds as he took the dimly lit concrete stairs to the second floor. He entered a long corridor, turned right, took a few more steps, glanced over each shoulder, saw no one, unlocked the triple-bolted door to apartment 215 and entered.

He walked to a sideboard and carefully poured two fingers of rum into a glass. He removed his coat and cap, tossed them on a chair, reached for his drink, straightened himself, turned and faced a full-length mirror.

United States Delegate to the Organization of American States, Carlos Santiago Dominguez, Jr., suddenly looked a boyish forty. On the verge of six feet, dressed in a demure gray suit, a tie centered tightly on a blue-striped shirt, with a silk scarf casually cross-shoulder, he was Miami, Bimini, Buenos Aires and Quito tanned, rich-casual and, quite unnaturally, novice-nervous.

Born 54 years ago in Argentina to United States Ambassador and Mrs. Carlos Santiago Dominguez, Sr., Carlos Jr., was the last in his family; the sole survivor. His parents were killed in an airplane accident while on a fishing trip to the Plateau of Patagonia in southern Argentina.

Victoria, his wife of three years, was killed by terrorists in Tegucigalpa, Honduras. His stepson died in a car accident shortly after graduating from middle school. All five of his brothers were dead.

All gone, long gone, just like his life of affluence as the son of a U.S. Ambassador.

He took all the money he inherited from his parents, every penny he got from selling their Maryland estate, every dollar he got by cashing their CDs, IRAs and stock, and nestled all of it safely in various banks in the Bahamas, Geneva, Toronto, and the Caymans.

The initial deposits totaled $13.7 million. That was 28 years ago, after his wife's murder, and the incident with the Baltimore and Ohio Railroad.

Carefree and feeling his oats, young and adventurous Carlos decided to leave his parents' spacious hacienda in Buenos Aires and get a job on the first railroad that would hire him. How was young Carlos to know that his father was a former Chairman of the B&O Board of Directors?

After a few years in Cincinnati, Carlos had his union card and a beautiful but adventurous wife whose passion was before its time: saving rain forests.

Then the damn accident. The loss of his left foot at the ankle because of a land mine while on vacation in Colombia.

Carlos qualified for a B&O medical retirement of $4,500 a month, a $3,250 monthly disability from his union, a railroad involuntary monthly retirement of $2,750, and Social Security Disability of $1,800 each month.

Each tax free check was deposited in rotation among his banks.

But he wanted more, and he wanted it at low risk.

His well-developed scheme was foolproof.

First, he had to be elected to a municipal office from a district that had a substantial Latino population. He did not want to spend his valuable time catering to whims, whiffs and whinny crazes of poor white trash constituents.

Second, he would maneuver himself into a position of leadership in the city's Sister City Program.

Third, he would become an expert on developing Sister City Programs in Central and South America.

Fourth, and most important, he would use his influence with his late father's colleagues and cronies to obtain a Presidential appointment as a senior cryptology intelligence level U.S. Delegate to the Organization of American States. The senior Delegate status was important because it carried White House prestige, and provided Dominguez with worldwide amenities, privileges, courtesies and, most importantly, political immunity.

Those four steps would provide him with the foundation to build an empire larger than Colombia's Cali cocaine cartel, more profitable than all the mafia assets of Gambino, Gotti, Colombo, Luchese and Genovese crime families in New York, Newark, Fresno, New Orleans, and Phoenix combined, and safer than traveling on Air Force One.

A six-month search of Florida cities revealed the first step would start in District Two, City of Dos Bayou, Escambia County, in the Florida Panhandle.

The second and third steps fell into place faster than expected.

The fourth step was accomplished with three phone calls. That was twelve years ago.

Since then, each year had proven more profitable beyond expectation as Carlos Santiago Dominguez, Jr., traveled hundreds of times to and from each of the thirty-five OAS countries, with major emphasis on the twenty states in South and Central America.

With the trappings of full diplomatic immunity, and in the service of his President, Dominguez was impervious to reproach, question, interrogation, search, seizure or detention.

Likewise, every briefcase, letter, suitcase, pouch, box, crate or shipment he sent or received was protected from search or seizure.

Any variance of that standard by a law enforcement officer would be a flagrant violation of U.S. and international law.

Mayor Carlos Santiago Dominguez enjoyed attending quarterly meetings of the Board of Delegates in the OAS headquarters on 17th Street, just off Constitution Avenue, in Washington, D.C.

From the Capital Hilton Hotel on 16th Street, where he retained a penthouse suite, he was chauffeured in a White House limo to his appointments.

He regaled and delighted his fellow delegates by communicating with them in the four official languages of the OAS – English, Spanish, French and Portuguese. And he rejoiced in manipulating them with stories and actions that reflected the rich diversity of the peoples and cultures across the Americas.

Last year, in recognition of Mayor Dominguez's dedication to the OAS's Inter-American Drug Abuse Control Commission and its work with member countries to strengthen laws, improve law enforcement and stem the illegal trafficking of narcotics and related chemicals and arms, he was chosen by his fellow delegates to sit on the Permanent Council. His title: Executive Secretariat of the

Court of Human Rights and Integral Development of Hemispheric Security.

It was the highest, singular honor that could be bestowed on a member delegate. The status had no equal in the OAS family.

Each member state had one vote on the Permanent Council. The U.S. population, with nearly 300 million people, represented only 25 percent of the OAS population, but the U.S. vote had broad coattails.

Mayor Carlos Santiago Dominguez possessed the sole U.S. vote, and the majority votes in his pocket, to lead and direct the political and economic affairs of North and South America.

Each day brought Dominguez closer to his goal: Why be President of the United States when you can control two continents—North America and South America?

Member nations on the Permanent Council had exhibited their fondness for Dominguez's election by exalting him during a three-hour Summit of the Americas banquet at the Four Seasons Hotel in Georgetown. Every member nation from Canada to tiny Belize in the Caribbean was represented.

Everyone knew Senor Mayor Carlos Santiago Dominguez, Jr., was the best of the best.

Such was the life of the masterful mobster who wore the pinstripes of an OAS Latino diplomat with retained non-pretentious apartments in Quito, Bogota, Buenos Aires, Tegucigalpa, Lima, Mexico City, Caracas, Bolivar, Santiago and Montevideo. Those did not include his leased hotel suites in nine other countries.

Each apartment and suite were self-contained with a full wardrobe, a computer center with all the amenities, phones with scramblers, and, except for three of his suites, a helicopter pad. And there was no need to become familiar with a strange, new environment at the different respites because they were all cloned. Each had 1500 square feet, with some minor exceptions in Lima and Buenos Aires which were larger, and each had the same furniture, the same amenable features, in the same location, and, the same inventory.

Dominguez did not have the patience it took to open various drawers and search for socks, rum or ammo clips.

It was no coincidence that his apartment in San Jose, Costa Rica, was directly across the street from the OAS Inter-American Court of Human Rights.

No visit to San Jose was complete without a stopover at the OAS office to lend his voice to people who had suffered human rights violations, reaffirm his support for women's rights, and call for better housing for indigenous people.

Those visits also afforded him the opportunity to receive any new classified code changes for OAS diplomatic immunity shipments or postings.

No one knew that the fox who controlled the political and financial direction of two entire continents also had the keys to all the hen houses.

By careful and precise planning, he neither knew, nor cared to know, the names or faces of the second or third tier of employees, retainers or independent contractors who worked for him. And they, in turn, did not know him.

All they knew was they were paid well, very well, indeed, each Friday for accomplishing their assigned jobs.

If a job meant bribing the captain or crew on vessels bound from the United States to Israel or Egypt and stealing hundreds of U.S.-made antiaircraft Stingers, so be it.

If it meant the destruction of the Contra supply depot at the Ilopango airfield in El Salvador, so much the better.

When OPEC oil ministers refused to negotiate, Dominguez's specialized henchmen kidnapped and tortured the ministers until they changed their minds.

Close ties with leftist insurrectionist groups in Iran, Iraq, Libya, North Korea, Sudan and Syria resulted in Dominguez's association with Osama bin Laden in the master planning of the bombings of U.S. Embassies in Kenya and Tanzania. Those actions took the lives of 291 people and wounded 5,000 others.

That plot was preceded by Dominguez's introduction to Libya's Muammar Qadhafi who needed assistance.

Qadhafi wanted to avenge America's bombing of a terrorist camp in Libya, and would pay a handsome retainer for "a proportionate response."

Two days later, Qadhafi did not question the plan presented by the Dominguez team.

It was a simply arrangement: A C-4 bomb would be placed inside a Toshiba "Boombeat" radio, packed in a Samsonite suitcase and stuffed with clothes, loaded on a plane in Malta, transferred through Frankfurt, then shipped onto London where it would be placed aboard Pan Am's clipper Maid of the Seas Flight 103.

The next day, when CNN televised the burnt debris on the ground at Lockerbie, Scotland and reported the loss of 270 lives, a sizable transaction was electronically debited from a bank in Tripoli and credited to an account in the Bahamas.

A month later, Qadhafi required additional services from his old friend, Carlos Santiago Dominguez.

Qadhafi needed strategists to brainwash Libya loyalists Abdel Basset All al-Megrahi and Lamen Khalifa Fhimah to take the fall for the bombing of Pan Am's clipper Maid of the Seas.

Within 24 hours, psychiatrists, hypnotists, acupuncturists and a video crew were dispatched.

When San'a, Yemen Islamic militants, needed bin Laden's financial backing to blast a massive hole in the side of the USS Cole and kill American sailors on board, bin Laden credited Dominguez's Swiss account for assistance rendered.

It was a cold, misty Thursday afternoon in Bogota.

Carlos Santiago Dominguez walked around his apartment and forced himself not to sit in the large, inviting Lazy Boy chair. He had been in a business mode for 15 consecutive hours, and he had one more important appointment to keep before he could call it a day.

He was aroused from a deep sleep very early in Quito and had his usual routines to accomplish before catching the midday flight to BOG.

However, none of his priorities were shared by the young starlet.

The beautiful senorita, who was the charm on his arm at the ballet, had kept him busy well past midnight after they returned to his apartment. And then, only five hours later, she insisted on nibbling around his lower stomach and loins while she cradled and massaged his testicles. How could he sleep? How could he deny her what she was paid to do? She did not stop until she had squeezed and swigged his last drop.

He doubled her fee and locked the door after her.

He had only five minutes to prepare for the first of six conference calls. Four hours later, he would be lifted off the helo pad and flown to the airport.

He looked at the large gold Rolex on his left wrist. He had less than an hour. He sipped his drink as he walked by an IBM computer. It constantly updated assets in the al-Qaida bank accounts, decoded progress statements and requirements by mission leaders on various international assignments, analyzed the current status and assets of old clients, and described current situations worldwide with a listing of potential new clients and their assets. Next to the IBM was a wall panel of six TVs that carried news from the different continents, a Fax machine and a table with four secure telephones filtered by scramblers.

He turned and looked again at the full-length mirror and examined his neatly trimmed facial brushery and tanned skin.

Somehow, Carlos Santiago Dominguez, the terrorist and drug kingpin with broad geographical reach and political immunity, was disgustingly Florida-and-Caribbean-handsome.

The voice, when he rarely spoke, was rich and deep, marinated by four decades' worth of rum, tequila and cigars. His hair, which couldn't be called groomed, was semi-spiked and kept winging down onto his temples. When he wiped it back, it always flopped forward again. His sleepy lids were usually hidden behind tinted glasses. That was another Dominguez don't-give-a-damn-trademark; wearing dark glasses on cold, cloudy days.

Carlos Santiago Dominguez was the exemplar of Latino leadership, the self-reliant nobleman of nature who trail-blazed into a wilderness of the spirit and emerged stronger and wiser. How else could one with a flair for the ballet, dancing and seduction survive as a mastermind of criminal enterprises such as drug trafficking, deadly bombings, assassinations, extortions and hostage dramas?

And where else could one be invited to a black-tie dinner at the White House, sit at a table with the Secretary of State, and look equally content in blue jeans and flip-flops the next day shopping with a statuesque redhead at Tyson's Corner?

Part of his success was that he was as personally charming, intellectually brilliant, bureaucratically masterful, culturally suave and politically well connected as he was ideologically unyielding.

A diverse world leadership structure that included Muammar Qadhafi and Osama bin Laden proudly described how Dominguez was, "All things, all knowing, and all caring, to all the people who suffered."

But Qadhafi's second description of Dominguez required not only a rewrite of history but a long stretch of imagination: "A professional revolutionary in the old Lincoln and Leninist tradition who fought for humanity, for the people of Palestine, for the people of Cuba, for the people of Libya, and against American imperialism and the Zionist state."

Dominguez took another sip of the warm rum and glanced at his watch. He would leave in 23 minutes. But first he had to change for a special occasion.

He opened a side, closet door, reached down and pulled out a pair of jungle boots. He lifted them eye level and closely examined the large metal plates attached to the inside heels. A rueful grin flashed across his face. He slammed the heels together and a loud metallic clack reverberated off the walls.

He sat on the side of the bed, unbuckled his belt and yanked off his pants. His prosthetic left foot was the result of a land mine near El Prodigio in southern Colombia when he led a Sandinista combat mission against Contras. The explosion ripped off his foot and his left leg was amputated below the knee. He was on a "working vacation" at the time.

The prosthesis was never an impediment to his lifestyle, and physicians, therapists and lovers were the only ones who knew of it.

By the time the knock sounded on the door, his attire from Brooks Brothers, Land's End, Neiman Marcus and Johnson & Murphy was replaced by a battle dress uniform, a beret, jungle boots and a double-holster ammo belt with 9 millimeter pistols.

The only things that remained in place were the dark shades and a cigar.

The lead helo skimmed over the trees and hill tops at a constant left and right maneuvering ground speed of 175. Trailing behind were four other identically marked helos that also mixed their formation so each craft switched position every three to four minutes.

Dominguez and his crew knew that a moving target was harder to hit.

As the rotors cleared the highest peak, Dominguez and his colleagues had an unobstructed view of several American-made fighter jets parked nose to tail in a line on a small patch of cleared land. The surrounding growth of bushes and small trees that appeared so permanent, suddenly parted and a long, open runway appeared.

The young Afghanistan Islamic militant seated next to Dominguez pointed to the military jets and asked, "How is that possible, even for you, my father's friend?"

"Ussama, anything is possible," Carlos Santiago Dominguez said to the son of Osama bin Laden. "Anything is possible."

To young Ussama, even at age 16, everything was possible. All he needed was a keyboard and modem.

He was already an accomplished computer hacker. During the past two years, he had stolen the U.S. Navy's source codes to missile guidance programs, changed American, NATO and commercial satellite orbits which destroyed communications capability, altered the rabbet formula at General Motors and Ford manufacturing plants that forced the recall of millions of new vehicles, re-calibrated rotary cycles of the U.S. Marine Corps' MV-22 Osprey which forced a realignment of the $41 billion aircraft program, and siphoned the entire inventory of intelligence data from Army, Navy and Air Force War Colleges.

Ussama's eyes widened as he looked at the American-made F-4 fighter jets. "Are they yours, my father's friend?"

Dominguez smiled at the young man and nodded. It was a Dominguez brainstorm that acquired the jets and fattened the OAS coffers. It was not a complicated scheme.

The fighter aircraft, and all available spare parts, were purchased by the World Bank from the United States Air Force's

Davis-Monthan surplus site at Tucson, Arizona. The Air Force used the income to repay the World Bank for R&D funds borrowed to supplement stealth research. The World Bank transferred the aircraft inventory to the Royal Canadian Air Force which, in turn, sold it to the Permanent Council of the Organization of American States. The OAS then credited the Canadians' account, turned the fighter aircraft, and parts, over to the National Sister Cities Program for municipal static exhibits in Central and South American, and debited each member's account for administrative services rendered.

"This will be your introduction to our Sister Cities Program," Dominguez said to young Ussama.

The left wing helo in the trailing formation banked suddenly, zoomed by the aircraft on the ground and landed a few hundred feet to the rear near some bleachers.

Carlos Santiago Dominguez deplaned first and was followed by 15 of his most distinguished guests. The other helos landed nearby, the passengers got out, joined the others and climbed onto the bleachers.

Their heads all moved in unison as a strange-looking, large mechanical contraption with two vertical exhaust outlets was hauled from a camouflaged tent. Technicians attached the contraption to the first fighter jet, nodded to their boss, then ran back to the tent.

The nods from the technicians signaled that the first drone flight was ready. The catapult was in place.

Host Senor Dominguez stood in front of the bleachers in his battle dress uniform. He held at port arms a U.S.-made Stinger, Model D, the most advanced antiaircraft ground-to-air-missile known in the terrorist community.

It was his favorite weapon.

The Stinger was a heat-seeking missile. Any aircraft was vulnerable to its deadly accuracy. It weighed only 34.5 pounds and had a range of 3.1 miles. And, as Dominguez knew, the Stinger was mobile and extremely effective as a small arms shoulder-mounted weapon; sophisticated and adaptable for terrorist use.

Years earlier, for Dominguez and his amigos, the skies over

El Salvador and Honduras, where troops were massed to attack Nicaragua, were target-rich areas for the Stingers.

Dominguez was a master in teaching his Sandinista troops how to balance the launcher in their hands, punch the forward button with a thumb which released the missile to give the infrared seeker-head its first look at the heat radiating from aircraft engines.

Carlos Santiago Dominguez, the salesman who had hundreds of Stingers to sell at his usual exorbitant markup, stood at attention with the heels of his jungle boots touching and toes at a 45-degree angle. He looked at his guests in the bleachers. They had formed small clusters as they talked, waved, shrugged, nodded and gestured.

The host moved his right foot sideways about eighteen inches. Then, with a quick motion, he slammed his right heel hard against the left heel. The loud metallic sound was an immediate attention-getter.

Carlos Santiago Dominguez suddenly faced the quietest and strangest collection of rogues he had ever seen.

In the bleachers were Yemen Islamic militants, black power advocates, Neo-Nazis in their jackboots, right-wing extremists from Western Europe, hoodlum gang leaders from Russia, Hutu rebels from Burundi, Taliban agents, al-Qaida network enforcers, militiamen from Montana and Vermont, Bosnian Serb commanders from the Zvornik Brigade, leaders of Iran's New Republican Guard Corps, Palestinian suppliers, Syria's Hezbollah guerrillas, drug lords from Thailand, Turkey and Pakistan, and Chinese brokers from Hong Kong. The unholy alliance also included the usual camp following hangers-on; the dot-coms, the non-coms and the hot-moms.

Dominguez knew he did not have to conduct a hard sell. The customers in the bleachers already wanted the Stingers. Especially those who had drug interests in South and Central America or the golden triangle.

The customers were well aware of the U.S. "mercenaries" who were flying missions over guerrilla-infested coca fields, manning remote radar stations, and working perilously close to the front lines of the U.S. initiated drug war in Colombia.

Everyone knew the U.S. government had a $1.3 billion contract with D.C. beltway companies to supply equipment and a rowdy group of daredevils, mechanics and pilots to eradicate coca crops and heroin-producing plantations.

However, as is the case in most U.S. operations abroad, there was a hitch.

U.S. contractors conducted a massive aerial drug fumigation of 75,000 acres in northern Colombia to exterminate the coca fields. The operation was a costly, dismal failure because the sprayings killed only vegetable and orchard crops, and left thousands of farmers and villagers sick with no other source of income.

In the meantime, leftist guerrillas and rightist paramilitaries take turns protecting the cocaine traffickers for a share of the profits.

It was just a matter of time, Carlos Santiago Dominguez knew, before his income would at least double, with no heavy lifting on his part.

His profits would increase dramatically because the United States could no longer play strictly an advisory, albeit a financially draining, role. It was being unequivocally sucked into the vortex of a 40-year civil war. And the sooner the better.

Dominguez needed a Central-and-South-America "Vietnam War IP" issue to create the new position of President of the Organization of American States.

Why rule a country, large or small, when one can dominate an entire continent?

Carlos Santiago Dominguez looked at the customers in the bleachers. Without the heroin and cocaine plantations, a huge portion of their funds would be eliminated. With a U.S.-financed war in Colombia and neighboring Ecuador, Bolivia and Peru, the price of a kilo would triple.

It was time to merchandise the Stingers.

He smiled at his guests, bowed, turned to the tent and yelled, "Launch the first drone."

The catapult seemed to explode and the unmanned F-4 fighter jet was thrust into the air with the force of an afterburner.

As the technician in the tent manipulated the drone's remote control panel, the F-4 climbed vertically, made a giant loop, circled twice overhead and started a high-speed, diving attack at the bleachers.

The customers, who were the most feared terrorists and mercenaries in the world, started scrambling for their lives.

Carlos Santiago Dominguez raised the launcher, pointed it toward the approaching aircraft, punched the forward button and felt the quiver of the seeker-head at work. The missile screamed its readiness as the sight was elevated and the trigger engaged.

The Stinger's noise caused the customers to stop in their mad rash. They looked at Dominguez who stood in the path of sudden death. Young Ussama stood beside him.

The customers watched as the Stinger looped slightly before it deployed its maneuvering fins and dropped slightly to home-in on the target. The fins moved only fractions to obey signals from its onboard computer brain, a coin-sized microchip.

The explosion was deafening.

The customers were awe-struck as they gawked at each other and slowly returned to their seats.

Dominguez looked at them and smiled. Again, he slammed his metal-plated heels together and came to attention.

He then bowed.

The customers thought the show was over. They stood and applauded.

"Launch the second drone," Dominguez yelled.

The assassins and mercenaries on the top bleacher rows looked nervously at each other and moved quickly to the front rows, closer to the ground.

The explosion from the catapult was louder than before.

The F-4 drone climbed to 10,000 feet, leveled off, did a 180, and started its approach toward the bleachers at 450 MPH.

The customers froze in sheer terror. They did not know if they should run or risk their lives on another lucky shot from Senor Dominguez's Stinger.

Dominguez lifted and balanced the launcher. He punched the button and felt the quiver. It screamed and the fins deployed as it honed in on the target.

The F-4 was at 1000 feet and gaining thrust when the impact occurred. The Stinger hit the left wing near the fuselage and the fuel tank exploded. The F-4 flipped over and started a port-induced pull that rocketed it directly toward two helos parked 300 meters south of the bleachers.

The giant fireball was intense. The collision ignited the fuel tanks in the helos and tossed the rotor crafts 30 feet into the air. When they crashed to the grown, live rounds of ammo exploded and the customers scattered in all directions.

Dominguez never moved.

He finally turned toward the tent, and in the nonchalant tone of a novice who had just hit two consecutive golf balls into the water, yelled, "Send for two more helos."

The obnoxious odor of burning jet fuel sent a massive dark cloud into the sky.

"Come, ladies and gentlemen," Dominguez beckoned with his hands, "please take your seats and we will conclude our little demonstration."

"What more is there to see, Senor Carlos," a man's voice shouted from the bushes. "You have convinced all of us. How many can we buy?"

The customers formed small circles near Dominguez. Animated discussions were conducted in whispers as many of them shook their heads in disbelief.

After a few minutes, Carlos Santiago Dominguez raised his hands skyward and said, "My friends, there are plenty for all of you. Please pass along the table over there," he pointed toward the tent, "and give my people your name and electronic transfer number. If you don't have the number with you, phones will be provided.

"In a day or so, your account will be debited. Consider that your bill. You will be notified in one week where you can recover your Stingers and missiles."

Dominguez smiled. "There will be no charge to you for the two helos that were destroyed." Then, with a larger smile, he said, "Those were on the house."

A roar of approval erupted.

He bowed and graciously pointed toward the table.

The customers hurriedly formed lines on each side. A basket of cell phones was carried from the tent and placed beside the table.

Each phone was in use within seconds.

The day was profitable for the al-Qaida. And Carlos Santiago Dominguez was pleased with his usual twenty percent cut of gross profits.

He would calculate into the price of each Stinger a pro-rata share for replacing the two helos.

That evening when he checked the bin Laden al-Qaida network asset base on his IBM computer, the data showed that he had increased the network's bottom line net by $643 million.

It was time for him to go home to Dos Bayou and earn his keep. The monthly City Council meeting was scheduled for next Tuesday.

He was sure that he and his colleague, Council Member Libby Washington, would be asked to explain their votes against the new city manager, whatever his name was.

The hell with the majority members on the council, he thought, they should have expected the two no votes because there were no black or brown candidates on Mayor Phillip Garrison's list.

The Latino population in District Two had to be protected, and Dominguez would do just that, just like Libby Washington had to protect the blacks in District Three.

It was time to go back home and start a little fight.

CHAPTER 2

Hurricane Raymond had turned Highway 98 into a daring obstacle course for the Honda Acura that Greg Robertson slowly and cautiously guided down the road.

The storm had bellowed out of the Gulf of Mexico just after nightfall, slammed into the northwest Florida panhandle, damaged his house, pissed off his wife, and delayed his departure by an hour.

Greg was almost two hours into his drive for the most important appointment of his life, but had traveled only 41 miles.

He had seen battlefield destruction, but nothing he had ever seen in combat compared to the widespread damage he gawked at through the whipping windshield wipers. The storm had vented its fury on the Gulf Coast by toppling trees and power lines, stripping roofs off buildings, and shoving a roiling sea onto the streets.

Hurricane Raymond had flung utility poles, vehicles, boats and parts of houses and businesses hundreds of yards, and strewn them along the winding road Greg had to travel; the only direct link between Sandestin and Dos Bayou.

Greg and Brenda Robertson had experienced more than their share of Southern California earthquakes before moving to Florida, but they had never felt the eerie, helpless and victimized feeling of a violent and destructive storm.

The leading counterclockwise whirl of Hurricane Raymond hit just before dinner with gale force winds of 120 miles an hour, and its trailing clockwise power gusted to more than 135.

There was a personal urgency in what Greg Robertson had to do, and Brenda reluctantly agreed. They had refused warnings to evacuate, and the stern-sounding voice on the radio announced that a curfew was strictly enforced by the county sheriff.

Greg had to get to the city of Dos Bayou by 10 a.m. and it would take more than a storm or a curfew to stop him.

As he maneuvered the Acura around debris and a demolished trailer house that blocked half the highway, the voice on the car radio warned of knocked-out power lines, looters, flooded streets with drenching rain, hail and tornadoes spun-off by the hurricane.

Greg Robertson swerved past the latest obstacles and accelerated back up to 25 miles an hour when the left front tire hit a deep pothole and his head bounced against the steering wheel with a painful thud. He rubbed his head, examined his hand, found no blood, and continued his glaring stare through the whipping wipers.

He gripped the wheel tight as the headlights illuminated the pounding rain and the trash-covered road ahead.

There was no traffic in either direction as he poked along westward toward the city of Dos Bayou.

Greg knew two things for sure. First, he was going to be late, very late, for the appointment; and, second, why was he the only one on the road?

He carefully released his right hand from the wheel and pulled his left coat sleeve up until it was higher than his wristwatch. "Nine fifteen," he announced with a frown. He figured he would be at least an hour late for the appointment.

He knew he couldn't call and tell the mayor he was going to be late because the telephone lines were down, and he had left his cell phone with Brenda. Schools were closed, and there were no classes to teach. She had said, in her usual well-organized manner, that she would start the claim process with their insurance company, and take pictures of the damage. She needed the cell phone.

The voice on the car radio kept describing the destruction of

Hurricane Raymond. Greg Robertson did not need any more bad news.

The voice said more than two hundred thousand people had evacuated the Florida panhandle, and about half of them would return to concrete slabs where their homes and businesses once stood.

Thank God, Greg thought, he and Brenda had survived the crashing, terrifying sounds of damaging jolts of pine and oak trees that fell on their roof, ceilings that leaked, blown-out windows, and ruined carpet. But they were not injured.

Before Greg left for Dos Bayou, he did not have time to look for any structural damage to the house. The damn flat tire took what little patience he had left.

As he drove, Greg's face displayed the shock of horror, then faint quick grimaces, as he recalled the terror of their first hurricane.

He thought Brenda would go ballistic when the storm-tossed trees slammed against the roof, but she didn't. She calmly went into the kitchen, pulled out all the pots and pans, lined them on the floor in order of size, and lit a Coleman lantern.

He knew she would go berserk when all the ceilings started to leak, but she reacted with calm resolve. She patiently examined the drop zone of each leak, the volume of dripping water, and placed a pot under it. The size of the container she selected depended on the amount of falling water.

He was certain she would have a temper-tantrum when the power was knocked out, water poured down the walls, rain blew through the broken windows, and the new carpet was soaked. But her composure was unruffled. She lit another lamp, refilled her wineglass, and asked him to set up the backgammon game.

Greg arranged the backgammon board with the trepidation of a steward rearranging deck chairs on a sinking ship.

He also obediently complied with Brenda's directions on emptying the pots and pans. Like a magician pulling something out of thin air, she always had a backup vessel to replace the one being dumped.

As he drove, he thought of Brenda's toned and lithe body, her calm demeanor and her words of encouragement.

"The backgammon will help us pass the time until you have to leave," Brenda said as she loaded film into their two cameras. "Besides, there's nothing we can do until daybreak, unless you want to make love on a soggy bed covered with pine straw."

It had been a long, fearful night with no sleep and no sex.

Brenda won all four games of backgammon as she sipped white wine and kept Greg's coffee cup topped off.

Greg remembered how the storm brought out a defiant act of bravado that was true to Brenda's form. He still had a hard time believing what she did and how she did it.

He was amazed at how stable and decisive she was at handling multiple tasks. She was steadfast in her determination to control the damage, rational in her actions to salvage what she could of their property, and patient beyond Biblical Job.

Greg had been a nervous wreck all night.

"We're not going to lose this battle," he remembered yelling at the top of his lungs until he was hoarse. An upset stomach followed. Then a headache. Brenda had a pill or a teaspoon full of something for each of his ailments.

He could never understand her damn composure.

Like when she used her new T-Fal pots and pans to catch the dirty steams of storm water and pine straw that poured through the holes in the ceiling. She never complained.

She maintained her normal polite, soft-spoken, self-disciplined, sleekly gorgeous assistant-principal-and-third-grade-teacher-disposition even when a gushing downpour hit, the rain increased, and they could not empty all the pots and pans fast enough. Gallons of dirty water had spilled onto the carpet.

It was the first time in their three-year marriage that they had been in such a disastrous situation, and Greg was dumbfounded at how calm and practical Brenda handled the chaos.

He was out of his element when it came to ground warfare.

Greg's experience as a former Air Force fighter pilot with 68 combat missions was no match for Brenda's rational leadership in crisis management, disaster preparedness and damage control.

It was not the hurricane, the destruction, or the odorous mess that upset her.

What really sent her into a berserk, booster-rocket orbit was when he was ready to leave in his new three-piece suit and discovered that his damn Chevrolet Blazer had a flat. He had to take her Acura. That pissed her off. The Acura was her first true love, a gift from her parents when she left home in Atlanta to go away to college.

When they kissed good bye, he said with all the Alpha-male leadership voice he could muster, "I'll change the tire when I get back."

Brenda's hazel eyes quickened, and her shoulders relaxed. With her ethereal beauty and steely authority, Princeton-educated Brenda, at 5 feet 7 inches tall, nodded with an opaque gaze.

She flashed a canny smile, cupped her hand and grabbed his crotch in a firm grip. "I'll believe it when I see it," she smiled.

Her laughter and eyes followed his familiar gimpy swagger as he got into the car and drove away.

More bad news from the radio: Hurricane Raymond, rated a Category 4 on the Saffir-Simpson Scale, with 5 the most intense, hammered its worst storm surge into Pensacola where water rose 4 feet above sea level.

Escambia County Emergency Management officials reported 238 deaths so far, shelters were overcrowded with 53,000 people whose homes were destroyed, and a preliminary damage assessment to Pensacola, Gulf Breeze, Dos Bayou and other nearby cities was placed at $970 million.

Greg Robertson's eyes widened in disbelief as he heard the words "Dos Bayou."

He had been in the city only once, about three weeks ago, and that was for an evening meeting with Mayor Phillip Garrison. It was too dark to drive around the city and view the neighborhoods. He knew nothing about the city, except what he had researched before that first meeting.

The voice on the radio continued: The storm, after dumping 16 inches of rain, headed toward Montgomery, Alabama, and forecasters predicted further catastrophic losses as it moved into Georgia, the Carolinas, Virginia and the nation's capital.

"Screw it," he yelled, as he turned off the radio. "Okay, I'll be late but I'll make it. This isn't as bad as night missions during Desert Storm."

He thought about his sorties over the Iraqi desert and how his A-10 Warthog had wiped out scores of Saddam Hussein's tanks. A big grin split his face. But the grin quickly disappeared when he thought about Hurricane Raymond, their damaged house, how Brenda had been such a strong inspirational leader, and how, in hindsight, he had been such a wuss.

The sudden glare of road flares and flashlights blinded him. He slammed on the brakes, the tires skidded on the wet pavement, and the Acura started sliding sideways. He saw an orange blur of a figure jump from the path of the careening car as it seemed to gain speed on the wet pavement.

The bone-jarring collision jerked Greg's body forward, his head slammed into the steering wheel, then he was thrown backwards by the violent force of the air bag.

He wiped the blood from his forehead and looked wide eyed through the windshield wipers that whipped back and forth at top speed. He saw four people in bright orange rain gear approach. As they got nearer, he saw their badges, the contemptible look on their faces, and, worst of all, their shotguns pointed directly at him.

A fist pounded on the window and a voice yelled, "Get out of the car with your hands raised high above your head. Now, goddamn it, now."

Greg Robertson, who never liked the sight of blood, especially his own, stared at his blood-soaked hand.

A rifle butt slammed through the window and glass fragments stuck to his bloody face.

"I said now, goddamn it."

He unbuckled the seat belt, opened the door, and was immediately yanked out of the car by two powerful hands. The hands dragged him through the mud and rain like a trash bag, and threw him on the ground face down. A swift boot slammed into his rib cage.

His wrists were held tightly behind him as cold steel handcuffs pinched the skin as they were snapped shut. A hand rubbed his torso and buttocks until it found his wallet and yanked it out.

"Well, now, let's take a look at what we have here," a voice said, as the end of a gun barrel hoisted Greg's limp body and rolled it over.

A huge mountain of a man in orange rain gear leaned down and looked into a face smeared with blood, broken pieces of glass and mud.

"Bet we have us another looter, all right. This one's in a three-piece suit."

The huge man turned, tossed the wallet to another orange-clad figure, and yelled, "Run a make on him and his car and check it for stolen property. Hurry, we ain't got all day."

Greg was in the worst pain he had ever felt, but he knew how to conceal agony and control the urge to kill. He was outnumbered and unarmed. He bit down hard on the inside of his cheeks to keep his mouth closed.

"Well, well, howdy doodie," a voice shouted a moment later. "Yessiree, Sergeant Billy Ray, he broke into some school. A lot of books and school supplies are on the back seat and floorboard. He's a looter, all right."

"Read him his rights and stuff him," ordered the orange rain gear that hovered over Greg's torso. "And get a couple tow trucks out here. Have the looter's car and the black and white unit he rammed hauled to the junkyard. Hell, they're both totaled and his belongs to us now."

"I can explain . . ."

A rifle butt slammed into Greg Robertson's stomach.

"Get up, you sonofabitch," a voice yelled as Greg was jerked to his feet. "You're gonna get three hots and a cot in the county jail. The charges are looting, violation of curfew, destruction of county property, speeding, driving a stolen vehicle, resisting arrest and a few other things I'll ponder on between here and Milton."

Two burly men in orange rain gear dragged him toward a police car, shoved him headfirst into the back seat and drove away.

Greg knew he was in the Deep South and in deep trouble.

His stomach throbbed. His ribs ached. There was a warm liquid in his mouth. His tongue felt a gap where a tooth was missing. He spit a mouthful of blood on the floorboard. Each breath he took brought a sharp pain from his ribs. The tight handcuffs had cut off circulation and he could not move his fingers. He wrinkled his nose and felt the broken glass dig deeper into his facial wounds. He felt blood draining down his cheeks. He spit again.

An orange-clad passenger in the front seat turned and looked with scorn at the backseat scumbag. "You want something?" the deputy sheriff asked.

Greg did not respond.

"Look at me when I'm talkin' to you, boy."

Greg looked up.

A clinched fist slammed into Greg's left eye. Another jab caught him on the right jaw.

"That'll give you a low-grade toothache," the deputy said. "Now don't spit in this car any more. You hear me, boy?"

"Yes, sir."

The driver smirked with a twisted smile, giggled, and glanced at his fellow officer who was rubbing the pain out of his right hand. "Guess he won't be lootin' anymore for a while, Timmy Dee."

Greg was now a prisoner of war for the second time. Except now, there was no Geneva Convention to protect him from brutality by his own countrymen.

He closed his eyes. His self-talk kept repeating the names he had heard. Billy Ray and Timmy Dee. Billy Ray and Timmy Dee. Billy Ray and Timmy . . .

His body quivered in shock until he lost consciousness.

Merciful sleep ended when the car braked to a hard, abrupt stop and Greg Robertson's body slammed against the front seat. The door opened and the two men in orange rain gear pulled him out. They dragged him toward other handcuffed prisoners who stood in a long row. Deputies with shotguns patrolled each side of the line.

Greg forced his eyes to open as wide as the pain allowed. His vision slowly focused on a group of mangled humanity. He saw about 15 men who had been battered, bruised and beaten. Every one of them needed medical help.

He studied the two persons at the front of the line. Their hunched bodies could not hide their arms, legs and torsos that quivered and jerked with each convulsive movement. They were black women, maybe in their late 20s or early 30s. Their clothes were torn and soiled. They tried to move their shoulders and legs so the shredded pieces of cloth concealed their bruised bodies, but the handcuffs and spasms made the tasks impossible.

Greg also noticed something very weird about how a couple of the armed guards hovered around the two women. The guards were doing something that intrigued Greg's curiosity. He squinted his eyes and kept looking until the horrid realization hit him like another rifle butt in the stomach.

He noticed the guards took turns and bumped against the women, pawed their exposed flesh, and whispered something. The women took the abuse as if they expected it from men who had just tormented them in a violent, brutal gang-bang.

Greg had seen raped and tortured women before. There were hundreds of them in Kuwait, and he could never erase the memory of such savageness.

He remembered how American and allied forces drove Dictator Saddam Hussein's barbarian rapists out of Kuwait and into the desert. Hatred showed on Greg's face as the memory of his A-10 Warthog, with the name Captain Gregory N. Robertson on the panel below the cockpit, took a heavy toll on the retreating bastards.

Greg's battered and inflamed eyes mirrored a deep and bitter anger, and frustration mounted into rage on his bloody brow.

His entire body was sore with multiple injuries, but his pride hurt worse.

Saddam's barbarians were just a few feet away. They wore orange rain gear over their uniforms and carried shotguns. They also wore heavy badges and hair-triggered pistols.

Greg thought of his frantic and desperate mission to Dos Bayou, and wondered how long Mayor Phillip Garrison would wait at City Hall before he gave up and offered the job to someone else. Somehow, Greg knew, he had to get a message to Mayor Garrison. But how?

Greg forced himself to turn his head and look away. He wondered how so many terrible things could happen to him since he kissed Brenda goodbye just a few hours ago.

When he left home in a dark flannel vested suit, Brenda said he looked like he had walked straight out of the pages of a Neiman Marcus catalog. He remembered how she had often complimented his "devastatingly blue all-knowing eyes, short-cropped blond hair, chiseled face, and familiar 6 feet 2 inch swagger."

Greg's hair was now matted with gobs of dried blood and broken pieces of glass. Scars stretched like time-lines across his face, and his left eye was bruised and swollen. His suit was beyond salvage, and he looked like all the rest of the handcuffed prisoners: Dirty froth from the bottom of the trash bin.

The line finally started to move, but Greg's gimpy swagger was gone. He limped slowly and painfully as he followed the human column up a flight of stairs, down a long hallway and into a courtroom. Guards pointed their shotguns to a long bench next to a wall.

"Sit there," one of the guards ordered, "and keep your mouths shut and don't move or talk until someone calls your name."

It was the first time Greg Robertson had ever been inside a courtroom.

He looked around and saw about a dozen people huddled around three well-worn folding tables near the front. They were in whispered conversations. A sign on the first table was written with a black marker and read, State Prosecutor. The next table's sign was Public Defender, and a much larger sign in bolder lettering on the third table read, BAIL BONDS (TRANSPORTATION WITHIN REASON TO HOME OR CAR).

A man came out of a front side door and carefully closed it behind him. He took a couple steps and glanced with a scowl at the miscellaneous assortment of handcuffed scumbags on the bench. The man turned abruptly to the distinguished ladies and gentlemen at the three tables, and said, "Rise and pay heed. This court is now in session. Come near and you shall be heard. The Honorable Chester D. Andrews, second circuit, presiding."

The lawyers and bail bonds people stopped their chatter, faced the front, and stood at rigid attention. The prisoners looked at their feet and never moved. Greg Robertson made a painful but futile effort to rise, but his body felt like rigor mortis had set in. He slumped back onto the bench.

He saw the stooped figure of an old man in a black robe enter from the same front side door. The aged soul walked in small, uncertain steps across the dais, stopped, reached down, pulled his robe up to his waist, and carefully seated himself.

The small frame in the black robe turned and nodded to the court stenographer seated at a small wood table beside the bench. She smiled politely and nodded back.

"Seats," the judge ordered, and made a faint tap sound with his gavel. The effort seemed to exhaust all his energy.

The stenographer started her silent pecking on the steno machine.

The noise from the three tables caught Greg Robertson's attention. The lawyers and the bond sellers had moved their metal chairs over to the far side of the courtroom and started to replace them with wooden chairs. Then they decided they did not have enough wooden chairs because there were more bond sellers than lawyers. After some hand motions, the lawyers took all the wooden chairs and the bond sellers got the metal ones.

When the lawyers and bond sellers finally settled at their respective tables, Greg saw two state prosecutors, both men, three public defenders, two women and a man, and nine bail bond sellers, six women and three men.

Greg noticed that each bond seller had a laptop, a stack of forms, pens, a bank deposit book, notepads and counter checks. He also noticed their strange behavior as they eyed the long line of prisoners with mercenary glances, then turned and snickered to each other with their quivering tongues.

They looked and acted, Greg thought, like starving, carnivorous hyenas that would rip the last remaining flesh off a prisoner's body if it meant a commission.

"This is a pre-trial hearing," the judge announced as he looked over his glasses that rested on the tip of his nose. "Is the state ready to proceed?"

A lawyer in a gray suit rose at the prosecutor's table. "Ready for the state, your honor."

"Counsel for the people ready?"

A large woman got to her feet. "Ready for the people, your honor."

"Proceed."

"Your honor," the state prosecutor said, "the first defendant is Mack Ernest Kemper. Mister Kemper is charged with breaking and entering and looting. Mister Kemper, please stand."

Greg Robertson leaned over and looked down the line of prisoners. A small, frail elderly man slowly got to his feet. There was blood on his torn shirt, his right hand dangled grotesquely from the wrist, and part of his hair looked like it had been pulled from his scalp. A patch of dried blood dotted his forehead.

Judge Andrews adjusted his bifocals and looked at the defendant. The judge stared at the man's torn, bloody shirt, his right arm, and the bloody spot on his head. The judge shifted his vision to the other defendants.

"Why are all these defendants injured, Mister Prosecutor?"

"Resisting arrest, your honor. They were violent and belligerent. Most of them were looters. Those who want medical attention will get it."

"I see," the judge said, turning again to the still-standing Mr. Kemper.

"How do you plead, Mister Kemper?" the judge asked. "Guilty as charged or not guilty?"

The man shook his face. A look of disbelief glowed in his eyes.

"Guilty of what, judge? I own that house and live there. I locked myself out when I went to inspect for hurricane damage. I was trying to climb through a window when those yahoos over there," he said pointing to the deputies, "arrived with their shotguns and all hell broke loose."

"Your honor," interrupted the state prosecutor, "the officers only tried to help Mister Kemper until they discovered he had looted his neighbor's property. Mister Kemper became belligerent, argumentative and hostile. While resisting questioning and arrest, it took three officers to subdue him."

Greg Robertson looked again at the small man. He weighed about 115 pounds, if soaking wet.

"The court, by its own motion," the judge said, "enters a plea of not guilty for the defendant, sets bail at $10,000, and sets the trial date for 10 a.m. two weeks hence. Bailiff, escort the defendant to the bail bond table and if he makes bail, remove the handcuffs. Court stands in recess until the process with Mister Kemper is completed."

Everyone could hear the conversation at the bail bond table.

The defendant owned mortgaged property in the county. He did not have his checkbook with him. He had a checking and savings account at First Central Bank.

A bond seller punched some keys on his laptop and filled out a counter check for $1,000.00 which was 10 percent of the bond. The laptop then placed a court-ordered freeze on all transactions on Mr. Kemper's bank accounts until the $1,000.00 check cleared.

While that was going on, another bond seller filled out the bail application, and made an entry in the bank deposit book. Mr. Kemper signed the application and the counter check, turned to the bailiff and held out his arms. The cuffs were unlocked and the man started to leave.

"Do you want medical treatment, Mister Kemper?" the prosecutor in the gray suit asked.

Mack Ernest Kemper stopped, turned and looked with disdain at the prosecutor.

"Mister State Lawyer," Kemper said loudly with words that dripped in sarcasm and bounced off the walls, "the injuries I got in Vietnam did not cause as much pain as I have now. You have given me a broken heart. Over there, they gave me a Purple Heart."

Kemper raised his left arm and pointed at the deputies. "I fought for them in Nam. I did not fight with them here. No, Mister State Lawyer, I will call my own ambulance. I will see my own doctor. And I will file my own law suit."

Kemper turned, looked at the deputies, and turned again to face the prosecutor. "And I'll see you and your goons in another court real soon. Good day."

The entire process with Kemper took about three minutes and netted a $1,000.00 fee.

During the next thirty minutes, Greg Robertson watched as the worse scum in the courtroom took an additional $14,750.00 in fees as they sat at the tables.

Greg and the two black women were the only prisoners left.

"The next defendant, your honor," announced the prosecutor, "is Gregory Nathaniel Robertson who is charged with violation of curfew, destruction of county property, excessive speed in unsafe driving conditions, driving a stolen vehicle, resisting arrest and looting. Mister Robertson, please stand."

It took every ounce of energy Greg had to slowly and painfully rise.

"How do you plead, Mister Robertson, guilty as charged or not guilty?" asked the judge.

It was a long shot, but Greg had no other choice. He and Brenda did not have thousands of dollars in a bank account that the worthless mercenaries could suck out and transfer.

He was unemployed. His job as Operations Manager was eliminated by a conglomerate that waged a costly but successful hostile takeover of his company. The company had recruited him four years ago when he left the Air Force. The takeover was Greg's first real-world corporate experience that threw 372 people out of work.

That experience also caused Greg and Brenda to leave Long Beach, California, pack everything they had on a U-Haul, and move 2,300 miles away to Sandestin, Florida.

He and Brenda eked by on his severance package and her teacher's salary.

They were too independent to use the blank check her father signed and gave them. "Just date it and fill in whatever amount you want," he had told them.

His mouth ached with agonizing pain, but he forced himself to speak as loud as he could.

"Your honor," Greg said, "I beg the court to telephone the honorable Phillip Garrison, Mayor of the city of Dos Bayou. He will enlighten the court on my situation. May I be seated, your honor, while that call is placed?"

Every face at the three tables turned and looked with astonishment at the worthless tramp defendant who dared to order the court to change its standard pre-trial procedure.

Greg slumped on the bench, lowered his head and spit a mouthful of blood on the floor. He raised his cuffed hands and wiped his mouth.

Second Circuit Court Presiding Judge Chester D. Andrews, who had served 31 years on the bench and had never been overruled, opposed for reelection, or lectured to in his own courtroom, leaned his frail frame forward.

"Sir, do you want to be held in contempt of this court?"

Greg Robertson knew he had no more trump cards to play, but he also knew how to play with the cards dealt him.

"Your honor, I respectfully and earnestly plead with the court to make the call to Mayor Garrison. I mean no disrespect to the court."

The state prosecutor in the gray suit turned and whispered to his colleague, "That poor bastard just got himself sometime in the slammer. By the way he talks, y'all know he's not from around here, this being the birth of the blues and the sound of soul. He's fixin' to be on all fours with about ten horny studs all lined up behind him waitin' for their turn at some fresh meat."

Judge Andrews looked quizzically at the public defenders. They appeared as surprised and bewildered as the prosecutors.

"Can any of you shed some light on the defendant's unusual request?" the judge asked.

A large woman, whose expression revealed she wished she was anywhere else but where she was, rose awkwardly from her chair and leaned on her outstretched hands that pressed against the table. She cleared her throat with a nervous cough and looked sheepishly at the judge.

"The people, your honor, do not know the defendant. We just have his file, which we have not had time to peruse. We have never spoken to him although we do, in fact, represent him at these proceedings. The people can shed no light whatsoever on his request. We trust that pleases you, your honor."

The gray-suited state prosecutor twitched like a tiger on the prowl. He smelled blood. He jumped to his feet. "This nonsense is totally . . . "

"Take your seat, counselor," the judge ordered with a shake of his head. "You do not play a role in this particular matter."

Greg Robertson could feel the beads of sweat on his face as he maintained eye contact with the judge.

The courtroom was eerily quiet as the judge gazed forlornly at the poor miserable wasted specimen of manhood who had just ordered the court to do something it had never done during more than 30 years on the bench.

The judge was in deep thought. He wondered how this character knew Phil Garrison. Could he be some relative? No. Phil had no relatives. Maybe he's Martha Sue's relative. She was a widow when Phil married her twenty years ago. Why wouldn't Phil have mentioned a relative? Hell, he and Phil had fished and played cribbage together since they were kids. They grew up together. Went to the same schools. They knew everything there was to know about each other.

Is this guy trying to oogedy-boogedy me? The judge wondered.

Better call Phil and get to the bottom of this.

"Bailiff," the judge ordered, "get Mayor Garrison on the telephone."

Judge Andrews looked at the large woman at the public defenders' table. She had been in his court several times and he could not remember her ever winning a case. Seated next to her was a young woman who could not have been more than a year out of law school. Next to her was a nervous sort of young man who looked like he should still be in school.

"Counselor," the judge said to the large woman, "approach the bench and give me the defendant's file."

The woman looked at the three stacks of files on the table and started pawing through them. Her two young assistants sat glued to their chairs. The large woman kept pawing.

"It's the one with his name on it, Counselor Phillips," Judge Andrews said slowly with derision.

Greg Robertson leaned back and took a deep breath as the phone was handed to the judge.

Greg slowly, mercifully, let the air out of his lungs.

The phone conservation seemed to take forever.

The judge talked in hushed tones, and occasionally flipped a page in the file.

While the phone conversation was going on, everyone at the bond sellers' table stole quick, hateful glances at the vagabond defendant who was trying to derail their gravy train and cost them a lot of money.

Judge Andrews finally shook his head up and down and said, "I concur." He handed the phone to the bailiff, and looked at the defendant.

Greg did not know what to expect as he saw the judge's face slowly turn from a stern, authoritative jurist into an expression that displayed compassion, benevolence and loving kindness.

"This county," the judge finally said, "and this court owes you a sincere apology, Mister Robertson."

The judge turned to the court stenographer. "I hereby order the seven deputy sheriffs, now present in this court, to be under the sole supervision of my bailiff, Sergeant Jefferson Thomas Jake Underwood. The deputies are advised that Sergeant Underwood is an officer of this court and is an extension of the jurisdiction of this court.

"Sergeant Underwood, and his detail of subordinate deputies, shall take Mister Robertson forthwith to Saint Agnes Hospital for medical treatment at the county sheriff's expense. Afterward, the officers, under Sergeant Underwood, shall expeditiously take and escort Mr. Robertson, code three, to the Dos Bayou city hall where Mayor Phil Garrison is waiting. All charges against Mr. Robertson are hereby dismissed, and any reference to his arrest in this incident shall be expunged from his record."

Sergeant Jake Underwood was seated at the bailiff's station, a spot he had dutifully occupied for nine years in Judge Andrews' court. Jake Underwood was a big, muscular, burly sort of a self-starter who had served a couple stints in the Marine Corps as a grunt infantryman with the stripes of a Gunnery Sergeant.

No one ever heard Jake Underwood complain. Not even the Navy doctors heard a sour word from him when they decided it was too risky to remove a piece of Iraqi shrapnel embedded in his back, next to his lungs.

The former Gunnery Sergeant had a raspy voice, with all of its cadences and varying volume, and he knew how to bark an order and when to keep his mouth shut. He also knew most of the deputies who were standing in the rear of the courtroom.

Prisoner abuse, intimidation, assault, harassment and sexual attacks came with the territory for most of them, especially Sergeant Billy Ray Lewis who stood in the back corner next to his partner, Deputy Timmy Dee Roland.

They were now under Sergeant Jake Underwood's command and old Jake had the power of the court behind him.

The judge looked again at Greg Robertson.

"Mr. Robertson, Mayor Garrison gave me a report on your background and status. I am impressed. You are an Air Force Academy graduate with a distinguished combat record as a fighter pilot during Desert Storm. Because of your status at the city of Dos Bayou, the car you were driving at the time of your accident, and subsequent arrest, was a public service vehicle, as covered under state statute. Therefore, you were not in violation of the curfew law.

"The report in your Public Defender's file described how you totaled the alleged stolen car you were driving, and how you also totaled a sheriff's car. Can you briefly describe what happened?"

"It was not stolen, your honor," Greg responded. "It was my wife's car. I was beaten by the arresting officers."

"What kind of car was it?" the judge asked as he picked up a pen and turned a page in his tablet.

Greg Robertson, who knew he was not under sworn testimony, looked at the judge and said, "It was a late model white four-door Honda Acura, fully loaded, your honor. It belonged to my wife, Brenda, who is assistant principal and third grade teacher at Lincoln Elementary School in Sandestin."

The occupants at the three tables sat in stunned silence.

The judge finished his notes, placed the pen in front of him, and scowled at the people seated at the tables.

"My eyes have been opened here today," he said, "and I don't mind telling you folks that I don't like what I have seen and heard."

The judge turned his attention to the two black women.

"Now, while I'm at it, your charges, whatever they were, are dismissed. You will also be taken to the hospital for treatment and escorted home.

"All charges against the ladies and Mister Robertson shall be expunged from their records."

The judge looked with a stern and unsympathetic glare at the lawyers and moneychangers seated behind the tables.

"I will take under advisement the court's own motion to dismiss all charges against those who appeared during these proceedings, and the full refund of their bail money. You will get the decision later today on the court's web site."

The state prosecutor in the gray suit nervously straightened his tie.

"And for you bond sellers," Judge Andrews said sarcastically, "I shall exercise my option under state statute and henceforth prohibit your presence in my court. You shall do your business in your respective offices and out of my sight, but not out of my jurisdiction as long as you are in the second circuit."

Judge Andrews was not finished with his admonishments. He turned toward the deputies.

"I shall ask the attorney general's office to conduct an immediate investigation of injuries I have seen today on the plaintiffs. None of you deputies shall leave the jurisdiction of this court until the investigation is completed.

"Sergeant Underwood, you know what to do. This court is adjourned."

The five police cars traveled code 3 to Saint Agnes Hospital and pulled to a skidding, water splashing stop in front of the emergency entrance where a medical team was waiting in the rain with wheelchairs.

The two black women were wheeled into separate rooms as Greg was triaged and taken to electroencephalography.

"This is a painless procedure for recording electrical impulses of the brain," the doctor said. "The next exam will be in electrocardiography. It, too, is a painless procedure for making a graphic recording of the electrical impulses that pass through the heart to initiate and control its activity. After that, we'll do Magnetic Resonance Imaging which will fill in any gaps, then a complete physical, and run some lab tests."

Two hours later, a nurse wheeled Greg down a long corridor. Behind them, Sergeant Jake Underwood led a single-file formation. The line of humanity contained the supervisor of accounts receivable, a dietitian, a cardiologist, an ophthalmologist, an internist, a vascular surgeon, a dermatologist, an otolaryngologist, a rheumatologist, a neurologist, an oral maxillofacial surgeon, a periodontist, a urologist and seven deputies.

They each wore a grim face except the supervisor of accounts receivable. She carried a cell phone, a calculator and a file that she constantly scribbled in as she walked. The file contained hospital charges, lab costs, and fees from all the specialists who treated Greg Robertson during the past couple hours. The tabulation of costs did not include the next appointment, which was three doors away, or prescriptions.

Sergeant Underwood moved briskly ahead of Greg's wheelchair, held the door open, and motioned to the deputies to wait outside.

It was a spacious office with a conference table. The nurse wheeled Greg to the end of the table, and everyone took seats except Sergeant Jake Underwood who stood by the door with his arms folded across his chest, just below his shinny badge. His utility belt contained the usual gear; a 9-millimeter Walther, shells, mace, cuffs, knife, flashlight, baton, sunglasses and phone.

A doctor rose from his desk on the far side of the room, picked up a recorder and a file and walked over to Greg.

"I'm Bill Jacobs, chief of emergency medicine," the doctor said with a forced smile.

"Mister Robertson, you were worked over real bad, but we'll put you back together in no time. You'll stay here in the hospital for a few days and get some much needed rest and treatment."

Greg nodded against the order. "I have to get to the city of Dos Bayou today."

"How will you get there?" Doctor Jacobs asked. "You certainly can't drive."

"Sir," Sergeant Underwood said in a husky voice, "I'm an officer of Judge Andrews' court, and it is my duty and pleasure to provide Mister Robertson a proper police escort, code 3, to Dos Bayou."

The chief of emergency medicine stared wide-eyed at the sergeant.

"I see," the doctor said with a look of disappointment. "Well, in that case, do you mind if I have an advanced life support ambulance follow you? A nurse, a paramedic and a couple emergency medical technicians may come in handy."

"They are welcome, of course, sir," Jake Underwood said.

"Thank you, sergeant. Won't you have a seat?" the doctor asked as he waved his arm at an open chair at the other end of the table.

"Thank you, no."

"Very well. We shall begin. Mr. Robertson, please listen while I dictate what we found during our examinations, x-rays and lab tests. When I conclude, the doctors present will give you appropriate prescriptions and respond to any of your questions. Our pharmacy will fill the scripts and you can be on your way. I will try to be brief but thorough. Okay?"

"Thank you," Greg uttered. "I appreciate your understanding."

The chief of emergency medicine started his dictation into the recorder.

"Damage to the third, fourth and fifth lumbar vertebrae. Scrip for cerebrospinal fluid buildup. Fecal impaction. Scrip to dissolve hard mass that blocks the passage of waste. Hematoma, rectus abdominis. Occlusion. Needs adjustment for bite. Number three molar missing. Bone fragments removed. Number six canine missing. Bone fragments removed. Number nine incisor loose. Vision in left eye impaired. Scrip for infection. Obstructed passageway, left atrium. Paraumbilical hernia. Peak-flow meter detected low lung efficiency. Hematoma on pectoralis major muscle. Numerous abrasions, lacerations and contusions on head, back, shoulders, sides, legs, arms and stomach. Glass fragments removed from skull, forehead, cheeks and nose. Script for infection. Dietary menu required for two weeks. Follow-up treatment by specialists is imperative. Repeated hits by a blunt instrument, and fists, suspected cause of injuries."

After the perfunctory farewells, the supervisor of accounts receivable opened her file and walked over to Sergeant Underwood. She gave him a stapled bundle of papers and held out a pen. He thumbed through the 27 pages and noted the consultation fees and hospital charges by all the specialists, the dietitian, the chief of emergency medicine, prescriptions, pharmacy costs, examinations, x-rays and lab work. The balance due was $26,839.04.

Sergeant Underwood took the pen from the supervisor's out-stretched hand and initialed the cover page. "Not bad for two hours' work," he said handing back the papers. "Send the bill to Sheriff Homer Jedbow Cogburn for payment per orders from Judge Chester D. Andrews."

"The ambulance and crew will be a separate bill," the supervisor said in a curt tone. "It's six thousand dollars per eight-hour shift, plus mileage."

"How much is mileage?" Sergeant Underwood asked as he stood ramrod erect.

"Fifteen dollars per mile."

"Send it to Cogburn per Andrews."

The supervisor of accounts receivable stepped directly in front of Sergeant Underwood. She straightened her 5-2 frame to its full vertical position, rose on her tiptoes, tilted her head skyward, but could see only the bottom of Underwood's nostrils.

"What gives you the authority to approve these expenses on behalf of the county?" she shouted.

Underwood removed his hat and bent his head down. Their faces were ten inches apart. He leaned closer until their foreheads almost touched. "I am an officer of the court and an extension of the court's jurisdiction. Proceed as directed, ma'am."

The supervisor of accounts receivable looked wide-eyed at the square jawed, crew cut, muscular black man who spoke with a deep, bass tone of explicit authority.

"You have a nice day now, you hear?" the supervisor said through tight, nervous lips as she stepped back, slammed her file shut and snatched the pen from Underwood's hand.

The six-vehicle convoy departed the hospital with Sergeant Underwood driving the lead car.

The ambulance was the second unit in the convoy. The new, shiny Braun vehicle was the most expensive cost-per-mile ambulance in the hospital's emergency transport fleet. It was outfitted with a double inventory of advanced life support equipment that left little comfort space for the four personnel inside; two emergency medical technicians, a paramedic, and a nurse from the hospital's emergency room.

After a left turn on Opt Road, Sergeant Underwood went code 3 with lights flashing and sirens blaring. He slowed as he cleared an intersection on a red light, turned right on a frontage road and accelerated as he veered onto the entrance lane to Westbound Freeway 10. He glanced in the rearview mirror, moved to the passing lane, and counted the code 3 vehicles behind him.

Sergeant Underwood was in command and on the final leg of his mission. His patient, who should be resting in a hospital bed, was in the back seat. Underwood adjusted his mirror, turned on the car radio for the news, and looked at Greg Robertson. He appeared to be dozing. He was all bandaged up and, to Jake Underwood, looked like a mummy.

The speedometers never climbed higher than 45 miles an hour. Low areas on the highway were still flooded from Hurricane Raymond's torrential rains and debris, and traffic gridlock at higher elevations caused scores of rear-end collisions and road rage among motorists.

As officer-in-charge, Sergeant Underwood ordered the convoy to switch to code 6 and turn south on Martin Luther King Boulevard for the remaining twelve miles to Dos Bayou. The route had less traffic, but more hurricane destruction.

Greg Robertson awoke to a familiar voice on the car radio. The voice was still describing storm damage.

The voice said rainfall had flooded most of the streets in Dos Bayou, had ruptured a dam and the city's main sewer line, and pushed up the Nelli and Blackwater rivers. The rivers, which contained millions of gallons of raw sewage, would crest within 12 hours.

The hurricane death toll climbed to 438 in Escambia County, property loss would exceed $2 billion and 71,000 people remained in 54 shelters.

Gulf Utility officials said it would take weeks to restore electric power, and that snakes were a constant menace because many of them left flooded areas for shelter under cars and houses.

The National Guard was activated to sandbag against rising flood waters and patrol for looters.

The area's squash, cotton, pole beans, corn, tube peppers, melon and tomato crops were a total loss.

The voice continued: A representative from the Reverend Jesse Jackson's Rainbow Coalition toured the flooded areas late Wednesday and held a press conference at the Pensacola NAACP office. The representative, the Reverend Willie Matthews, said the Florida panhandle needed not just flood relief, but a top-to-bottom reconstruction because its economy, especially in black neighborhoods, lagged even before Hurricane Raymond.

Officials from the Federal Emergency Management Agency announced plans to speed up the distribution of $60 million to buy or rent about 4,000 mobile homes for displaced flood victims to live in while their homes are repaired or replaced.

Residents would face several more days of rain, tornadoes and flooding in the hot August temperature without electric power.

Sergeant Underwood reached over and turned off the radio, made a tire-screeching right turn on Andalusia Street, and came to a water-splashed stop in front of city hall.

Mayor Phillip V. Garrison's droopy, creased hangdog face with soulful brown eyes looked out the front window and saw Judge Andrews' long-time bailiff get out, wade through mud and water, and open the right rear door.

An ambulance and several black and white units splashed to a stop in the circular driveway.

The mayor watched anxiously as Sergeant Underwood leaned into the back seat and carefully pulled out a bandaged and gauze-covered cripple with a patch over one eye.

The disabled figure of a man, the mayor thought, looked like a sure candidate for permanent residence in an intensive care unit.

"Oh, my God," Mayor Garrison said as he pressed his face against the window. His lower jaw sagged in disbelief. "He looks like death warmed over."

The mayor walked to the front door and pulled it wide open.

Sergeant Underwood had a big beefy arm around Greg's waist to support his weight as they slowly inched their way up the front stairs and into the foyer.

"My God, Greg," the mayor said, "you look like you crashed and burned."

"Mayor Garrison," Sergeant Underwood said, "Judge Andrews asked me to escort Mr. Robertson to you. He was roughed-up by our deputies. We just came from Saint Agnes Hospital. The docs said he'll be as fit as a fiddle in a few days."

The mayor raised his head to look through his bifocals for a closer examination. The mayor's mouth opened, his lips moved, but nothing was uttered. His face mirrored absolute, horror-stricken nausea.

He looked at the crumbled body of Greg Robertson. Plots of hair on the poor guy's head had been shaved, and strips of tape covered the stitches. A black patch with a tiny horizontal slit covered his left eye. His face was obscured by bandages. His mouth looked like raw hamburger. He wore a neck brace. His legs appeared so weak they couldn't support the weight of a butterfly. His left arm was in a sling. His shirt and coat were unbuttoned and a large elastic tape stretched across his stomach. Dried blood and mud covered his torn and wrinkled suit.

Mayor Garrison had seen scores of beaten-up hobos in his town over the years, but he had never seen anything like the object before him.

"Let's take him into my office where he can be comfortable," Mayor Garrison said as he helped guide Greg toward a large leather chair.

"I'll leave you two to talk and I'll wait outside with the ambulance crew and deputies," Sergeant Underwood said. "Judge Andrews should be here shortly. He's bringing something for Mr. Robertson's wife."

The bailiff closed the door behind him.

The mayor leaned down and looked compassionately into Greg Robertson's face. Some eye movement was noticeable through the slit in the patch.

"I am so sorry. So sorry for you. It surely hurts me to see you like this. You don't have to talk if it's too painful."

Greg mumbled something with an affirmative nod.

"First and foremost," the mayor said, "I'm very pleased to inform you that the city council voted four to two to accept my recommendation to hire you as our new city manager. Welcome aboard."

Greg leaned against the back of the soft leather chair and reached out his right hand. The mayor took it with a warm but gentle grasp.

"I told Chet, I mean, Judge Chester Andrews, about your appointment when he called me. He and I go way back. Chet's my closest friend. After our conversation, I called your wife and brought her up to speed. She knows you've been banged-up, and you'll be home soon.

"I'm starting your salary at eighty-five grand plus benefits and an expense allowance effective today. Your administrative staff all evacuated out of state before the hurricane hit. There will be plenty of work to do when you're back on your feet. I don't need to tell you what kind of a mess this city is in. Hire and fire anyone you want. Everyone serves at your pleasure. You need no reason to let someone go. There are no unions or bargaining agreements. I'll fill in for you until you're ready. I'll wear both hats. Take your time. I'm civil service over at Pensacola Naval Air Station and I'm just waiting for my retirement to kick in."

The noise of cars splashing through mud and water in front of city hall caught Mayor Garrison's attention.

The office door opened and Sergeant Jake Underwood entered.

"Shall we show him? Underwood asked with a broad, toothy smile.

"Let's do it," the mayor said.

They gently pulled Greg from his seat and helped him walk to the front porch. Second Circuit Court Presiding Judge Chester D. Andrews was standing in a puddle of water beside a mud-bathed, but brand new white, fully loaded, four-door Honda Acura.

"What we're going to do, Mr. Robertson," the judge said, "is drive you home in your wife's new car. We'll help you get in the back seat and Sergeant Underwood will drive. Mayor Phil Garrison and I will ride with you, if you don't mind. We'll deposit you safe and sound at your home. Your wife will have help taking care of you because we've hired a full-time, round-the-clock nursing staff, maids and cooks to assist. Plus, you'll have the ambulance and the medical staff on duty at your place just in case you need them."

Sergeant Underwood heard the judge and ran a quick mental tabulation of weekly costs Sheriff Homer Jedbow Cogburn would have to pay. Underwood stopped counting at thirty-two thousand. Another half-week, Underwood knew, would match his annual salary.

Greg was dumbfounded. Just a few hours earlier, the judge had threatened contempt of court and a jail cell. He was now giving Brenda a new car and a house full of hired help, not counting an ambulance and all those medical people standing in the mud beside it.

Sergeant Underwood put his arm around Greg's waist. "I'll help you so you can walk around and examine your brand new car."

Mayor Garrison waded through the mud and water toward Judge Andrews, leaned over and whispered, "Who paid for it, Chet?"

"Sheriff Homer Jedbow Cogburn," the judge whispered with a wink. "But old Homer, the ignoramus Bluegrass crooner, doesn't know it yet. I figured a little Southern hospitality might head off a big-time lawsuit that could very well bankrupt this whole county."

"What do you mean?"

"Well," the judge said in a low voice, "if your new city manager is half as smart as you described him, he could file the biggest goddamn lawsuit you could ever imagine against the county. And old Homer Jedbow Cogburn and all the deputies and everyone else listed as defendants would not have a Chinaman's chance. Mr. Robertson would own this whole damn county. It would be bankrupt, and the state would bail it out, but your man would own it lock, stock and barrel. That's what I mean."

"What makes you so sure Greg has such a good case?" the mayor asked.

Judge Andrews' face wrinkled into alarm as he eyed his life-long friend.

"It's not a good case, Phil. It's a slam-dunk case if I ever saw one. If Mr. Robertson files against the county, he's got a rock-solid case that's any lawyer's dream. The county would have absolutely no defense. That's why our hospitality is so important."

The judge's words sunk in. Mayor Garrison nodded.

The judge thought for a moment.

"What are you paying him, Phil?"

"Eighty-five grand, plus perks."

Judge Andrews shook his head, and looked at his old friend and fishing partner.

"Let's sweeten the pot, Phil. Let's make it an even hundred grand. I'll throw in the additional fifteen thousand from my budget. Hell, no one has to know."

"Yeah, I suppose we should," the mayor said. "Besides, Greg is not just half as smart as I described him to you. He's as sharp as a tack and his wife may be even smarter."

"What do you mean?" the judge asked with a quizzical expression on his face.

"Well," the mayor said, "Greg graduated first in his class at the Air Force Academy, and graduated with honors when he got his master's from Oxford as a Rhodes Scholar. I read his citations for receiving the Distinguished Flying Cross, a Silver Star and two Purple Hearts during Desert Storm. The guy is a Rambo with brains. He doesn't know what fear is."

Mayor Garrison thought for a moment, then leaned even closer to the judge's ear. "His wife, Brenda, has her bachelor's and master's degrees from Princeton. Chet, I'm sure you've heard of her father."

"Who's her father?" the judge asked with a wrinkled brow.

"Jeffery Adam McCormack in Atlanta. That's who."

Judge Andrews rubbed his chin. "McCormack's law firm has at least two hundred lawyers. Oh, my God." He thought for a moment. "And I remember that they're admitted to practice in every state in the union. Christ, Phil, we're sunk. McCormack's firm is known around the country as old shake, bake and radiate."

The mayor could not resist.

"How did it get that name?" he asked.

"Well, when they win, and win big which they usually do, it takes the losing party as long to recover economically as any sucker would after a nuclear explosion.

"That's what they mean by shake, bake and radiate."

"Guess what Greg Robertson's daddy does for a living?" the mayor asked.

"I'm afraid to. But go ahead and give me both barrels. What?"

The mayor flashed an impish grin. "He's an appliance salesman at Sears."

Judge Andrews took a deep breath and exhaled slowly.

"Well, that's good news," he said as his face turned into a quirky smile. But it disappeared fast.

"Did your man Robertson have any storm damage at his house?" the judge asked. "Yes, his wife said they had extensive damage."

"Let's take care of his deductible and whatever the insurance doesn't cover. You agree?" the judge asked.

"Hell, why not," the mayor said. "I'm going to do some fancy dancing to keep the council, and especially the two council members who voted against Greg, from finding out about all these little side deals we've arranged."

"Who were the two who voted against him?"

"The same minority we always have on damn near every vote," the mayor said with a wave of his arms, "Carlos Santiago Dominguez and Libby Washington."

"I know a little about Carlos and Libby," the judge said with a nod and an all-knowing wink. "If they get out of control, just let me know. I'll yank their chains and no one will be the wiser. Besides, I understand federal agents are quite curious about Mayor Pro Tem Carlos Santiago Dominguez's frequent trips into South America, especially with his diplomatic immunity. It seems no one can figure out his sources down there."

"No one, my ass," the mayor said shaking his head. "Hell, no one can figure out how Carlos Santiago Dominguez lives so high on the hog with only his railroad disability retirement.

"The guy travels all over the South American continent for the Sister City Program and the Organization of American States, and he never bills Dos Bayou for expenses. And with no bills, we can never figure out where he goes. There's no record of anything he does."

"Maybe he came into some new money," the judge said.

"No one from around here has won the lottery in a long time, Chet, and you know that to be the truth," the mayor said with a shrug.

"And what's more, Chet, listen to this," the mayor said with a look of exasperation. "Dominguez voted against Greg Robertson, and Dominguez has never met Greg. Hell, I think Dominguez would vote against his own mother, if he had one."

"That is strange behavior," the judge said nodding.

"Well, anyway," the mayor said as he leaned over a little closer, "after Dominguez voted against Greg, old fancy pants Dominguez left city hall and disappeared before Hurricane Raymond hit. Two days later, his Porsche was found under a huge pine tree at the airport. It was totaled. A security guard said Dominguez paid cash for a first-class ticket to Colombia down in South America."

"Well, now," Judge Andrews said rubbing his chin, "why am I not surprised?"

"There's more," the mayor said. "The security guard said that Dominguez flies down to South America just about every month. Sometimes in a private jet."

The judge's face wrinkled into a worried expression. "We sure have our plate full with the likes of Carlos Santiago Dominguez and Sheriff Homer Jedbow Cogburn."

"What's that crazy bluegrass singin' sheriff up to now?" the mayor asked.

"Well, it's hard to believe, but old Cogburn was the featured bluegrass entertainer last weekend at the annual international mullet festival over in Niceville."

Mayor Garrison closed his eyes in disbelief.

"Oh, there's more," the judge said. "Playboy magazine photographers and centerfold bunnies were there and the magazine's reporter announced that Playboy is running a big spread in a future issue featuring Cogburn's bluegrass songs and the bunnies in what the reporter called 'the cultural highlight of the year in the Redneck Riviera.'"

"Oh, Lord," the mayor gasped, "did Cogburn have his clothes on?"

"Yes, and he was apparently the only one, according to one of our bailiffs."

The mayor's hangdog face shook in a look of wonder and his jowls quivered. He turned and flashed a big smile as he walked over to Greg Robertson. "Your troubles are over, Greg. Welcome to Dos Bayou, Mr. City Manager. Shall we go?"

The mayor was wrong. Trouble in Dos Bayou had just started.

CHAPTER 3

Deputy Sheriff Timmy Dee Roland's small, skinny body was slumped deep in the driver's seat as his left arm dangled over the steering wheel. Wrist movement guided the patrol car as it maintained a steady pace behind the white Honda Acura.

Timmy Dee had not spoken to his seatmate and partner, Sergeant Billy Ray Lewis, since they pulled away from Dos Bayou City Hall, followed the Acura down Spring Parkway, turned east on Highway 98 and headed toward Sandestin.

Timmy Dee's face glared through the window at the Acura. His brow and cheeks bore their usual lines of hate-filled creases whenever something went wrong. And Timmy Dee had just witnessed a terrible wrong, an unheard of order from a junior officer to a senior officer. That was exactly what Sergeant Underwood did. He had given an order to Billy Ray. It was wrong because Underwood was a junior officer. The order was for Sergeant Billy Ray Lewis and his partner to follow the Taurus to the city manager's house in Sandestin, and take Underwood, Judge Andrews and Mayor Garrison back to Dos Bayou City Hall.

It was not just the order that irritated Timmy Dee. It was the way Underwood had barked the words so everyone, including Judge Andrews and Mayor Garrison, could hear the command.

Timmy Dee knew that Underwood's order was nothing more

than a nuisance trip or baby-sitter job that Underwood should have given to a junior deputy, not a senior, superior leader like Billy Ray. Timmy Dee and everyone else knew that Billy Ray was senior to Underwood in time in grade, and Timmy Dee, like all the other white, team-player deputies in the Sheriff's department, hated Sergeant Jefferson Thomas Jake Underwood.

But Timmy Dee kept quiet. Just like Billy Ray had done since they left city hall and headed toward Sandestin.

Timmy Dee knew the importance of being submissive.

He grew up along the Gulf Shores of Flora-Bama, a small rural area of sharecroppers west of Perdido Key. He had shifted gears after high school and had left the physical, no-frills Alabama grind for a Pensacola, Florida lifestyle more to his liking. He enjoyed the genteel mannerisms of his new body language and the prepping sessions he went through for loosey-goosey Jimmy Buffett concerts, and hanging-out with new friends as they listened to hours of the eardrum-pounding boy band 'N Sync.

Timmy Dee's dark and murky, grainy and grim, lifestyle had not changed when he became a deputy sheriff seven years ago. He just became more discreet with his partners in the loose-knit Redneck Riviera.

He decorated his Palafox Street apartment into a gorgeous pink and blue pad with aromatic candles and Japanese-scented massage oils. The expanded kitchenette became a gorgeous chef-friendly kitchen, and one day, he knew, someone would find him gorgeous enough – street-smart, savvy, flirtatious and womanish enough – to love forever.

Until then, he knew that in law enforcement, as in local politics, slickness would prove more enticing than profundity. And he was as slick as they came. He had mastered the superficial allure of a well-oiled, obedient disciple on Sheriff Homer Jedbow Cogburn's staff.

But Timmy Dee was never a leader. A leader needed followers, and Timmy Dee was a good, devoted follower. He did whatever Sergeant Billy Ray Lewis ordered, needed, wanted or desired.

When Billy Ray needed a young, frightened female prisoner controlled, Timmy Dee would hold the slut's shoulders and arms to the ground, grin at her as she screamed and moaned, while Billy Ray's hips pounded against her flesh.

Timmy Dee also hated each bitch with a jealous rage.

As Timmy Dee drove, his mind wondered back to the beginning of his shift, only a few hours earlier, when he did what Billy Ray ordered. Timmy Dee had done it many times before. He had struck the prisoner several times with the butt-end of a shotgun, slammed the point of a baton into the guy's gut and ribs, kicked him in the back and sides with a swift boot, and connected hard with a clinched fist to the guy's face.

Timmy Dee knew that Billy Ray had no way of knowing the guy was a city manager with political connections all the way to Judge Andrews. Oh, what the hell, Timmy Dee thought, that's the way the mop flops sometimes. A poor, hard-working, unappreciated cop is out on patrol just doing his job when some yahoo breaks the law, wrecks a patrol car, resists arrest, gets hauled in and some pencil-neck judge lets him walk.

Timmy Dee looked in the rearview mirror and carefully examined his hair. It was slicked back as usual with a broad part on the upper left side. Not one hair was out of place. He squinted his eyes and the creases disappeared from his brow and cheeks. The worried-look vanished. A quick smile flashed across his weasel-shaped face.

He thought about tough, black, ex-marine Jake Underwood and how he would have to go down. The smile broadened.

His mind switched to what he would prepare for his dinner guest tonight, what candles he would light, and, afterward, what oils he would use for the massage.

Timmy Dee decided he would serve sirloin tips en brochette. He would marinate the beef in a consommé with sherry, soy sauce and crushed garlic cloves. Twice-baked potatoes, or parsley rice, would accompany perfectly sliced Italian squash. A fine, mellow Napa Valley Merlot or Cabernet Sauvignon from his rack would add the perfect complement. A bottle of California Talus Chardonnay would be waiting in an ice bucket by the hot tub.

Oh, my, Timmy Dee thought to himself as he considered a more difficult decision. What, oh, what shall I wear?

He stole a glance at his partner. No, Timmy Dee, he said to himself, you have no cause for alarm. Not with a big, strong partner like Sergeant Billy Ray Lewis, whose uncle is Sheriff Homer Jedbow Cogburn.

Timmy Dee knew the sirloin tips would be a lovely start to a lovely, relaxing evening.

It was Billy Ray's favorite meal.

~ ~ ~ ~ ~ ~

The prescribed drugs from the hospital had circulated through Greg Robertson's body and he was blessedly free of pain except when he tried to shift his weight in the back seat. The broken ribs reminded him to stay still. He had dozed off when they left city hall and he wondered how long he had slept. He peered through the window of the moving car and saw blurry objects pass by. He could not determine his location. His pilot's instinct told him that he needed to know where he was and where he was heading. Then he saw it. Hurlburt Field, his old Air Force special operations base. He was only 11 miles from home. Eleven miles from Brenda.

A quizzical expression slowly formed on Greg's face as his mind reminisced about the events at city hall. He recalled how the judge's bailiff, Sergeant Underwood, helped when they walked around and inspected the new car. He remembered what his starting salary was as city manager. Then his mind drew a blank. His memory faded. The drugs made him sleepy. He forced himself to think. What did Underwood say after he made sure everyone was buckled in? What were the words he had spoken in such a strong, command voice just before the car doors closed? Greg had to remember. He shut his eyes and tried to visualize the scene.

A light flashed in Greg's mind. His eyes opened and he could hear the command from Underwood.

"Billy Ray, I want you and Timmy Dee to follow. I'll be the point. You'll be in the middle, between me and the ambulance. You and the ambulance will stay on code five. After we take Mr. Robertson home, you'll bring me, the judge and the mayor back here to city hall. Any questions?"

Greg had to fight the drugs. He tried to think. The names Billy Ray and Timmy Dee sounded familiar. Why? Who were they?

The drugs won. His head dropped into a deep sleep.

Second Circuit Court Presiding Judge Chester D. Andrews turned halfway around, looked back at Greg Robertson's slumped head, and gave his old friend, Phil Garrison, a nod. "He's sleeping like a baby, isn't he?"

Mayor Garrison shook his head. "He's had one long, hard day and that's for sure."

"Haven't we all," Judge Andrews said with his signature wink. He turned back, resettled in his front seat, and looked at his bailiff. Jake Underwood's hands were on the steering wheel and his big eyes were glued to the road.

"Jake, I was thinking just the other day about how long you have been my bailiff. Has it been eight or nine years?"

"Sir," Underwood said without changing his stare, "it was nine years on the thirteenth of last month. Nine good years, sir."

Andrews turned halfway around again and looked at his old friend, Phil Garrison.

"You know, Phil," he said with another wink, "the Governor just signed a new statute that deals with judiciary issues. The law gives the presiding judge in each circuit court the power to appoint a Chief of Bailiffs. The position carries the rank of lieutenant, and whoever gets the job reports directly to the presiding judge.

"Phil, who do you think I should appoint to that position?"

Jake Underwood's eyes grew even larger as the words sunk in. Jake knew the judge had a dry, subtle sense of humor. A promotion to lieutenant was no laughing matter. The rank was few and far between, especially in Escambia County. Jake saw no humor whatsoever in the judge's comment. Besides, why was he asking Mayor Garrison for advice? Why would the judge even mention such a thing? No, there was no humor in it at all that Jake found. But the judge's comment and his question to the mayor sure got Jake's full attention.

"Well, Chet," the mayor finally said in a very slow, deliberate manner that had to speed up to be considered a drawl, "I suppose I would have to think on that long and hard for sure."

Jake was going crazy. How could he drive and listen to his future being decided by two likeable old codgers who fished together all the time? The guy seated beside him had the power to promote someone to lieutenant. The politician in the backseat suddenly lost his ability to speak. Now he has to think on it. Think on what? There was a simple answer.

Jake had to go to the bathroom. Hell, this was no time to stop. Why didn't the mayor just continue his sentence and get it over with? Jake wanted to say something. No, he didn't just want to say something. He wanted to scream as loud as he could. "Don't think about it. That could take days. Don't study it. That could take weeks. Me," he wanted to yell. "I'm your man. Appoint me. Oh, Lord, I have a vision. The vision has me wearing lieutenant bars. Me, a black man in Escambia County in a lieutenant's uniform. I'll do you proud, judge, and you, too, mayor. Thank you. Thank you very much, indeed."

Jake's mental outburst on what he wanted to proclaim was interrupted by some words coming from the back seat. It was the damn, slow-talking mayor again.

"Well, Chet, I have pondered your question and all the ramifications that go into making a reasonable and sound practical response," the mayor said in a slow cadence that drove Jake Underwood absolutely wild. "I would have to say, now hear me out Chet, you know, I would have to say why not give serious thought to, ah, to, well, like give serious thought to Sergeant Underwood?"

Jake had to pee. Pee, hell, he had to piss like a racehorse on a flat rock.

"Well, Jake," the judge said as he turned and faced his bailiff, "what do you think of Mayor Garrison's recommendation?"

"Good choice, your honor," Jake heard himself say.

"All right, then, that's done. Phil, would you get Sheriff Homer Jedbow Cogburn on your cell phone?"

"Glad to."

Several moments passed and Jake was even more nervous than before. He wondered if the sheriff had seen the hospital bill with Jake's initials on it. How about the bill for the new Acura? And the eight-hour per shift cost for the ambulance?

It seemed to take forever for the department to locate the sheriff. Finally, Jake heard the mayor ask, "Is this Sheriff Cogburn? Please hold for Second Circuit Court Presiding Judge Chester D. Andrews."

Jake took a quick glance as the phone was handed to the judge.

"Hello, Homer, you doing okay?"

There was a pause.

"Good. Yes, I'm just fine. Thanks. I wanted to tell you that I have just promoted Jefferson Thomas Jake Underwood to the position of Chief of Bailiffs. The job calls for the rank of lieutenant. Make that first lieutenant. Under a new state statute, I make the appointment. As of this time and date certain, Underwood is hereby a first lieutenant.

"Please process all the necessary paperwork and have the file on my clerk's desk first thing tomorrow morning. Good to talk with you Homer. Good-bye."

Only a few seconds had gone by when the cell phone sounded.

"Hello," Judge Andrews said. "Yes, this is he. Yes, I'll hold."

The judge covered the mouthpiece, turned and whispered, "It's Homer." Jake and Phil watched impatiently as the judge held the phone to his ear. "Get a pen and paper, Homer, and I'll dictate the number of the statute." That seemed to take forever.

"It's seven, zero, niner, two, niner . . . what? How do you spell it? Spell what?" Jake and Phil were lost.

"It ends in e-r not o-r," the judge said with exasperation. "Call the state attorney and have him fax it to you."

The judge pushed the END button and handed the phone to Phil. "What were you spelling for him?" Phil asked.

Judge Andrews shook his head. "Poor old ignoramus, Bluegrass Homer did not know how to spell niner."

The judge thought for a moment. "Hell, Phil, I'll go him one better. Get him back on the phone for me, please. Let's have some fun."

Jake knew he had to stop real soon and piss. It would be a long, full-stream piss just like any lieutenant would do it.

"Homer, have one of your deputies go to Lieutenant Underwood's house and have his wife give your deputy one of Underwood's uniform shirts. Then have the deputy go to the Army-Navy store, or whatever, and buy a set of first lieutenant bars. Have the deputy deliver the shirt and bars forthwith to three, six, niner Foxwood Drive in Sandestin. Now hurry. Do you copy?"

There was a long pause.

"Thanks, Homer. That will be all."

~ ~ ~ ~ ~ ~

Sergeant Billy Ray Lewis glanced at his side mirror and saw the ambulance behind him. He looked ahead with a sarcastic grin and saw the damn white Honda Acura. The carpetbagger city manager was slumped in the left rear seat and Billy Ray could see the large, black short-trimmed head of Jake Underwood, the biggest prick in the department, behind the steering wheel.

The head and shoulders of the ass-licking, brown-nosing, trough-feeding federal bureaucratic small-town mayor was in the back seat. The way his head kept bobbing, Billy Ray knew the lily-livered bastard was yes-siring everything that was coming from Judge Andrews' mouth.

Judge Andrews! Now there was the poorest excuse for a judge the Florida panhandle ever had. Cops hated him, Billy Ray knew. At least the good cops did. The others didn't matter. The others, the dumb cowardly ones, went straight from shift briefings to their patrol cars and left for their beats. When their duty-day ended, they went directly home to haughty details like coaching black Little League games, attending PTA meetings or continuing old tribal customs they should have left in Africa.

They never socialized at the Gator Pit Bar, the watering hole where the good cops got their first three beers on the house, and their robes hung on hooks in the storage room closet.

The good cops were the ones Billy Ray had molded into tough, crime fighting protectors of God-given southern rights; cops like Timmy Dee Roland, a God-fearing Christian, and a state's rights fundamentalist member of the Ku Klux Klan.

Timmy Dee was the latest example of Billy Ray's selection

process. Timmy Dee had proven to be a good disciple on many occasions. After four years of rock-solid performance, Timmy Dee, three years ago, became the 27th member of the family.

Each family member attended the night meetings Billy Ray called, swore their allegiance to the burning cross, and their obedience to the Grand Dragon, the huge, brawny, explosive-tempered Billy Ray Lewis.

The Gator Pit Bar was the property of Billy Ray's older sister, Mary Jean, and Red, her common-law husband. It had a tin roof, long bar, cold beer, hardwood floors, three pool tables and a pine clock with a "6" at every position.

The inscription on a small plaque under the clock read: "I never drink till 6." The clock and plaque were Mary Jean's idea when they took over years ago.

Mary Jean, in her usual denim jumpsuit, was always friendly as a veteran bartender should be, and she was Billy Ray's only confidant. She proudly funded his Klan expenses and provided unlimited quantities of kerosene for their meetings and cross-burning rituals.

The bar was a hangout for crawfish fishermen from the swamps, a few bikers, a hooker now and then, and good cops who met in the large, windowless back room that Mary Jean and Red used for storage.

Billy Ray was as Cajun as the bar's nearby fauna-infested bayou. He didn't cotton to exotic food, strangers, or the welfare animal-types who lived in the projects.

He lived alone in a trailer park, had his own brand of hillbilly music, a sizable gun and knife collection with plenty of ammo, a boat and two trucks. He didn't move around too much on his free time except to inspect crawfish boats for sale after the season.

So there wasn't too much that occupied Billy Ray's mind except his neighbor, the cripple Bull Hussey, and his laying hens that kept terrorizing Billy Ray's fighting cocks. Billy Ray knew that he and Timmy Dee would have to deal with the cripple guy real soon.

Billy Ray and Mary Jean were raised in Century, a small white incest-ridden community short of gray matter on the northwest tip of Florida. He and Mary Jean never knew their parents. The people around Century who raised Billy Ray and Mary Jean called themselves uncles and aunts. The only thing ever mentioned about their parents was when Billy Ray and Mary Jean heard an uncle say they were killed when their car slid out of control on a wet road near Cantonment and hit a telephone pole.

Billy Ray worked in the fields since he was old enough to remember. When he was 12 and Mary Jean was 14, they were separated and lived with different aunts and uncles. Mary Jean never complained about having to live with so many different men. It was years later, after she ran away with Red that she confided to Billy Ray her long-felt depression and grief about what the uncles did to her.

The only secret Billy Ray ever kept from his sister was what the aunts had done to him.

One year after Mary Jean ran off with Red, Billy Ray dropped out of high school during his junior year to work as a janitor and gardener for his uncle Homer at the police station.

Everyone knew Police Chief Homer Jedbow Cogburn had a marker on just about everyone in the north county. It was no contest six years ago when he ran for sheriff and won by a landslide. His reelection two years ago was a close contest, but he squeaked by and remained in office. Billy Ray was the campaign manager.

Billy Ray had worked for Uncle Homer Jedbow Cogburn for the past 18 years. During that time, Billy Ray went from janitor-gardener-gofer, city trooper, to senior sergeant in the Escambia County Sheriff's Department.

During those years, Billy Ray survived two dozen investigations by his own proud count. The indictments were for extortion, illegal campaign solicitations, prisoner abuse, racketeering, drinking on duty, mail fraud, gambling and civil rights violations.

In each case, the charges were dismissed because of hung juries, witnesses had suddenly refused to testify, or they just mysteriously disappeared.

Folks in the north county area eagerly awaited Billy Ray's response on each charge because he always had a droll and disarming answer.

When the most recent indictment was dismissed, a reporter

asked Billy Ray if he thought the government would ever give up. His response: "Maybe when I die and I'm buried. Then they'll dig me up three days later and say I was in the wrong grave."

North County people who followed Billy Ray's career were as impressed with his sly, Houdini-like ability to get out of trouble as they were with his political skills.

What little brain he had kept his uncle in office. And his uncle always returned the favor by using his deep, well-oiled slush fund to pay lawyers and hoods to fish Billy Ray out of trouble.

Sergeant Billy Ray Lewis was an incongruity to the norm and a paradox to everyone who knew him. Everyone, except Timmy Dee.

Billy Ray scowled as he looked again at the Acura. It had moved into the left lane with its single on.

Billy Ray looked over at Timmy Dee and grinned. Billy Ray moved his left arm down on the seat, opened his fist, palm up, and extended his fingers. Timmy Dee slowly took his right hand off the wheel, straightened his long, lean fingers with manicured nails and tenderly formed an entwined grasp.

~ ~ ~ ~ ~ ~

The first decision newly promoted First Lieutenant Jefferson Thomas Jake Underwood made was to take a piss.

Jake did not ask the judge, the mayor or the city manager for permission to stop the three-vehicle convoy at the Chevron station. He just flipped the signal, changed lanes, braked in front of the men's room, and unzipped as he trotted.

The powerful horizontal geyser would have made any lieutenant proud of his rank.

He was washing his hands when Billy Ray and Timmy Dee entered. Timmy Dee went directly to a stall and closed the door. Billy Ray walked behind Underwood and bumped him with a "get out of my way" elbow push.

Billy Ray walked to the urinal, shook his hips a couple times to loosen his shorts, opened his fly, poked a hand inside and started the usual search for the Vienna sausage-shaped object. He turned his head and looked at Underwood.

"Don't you ever again, I mean, never, ever, never again yell an order at me. You hear me, bailiff boy?"

A giggly sort of snort came from Timmy Dee's stall.

Underwood finished wiping his hands in a slow, deliberate manner and tossed the paper towel in the trash can.

Jake Underwood knew very well what Billy Ray meant, and the bias in his words.

Field troops, over the years, had often expressed opinions that bailiffs had arm-chair jobs, short hours and long breaks to play their cribbage games, plan weekend family outings, shop, or study for promotional exams.

The troops complained that they did not have "bankers' hours." They had to work. They had to chase speeders, man roadblocks, assault pot houses, serve extra duty on SWAT Teams, and miss family birthdays and anniversaries.

Jake Underwood also knew something else. He came from a middle-class Tupelo, Mississippi Methodist minister's family with deep feelings and respect for personal space. But most of all, he knew what "boy" meant. His great-grandfather was once one on a plantation.

Billy Ray had just committed four wrongs that violated Underwood's space, status, rank and civil rights.

Flip the brim on a black man's hat? That was sacrilege.

Caress the well-coiffed hair, or offer an embrace that might wrinkle a crisply starched shirt? Don't even think about it.

But a swift elbow in the back? A simple 'scuse me would not suffice. You paid.

Insolence to a senior officer? You paid dearly.

Insubordination? You paid big time.

Contempt to an officer of the court who was an extension of a court's jurisdiction? You paid time and money.

Call an African-American "boy?" You don't have anything left to pay, except more time.

"Sergeant Lewis," Lieutenant Underwood said slowly and deliberately as he walked to the door, "if and when you ever find your cock and complete your mission, get in your car and follow me. Report to me immediately after we deposit the city manager safely in his house. Any questions, sergeant?"

A throaty gasp emitted from Timmy Dee's stall.

"Hearing none," Underwood said as he stepped outside, "carry on." The door slammed shut.

Billy Ray looked down and saw large urine spots on the front of his pants.

"I'll get that black son-of-a-bitch if it's the last thing I do," he yelled.

~ ~ ~ ~ ~ ~

The rapid shish-shish sound of rotor blades hovered overhead as Jake Underwood turned off Highway 98 and onto Foxwood Drive.

Judge Andrews lowered his window, leaned his head out and studied the helicopter. "It's from the sheriff's department," the judge said as he repositioned himself.

"Phil, would you get on your phone again and call Sheriff Cogburn? That might be my delivery service."

Jake Underwood could hear the dial tones.

"Hello. Second Circuit Court Presiding Judge Chester D. Andrews wants to speak with Sheriff Cogburn, please. It's important."

Oh, for Christ's safe, Jake said to himself as he rolled his eyes. Can't these two old curmudgeons just make a simple telephone call without making a damn federal case out of it?

"One moment, please."

"Hi, Homer," Judge Andrews said. "One of your helicopters is overhead. Is that my delivery service?"

There was a long pause.

"Okay, I'll have a unit meet them at the Wal-Mart parking lot. But when I told you to hurry, I didn't mean you had to scramble your helicopter."

Another pause.

Jake shook his head in disbelief.

"Homer, how much does it cost to fly one of those things for an hour?"

Jake glanced over at the judge.

"Well, that's a lot of money, Homer. You've got some more costs coming your way."

The judge listened.

"Oh, I kind of lost count, Homer," the judge finally said. "There's one from Saint Agnes Hospital, one from Jim Clark Honda Acura and another one from the hospital for an ambulance. There might be more along the way but that will be all for now."

Jake Underwood pulled into the driveway just as Greg Robertson opened his eyes.

A crowd was standing in the front yard.

CHAPTER 4

Sergeant Billy Ray Lewis nodded his head up and down in one quick gesture. He did not open his mouth to utter a word when he got the order. He didn't say, "Yes, your Royal Back-Stabbing Highness," but he thought about it. He didn't snap, "Why don't you have your black, bailiff boy run your silly, little errands," but he wanted to. And he didn't say, "Kiss my ass, judge, you're not in my chain of command," but he sure felt like saying it. No, Billy Ray just nodded, raised the car window, lifted his left hand in a fist with the thumb pointed backwards and Timmy Dee knew what to do.

The patrol car backed out of the driveway, dodged the ambulance, went code 3, and headed north on Foxwood Drive toward Wal-Mart.

"What do you think the helicopter is carrying that's so damned important," Timmy Dee asked as he checked for oncoming eastbound traffic, saw none, and made a skidding right turn onto Highway 98.

"Beats the shit out of me," Billy Ray dead-panned. "Uncle Homer has to approve any chopper flight that's not on a life-support mission. We'll just have to wait and see. Guess we'll find out real soon the way you're driving."

Timmy Dee cut the lights and siren as he pulled into the Wal-

Mart center and headed toward the helicopter in the far-left corner of the parking lot. The rotors were in slow mode as they twirled, and a crewman was standing beside the craft. He held something in his hand.

Billy Ray was unbuckled and half way out of the car when it came to a hard, braking stop. The crewman handed Billy Ray something on a clothes hanger. A dark plastic wrap covered the contents.

"What's this?" Billy Ray asked with a quizzical expression.

"It's a shirt." The crewman reached into his flight jacket pocket and pulled out a small jewelry box. "This goes with it. Now, if you don't mind, we'll get this bird back in the air for missions we're suppose to handle. We're outta here."

Billy Ray had an open-mouthed, blank expression on his face as he held the shirt-hanger in one hand and the box in the other.

The crewman climbed into the craft and gave Billy Ray a half salute. The rotors revved, the machine lifted off in a swirl of dust, banked hard left as it cleared the Wal-Mart roof and disappeared.

"Goddamn it," Billy Ray yelled as he got into the car, placed the hanger on the side hook, and tossed the box on the front seat.

"What's that?" Timmy Dee asked.

"The guy said it was a shirt. He also gave me that box."

"Open it, Billy Ray. Let's see what's in it."

Billy Ray snatched the box and tried to open it with his thumb. Nothing happened. He tried to twist it open. Same result. He used his fingers and tried to pry it open. It was stuck. He held it up to his face and saw transparent strips of tape wrapped around it. "Oh, hell, no one said it was secret." He took out his switchblade, clicked it open and cut the tape. "Now we'll see what this fucker is." He opened it, looked at the contents, and his large brown eyes froze in an eerie glare.

Timmy Dee watched as Billy Ray's face turned slowly from shock, to astonishment, a hint of kindness, and finally into a glow of serene happiness.

"Timmy Dee, you won't believe what Uncle Homer has done for me. Look at these."

Timmy Dee craned his neck and looked down at the out-stretched hand that held the open box. It contained two shiny, brand new, silver first lieutenant bars. Timmy Dee's face split into a broad grin that grew in length as the realization set in.

"Billy Ray, you didn't tell me you were on the promotion list for lieutenant."

"Hell, I wasn't. I flunked the test. Shit, I've flunked it three times in a row. "

"Well," Timmy Dee said, "this means the sheriff ordered your promotion to skip the rank of second lieutenant, and for you to go directly to first lieutenant. That makes sense."

Billy Ray held the little box in the palms of his over-lapped hands as he continued his awe-struck gaze at the silver bars.

Timmy Dee reached back, took the hanger off the hook, pulled up the plastic cover, and examined the shirt. He raised the collar off the hanger and carefully checked the size. "Yep, it's yours. Size extra large."

Billy Ray looked at Timmy Dee. "How does it make sense?" Billy Ray asked with a brain-dead utterance.

"What do you mean?"

"How does it make sense that anyone should skip a rank?"

"It's a payback for managing your uncle's successful campaign," Timmy Dee said matter-of-factly. "It's called quid pro quo. That's why it makes sense."

Billy Ray, the high school dropout, looked more puzzled than before.

"What's quick, prod. . . . what did you say?"

"Quid pro quo," Timmy Dee said. "It means you scratch my back, and I'll scratch your back. It's like returning a favor. That's what your uncle just did."

Billy Ray straightened himself in his seat, thought for a couple moments, and looked at Timmy Dee. Billy Ray was about to make his first command decision.

"As soon as we take our passengers back to Dos Bayou city hall, we'll go to Uncle Homer's office and let him put the bars on me. In the meantime, we won't say or do nothin' 'till I'm in full uniform."

A twisted, derisive grin formed on Timmy Dee's face. He knew exactly what Billy Ray meant.

Sergeant Jefferson Thomas Jake Underwood was going down. Real soon.

~ ~ ~ ~ ~ ~

Vigilant observer Brenda Robertson stood in the living room with her school teacher's perceptive gaze. She looked apprehensively around her storm-damaged home and saw more strangers than she could count. The ambulance crew, hired help, contractors, subcontractors, an insurance adjuster and unexpected guests were everywhere.

One was in the kitchen cooking. One was setting the table. One was vacuuming. Two contractors, five subs and the adjuster were examining rooms, walls and ceilings for hurricane damage, taking photos and writing estimates.

Five medical types were in the master bedroom with Greg. They were taking his blood pressure, evaluating his vital signs, changing pads and bandages, and inventorying the various containers of prescriptions.

One was in the bathroom taking a piss. Brenda could hear him.

Greg's boss, the mayor, stood like a stone Buddha at the front window.

Another one, who acted like a Royal Potentate, was seated in the Lazy Boy recliner in the living room. Brenda remembered her introduction to him. He was a judge. He appeared to be a self-appointed supervisor who directed everything that was going on.

Judge Andrews, Brenda thought, looked like the type who was born standing up, talking back and supervising his own delivery.

Brenda shrugged her shoulders. Everything looked so disorganized, but everyone was busy doing something. Except the judge.

Brenda took another glance in the master bedroom. The medics were looking at charts and a clipboard. Greg was sleeping.

Brenda turned, walked into the kitchen and poured herself a glass of wine.

Mayor Phil Garrison maintained his sentry-duty position at the front window. His eyes were glued on the driveway. He was carrying out, as usual, his part of a Judge Andrews' plan. Finally, the patrol car appeared. Garrison turned and looked at the judge. "They're here, Chet."

"Good. Let's do it," Judge Andrews said with a wink.

The mayor opened the door, walked to the car and asked, "Would you two please come with me to the backyard? I need your help."

"This old shit is gonna end real soon," Timmy Dee whispered as he and Billy Ray followed Mayor Garrison through the gate.

Judge Andrews pulled the side lever on the recliner, the footrest folded up, he eased himself out of the chair, and went out front. He opened the car door and looked in.

A small jewelry box was on the front seat. He opened it, examined it, closed it, and put it in his pocket. He took the shirt off the hook, walked back inside and headed for the kitchen.

"Miss Brenda," the judge said in a mild but judicial-type command, "please come with me into the living room. I need a witness for a swearing-in."

Brenda refilled her glass and followed her leader.

Jefferson Thomas Jake Underwood stood at attention in his crisply starched helicopter-delivered shirt as Second Circuit Court Presiding Judge Chester D. Andrews pinned on the bars.

Brenda took another sip as the judge administered the oath. No one heard what he said because the cleaning lady with the vacuum cleaner had moved into the living room.

Hands were being shaken as Mayor Garrison walked in. "They're in the car waiting. The other car just pulled up."

"I like it when a plan comes together," Judge Andrews said with a wink and a broad smile.

"Miss Brenda," the judge said with an out-stretched hand, "please let me or Mayor Garrison know the minute you need anything. Your husband is in fine hands and your house should be as good as new in no time."

The judge turned and faced Lieutenant Underwood. "Okay, Jake, go do what you have to do with Sergeant Lewis. We don't need him or his partner anymore. They can leave. We'll wait a couple minutes until they're out of sight, and then we'll be on our way."

"Yes, sir. I'll be right back."

Underwood marched out the door like a man on a mission.

"How long do you think Jake will take?" Mayor Garrison asked.

"Oh, I'll say a minute."

The judge was wrong.

Sergeant Billy Ray Lewis was told when and where to report, and Timmy Dee burned rubber. Lieutenant Underwood watched as the car disappeared down the road.

The one-sided conversation took 24 seconds. There were no questions.

Brenda's usual perky, happy mood had turned melancholy as she waved and watched her three guests leave.

She sensed something unusual had happened between Lieutenant Underwood and the two officers who departed in such a hurry. She had overheard their names, and she wondered if Billy Ray Lewis and Timmy Dee Roland had anything to do with Greg's condition. She forced herself to stop the self-talk. What was she thinking? They were cops. They protected people. But she could not help from wondering and worrying.

She also had a strange and uneasy feeling about the judge and the mayor. They were kindred spirits. Two likeable old sorts and their personalities had a fervent touch of southern graciousness. But what bothered her about them was the way they connived, plotted and schemed, and how they seemed to read each other's mind.

During an hour or so of observing Judge Andrews, Brenda saw first hand how he presided over everything, huddled now and then with the workers, received hushed briefings from the bailiff and the mayor, and told everyone "what to do."

It did not take Brenda very long to form a conclusion about Judge Andrews. There was no man behind the mask.

Her discovery did not mean he lacked substance or depth. Nor did it reveal the man in the expensive but casual attire as a con hiding his essence behind the ice-blue gaze of a glacier.

Sage old Andrews inspired mystery in Brenda because she had to assume there was more to him than met her eye. What met her eye during the past hour of observation was a man whose game face had been cast in marble.

An assumption arose in her that a different personality lay behind the mask. Maneuvering, cunning and manipulating, old foxy Andrews was hiding something he didn't want anyone to see. And Brenda knew what it was. Namely, it was himself. The real him. The real lethal and likeable Chester Andrews.

But she also had a strong inkling that if he let down what was left of his hair, someone else would jump out.

She also knew he had an insatiable ego. He invited intimacy and small talk, but for so public a figure, he still cast a lone-wolf shadow. His ego, Brenda felt, did not leak into conceit. He did not brag or gloat. He used his ego as a competitive weapon to see who was best.

Judge Andrews' joined-at-the-hip-friend, Mayor Phillip Garrison, was nowhere near the best. Brenda knew it. She had already heard from other teachers at her school too many sordid details about the chiseling, beguiling, back-slapping Garrison.

Half bad-ass, half kiss-ass, asshole Garrison was a big man with a big appetite.

Any night, the teachers said, he could be found at Pascali's, a gastronomically renowned restaurant in Pensacola, where his corner booth, No. 10, was called "Phil's Folly."

The maitre d' bowed and called him "Mr. Mayor."

For years Garrison had been the public face of the city of Dos Bayou, and he had come to bask in the pleasure of being quoted, cited, courted and pictured in all the power centers in Northwest Florida, from Fort Walton Beach to Pensacola. He liked the routine. His usual at Pascali's was: Start with ice-cold martinis the size of doggie bowls, move to aged steaks as big as Buick hubcaps washed down with bottles of choice French wine, followed by strong, sweet liqueurs.

The only thing that irked Mr. Mayor was a waiter who mistakenly handed him a check.

His hearty, gruff voice rumbled across the restaurant. Lobbyists and old pals would stop by to shake the hand of the senior bureaucrat at Pensacola Naval Air Station that awarded hefty contracts; the same hand that granted zone changes to sub-dividers, building permits to developers, and ruled the tax laws at Dos Bayou.

He was a burly, swaggering man with the face of a hang dog. During his 18 years as Mayor of Dos Bayou, Garrison did some occasionally good work for the people, and a lot more for his deep-pocket friends.

And his deeds to his friends had become the talk of the town. He was now routinely second-guessed on talk radio, critiqued in print and booed by those often-disharmonious Dos Bayou taxpayers. Garrison's aw-shucks country-boy demeanor had become accustomed to weathering storms. But the storms were now growing and circling him in the form of Internet gossip and newspaper editorials and cartoons in adjacent counties.

His enemies knew that the information highway that kept hammering away at Garrison and comparing him to roadkill also knew that Internet roadkill was never really dead.

The teachers at Brenda's school told her that Garrison symbolized what people hate in local government.

It was not the bribes from defense contractors at the navy base, petty-cash chiseling of taxpayers' money at Dos Bayou, illegal gifts or a snazzy Cadillac that the teachers hated.

What the teachers did not like was arrogance of power.

They talked about the system that hands barons such as Garrison muscle to run roughshod over rules and people. They talked about the times when Garrison seemed to be cornered, and there was no way he could explain away what he did.

He just played the martyr, a heavy jowled Joan of Arc torched by heretics.

Arrogance, to Garrison, meant never having to say you're sorry.

The teachers had convinced Brenda that someday Garrison's

penalty would be a burden of disgrace for anyone who touched him.

Brenda knew that Greg would be an excellent city manager. But why Dos Bayou? She would not let Greg become a member of "Phil's Folly."

How could she interpret, how could she unravel, all the other peculiar things that had just happened right under her own nose?

When she called the insurance company, reported the storm damage, and requested an adjuster, she was told they could not have one there until Monday or Tuesday of next week. Two hours ago, when the adjuster showed up with two contractors and three subs, the adjuster told her that someone "with influence" had called.

Brenda knew the judge and the mayor had plenty of "influence" between them.

When the contractors made their cell calls and ordered thousands of dollars in building materials, Brenda asked them if the orders were approved. One of them told her, "The little lady of the house need not worry about particulars or complicated cost figures."

He explained that everything was under control, that they were just following orders, and "the little lady" had her hands full with a "badly beaten-up husband who was a city manager."

It was the first time Brenda has been addressed by that old, oft demeaning expression "little lady." She hated it even when Rhett Butler said it!

How in the world, Brenda thought, did so many busy contractors know about her husband?

Brenda thought about the maid. She showed up three hours ago in a Chrysler Town & Country LX van and unloaded a Rainbow vacuum cleaner, mops, brooms and enough household cleaning supplies to last a year.

Brenda never had a maid before, and Wendy Watters – as she called herself – was the most atypical cleaning-type Brenda had ever seen. She was in her early 30s, had a sad, weary brow, casual dark blond hair, and a petulant, ripe and mischievous mouth that never closed. She also had enormous cleavage.

Brenda tried to avoid her, but they always seemed to bump into each other.

Wendy's comments were usually just echoes of her previous statements.

Wendy said she was just doing what she was told to do, there would be no charge, and she was glad to help. "Besides," she said too often, "your husband is an important part of our community."

Then a young nurse, who introduced herself as "Miss Freehand," arrived in a new Mercedes. She unloaded two suitcases, a garment bag, several large containers of medical supplies, a defibrillator, a bed pan, sponges, liquid bath soap, lotions and powder. After Miss Freehand put everything away, she asked to be notified, "when my patient arrives with Phil and Chet."

The cute young thing, who Brenda thought looked more like a free-spirited, beach-bunny centerfold than a nurse, made herself at home in the guest bedroom.

Brenda wondered how the nurse knew that Greg was being accompanied by Mayor Phillip Garrison and Judge Chester Andrews. How many other public officials did the nurse know by their first names? And why?

Brenda could not discern another mystery about young Miss Freehand who wore an elegant-yet sexy ivory pantsuit, black flats, and had silken brown locks held captive by a black headband.

The Mercedes she had was the same model but two years newer than the one Brenda's father drove. And he was the founder and senior partner of Atlanta's largest law firm!

Brenda also wondered how all that sophisticated medical equipment could emerge so quickly by a nurse, even one who proudly proclaimed, "I always keep bags packed for emergencies."

Brenda smelled more "influence" than she cared for.

Then there was the cook. Oh, yes, the big Italian matronly cook who parked her Ford Excursion SUV in back by the kitchen door.

After she introduced herself as "Momma Lou," she carried in bags after bags of various cuts of meat, fish and poultry, vegetables, canned goods, fruits, juices, dairy products, assorted groceries and four cases of wine; two Chianti and two Chablis.

The wine selection, Brenda thought, was an unusual coincidence. Greg loved Chianti, and Chablis was Brenda's favorite.

When Brenda asked Momma Lou how much all of it cost, the woman wiped her hands with her apron and said in a thick Sicilian accent, "Its'a all taken care of so don't you worry yourself none about it. Momma Lou is here."

Brenda also remembered another Momma Lou comment: "You just concentrate ona fixin'-up your husband so he can handle his new job, and you can go back to teachin' our little bambinos."

By then, Brenda knew that too many people knew too many things that were none of their damn business.

But they kept coming.

Electric and gas lines were out and radio news reports said that customers should not expect any help for at least two weeks. The bad news from the radio was still ringing in Brenda's ears when there was a loud knock on her front door.

It was a 12-man crew from Gulf Power.

She had electricity in ninety minutes.

The gas came on 30 minutes later.

While she was on the porch and took a cell call from her mother, and worried about the high cost of her next phone bill, she saw three Sprint trucks pull up. Her phones were working 40 minutes later.

Then there was the large maintenance van from Chuck's Auto, Fuel and Detailing Shop. Three men said they were glad to provide a "complimentary courtesy call." They washed and detailed her new Honda Acura and filled the tank.

When they finished the Acura, one of them said, "Guess while we're here, ma'am, we'll remove the flat on your hubby's Chevy Blazer and put a new tire on. We'll go ahead and check his fan, belts, wipers, hoses and tubes and do any maintenance that's needed so the Blazer's in top condition for trips to and from Dos Bayou."

Brenda was in the front yard when Chuck's van left. She noticed a Hummer approach from the same direction. The strange-looking green olive drab colored vehicle moved slowly down the street toward her. The driver looked like he was trying to find an address. He saw Brenda and stopped.

"Ma'am, I'm looking for Greg Robertson's wife."

Brenda could not believe her ears. How did everyone in the world seem to know where they lived?

"Yes, I'm Mrs. Robertson."

"Is your husband the Dos Bayou City Manager?"

"Yes."

The driver picked up a cell-phone, dialed some numbers and spoke to someone.

Brenda watched intently as the man finally got out and walked toward her. As he approached, he appeared to be an Arnold Schwarzenegger lookalike in a civilian uniform with logos, badges and a name tag. He wore an ammo belt and pistol, and carried a bag in one hand and a clipboard in the other.

As he neared, he tipped his hat politely and said, "Ma'am, I'm Bart Grant."

"How can I help you, Mr. Grant?" Brenda asked in a voice full of trepidation.

"Well, the Mayor of Dos Bayou thought that your husband might need his first month's salary paid in cash because all the banks are closed due to hurricane damage. Around here, cash comes in handy when we have a storm, ma'am."

The man handed her the bag, the clipboard and a pen. "Please read and sign the paper, and I'll be on my way, ma'am."

Brenda read the form and could not believe her eyes. The paper was an acknowledgment of receipt for an after-tax sum of $7,843.52 based on an annual salary of $100,000.00.

"We can go inside so you can count the money before you sign, ma'am, if you desire."

Brenda opened the bag and thumbed through more $100-dollar bills than she made in more than three months of teaching.

"I don't think that will be necessary," she said as she scribbled her name and returned the paper.

"Thank you, ma'am. Oh, by the way, Mayor Garrison told my security firm to tell y'all that if y'all needed an additional advance, just let the mayor know. He said there was plenty more where that came from, ma'am."

"I'll bet there is," Brenda said with a slight tone of sarcasm. "Thank you."

She watched from the front yard as the Hummer backed onto a neighbor's driveway, pulled-out, and headed toward Highway 98.

She turned slowly and gazed at the workers on her roof.

Her shoulders slumped and her head drooped in an uncharacteristic manner. She felt a weariness, numbness and hopelessness she had never felt before. She had not taken a bath since yesterday morning.

Brenda looked at her scuffed shoes. She had not taken them off since she put them on 14 long, gruesome hours ago. Her faded denims were soiled, and her favorite old plaid work shirt reeked from cleaning polluted water off floors. The red-striped bandanna she had tied around her head to hide her hair was loose, and long dirty strands of twisted mats clung to her neck.

The bag felt heavy in her grip.

For the first time in her life, Brenda felt what it was like to be a grubby, slimy, miserable whore.

Two of them were inside her house with their madam.

There was no way, Brenda knew, that a young nurse could own a new Mercedes 500 SL unless she spent a lot of time on her knees and back with high rollers.

And the crude, raw Wendy, who couldn't assemble the Rainbow vac without Momma Lou's help, drove a new Chrysler van, and had a mouth any john would pay for.

The mouth had emitted a constant rat-tat-tat verbal barrage that was too risqué for a Howard Stern gig.

The new Ford Excursion SUV that Momma Lou drove did not make her a madam. It was the small appointment book she kept scribbling in when her cell phone constantly rung, and she described in her Sicilian voice the lurid details and fees for sex utensils named Sandy, Alice, Wendy, Marge, Virgie and Lolley.

Wendy's description fit the maid to a tee.

Lolley was the nurse, Miss Freehand.

Brenda glanced at the bag full of 100 dollar bills.

She looked at the large roll-off commercial trash bin beside her house. It was almost full of storm-related debris workers had tossed from her property.

She looked up and saw two men on her roof with a large hydraulic vice-wrench. The men looked filthy and sweaty as they realigned the joists that supported the roof.

Four other laborers toiled at stripping off dingy, slimy, broken pieces of composition tile that they tossed into the bin.

They were, in Brenda's eyes, hard workers who put in a full day for their pay. They had parked their old, battered pickups on the street near the Mercedes and Chrysler. The SUV was still in the back yard.

Brenda looked again at the bag.

Everything that was trash, filth or garbage went into the bin.

Brenda turned her head and saw Greg's Chevrolet Blazer with its new tires. Beside it was the new Honda Acura that the shifty-eyed, crooked judge, who knew how to cater a blowout, had given her as if it was another stocking stuffer. Brenda knew it was not as expensive as Miss Freehand's Mercedes, Wendy's Chrysler van or Momma Lou's Ford Excursion, but it was unearned, unwanted and un-welcomed.

Brenda was at the end of her rope.

It was time to call her father.

She felt a queasiness in her stomach.

She ran into the house, went directly to the bathroom, locked the door, dropped the bag on the floor and vomited.

CHAPTER 5

If Sheriff Homer Jedbow Cogburn were still a betting man, he would bet anything, even the goat farm if he still had it, that nephew Billy Ray Lewis would come busting through the door at any second.

Every time Sheriff Cogburn knew he had a sure bet he thought of the goat farm, and how the loss of it got him into the lucrative, southern-style profession of law enforcement in the Florida panhandle.

The dreams of men like Cogburn are often preposterous, especially when they come true. And Cogburn had his dream.

He owned Century's only goat farm and had within his grasp a fortune from restaurants and the upper crust in Pensacola, Panama City, Montgomery and Mobile who loved his goat cheese. The more the better. He couldn't make it fast enough.

But one day, young and impetuous Cogburn got drunk and made what he thought was a sure bet. It seemed reasonable at the time, and it had the potential for the expansion he needed to meet customer demands.

He bet the goat farm against his neighbor's dairy that he could run 100 yards, circle the salt lick, and return to the starting point before his neighbor could do the same on horseback.

That's how C. D. Atkinson lived out his days on his cow and

goat farms staffed by people who knew how to stoop and scoop, and a pretty young domestic-type who knew how to make a tangy mint cocktail, and cocktailing wasn't even her best feature!

That's also how Homer Jedbow Cogburn, at 24, became a mandolin-picking, banjo thumping, guitar-strumming, fiddle fiddling, song-writing, tenor-singing, coon-hunting, rookie cop in Century.

And Century is not a bad place to start. It's at the exact northwest corner of the Florida Panhandle, and they used to say of Century that it was a place outsiders could go to lose a weekend or misplace an afternoon.

The local folks still took a perverse pride in the little town's rip-snorting, hell-raising past.

And some of the locals who don't like Homer Jedbow Cogburn say it's difficult to see Cogburn as anything but a wastrel and a fool. To many, he was both. But the others who supported him took another view. In light of his circumstance, they saw him as they saw themselves; a dreamer, too.

How else to describe an unemployed man who lost it all with the grit to venture into the unknown territory of the Century Police Station, a snake pit of vultures in a shack that was hotter than a tin of camp coffee, eyeball the Chief, play a bluegrass ditty better than Bill Monroe, and ask for a job?

Three years later, Cogburn's bluegrass stompin' ground was the entire City of Century where he ruled as the pickin' an' singin' Chief of Police.

That's when he hired his nephew, Billy Ray Lewis, to tidy up the station as the department's first gardener, janitor and gofer.

Cogburn had no choice. He had to hire Billy Ray. That was part of the deal with Billy Ray's sister, Mary Jean.

Before Mary Jean ran off with an AWOL sailor from Pensacola, she threatened Cogburn with a few well-chosen words he never forgot: "Keep Billy Ray employed for the rest of your life, never contact me or try to see me again or I'll tell the world what you did to me and forced me to do to you."

Cogburn envied that sailor.

How often does a scalawag run away with a pretty young thing who's haired-over and broken-in?

So far, they had kept their promise.

Not so with Billy Ray. He was born with enough chips on his shoulder to make up a two-by-four. Each time he got into trouble, and Cogburn fished him out, Billy Ray promised it would be the last time. But each day with Billy Ray was just another 24 hours of assorted outrages. And sometimes, when he turned his vacantly pious glare on people of color, he acted crazier than a sprayed roach who didn't know diddly about doohickey.

And he was a master at exaggeration. He exaggerated so often that he frequently had to hire a stranger to call his dog.

Billy Ray was a constant bone in Cogburn's throat, but he was family, and most of the time he meant well.

It was Billy Ray who convinced Police Chief Cogburn to run for Escambia County sheriff six years ago, and now, as Sheriff Homer Jedbow Cogburn sat in his cushiony leather swivel chair between a cluttered knotty pine credenza and a matching executive desk in his spacious air-conditioned corner office, he wondered what kind of trouble Billy Ray had gotten into this time.

Billy Ray had called a few minutes ago and said he had to talk.

When Billy Ray had to talk, that meant he was in trouble.

Cogburn knew that Billy Ray's stupidity sometimes was enhanced by his own ignorance, which was excessively intensified by a personal vacuum of common sense that caused him to repeatedly engage in irresponsible behavior. But that did not make Billy Ray a bad boy in Cogburn's eyes.

Cogburn firmly believed that God had a special place in his heart for people like Billy Ray, because he made so many of them, especially in the Florida panhandle.

And Cogburn knew that the good Lord had also made a bad neighbor who lived next door to Billy Ray. The trailer park neighbor, Bull Hussey, was a cripple with one leg who raised laying hens and some fancy-type chickens he showed at state and country fairs. Billy Ray had often complained that the cripple's chickens were always creating a noise that kept Billy Ray's fighting cocks awake at night. And Billy Ray was afraid that if his fighting cocks got amnesia, insomnia, staph or whatever disease fighting cocks got when they didn't get their sleep, they just might lose their interest in fighting, crowing and killing, and that would be a financial loss to Billy Ray.

Cogburn knew only too well that Billy Ray had a quick temper, and Cogburn worried even more when Billy Ray, during his last visit, said that he might have to do something with "that cripple guy Bull Hussey."

Another one of Billy Ray's problems was that he loved to celebrate; celebrate basic freedoms which to him were kegs of beer, screwing in the bushes, fistfights, and bonfires during Klan rallies.

And Billy Ray seemed to have a strange way of showing up at places where he was not invited.

Like the time during Cogburn's last re-election campaign when he hosted a sedate cocktail party in Pensacola at West Florida University for delicate literary types and their proper wives and Billy Ray appeared very much unannounced and dressed like he had left the house on Sunday morning to pick up a six-pack and the newspaper and simply forgot to go back.

Billy Ray started imitating the struts and lisps of Pinot Grigio-sipping academicians. He stomped around, stepping on long gowns and howling for another Coors. When he asked a highly placed faculty wife her relative expertise and stamina in the cocksucking discipline, she answered in a Mae West throaty start-stop voice, "If you think....you can....handle it....come up....and see me.... sometime, big boy."

The delicate and learned folks thought Billy Ray was doing a little comedy gig and nervous laughter broke out.

Cogburn carried the faculty vote by a slim margin but received overwhelming re-election support from the faculty wives.

Cogburn thought about the Klan rallies. Then he thought about Billy Ray's dark skinned neighbor, Bull Hussey. That thought was just another reason, reason on top of reason, why Cogburn had to get the hell out of Florida.

Sheriff Cogburn wondered how long Billy Ray needed to talk,

because it was already late, and the bluegrass festival over in Gulf Breeze at the high school's Dolphin stadium started in two hours.

It would be a long two hours, Cogburn knew, because a hurricane was heading toward Pensacola and if the festival had to be cancelled, disaster officials should make that decision in the next few minutes.

The Cogburn Codgers were the featured act at the festival.

Bluegrass, Cogburn firmly believed, got him elected seven years ago, and reelected last year. If it got him reelected one more time, Cogburn would qualify for his retirement, and so would Billy Ray.

When both of them retired, Cogburn's commitment to Mary Jean would be over, and he could spend the rest of his years at music festivals so the world could appreciate his artistry.

The Florida panhandle was a mecca for bluegrass, country, R&B, pop, jazz, Doo-Wop, Bee-Bop, old gospels, rock-a-billy, and pop-to-rock crossover music.

Cogburn and his Codgers fit right in.

Homer Jedbow Cogburn was one of those artists people couldn't pigeonhole because he mixed his music and sounds.

He was a big-boned, fleshy, red-complexioned late 40s-something type at about 6-2 who could rearrange his mouth in whatever semi-vertical, oval or horizontal shape he needed to sing baritone, bass, tenor or high tenor.

He and his Codgers' band could astound audiences with a Dean Martin Neapolitan sound-alike, "Little Ole Wine Drinker, Me," or Ricky Nelson's "Lonesome Town," Glen Campbell's "By The Time I Get To Phoenix," or Merle Haggard's signature ballad, "I Take a Lot Of Pride in What I do."

Good-ole-boy Homer Jedbow Cogburn had developed a persona as a crooner-supreme during Friday and Saturday night gigs at sold-out high school stadiums and county fairs.

Some say he could beat on a tin lunch bucket with a rusty file, while calling up his hounds, and fawning music critics for the Pensacola Herald would proclaim a new native Art Form awash in social significance.

It was traditional of him before his first concert break of the evening to follow his bluegrass rendition of the Beach Boys' "Good Vibrations," with the honky-tonk sound of "Cotton-Eyed Joe," transfer ballad-style to the Bee Gees' "I Could Not Love You More," instigate a near riot with Mick Jagger's "Satisfaction," then calm the crowd down with a wailing Amy Grant inspirational gospel song.

The Codgers' introduction of the Rolling Stones song always started with an incredible, buzzing guitar riff followed by Cogburn purring, "I can't get no. . . . . sat-is-faction . . . "

The crescendo built until the other instruments dropped out and it was just the mandolin and Cogburn's "Hey hey hey, that's what I say . . . "

Cogburn was a showman with stage presence and an infectious pie-eatin' grin.

After two hours of Cogburn, festival-fans didn't know if they should boogie, smoke a joint, light a Winston, dip Skoal, spit, pop a keg, throw a bra, screw or evangelize.

Bluegrass, alone, just wasn't big enough to hold a voice like Cogburn's. He would mesmerize souls with an intimate, sensual ballad, or have them clapping their hands high over their heads to a Hip-Hop beat that caused transformers to explode.

And, if he wanted to, he could perform an entire gig in falsetto, even better, some said, than Frankie Valli did with the Four Seasons.

Cogburn's falsetto rendition of "Big Girls Don't Cry," "Walk Like a Man," or "Oh, What a Night," watered the eyes of thousands who stood with arms waving high over their heads.

He never gave the folks a hint on what crossover style he would play and sing next, but the crowds always raved.

He could drop his lower jaw and slant it a bit and croon just like Perry Como. And anyone old enough to have an ounce of nostalgia appreciated the smooth as silk, soft as down, grown-up man a la Como you could trust with sentiment.

Cogburn's way of singing Como's "Hot Diggety, Dog Ziggety, Boom," was a real crowd pleaser, and "Juke Box Baby," had the aisles filled with dancers.

His finale was Johnny Cash's "Folsom Prison Blues," followed by "I'll Walk the Line."

Cogburn could drop his jaw and tilt it in the opposite direction and sound eerily close to the Man-In-Black.

Then, as the stage curtains slowly closed, the crowd always stood in unison and erupted with jubilant shouts, shrill whistle sounds and calls for an encore.

After a few more minutes of bedlam, the curtains slowly parted to display a piano. Next to it, in the glow of three spotlights, stood a likeness of Elton John. Or was it really him?

The house went wild. Was it Elton?

He wore extra-large horn-rimmed glasses, his blondish hair was combed down on his forehead, he had on high heeled boots with plaid socks that touched his Four-Squares, and his pinkish Bermuda shorts complimented his almost florescent flashy red and orange open, extra-high collar shirt.

The crescendo increased into a deafening roar as the Elton John impersonator tip-toed in slow motion to the piano, seated himself, pulled the mike down until it almost touched his lips, and bellowed, "Don't Let The Sun Go Down On Me."

The second encore was always "Bennie and The Jets."

"Philadelphia Freedoms," ended the third curtain call with lights dimming.

Then, suddenly, the lights flashed on stage and the Elton look-alike took a deep bow.

The crowd roared louder than ever.

When he slowly straightened himself, the horn-rimmed glasses were gone, as was the hair piece, and there he was: Homer Jedbow Cogburn.

It brought the house down.

Some newspaper music critics tried to ignore Cogburn's position as the only entertainer in the Florida panhandle who consistently played to SRO houses. After all, he did not represent social rebellion or personal angst, favorite topics of liberal writers looking for social relevance in popular music. Yet it was precisely because Homer Jedbow Cogburn was great fun and guaranteed to give a good time at gigs that folks from throughout the panhandle and southwest Alabama loved him.

Cogburn and his Codgers were a bluegrass band, to be sure, but they infused rock with jazz and all the other sounds, and combined classic melodies with undeniable beats and rhythms that distinguished them from other bands.

Homer Jedbow Cogburn just had his way with music. Even before he went into law enforcement, when lawmen discovered him driving with his eyes unusually aglow, he'd hand them some cheese and a big country grin and he goes on his way as free as Drew Scott.

He could have been arrested numerous times just on the evidence of his eyes; they appeared to be made of red glazed tile and probably could have fooled a ceramics expert.

Cogburn also had a knack for writing little musical plays and short stories that were usually just a shade out of kilter. Each catchy tune with Cogburn's unique sound had a protagonist the audience cottoned to.

Whether it was a drunken dentist with a banjo problem, or a lawyer who lost his memory and never missed it, his down-home style drew encores.

Cogburn always had a story behind his music. Someone was hurtin' or lookin' or findin' a beer to get over it. The words had feeling.

The mandolin was his favorite. He could make it soar, glide, pop, hiss, astound and amaze.

He had spent a lot of time on his opening line and his new short story for the Gulf Breeze festival gig. It was a sure bet to get things off with a loud chuckle. And he would introduce it with his usual flare for modesty: "I writ' a new little ditty for y'all tonight and I hope y'all like it and it goes something like this."

It would be his newest and best creation: "Escape from Milton."

The song was a play on words, because what Cogburn really wanted was to escape from Escambia County and the state of Florida.

In just a little over five years, Sheriff Cogburn would give up his day job.

Or his half-day job. Or the job he rarely went to. But it sure paid well.

"Two grand less than six grand figures each year for a grand person," was how he described it.

But even some of his supporters had reason to doubt his grandness. Or work ethic.

During the past several months, Cogburn's staff never knew his whereabouts or if he would come to work. They tried to cover for him, but a lot of things that needed his attention fell through the cracks. Things like envelopes with fake anthrax, terrorist threats on schools and the numerous, mysterious first-class trips the Mayor Pro Tem of the City of Dos Bayou made to countries throughout South America. Some suspected the distinguished Mayor Pro Tem, Carlos Santiago Dominguez, was a major drug dealer, or worse, an arms dealer to terrorists.

But the Sisters at his catholic church, St. Mary's near the projects, knew him as a lay leader in the community's Sister City Program, and a highly acclaimed senior official with the Organization of American States. After all, the vicious rumors of his alleged criminal activity flew in the face of his significant monthly contributions that supported the church's St. Vincent dePaul outreach program into poverty-stricken areas.

Sheriff Cogburn's administrative staff just rolled their eyes in disgust when someone on the Board of Commissioners called with a constituent problem, or a reporter called for an interview, or the County Manager dropped by to visit.

Sheriff Homer Jedbow Cogburn could not be found.

No one knew where he was most of the time.

But he did.

He spent his nights coon hunting, and during the day he secluded himself in a little cabin in the hollow near his home in Pace where he wrote songs and practiced new hiss-sounds on the mandolin.

And he studied chamber of commerce brochures on towns in North and South Carolina; two sane states that fit his comfort zone. Places where he could play his music. And enjoy his monthly retirement checks.

In five years, he would move to one of those states because Florida had become too weird for the likes of Homer Jedbow Cogburn. Florida was just not the way it once was and it would never go back.

How could it return to its glory days? Inflation was running at the fastest pace in 23 years, the job market was under further strain, and foreclosure filings were surging.

He hated the mix of problems; a mix that included too many strangers.

Immigrants from all parts of the Caribbean, generations of pissed-off, encroached-upon Southerners, newly arrived, new-money Northerners, Native Americans with their gaudy, turquoise-colored casinos, three million Jewish retirees who voted on New York absentee ballots, and 50 million European tourists with communication problems at K-Mart sidewalk sales.

All of them were trouble.

Cogburn was tired of troublemakers.

And he didn't know which were the most dangerous trouble-makers, the glut of lawyers or the overabundance of venomous snakes. For every coral snake, there were ten thousand probate lawyers. For each pygmy, timber or diamondback rattlesnake, there were fifty thousand ambulance chasers, and for each cottonmouth water moccasin, there were two hundred thousand criminal "cash up front" lawyers.

There were also troublemakers in new Florida, the glitzy Florida, the old Florida, the tourists' Florida, the developers' Florida, the Versace Florida, the Cuban-Latin Florida, the swamp-infested Florida, the cracker Florida, the back-woods Florida, the panhandle Florida, the fishermen Florida and on and on and on.

It was a recipe for the unexpected.

Cogburn liked things in neat little packages with known contents and no trouble. He didn't read the papers anymore or watch the evening news.

Why?

He had already seen and heard it all.

A dead man voted, three consecutive husbands died from eating mushrooms and the fourth died from hammer blows because he refused to eat mushrooms, a parrot was choked and dunked in a margarita at a bar, a swamp snake swallowed an adult gator, a man fed his roommate's kittens to his pet hyena, and a warden resigned after allegations he slept with the wives of 34 different inmates.

Could Cogburn take five more years of Florida?

Florida had to be the only place in the world that had a governor who called himself a "He-coon"-the wiliest raccoon in the forest. Florida was the place where a State Senate candidate claimed her opponent died three years ago, and an optometrist who moonlighted as an alligator wrestler got trapped in his foe's jaws only to return to work two days later with a bandaged head.

What came in second on Cogburn's ire list was a paraplegic in Milton who didn't realize his dog chewed off most of his foot.

That incident was the inspiration behind "Escape from Milton," his opening tune for the Gulf Breeze gig.

The waggish discourse was a four-minute, high-tenor saga of the unpredictable trials and tribulations of being a live-alone Milton cripple who blended in nicely with the panhandle community because of their mutual mental and emotional sterility.

Cogburn envisioned "Escape from Milton" as a chart topper, a radio staple, a CD bestseller, a festival standard, a Country Music Hall of Fame winner, a Grand Ole Opry highlighter, and, glory be, platinum! It would be his ATM cash cow.

Cogburn had a sure bet. That Milton cripple would be Cogburn's crutch to stardom!

Cogburn tried to write something on the weirdest and wackiest thing that made number one on his wrath list, but he gave up. It wasn't because he was too embarrassed, or that it happened in his own courthouse. He just had a bad "feel" on the whole thing.

The damned janitors had formed a "Voodoo Squad" that scoured courthouse grounds for sacrificed animals used in Santeria rituals. Their discoveries: dead chickens, beheaded doves, a dead llama, cows' tongues wrapped in twine, a mule's middle torso, shell-less turtles, a cow's head, and lizards with their mouths tied shut.

That was when he first started sending away for brochures

on the Carolinas. Cogburn had to be reelected. He wanted that retirement. He had to escape.

He had narrowed his choices to Williston, South Carolina, and, just over the state line, Lincolnton, North Carolina.

He had visited both places and found much to his liking. Each had a VFW hall, an American Legion, a Progressive Home Club for lonely widows, a Daughters of the Nile for Masonic Shrine widows who were still ambulatory, flea markets, parks with bandstands, a high school with a large arena, hard-shell Baptist churches that hosted potluck suppers with watermelon on the ground, moonshiners and Saturday night destruction derbies at the fairgrounds.

Each place was a natural fit for Homer Jedbow Cogburn's bluegrass festivals, but Williston had a slight lead. It had a Piggly Wiggly, a super market that always maintained a good supply of sweet tea, tripe, salt pork and toothpicks, four of his necessities.

The blinking light on Sheriff Cogburn's private line interrupted his blissful thoughts of resort retirement in Williston. He pushed the speaker button.

"Uncle Homer," Billy Ray said, "I'm leaving here as soon as possible to come see you. I need to talk."

"Leaving where, Billy Ray?"

"Sandestin. Wait for me."

The phone went dead.

Sheriff Cogburn's brow furrowed and his mind was in deep thought.

He held out his open left hand and with his right index finger started counting.

"My jurisdiction is Escambia County," he murmured. "That's one," he said, touching his right index finger to his left pinky finger. "West of us is Santa Rosa County." He touched another finger. "That's two." He thought for a moment. "Next is Okaloosa County." He touched another finger. "That's three." He thought again. "The next one is Walton County where Sandestin is. He touched another finger. "That's four."

The creases in his brow deepened as he slowly closed his eyes and pondered.

What shenanigan is my chief deputy and nephew, Billy Ray Lewis, into this time?

- - - - - - - - - - -

"Uncle Homer," brash and ready to brawl Billy Ray Lewis said as he stormed through the door, "I have to talk."

Sheriff Homer Jedbow Cogburn's pleasant daydream of building a large grandstand at the fairgrounds in his retirement paradise of wild, wonderful Williston, South Carolina was over.

Billy Ray looked grim. And very serious.

"A real weird thing just happened, Uncle Homer. Come to think of it, I have to talk about several weird things that just happened to me and Timmy Dee."

Cogburn didn't need to hear of any more weird things to confirm his move to Williston, South Carolina.

"Can Deputy Roland come in, Uncle Homer?"

"Guess so. It's all right with me."

Timmy Dee stood in a sweat and leaned against the wall near the office door. He looked on the verge of a fidgety hissy-fit breakdown.

He had never been on the sixth floor before, had never given a thought of seeing what was on it, much less the inside of the sheriff's executive corner suite.

A plain, low-rung, ordinary deputy sheriff like Timmy Dee Roland did not belong on the sixth floor. He had no business on the sixth floor. A deputy never rode the elevator that high in the courthouse except on a very rare occasion when ordered to by proper authority for a specific purpose.

A proper authority was a lieutenant or higher rank.

A specific purpose meant that you did what you were told to do, you got out fast, and you got the hell back on your beat where you belonged.

The sixth floor was sacred territory for lieutenants, captains, the undersheriff and sheriff.

Timmy Dee had a problem.

Sergeant Billy Ray Lewis ordered Timmy Dee to come along for the meeting with Uncle Homer.

Billy Ray did not have proper authority, except through kinship.

That's how Timmy Dee rationalized it, and that's why he was so nervous.

He knew it wasn't an order.

Billy Ray had begged, pleaded, whined and cajoled all the way from Sandestin before Timmy Dee finally gave in and said he would tag along. But he had a caveat.

"If," Timmy Dee had said.

"If what?" Billy Ray had asked.

"If you let me give you a massage after dinner."

"You're on."

"I'm in."

But Timmy Dee was nervous. Real nervous.

He saw an arm poke through the open door and a hand waved him to come inside.

"Come on in, Timmy Dee. Uncle Homer said it was all right."

Timmy Dee stepped through the door and saw a face behind the desk that he had seen only in newspapers and on TV. He gave a quick salute, glanced around the room, saw of line of chairs against the wall, nodded as he hurried by the sheriff's desk, walked posthaste to the first chair, and took a seat.

Timmy Dee could not believe that he was next to Sheriff Homer Jedbow Cogburn, the papasita, the grand old man, the Charlton Heston, the Hemingway, the Moses and, Timmy Dee's absolute favorites, Barney Frank and Clay Aiken. To Timmy Dee, Cogburn was a panhandle folk hero, second only to Jack Nicklaus who used to live at Perdido Key, and they still play golf and pitch horse shoes and eat Mexican food together three times a week when Jack comes to town.

Timmy Dee stole a quick glance at the sheriff. When their eyes met, Sheriff Cogburn gawked at the bluest eyes he had ever seen on a man. They were bluer, Cogburn thought, than a bottle of window cleaner.

Sheriff Homer Jedbow Cogburn watched as Timmy Dee crossed his legs and hooked his right foot around his left ankle.

Sheriff Cogburn eyed Billy Ray and glanced back at Timmy Dee. The sheriff had seen a lot of peculiar things in his time but he had never in all of his born days seen a grown man sit like that.

What was even more peculiar was that Timmy Dee looked comfortable, but a little tense.

"Well, like I was saying, Uncle Homer, a lot of weird things have happened to me and Timmy Dee today. I have to talk."

Sheriff Cogburn leaned back in his chair as Billy Ray stood in the center of the office.

Billy Ray was a huge sort, with an expanded girth, a bit zany in conversation because he was a scatterbrained exaggerator, and an assiduous bore who wore an expression that looked like a starter kit for a Neanderthal.

Billy Ray stood with his feet far apart and wore a dreamer's smile and a sagging gun belt as he swayed in invisible breezes.

He cleared his throat and started to talk. His voice had the texture of a toilet flush.

He talked a few minutes about the need to fight the al-Qaida network over in the old country before they come to our new country without an invite and surprised us again.

Cogburn shook his head now and then in disinterested agreement.

Billy Ray then went into a long, meandering diatribe. He waded through subjects on relief for Afghan women, litter on highways, the need for bigger roosters with longer spurs for cockfights, why they should have more gun and knife vendors at the county fair, and more parades, sidewalk sales, rallies and Klan membership drives.

"Tell 'em who you're inviting to entertain during the membership campaign," Timmy Dee said.

"Well, Uncle Homer, I decided to invite the Pointer Sisters to entertain. But I didn't tell them what it was for. It's gonna be a surprise," Billy Ray said.

"Tell 'em how much the manager for the Pointer Sisters wants," Timmy Dee said.

"Oh, well, three hundred dollars, or maybe thirty-three thousand dollars or three hundred thousand. I just remember it had a three in it."

Cogburn's mind was on the bluegrass festival.

Then Billy Ray talked about his neighbor the cripple guy Bull Hussey who had regular laying hens and some grand prize award winning chickens that disturbed Billy Ray's fighting cocks so much at night that they couldn't get their sleep, so Billy Ray and Timmy Dee were going to have to take care of the cripple guy real soon.

Cogburn's mind was disengaged. He was blissfully unaware of what Billy Ray said. Cogburn had floated into another zip code: Gulf Breeze, the bluegrass festival and SRO at Dolphin Stadium.

Timmy Dee sat with a dumbfounded look on his face. His legs remained twisted around each other. His left foot started a nervous tap-tap on the floor. His brow and cheeks had their usual worried creases.

Timmy Dee was perplexed. What Billy Ray talked about was not what they had rehearsed in the car or at the Waffle House when they stopped for sweet tea.

Big Bubba Billy Ray relished his Southernness and all things Southern at a Waffle House. He had three favorites. They were extra-sweet tea, a double pecan waffle, and hash-brown potatoes grill-scattered, smothered with onions, covered with cheese, chunked with ham, topped with chili, diced with tomatoes, and peppered with a generous amount of green jalapenos.

While they downed their third helping of sweet tea, Timmy Dee explained his simple plan to Billy Ray's simple mind.

There were only four subjects that Billy Ray needed to tell his Uncle Homer.

The first one was that they were following orders when they set up the roadblock to catch looters. The second was about the speeding car that crashed into Billy Ray's patrol car, totaled both vehicles, and the driver got banged up real bad in the collision. The third subject was about Judge Andrews who let the guy off. The fourth item was a little more complicated. It covered the helicopter, the shirt incident, the lieutenant bars, and how Sergeant Underwood threatened Billy Ray.

They rehearsed the plan over and over in the car and at the restaurant. But as they neared the courthouse, Timmy Dee had a gut feeling that Billy Ray had something else stuck in his craw.

As Timmy Dee listened while Billy Ray talked on and on, it was clear that Billy Ray had stored up a lot of things that rankled his stomach.

Billy Ray said he wanted the county curfew on kids under 18 moved back from midnight to 8 p.m. on Saturday nights, that there was a growing unrest in the county over the need for more rodeos, and he wanted the parade permit fee waived for a Klan march and rally the day before Martin Luther King's birthday.

Billy Ray took a deep breath and stopped talking.

Timmy Dee re-crossed his legs and hooked his left foot around his right ankle. The tap-tap-tap sound continued.

Cogburn's eyes were half-shut, and his mind rattled-off the words to "Escape from Milton."

The silence got Cogburn's attention.

"Very good, Billy Ray. Is there anything else?"

"I need to talk some more," Billy Ray said.

Billy Ray talked about the helicopter.

Now, Timmy Dee thought, he's doing what we rehearsed.

Billy Ray talked about how the chopper delivered his shirt and the silver first lieutenant bars, and how proud he was for the promotion, "but Sergeant Underwood made off with the whole kit and caboodle."

Timmy Dee slowly shook his head in disbelief.

Cogburn's mind was on the third verse of "Escape from Milton." He wondered about the effect that it might have if he put three hisses, instead of two hisses, after the part where the cripple boiled his dog.

Timmy Dee's tap-tap-tap sounds got louder when Billy Ray got off track again and explained, "One of my plans is for the Ku Klux Klan to sponsor Adopt-A-Highway cleanup programs around public schools, black churches and the NAACP building."

Timmy Dee got real confused when Billy Ray mixed in the cleanup programs with the city manager's arrest, what Judge Andrews did, the Underwood incident, why Underwood should be fired, why someone should take the lieutenant's test for Billy Ray and put Billy Rays' name on it so he could be promoted, and if Underwood wasn't fired yet, Billy Ray would kick his big, black ass all the way to Montgomery.

Billy Ray also said, "Something should be done about legalizing cockfights like they do in Old Mexico, New Mexico, Honduras, Iraq and Argentina, and protect gamecocks from coons, possums, hawks, owls, laying hens and snakes."

Cogburn slowly opened his eyes and decided he would stay with two hisses. He glanced at his watch. The festival started in 45 minutes.

The tap-tap-tap was louder than ever.

"What about the test?" Billy Ray asked.

"What test?" Cogburn asked.

Billy Ray repeated the part about flunking the lieutenant's test three times and about having someone else take the test for him like they did in Century when he was promoted to sergeant.

Cogburn said he would work on it, and he gave a few examples.

Timmy Dee thought Cogburn's explanation was inspirational.

The sheriff explained that no one, not a nary soul, who grew up in Century had ever taken and passed an exam since they left high school through the back door, like Billy Ray had done during his junior year. The only exception, Cogburn explained, was when they took their driver's test. Some kinfolk who worked at the DMV office would read them the questions, mark down answers they thought they heard, and hand them a license.

Cogburn elucidated in a long, drawn-out story that tests were nothing more than unnecessary stumbling blocks to progress, improvement and success, and that Billy Ray would be an exception because he would be a lieutenant if it was the last thing the sheriff did.

What Cogburn said made sense to Billy Ray. And Timmy Dee.

What they didn't know was that Cogburn had just told a story about himself.

He had never taken an exam since he left Century High School and started raising goats.

By the time he got around to thinking about a driver's license, he was a rookie cop with the Century Police Department. That got him exempt from ever taking a driver's test because, as a police officer, he was grand-fathered-in under the Protective Services Statute of the State of Florida. His driver's license was good in any state and the expiration date read "For Life."

Cogburn may have been grand-fathered in other ways, too.

In his early 20s, he was an unrepentant, non-supportive, no-show father of three daughters born to different old high school sweethearts, and was named as a correspondent in two different contested divorces.

But how could he be shamed?

He was the pampered lead-tenor vocalist in the Garden Street Southern Baptist Church!

"You fellows want to come with me to the Gulf Breeze festival at Dolphin Stadium?" Cogburn asked as he rose.

"We would like to, sir," Timmy Dee said, "but Billy Ray has accepted my invite to come to my place for dinner tonight."

"I'm pleased about the lieutenant's test and the permit fee, Uncle Homer," Billy Ray said as he left with Timmy Dee.

"You boys come in anytime."

Timmy Dee ran to the elevator and pushed the button.

Sheriff Cogburn stood at his desk with a dazed expression.

The Voodoo Squad was on his mind. He thought about the incident and how he had spent two days in his cabin on a lyric style he had never attempted before.

He had planned to expand his musical repertoire by producing an over-the-top rap-rock-metal rendition on the Voodoo Squad. But after 12 drafts, he realized that his romanticized versions glorified those he reviled.

When he burned the drafts, he could not imagine himself as a musician commemorating any of today's dime-a-dozen assassins or hate-crime mongers.

As he stood in deep thought, he had a sudden urge to express in lyrics the bitterness that grew within him. To do it, he would need the same seediness that pulsated through his veins when he wrote the cartoon debauchery, "Escape from Milton."

He smirked as he relished the thought of doing a rap-rock castration and lynching of the little weasel-faced prickless wonder Deputy Timmy Dee who should have been smothered at birth.

He would start writing first thing in the morning, right after coon hunting.

He would write a heavy metal piece on the gay son-of-a-bitch who just contaminated the sixth floor.

He pondered for several moments.

How many other Timmy Dee Rolands were on his payroll?

Sheriff Homer Jedbow Cogburn was a man with two sides: a bogus, lucky corn pone trapped in a vaudevillian's body.

CHAPTER 6

Greg Robertson was asleep. He was on an IV drip of narcotics, sedatives and antidepressants.

The fatigued and famished ambulance crew was in the dining room. The food was plentiful as the nurse, paramedic and two EMTs started on a feast. It was their first non-fast-food meal in three days.

Brenda was an exhausted, dingy specimen of womanhood as she slept soundly on the living room sofa.

Miss Freehand stood midway down the hallway as she listened and giggled to Wendy Watters describe a john she dated.

In a spirited, hand-motion, animated manner, flapper-tongued Wendy flipped her hair, held her hands to demonstrate what 14 inches looked like, displayed gratuitous cleavage, simulated a big-gulp-swallow, closed her eyes, and licked her lips with a long, moist tongue.

Miss Freehand gasped, bent over, and held a hand against her mouth to conceal a roar.

Momma Lou came out of the bathroom, put an index finger to her lips and mouthed "Be quiet." She gave a satin negligee to Wendy, and handed Miss Freehand a mini digital video Camcorder equipped with a still camera.

"Be fast, provocative and lurid," Momma Lou ordered in clear English with no Italian accent.

"Lolley, I want you to shoot about two or three minutes of Wendy doing him. Take several stills. We'll shoot his face when he wakes up."

Momma Lou looked at Lolley Freehand, the whore-nurse. "I'll tell the ambulance people that you're watching over him while they eat, and that they should take their time and enjoy. I'll guard the bedroom door just in case his wife wakes up. Now hurry."

~ ~ ~ ~ ~ ~

Pascali's maitre d' glared at unoccupied table No. 20.

Mayor Garrison was 40 minutes late for his customary, glad-handed 7:30 dinner reservation.

The table could comfortably seat a party of six but Garrison always had just two or three at the table. He liked elbow room.

The maitre d' was impatient, as were the 12 groups lined up in the foyer. Most of them had waited for 20 minutes or longer.

The maitre d' walked by table 20, snatched off the Reserved sign, went to his station near the foyer, took six menus, and said, "This way, please, Doctor Mason. I have a lovely table for your party."

After the group was seated, the maitre d' bowed gracefully and said, "Please accept a complimentary round of cocktails. I deeply apologize for the delay."

The maitre d' returned to his station, pulled out the top drawer, removed a notepad and thumbed through it until he came to the page headlined MAYOR GARRISON. The maitre d' took his Mont Blanc pen and entered: Incident No. 15. Garrison reserved. No-show. Loss of business tonight, $300 plus. Loss of tips $60 plus. Losses to date this year $4,700 plus. Tips lost $1,000 plus. Big fucking asshole!

~ ~ ~ ~ ~ ~

Pascali's was not even a blip on Mayor Phillip Garrison's radar-calibrated-mindset as he parked his Cadillac by the back side door of city hall. He entered, flipped on the hall lights, walked to his office behind the city council chambers, and leaned over his cluttered desk.

He studied the stacks of stuffed files that he had worked on earlier, and the notes he had placed on the stacks. As he looked at the notes, he muttered the words the FEMA woman told him when he asked about sole-sourcing contracts to speed-up repair work.

"If it's in the public's interest, convenience, necessity, health and welfare, Mister Mayor, then proceed forthwith without competitive bids or permits and cure the storm damage."

Those were her exact words. He wrote them down on the same page that listed her name, her senior management title, telephone number, cell number, pager, and FEMA mailing address in Tallahassee.

Although Garrison had found her telephone voice a little standoffish, she reluctantly granted his request for a claim number to process Dos Bayou statements to FEMA for payments.

When she said there was a 25-day turnaround period for payments, he presented his case for a 5-day period. It worked. They compromised at 10 days.

Any government paper pusher who had been around the horn a few times and was worth his salt, knew the importance of a claim number and the benefit of a short turnaround payment period.

Phillip Garrison was an adroit, consummate bureaucrat when it came to knowing the system, accessing the system, and milking it dry.

He had circled the seven-digit claim number three times.

He examined the notes on top of each stack.

"Eureka," he shouted as he saw his note that read FEMA APPROVED HURRICANE RAYMOND DAMAGE REPAIRS.

He grabbed the stack, walked to the conference table on the far side of his office, took a seat, and opened the first file labeled ELIZABETH R. PRESTON RECREATIONAL PARK AND NATURE TRAIL.

He turned a few pages, smiled, and thought about the possibilities.

"It's beginning to look a lot like Christmas," he sung as he bobbed his head. "Everywhere I go."

He went to his desk, unlocked the bottom drawer, and took out a small, leather attaché case. He snapped it open, walked back to the conference table, lifted the cell phone from his belt and punched some numbers.

"Sam. Phil Garrison. Y'all doin' okay?"

He listened for a few seconds.

"Sam, I'm going to give your company a one-year extension on your contract at the Pensacola Navy Base. Now, I need a favor over here at Dos Bayou. Here's what I need you to do.

"In the next two or three days, get about 15 or 20 of your boys, all the carpenters, plumbers, bricklayers, painters, landscapers, gardeners, and electricians you can find, along with a couple backhoes, a trencher, about three or four tractors or small cats, dump trucks, the whole nine yards, and repair the storm damage at Preston Park and Nature Trail. It'll take you about two or three weeks. You'll have pictures to go by in rebuilding the site.

"I'll put you down for three hundred fifty grand. I have a 10-day payment turnaround with FEMA. That way, you draw interest and they don't. Are you in?"

Mayor Garrison listened to the happy voice on the other end.

"You want the same deal we have on my contract at the base?" Sam asked.

"I hear you, Sam. You betcha."

"Are permits required?"

"No."

"Okay. I'll add about twenty-five percent profit to the invoice which will cover your cut of the action. Count me in. Be there in two days."

"Sorry I can't talk more, Sam. I have to go."

Garrison was all business when it came to contracts. And percentages. And cuts. There was one more person he had to talk to before calling it a night. He lifted another bulky file off the stack and looked at the label. ANDALUSIA BOULEVARD EROSION, WATER MAIN DAMAGE AND SEWER LINE LEAKAGE.

"This one is big-time infrastructure," he said in a hushed tone.

The mayor turned a couple pages in his attaché case, picked up the phone and punched some numbers.

"Charlie. Phil Garrison. How y'all doin'?"

It didn't take long for Charles D. Williamson, owner of the largest general contracting enterprise in the southeast, to recognize the caller.

Charlie Williamson liked Phil Garrison from the get-go. A few years ago, Garrison awarded Charlie's firm the runway reconstruction projects at Pensacola Naval Air Station and Whiting Field. Those jobs grossed $19 million. Charlie's profit was 20 percent, minus the cut to Garrison.

Last year, Charlie's company completed a new commissary on the base and three 5-story dorms. That brought in $36 million, a 22 percent profit, minus the cut.

"I'm just fine, Phil. It's a pleasant surprise to hear from you again," Charlie said.

Garrison went right to business. He explained the storm damage, emphasized the urgency to fix the water and sewer lines, protect the underground water supply, stop the erosion, and re-pave Andalusia Boulevard which was Dos Bayou's main thoroughfare.

"We're lookin' at about an eight million-dollar job, Charlie. When can you start?'

"Let me think on it for a sec, Phil. Let's see now, twenty percent of six mill is one point two mill."

"That's right," Garrison said.

"Is it cost plus?"

"Yes."

Is there a cut?"

"I hear you, Charlie. You betcha."

"Okay, twenty-five percent minus five percent," Charlie said. "Is this a FEMA job?"

"Yes. I have a 10-day turnaround for your payment."

"All right. That's good. Do I have to pull permits?"

"No."

"I'll have a crew in Dos Bayou come first light."

Mayor Phillip Garrison turned off his cell phone and yawned. It had been a long day.

He would finish the stack of files later.

He put his notes into the attaché case, and locked it in his desk drawer.

Phillip Garrison had learned many years ago the advantages of concealment.

With his small frame, a hangdog's face, soulful eyes, and expressions that went with it, he had also developed a locked-in sense of perseverance.

When he started his bureaucratic career 32 years ago, he vowed not to copy the failed traits of classmates at the University of West Florida. Many of them were passed over during labor shortages, and victimized during job cutbacks. They hop scotched and skipped around from one job to another, and were often unemployed.

Not so with Garrison.

He was not born into the tech world, but he had a scarce talent for writing complicated contract specifications, negotiating prices with hungry, low bidders, and an administrative knack that emboldened himself into an antihero daunting personality.

And his personality could change when it suited his purposes.

But down deep inside he knew he owed his success to his ability to fake, steel or copy from others. Nothing about him was original. He was a complicated fabricator, the type who does just well enough to survive in the federal bureaucracy.

Known as the "Cocky Rooster" because of his combative style and short stature, Phil Garrison was the "man to see" when contracts were needed at Pensacola Naval Air Station, or contacts were crucial for a council vote at Dos Bayou.

Those on the losing side – and there were many – referred to him as, "notorious for getting things done the way he wanted them done."

Woe be the person who ran against Mayor Garrison at reelection time.

The opponent's past was attacked in media ads and mailings that vividly described legal, spousal or financial troubles, a sporadic voting record or disciplinary actions taken against him when he served in the military—records that were closely guarded and marked confidential.

Many suspected that the dirt Garrison used was stealthily obtained by clandestine and surreptitious court-ordered subpoenas issued by his old cribbage and fishing partner, and life-long friend, Second Circuit Court Presiding Judge Chester Andrews.

How else could a third party obtain a veteran's 30-year-old military file from the Department of Defense archives in St. Louis? Records that showed he was summary court-martialed and busted one rank in Vietnam! Records that also showed the man changed his behavior, saved several lives during combat, and was awarded two bronze stars for valor, but only the guy's court-martial was used by Garrison in the mud-slinging political campaign.

Garrison's campaign victories represented an endorsement of his ethos by an apathetic electorate.

Every four years, the un-deciders, the occasional deciders, and the well-heeled donors with contract offers on the table, heard the same victorious, reelected Garrison rub salt into the wound.

"I want to thank the good Lord, and all the honest, God-fearing people in this great city who know the truth when they see it and don't believe all the lies, slander, innuendo and gossip that my badly defeated opponent must now choke on as he tries to salvage what he can of his reputation and career.

"All I did was provide a little voter education on the loser who tried to horn-swoggle all of us."

But the more he huffed and puffed, he began to sound to newspaper columnists just like a rapper on MTV; all strut and no strength.

Reporters started to write articles about how he dithered and ducked, coasted and claimed, primed but paused.

Garrison, the reporters wrote, could be crotchety, wisecracking or a rumpled old country-pumpkin at the drop of a hat, and furnish the hat!

Most of the time, they agreed, he was egalitarian to the bone.

Mayor Phil Garrison displayed a persona of one who had grown into a fat, almost happy politician. He was rich and rolling with a Rolex.

As he started to leave, he looked at three old plaques on his office wall and studied the one on the left; his favorite.

The big brown eyes on his drooping, hangdog face looked playfully and affectionately at the words. His slumped pose signaled a desire to frolic. His big, flabby ears appeared to perk, and his face relaxed into a complacent, serene disposition.

He read the words for about the millionth time.

"Luck is the residue of desire."

His face changed to a vulnerable display of trust and confidence.

It split into a big grin.

"I like all this residue," he sighed contentedly. "And I might add, I stole every bit of it, and that's a big yippie-kay-yo in my heart."

He looked at the second plaque, which he hated, for about the two millionth time.

His face wrinkled into an aggressive pose. He bared his teeth, showed a spiteful glare of vengeance, and his waffle-iron brow was hot-wired to his brain.

He read the words slowly.

"Have you ever put one foot in front of the other without the slightest notion of where you're going?"

Garrison scowled. His face flinched and drew back in anger.

"Fuck no."

He looked at the third plaque, which mirrored his personality, for only the second time.

His face took on the ghost-mask of a tired old bankrupt dirt farmer who had his second consecutive season of drought. Garrison stuck out his tongue and his entire face wrinkled into a rotten onion-blossom shape. He did his best to talk. He leaned in and cupped his ears as if taking a deathbed confession. He appeared to be talking in strange tongues.

He read the words in a hateful whisper.

"When in charge, ponder. When in trouble, delegate. When in doubt, mumble."

"That's me," he mumbled. "That's been my whole fucking life-style since day one."

CHAPTER 7

There was always something strange or even eerie about the inhabitants of Dos Bayou. Most of them were outdoorsmen such as bums, AWOL sailors, street urchins, rodeo has-beens, idlers, dreamers, fake rednecks, genuine shit-kickers and hallucinating artists. And not one of them could get stoned or drunk unless a high volume guitar was thumping in his ears. They failed to shave, wore earrings, racially intermarried, smoked other than menthols, snorted rather than dipped and sang of more than calico visions, sweet fading mothers or honky-tonk angels.

Such was the conglomeration of swamp country humanity that gave Dos Bayou its peculiar odor of ambience.

Perhaps Dos Bayou folks were as backward as their Pensacola cousins claim. But who's to judge?

There was one thing for sure around Dos Bayou, in particular, and Escambia County, in general. That was: Don't mess with Deputy Sheriff Sergeant Billy Ray Lewis, Sheriff Homer Jedbow Cogburn's nephew, or ole Billy Ray will not only mess you up but he'll stomp your asshole until it's a mud hole.

Most of the folks in Dos Bayou have a life-long acquaintanceship with firearms, so whatever Billy Ray Lewis did with his guns was nothing new. But sometimes things got a little sticky especially when Billy Ray's fighting cocks contracted insomnia and started walking in their sleep. During one of their insomnia attacks, they invaded neighbor Bull Hussey's pen of prized Plymouth Rock laying hens and other award winning chickens that competed at county and state fairs, and molested every one of them, time after time, until the sun came up.

The trespassing, night walking love machines that strutted over to Bull Hussey's pen not only molested the hens and chased away the Araucana, Silver Seabright and Silver Phoenix roosters, but they killed the award winning White Silkie Bearded Cockerel, the Golden Laced Wyandotte pullet, the Golden Polish pullet and the one and only national champion Belgian Mille Fleur Bearded cock.

The whole thing was seen by Roselizabeth Stevenson, a trailer park neighbor whose space was on the other side of a small onion garden from Billy Ray Lewis and Bull Hussey.

When Bull complained that the Piggly Wiggly Market had refused to buy any more of his eggs because of the weird sizes and colors his prize winning Plymouth Rocks were suddenly producing, Roselizabeth explained to Bull what she had seen the other night from her bathroom window.

The next day, Billy Ray didn't pay much attention to Bull's complaints about the fighting cocks, so as soon as Billy Ray left for work Bull's shotgun wasted the entire inventory of Billy Ray's illegal hobby.

Roselizabeth and six deacons from the Church of Christ were the only ones who attended Bull's closed-casket mortuary service; a service prompted by Bull's mysterious death. A death caused, the coroner ruled, from self-inflected wounds.

Bull had drowned in two feet of water in Pear Blossom Creek near the west gate of Pensacola Naval Air Station after swallowing what appeared to be a hand-made three-pronged treble fishhook that was shaped like spurs worn by fighting cocks. What delayed the coroner's findings for a few minutes were chicken feathers; feathers that had been wrapped around the fishhook that Bull had supposedly swallowed.

What caused a few more minutes of delay in the coroner's findings was another rather unusual act by Bull. The coroner determined that Bull obviously had second thoughts about taking his own life because he had reached his hand deep into his mouth, grabbed the cord that was attached to the fishhook and yanked it out of his stomach and throat but the treble prongs got tangled into Bull's tongue and he drowned just before he would have bled to death.

Bull's brief obituary in the Pensacola Herald mentioned that he was retired from the United States Marine Corps, and had no known relatives. The last sentence in the article read:

> Mr. Hussey's body was discovered by Deputy Sheriff
> Timmy Dee Roland while on a routine patrol.

Roselizabeth was furious. She knew that Timmy Dee Roland was Billy Ray Lewis' sheriff's department patrol partner and gay lover. She had seen them together too many times at Billy Ray's place, and what they did on the front porch should not have been done by gays, straights or squares except behind closed doors.

Although her heart was torn apart by Bull's tragic loss, she was determined that despair and loneliness would not consume her, and that her uncompromising quest for vengeance would be realized. It would be just a matter of time before three persons would be in her cross-hairs; two bad cops with heavy badges, and Timmy Dee Roland's cousin, the scumbag incompetent coroner.

As time stood still in her mind, she thought back to late last year when she arrived in Dos Bayou and settled in at the Honeysuckle Trailer Park. Behind her were 15 years of dealing cards and mixing pleasure with business as she hobnobbed with the movers and shakers in Biloxi.

Every time she thought about how she got to Biloxi, she shook her head in disbelief. It was a part of her past that she could not forget, regardless of how hard she tried.

She was a southern girl orphaned at 16 when her parents and only sibling were killed in a car crash. A distant aunt and uncle in Flint, Michigan took her in and made her do all the house work and cooking until her high school graduation; then kicked her out.

While walking in a freezing rain to the bus station, Roselizabeth saw a United States Air Force recruiting poster.

A couple weeks later she was standing in formation as an Airman Basic at Lackland Air Force Base in mild and sunny San Antonio, Texas. She graduated at the top of her Basic Training class, enrolled in the Troy University Extension program, and was the only Airman who scored three consecutive ratings of Expert with different weapons on the pistol, rifle and machine gun qualification firing range.

Technical training at nearby Brooks-City Base School of Aerospace Medicine was followed by one year of hands-on advanced medical field work at Incirlik Air Base, seven miles out of Adana, Turkey.

Because her Incirlik medical unit was under-staffed, she often volunteered to work double shifts to assist with triage processing and apply her well-honed skills in emergency pre-hospital care to save the lives of hundreds of combat wounded American soldiers who arrived 24/7 from Iraq and Afghanistan.

After a year in Turkey without a weekend off, she was given her choice of any worldwide assignment. She opted for any base in the warm, southern part of the United States.

Known for her keen mind, self-starter attitude and drop-dead gorgeous Angelina Jolie look-a-like appearance and demeanor, Roselizabeth became the youngest Technical Sergeant instructor in the 78-year history of pre-hospital emergency medical care at Keesler Air Force Base in Biloxi, Mississippi.

On her first duty day at Keesler, Roselizabeth's Group Commander, a Colonel, hosted a surprise birthday party for her in the base club. Half-way through the party, a Color Guard marched in, posted the colors, and "Attention to Orders," was announced.

While the Group Commander read the citations that were processed from Incirlik, the Keesler Base Commander, a Major General, pinned on the highly coveted, but rarely earned, decorations.

On three separate occasions during the awards ceremony, the words "meritorious service above and beyond the call of duty," echoed around the SRO auditorium.

On her 20th birthday, and three years out of high school, she was the youngest E-6 Technical Sergeant in the United States Air Force with 18 U. S. and NATO military awards and decorations, with hardware clusters, that filled six rows on her Class A uniform.

But the Base Commander saved the best for last. Roselizabeth was presented two diplomas from Troy University; one displayed her bachelor's degree in Finance while the other noted her bachelor's in Hospital Administration.

She had completed each major field of study in three years with a 3.8 grade point average.

As she neared the end of his enlistment at Keesler Air Force Base, Roselizabeth started thinking of her future outside the Air Force. It was time, she felt, to think about herself, and her life as a civilian.

To find out what it was like "on the outside," she took a part-time job as a card dealer at the high-rollers' mecca, the Beau Rivage Resort and Casino. For the first time in her life she had a "personal banker" at Wells Fargo, a high-prime money market account, an IRA and a safe deposit box.

Another first was when she accepted an offer from a handsome deep pockets john who was staying in the Beau's Presidential Suite.

By the time she was discharged from the Air Force, she had established a small, reliable and highly profitable list of clients who paid her monthly "time share" four-figure retainers, and her circle of acquaintances grew to include a first-name relationship with the mafia kingfish of Biloxi's brotherhood of assassins.

For the brotherhood, the Gulf of Mexico had become an even safer place than the Las Vegas desert to dump their human garbage.

But after awhile, Roselizabeth changed. She developed an over-the-top guilt trip that forced her to leave it all. She knew she was tough enough to recover, and the stains would fade over time. She knew she would have no trouble in showing her resiliency; and she would not waste her time searching for economic direction or over-thinking her appeal. And, above all, she would do it with tongue in cheek or smiling through gritted teeth—whichever it took.

Roselizabeth had seen more than her share of "local justice" in the southern Mississippi casino town of Biloxi, but none like the heinous murder of her new special friend, Bull Hussey, in Dos Bayou.

Bull made Roselizabeth feel welcomed in the trailer park from the first day she arrived driving a Winnebago and towing a Dodge Ram SUV.

It was her spontaneity, pleasantly teasing personality and the giveaway smile that stole Bull's heart from their first, "hello."

Bull was a kind and gentle Operation Iraqi Freedom combat veteran who maneuvered around his trailer and chicken pen on crutches or on a scooter, and wore his prosthesis right leg only when he went to town on business or to church with Roselizabeth on holiday Sundays. The missing limb never kept Bull from living a full and active life.

And to Roselizabeth's daily surprise, after their morning ritual of gathering eggs and feeding and watering chickens, Bull always had an outing planned.

On some days it was a stroll around the near-by lake, a concert in the park at Fort Walton Beach Landing, or a late picnic in a quite mesa so they could watch the sunset dip into the horizon. And for a real hoot, one afternoon they rooted for both sides at a minor league baseball game.

A fascinating culinary treat was enjoyed at the Gulf Breeze community festival during a leisurely afternoon where they tasted foods from different cultures that made them diet for two days. But that was fun, too, because he introduced her to painting ceramics.

Each activity that Bull planned encouraged conversation; an opportunity to grow in compatibility with a clearer picture of the other.

Bull's general knowledge of so many subjects--science, culture, sports and the arts--continually amazed Roselizabeth because he was never braggadocios or flashy about what he did or said. Everything about him was steeped in honesty, warmth and cordiality.

He was the perfect companion.

Roselizabeth felt blessed that she had Bull as her special friend; a friend who frequently felt her warmth and tenderness as they satisfied each other's needs and desires.

She had approached her new life improbably convinced that adventures both spiritual and carnal would seize her, hug her and make her lights shine.

But now she had deep regrets that she had helped Bull maneuver his scooter over to Billy Ray's backyard, had loaded Bull's double-barreled 12-gauge shotgun and helped him aim it and fire it and reload it again and again until every goddamn fighting cock was killed.

After Bull's mortuary service, Roselizabeth returned to the trailer park with the deacons. As the deacons disconnected her Winnebago from utility lines and hooked her SUV to the hitch, Roselizabeth walked over to Bull's place, unlocked the door and entered. She took four steps to her left, pulled out the bottom drawer of the china hutch, removed a large weighty square box, and left.

They made a quick stop at a flower shop on the way back to the mortuary.

As they entered the mortuary grounds, a Marine Corps officer approached Roselizabeth's vehicle.

"Ma'am," the officer said, "I'm Major Mathew Henderson. "The news of Command Master Sergeant Hussey's death reached us while we were en route from Iraq to our Air Station at Beaufort, South Carolina. Beaufort is Sergeant Hussey's old outfit. I diverted our flight to Pensacola Navy Base as we could get here as fast as we could, ma'am."

"That is so kind of you. Thank you," Roselizabeth said as she held out her hand.

"We will be here to guard Sergeant Hussey's casket until he can be flown to Washington where he will receive a proper burial with full military honors at Arlington National Cemetery. That is, ma'am, with your permission, ma'am."

Roselizabeth and the deacons got out of their vehicles and looked around the mortuary grounds. There were about 50 battle dressed marines in single file formation in front of the building.

"Yes, Major Henderson, those arrangements will be greatly appreciated," Roselizabeth said. "Will you please come with us to his casket?"

As they approached, Roselizabeth leaned-over and placed a long stem white rose on Bull's chest. She then opened the heavy square box. With watered eyes she removed Thomas Jefferson "Bull" Hussey's Command Sergeant Major rank insignias, his Navy Cross, the Silver Star, two Purple Hearts and three Bronze Stars, with Vs for Valor, and placed them beside the rose. She then removed from the box her own military insignias and placed them next to his.

She pressed the fingers of her right hand to her lips, then placed her hand on Bull's face.

After a moment, she stepped back.

"Ma'am, we will be here until Sergeant Hussey is taken to Washington," the major said. "I will recover the items you left and they will be with him at Fort Myer. The procession to Arlington will begin at the fort, and I have been told to inform you that we will fly you to and from Washington, and will arrange all of your accommodations while you're there.

"Is there anything else I can do for you, ma'am, at this time?"

"No, thank you," she said. "I'll be all right. You have been more than kind and considerate."

Major Henderson detected a voice with tension; a voice that did not convey absolute confidence. He sensed intense stress underneath her blithe spirit.

She looked at him with hesitant, searching eyes.

"Here," she said as she wrote on an envelope, "this will tell you how to contact me when you're ready."

"Ma'am," the major said as he took the envelope, "the McCormack law firm called my commander and told him the cause of Sergeant Hussey's death. We take it personal when one of our own is murdered. If you need us for any reason, just call the Marine Corps Barracks in Washington and ask for General Bradshaw, the Marine Corps Commandant. He is briefed on what happened to his old comrade-in-arms, Master Sergeant Hussey. They served together."

He looked at her with a sudden smile. "And ma'am, Sergeant

Hussey had an excellent lawyer. The Jeffery Adam McCormack law firm is nationwide and they do a lot of pro bono work for military personnel like Sergeant Hussey."

She held out her hand and their eyes focused on each other as if an invisible chain had locked them together.

"And if I can be of any help, or just be nearby so you can talk with someone who cares, you can reach me any time by calling the Corps Barracks. The duty NCO has all my numbers."

She dipped her head in a display of gratitude as their hands met and their eyes communicated volumes.

The major's sight followed every angelic step Roselizabth took as she walked with the deacons to their cars and left.

The deacons maintained a short distance behind Roselizabeth until she was westbound on I-10, over the Alabama state line, and well on her way to Mobile.

Roselizabeth knew what Billy Ray, and his partner, Timmy Dee Roland, would do to her if she had stayed. She also knew that she was now outside of Billy Ray's jurisdiction, but he was well within her range of vindication, revenge and justice.

Some crimes, she thought, were so horrendous and heinous that a life sentence was too kind. All she had to do was call in a marker she had hoped she would never have to use. The marker was a blank check given to her by the mafia kingfish of the brotherhood.

Her expressive eyes widened in anticipation as the towering cityscape of Mobile came into focus. She looked over at the open box on the seat and shook her head in disbelief when she saw the large manila envelope. It was Bull's last Will and Testament. Bull and his attorney had reviewed with her the 5-page document and the codicil attachment. She was Bull's sole heir.

But Bull saved his best idea for last. He had the law firm's notary public come in and with the entire legal staff as witnesses, a marriage ceremony was conducted.

She looked again at the box and saw the small jewelry case. She reached inside and removed the four caret marquise diamond band and slipped it on her left ring finger.

That, too, was Bull's idea.

He said their marriage was a fitting way to celebrate killing all those goddamn fighting cocks.

- - - - - - - - - - - - -

That evening when Sergeant Billy Ray Lewis returned home, a poultry truck loaded with Plymouth Rock hens and award winning, multi-colored chickens was leaving the trailer park.

As Billy Ray approached his trailer, he saw bold lettered No Trespassing signs posted on Bull Hussey's property, and armed uniformed Pinkerton Security guards were standing beside their company marked SUVs that were strategically positioned on all four sides of Hussey's property.

The security guys were not only armed, they were huge, mean looking Samoan-types and their baton sticks were big enough to please Teddy Roosevelt.

The look on Billy Ray's face prompted the officer in charge of the security detail to say on his cell, "He's not very bright. The wheel is still turning but the hamster's dead."

CHAPTER 8

Greg Robertson was restless and impatient. The drugs and sedatives had mercifully reduced the sharp, painful spasms, but he was angry with himself as he slowly inched his way off the bed. His energy was drained after only a few tortuous steps. He stopped and leaned on the bedpost for support, and took several deep breaths. He slowly moved his left foot forward and renewed his snail-paced mission.

Finally, his weak, slumped body wavered unsteadily over the bathroom sink. He leaned on his out-stretched hands to support his weight. He gradually raised his head, looked in the mirror and saw his reflection for the first time in three days.

A patch covered his left eye. A large fist-shaped bruise was on his left cheek. He opened his mouth as wide as he could and moved his tongue slowly over the top row of teeth. Some were loose. A right-front canine was missing. He moved his tongue over the bottom row and felt swollen, infected gums and two loose molars.

He leaned closer to the mirror. A large, bluish scar was on his forehead. His head had several shaved patches where bandages covered abrasions, lacerations and contusions.

He raised his head and carefully   examined sutures he saw on his left nostril. The stitches ran from the base of his nose to the inside edge of his left eye.

His face quivered and he clinched his teeth as he looked searchingly at his battered image in the mirror. The worst hate he had ever felt in his life ran through his veins. He leaned closer and whispered, "They should have killed me when they had the chance."

He tried to straighten his body, but his ribs hurt and his back was in agony.

He glared again at the mirror. A deep, searching frown of curiosity quickly replaced his reflection of anger. Something was missing. What was it?

He leaned over and moved his head up, down and sideways. He pulled the top of his robe away from his neck and examined his skin for several moments.

His face formed an expression of disbelief. Mind-games raced through his brain.

He looked again at his face and neck.

There were no burns.

Was he crazy?

The burns were there yesterday. He knew they were because he felt them. Or was it two weeks ago?

What happened to the burns?

He closed his eyes and his nose flinched with each deep gulp of air. He could smell the terrible odor of his burning skin.

In his mind's eye he could see the flames when the damn lucky Iraqi MG-25 air-to-air missile hit his left wing tank and caused the high flash point jet fuel to explode. He could see the flames engulf his A-10 Warthog. Heavy smoke filled his lungs as he pulled the handle. The canopy popped off in an explosive blast, and Greg was hurled out of the cockpit.

Thank God, he thought, that during his pre-flight routine he had changed his beacon's preset position from Manual to Automatic so it would become operational the split second his chute separated from the seat. The beacon was one less thing to think about.

He had a lot of things on his mind, and there was no time to spend on anything that required manual action. Everything had to click as he ran through his mental checklist, just like he was trained.

The first thing Greg saw after seat-separation was his Wingman circling the descending parachute. Greg knew his Wingman had notified Special Ops and a rescue mission would be underway.

But could the good-guys get to him before the enemy?

By now, Greg knew, everyone on General Norman Schwarzkopf's air staff, especially General Chuck Horner who directed the air war, had learned that Warthog niner-five had punched out and was in a float spiral that took him directly into hostile territory.

Greg smelled his burnt flesh as he drifted toward the tan moonlit desert near An Najaf, 60 miles northwest of Kuwait. On the southern horizon toward Kuwait, he saw the toxic fog and the oil fires, and wondered how many hundreds of oil rigs were set ablaze by Saddam's fleeing troops.

He forced his mind to rattle off the contents in his survivor vest: Compass, signal mirror, infrared flashlight, hand-held GPS, a 9-millimeter pistol with a spare 15-round clip, rescue flares, evasion map, knives, and a PRC-90 radio.

He saw a blacked-out stealth F-117 circle his chute's descent. The pilot tilted his wings in acknowledgement and headed northward toward Baghdad with his bomb load. Greg gave the plane a thumbs-up as it faded into the distance.

Greg knew that USAF Special Operations had locked onto his beacon when he saw his Wingman give two quick wing tilts.

Greg looked down, saw the earth coming toward him at about 33 miles per hour, and figured he had about three minutes before impact.

Then he saw them. Iraqi troops were about a mile away from his drop zone and they were closing fast.

Greg's mind began to function like a computer as he remembered his survival, evasion, resistance and escape training at Fairchild Air Force Base in Washington. He assessed his situation. He did not have time to bury the chute. The enemy was too close. He had to disengage the chute fast, and run south as quickly as he could to put some space between him and the advancing Iraqi force. He needed time because every precious second counted so Special Ops could find him. As he ran south, he knew he had to keep Venus over his right shoulder.

But first, he had to make the call.

He reached into his vest, withdrew the radio and yelled, "Mayday. Mayday. This is Warthog niner-five. Warthog niner-five. Mayday. Over."

Greg was wrong. He did not have three minutes to impact. He had two minutes, fifty-two seconds.

It was a hard landing. The radio flew out of his hand.

Greg quickly unhooked the chute, tossed it aside and started a desperate search in the sand for his radio. Then it hit him. "Hell, I don't have to look for it," he said. "I'll listen for it."

"Warthog niner-five, this is Warthog niner-six. Do you read?"

Greg followed his Wingman's voice to his partially buried radio, grabbed it, shook off the sand, and started his run south.

As he ran, he thought about survival school and the Isoprep form he and all the other flight crews had to complete. The four-statement form was his ticket for rescue in a hostile situation. Greg repeated each statement as he glanced at Venus over his right shoulder. He made sure he covered the three facts each statement required. He repeated them over and over in his mind. He also remembered his four digit number that did not match any consecutive series in his social security number. He repeated the digits in his mind.

Any one, or more, of the four statements, or the four digit number, separated Captain Gregory Nathaniel Robertson from an imposter.

Greg kept planet Venus right where she was suppose to be as he maintained a steady pace south.

But it was no contest.

Greg remembered the large Iraqi patrol that ambushed him.

He was at full speed when he hit the trip wire. He was beaten several times before he stopped his head-over-heels roll in the sand.

They took his pistol, tied his hands behind him, kicked him repeatedly, beat him some more with rifle butts, and tossed his thrashed, burnt body on a flatbed truck. But the Iraqis forgot something.

The beacon. It kept sending coded pulses to Special Operations.

It only took a few minutes.

Greg remembered hearing the familiar sound of twirling rotor blades from MH-53J Pave Lows.

His mind pictured the approaching aircraft. They were only a few hundred feet above the ground. He could see them.

The Pave Low gunships zoomed past as gunners blasted the Iraqis with 50-caliber firepower. The helicopters circled in rapid clockwise rotations around the hostile troops as Special Ops gunners zeroed in on their targets.

The flash of firepower from a different direction suddenly caught Greg's attention.

AC-130 Spectre gunships, the pride of Special Ops, shelled the enemy with Gatling guns, howitzers, cannons and machine guns.

Greg looked at the enemy troops. About 200 were dead or dying on the ground. About 50 were still standing. Greg watched as they fired their AK-47s wildly into the air at the fast-moving aircraft.

Missed shots from the airborne units carved large burning divots in the desert sand.

Black smoke and flying debris filled the air as the ground exploded around the few remaining Iraqi soldiers.

Greg saw some large mounds about 150 yards away. He tried to free his hands with some strong yanking motions, but failed. The cords just dug deeper into his wrists. He rolled off the flatbed, formed a low silhouette, and started a determined low-bent trot toward the mounds. As he ran, he glanced back at his captors. Only a dozen or so were still standing.

Then he noticed the enemy's reinforcements. They had taken some high ground, and by their shouts they appeared motivated. The longer the firefight dragged on, the more Iraqi insurgents showed up to fight.

The deafening sound of firepower filled the air.

Greg stopped and pulled his hands apart as hard as he could. No luck. The cords were too tight.

"Screw the low profile," he yelled. "I'm running tall. Let them hit the silhouette if they can."

He raced as fast as he could toward the mounds. He reached them at full stride, bounced off the first one and dived headfirst between two large moguls.

He heard a deafening sound.

He looked up and saw several helos directly overhead.

"Warthog niner-five," a voice sounded on Greg's radio. "Deduct one from your third digit and respond."

Special Ops had a copy of Greg's Isoprep form and they were making damn sure they were not picking up an imposter wrapped in a suicide bomb belt.

The digit question caught Greg by surprise. He ran his four digit number through his mind and deducted one from the third digit, which was seven.

"Six," was Greg's immediate response.

"What high school, what colors and what mascot?" were the next questions.

"Central High west of Fresno where our colors were black and orange and we were the grizzlies."

"What first car color?"

"It was a burgundy Ford Mustang."

"Your room service is here, sir," a voice sounded on the radio.

Greg knew his ordeal would soon end. The only other thing he had to do was follow his training and position himself in a submissive posture on the ground and await rescue.

Rope ladders were suddenly tossed out of the helos. Greg watched as scores of Special Ops troops quickly descended, the ropes were disengaged, the helos banked sharply and disappeared into a twirling dust cloud.

A large hulk of a man in battle dress uniform ran to Greg.

"Sir, I'm Lieutenant Kemper, Flight Leader, Special Ops. Looks like they roughed you up some."

"Roughed me up? They damned near killed me. What took you so long?"

"It took eighty-two seconds longer than expected to receive the electronic transfer of your Isoprep form," the lieutenant said.

"Sorry, sir, we couldn't take you aboard. The bad guys are in a sanctuary of the Hezeb Islamic al Gulbadin terrorist organization and have massed battalion-size two clicks from here. Our gunships are in the battle now and the pilot didn't want a passenger. He said you would understand.

"We have to join the fire fight and try to box them in. Can you run?"

"I ran here, didn't I?"

Greg turned and wiggled his fingers. "Cut the cords."

"We're going to run about two miles," the lieutenant said as he yanked out a serrated knife and began cutting.

"The bad guys are being reinforced real fast."

Greg had never seen a lieutenant like Kemper who spoke and acted like a combat seasoned colonel.

"We have Apaches for superior air power and Pave Lows for sophisticated navigational gear, but all of that is shit up a creek if we can't operate under the cloak of darkness. We love ink-black nights," the lieutenant said.

The lieutenant handed Greg an M-4. "You'll need this, sir. Follow me and you'll see how Special Ops caters a party with a desert theme."

Greg smiled at the waggish remark as he and the lieutenant joined the Special Ops unit in a southwestern grueling sprint across the desolate stretch of land. Each airman carried at least 60 pounds of gear on his back.

They were less than midway when a heavily armed force of insurgents launched their attack. Enemy soldiers who crawled like roaches seemed to pour out of the sand.

The Special Ops troops hit the deck and opened fire in one fluid motion.

High explosive rounds from M79 grenade launchers, and the distinctive sounds of shoulder-fired missiles, M4 carbines, M203 grenade launchers and M16s filled the air.

The Special Ops airmen began taking heavy sniper and rocket-propelled grenade fire from Iraqis on the high ground.

Danger-close air support strikes just a few yards away exploded all around Greg and the airmen.

Greg saw an inbound AC-130 Spectre and two Pave Lows burst into flames with deafening concussions. Burning bodies and debris crashed to the ground barely 50 yards away.

Greg watched as other Special Ops gunships veered away from the attack, changed their formations to figure eights, and rejoined the battle with a barrage of air-to-ground firepower.

When the Apaches hit their marks, the ground lit up like the Fourth of July. And overhead, F-15s, F-16s and A-10s screamed by to hit targets of choice.

Greg felt like he was back at the academy and sitting on the 50-yard line at an Air Force-Army game.

He and Lieutenant Kemper were as flat on the ground as they could get and still fire at moving targets.

Greg used his elbows and knees as he tried to keep up with the lieutenant who had a real knack for sliding over the sand like a big, nimble snake. Greg had a hard time keeping his ass down.

"Better get your butt down, captain," the lieutenant said, "or figure out some way to attach your helmet to your ass."

The lieutenant's Special Ops unit of about 30 airmen was slightly ahead and the troops were crawling fast.

"Airborne leader," the lieutenant reported on his radio, "they're trying to establish an offensive perimeter. I'm on the forward edge of the battle area. Need heavy surgical strike. Over."

Greg remembered the awesome display of American military strength. It ended so suddenly. His mind recalled how he turned slowly in circles and surveyed the smoldering battlefield destruction around him.

Then, suddenly, the enemy counter-attacked in force.

The lieutenant was four feet away when a shell hit his upper torso and exploded on impact. His face, chest and shoulders disappeared.

Greg immediately motioned for the airmen to follow him as he advanced. He knew from survival school that a combat commander stops leading when he stops talking.

He found a sand berm that provided some half-circle shelter. As they hunkered in, Greg assigned the airmen to positions with fields of fire in a reinforced tight perimeter. After each airman knew his field of fire, Greg demonstrated how to comingle all weapons and ammo in sequential pairs so each fire sector within the perimeter had multiple firepower; a well coordinated mix of shoulder-launched missiles, machine guns, rocket propelled grenades and rifles.

His last demonstration was how to fire an M4 carbine with an M203 grenade launcher on burst mode for deadlier impact, and, as a last resort, he held up his pistol.

The first enemy assault came from three different directions. But the perimeter held because of the variety of firepower.

After defeating two more assaults, Greg led a counter attack with grenades, missiles and small arms. The attack split the enemy force into two disorganized elements.

Three hours later, with Air Force F-15s, Marine Corps infantry, and an Army Stryker unit, Greg and four airmen were still firing at what was left of the retreating enemy.

Lieutenant Kemper and 25 other Special Ops airmen were killed. Eight others were wounded and were losing blood.

Greg's leadership in planning and managing the perimeter defense, organizing the successful counter-attack, launching an aggressive offensive strike that split the enemy unit, and determining the evacuation procedure for the wounded were cited by senior officers as, "Spectacular examples of combat leadership during intense hours of furious battle that tested a leader's mettle in ways even the most experienced had not seen."

The overwhelming ratio of enemy forces to Greg's Special Ops airmen was estimated at 18 to 1. The enemy body count after the battle was 466.

Hearing the enemy body count was the last thing Greg remembered.

He awoke the next day in the white, sterile world of an Air Force clinic in Saudi.

The burns were there. He saw them.

He saw them when the doctor held a mirror, described the transplant process, and what they would do to make the scars disappear.

Later that night, Greg and the doctor – and the rest of the

world – watched on television as an F-117 stealth fighter rolled in and put a bomb neatly down the Iraqi Defense Ministry's air shaft in downtown Baghdad.

Greg clinched his fist, shook his head and yelled, "Yes!"

He tapped the doctor on the arm and pointed at the TV.

"That pilot was on his bomb mission when he circled my chute after I punched-out," Greg said.

"Oh, I'm sure he did," the doctor said with an all-knowing smirk. "Now, you need to rest."

The doctor turned and whispered to a nurse, "I'll give him something to stop his hallucinations."

Was he crazy? Had he gone mad?

The burns were there.

"So, there you are."

The voice startled him.

He looked at her. His mind slowly put the broken pieces in his memory bank back together.

Brenda took his hand. "It's going to be all right. I guarantee it."

Greg looked at her with a quizzical expression. "Guarantee?" he asked. "How can you say that?"

"Daddy just called. He was over Panama City Beach and they just started their descent into Destin. He's bringing some of the top attorneys in the firm with him, and they're in his new Citation 10. He's dying for you to see it. And he said you should not worry.

"Now," she said with a broad smile and a pointed finger at his nose, "that's why I can guarantee it."

CHAPTER 9

The bellowing racket in the adjoining council chamber was growing louder and louder, and Dos Bayou Mayor Phillip Garrison's patience was getting thinner and thinner. He finally heaved a deep sigh and smacked his puffy lips in relief as he finished reading the last item in the City Council Agenda. The agenda was four pages long, but he knew there was no way he could shorten the meeting.

Mayor Garrison flipped through the agenda attachments, closed the bulky file and rose from his desk. He yanked his coat off the back of the chair, scooped up the file and walked toward the door that connected his office to the dais in the council chamber.

He carefully opened the door just a smidgen and cautiously peeked through the crack to survey the hullabaloo in the chamber. There was a mass of irate humanity about 250 strong crowded in the room. Mayor Garrison had never seen that many angry people in a space designed and built to seat 110 calm, docile souls.

The big brown sad eyes on Garrison's beagle-drooped face grew with confusion bordering on panic as he assessed the expressions on the people who stood closest to the dais. Each and every one of them looked mad. And confrontational.

With curiosity winning over trepidation, the Mayor opened the door a little wider and stole a long glance at what had all the sights and sounds of a surly mob.

His first instinct was right. All of the people looked and acted like they were just plain no-shit Sherlock pissed-off. The real nutty ones, he thought, were the ones doing all the yelling. The rest of them had expressions that Garrison associated with hemorrhoidal discomfort. They were the quiet ones.

Mayor Garrison feared the former, but absolutely, positively and without hesitation dreaded the latter. The quiet ones, the sore assholes, were the ones that worried him the most. They were like pit bulls compared to the Pekinese peewees that kept yelping all the time.

But there was something very peculiar about the crowd that he couldn't put a finger on.

Once again, his curiosity won over apprehension.

He looked again.

Then it hit him. There were a hell of a lot of unfamiliar pissed-off faces in the room. And the handful of lividly irate ones that Garrison recognized were obviously not there to slip him an envelope full of Franklins and Grants for his next campaign. Some were yelling. Others just fumed in silence. They filled every seat in the chamber, all 110. And those who couldn't find seats had taken all the folding chairs from other rooms and lined them in the middle and side aisles.

The late comers, about 75 who looked like Hun-type raw meat eaters, were standing impatiently along the back wall.

The late-late comers sat cross legged on the floor. Their knees rested on the thighs of those next to them. They all looked cramped and tired of waiting. And they were the lucky ones.

There were a couple hundred outside who couldn't get in. Many of them stood with faces pressed against the glass. They had arrived too late and the fire marshal would not let them in because the building was already overflowing.

Duke Hockbarth stood along the back wall and surveyed the huge turnout.

Duke's plan had worked better than he expected. He had used his plumbing business's customer list to mail notices of the meeting and inform people, "Of the mayor's underhanded attempt to spend millions of tax dollars on low priority storm damage items."

A planning technician in the public works department had heard about the mayor's plan, had seen a draft copy of the council agenda, and alerted Duke.

Duke's "eyes" and "ears" were everywhere in the Northwest Florida Panhandle where tax money was assessed, collected, budgeted, authorized, appropriated, programmed or spent.

Duke was the third generation Hockbarth to own Duke's Independent Plumbing. And town folks loved him. They loved him not necessarily because of fast, friendly service, lowest guaranteed rates, and senior and military discounts, but because he always had interesting news about political shenanigans in city hall and the courthouse. And he was always right.

Duke was also the darling of the Chardonnay-sipping stay-at-home soap-watching women whose artistically designed nails were too delicate to risk on a cranky faucet. And most Monday through Friday faucet problems Duke had grown accustomed to occurred in the master bathroom near the satin sheets and fluffy pillows on an unmade bed.

Duke was an enigma. He wasn't black or white. His skin was a light mellow rum.

His Jamaican great-grandfather was a seaman who saw no future for his family in St. Ann. He wanted a new life in a new country. It took four months in small boats, on small donkeys and on bare feet for Duke's ancestors to travel from St. Ann to Pensacola.

The craftsmanship of plumbing came easy to an old seaman who was accustomed to working with his hands.

Duke Hockbarth had an inner pride of his roots but never spoke of his color.

He looked pleased as he surveyed the crowd. He had mailed notices to each of his 723 customers, and nearly 400 of them – mostly women – showed up.

Mayor Garrison's hangdog ears seemed to point forward as he narrowed his eyes and strained the see the cluster of men in dark, three-piece suits who were seated in the far-left corner. They gestured passionately to each other as they carried on an animated conversation that blended in with the roar from others seated around them.

"Oh, shit," the mayor whispered to himself as he eyed the suits. "Why are so many lawyers here?"

The three-piece suits, Mayor Garrison thought, did not appear receptive to negotiate whatever it was that was stuck in their craw. And they all looked angry. Each and every one of them. All twelve!

The room was filled with the angriest and the most boisterous mob of people Garrison had ever seen in city hall. And they were getting louder by the second.

Mayor Garrison looked at the long, semicircular council table. City Attorney Victor Maynard was in his usual fantasy world as he sketched cartoon characters on his pad. Garrison, like many others, viewed Maynard as a certified cerebral lightweight.

Council members Curtis Wagner and Kevin Barnett were seated on Maynard's right. The other two Council members, Carlos Santiago Dominguez and Libby Washington, were in a huddle behind the table with a couple visitors. Carlos and the visitors listened as Libby talked and gestured with both hands.

Mayor Garrison knew very well that when Libby Washington was revved up and wanted to talk, those closest had to listen.

And as she talked, she did what she always does. She fixed her eyes on her listeners in such a way that made them feel as if they were the only persons alive. And she bounced from one subject to the next in an energized stream of consciousness, a natural trait that came in handy as Provost at the University of West Florida.

Mayor Garrison displayed a malicious leer as he studied Councilwoman Washington. She was the only person who had never accepted his invitation to join him for dinner at Pascali's; an invitation often repeated but never acknowledged.

She was a regal, petite and voluptuous woman whose sensuous mannerisms drove Phillip Garrison crazy. And, as usual, her perfectly coifed hair framed her high-cheeked chiseled face that was the color of mocha.

Her seat on the dais was on the far left, which was also her political leaning.

"Let's do it," Mayor Garrison said as he walked through the door, winked at Libby Washington, shook Carlos's outstretched hand, took his seat at the center of the table and looked serious.

Mayor Garrison took the gavel and pounded three quick raps on the table. "The meeting will come to order," he yelled.

No one paid him any attention. The noise was as loud as ever.

Three more raps sounded from the table.

"Let's listen up, my friends," a deep bass voice sounded from the rear.

Mayor Garrison looked around the chamber. The crowd was abruptly silent.

Without any waste of time or motion, the mayor distributed council agendas, directed the acting clerk to start the recorder, noted the date and time for the record, took the roll call, gave the benediction, led the pledge of allegiance, announced dump sites for storm debris, and blamed Hurricane Raymond for the agendas being late.

He acted and sounded like a programmed tyrannical robot. And he was.

He was in charge and no gang of hoodlums or hired mouthpieces would interfere with his position of power, delay the council meeting, or cause him to forego his usual cocktails and scrumptious dinner at Pascali's.

After a pause, the robot's long, droopy face looked even more serious.

"As most of y'all know," Garrison said, "our new city manager, Greg Robertson, is recovering from injuries and will not be present for tonight's meeting. Our city clerk is not here either because she and her family evacuated to Alabama before Hurricane Raymond hit and they have not returned. Unfortunately, she and her family don't have a house to return to. It was destroyed by Raymond. City Attorney Victor Maynard's secretary, Hazel Spencer, will handle the clerk's duties during this meeting."

Mayor Garrison nodded at a large, matronly woman seated among staff members in front of the council table.

No one could ignore Hazel Spencer's enormous growth of fire-engine-red-hair that was French rolled into a huge corkscrew on top her head. Her hair started with a foundation of small rolls and as it grew in height it widened considerably until it crested. The sculpture was precariously held together by some invisible means of support.

Hazel's hands were constantly fidgeting with items on the table but her head and back were ramrod straight. She had to balance a lot of vertical mass.

"If any of y'all want to address the council on any agenda item, or under oral communications, you'll need to complete the form provided at the table near the front door. No one addresses the council without the form being completed and handed to the acting clerk," Mayor Garrison said pointing to the matronly woman. "That way we know your name and address for the record, and the correct spelling. For your information, we follow Robert's Rules of Order around here. Now, we'll move to item one on the agenda and the corresponding relevant supplement."

"Point of information, your honor," a man's voice shrieked from the back wall.

"Sir, whoever you are" the mayor's paternal voice said, "I'm not a judge." Then, in a tone that turned self-righteous, the mayor proclaimed, "You may address me as Mister Mayor, which is appropriate here in the council chamber and in city hall. Your point of information is out of order. It is premature for anyone in the audience to speak on the item. We'll have staff members give their report on the item, next are council members who will address it and ask any questions they may have, then the principals involved may respond if they so desire. Finally, members of the audience who have completed their form will be heard for no more than three minutes."

Mayor Garrison, satisfied that his slowly enunciated lecture and stern admonition were fully understood by the poorly dressed folks who stood at the far wall, leaned back in his chair, looked at the staff and ordered, "proceed."

He looked and sounded like a man no one should tangle with. Especially on his own turf.

"Mayor Garrison," another man's low-pitched voice erupted from amid the people along the back wall, "a lot of us took off from work to be here for agenda items thirty and thirty-one that would cost us a lot of wasted money. We want to hear those items now and your explanation."

The audience turned in the direction of the familiar voice. They knew it belonged to Duke Hockbarth, a high-voltage personality they knew and trusted, but could not see.

The gavel pounded hard against the table. "You're out of order, sir," Mayor Garrison shouted. "I thought I had made my message clear when I addressed the other man who was also out of order. Is everyone now clear on when they can speak?"

"No, sir," Duke Hockbarth said sternly in a booming tone punctuated by a menacing scowl.

He stepped away from the wall and started a slow, zigzag path through the mass of humanity as holes opened for him to pass.

After he had walked around the people and made his way to the rows of seats, his rugged but handsome square-shaped face eyed the mayor. Duke was in his mid-30s and of medium build. His chin protruded just far enough to form a permanent resting place for a chip that no one dared knock-off, especially when taxes or the United States Marine Corps were discussed.

Duke's natural tanned skin was taut all over, evidence that every day conditioning with leaky pipes, clogged toilets and worn-out water heaters could turn a stocky man into a lean one with six-pack abs who was shaped up and trimmed down. He could bench press 385, just like he did as a grunt Marine on Okinawa 12 years ago.

Duke held a dirty baseball cap in one hand and wore his usual grease-stained faded denims and T-shirt that advertised Duke's Independent Plumbing. As his eyes locked on the mayor, Duke folded his muscular, bulging arms across his chest. He, too, had a clear message: He would not budge an inch.

"I'm not out of order, Mister Mayor," Duke said in a resonate voice. He unfolded his arms and pointed at the people around him. "Because as taxpayers who foot the bill for what you spend, we just want to know the procedure you followed on agenda expenditures thirty and thirty-one, and how you respond to a taxpayer's request at a tax supported council meeting."

"Hear, hear," a man shouted from the front.

"You're goddamn right," a woman yelled from the rear.

"You're the man, Duke," another woman screamed.

The room erupted in thunderous applause.

The mayor's face flashed a bright anger-filled crimson. He knew he had lost control.

He also knew there would be hell to pay if he did not follow orders from Sheriff Homer Jedbow Cogburn.

"Push the buzzer," the sheriff said at a recent league of cities meeting, "if you ever have an unruly crowd on your hands. Push the buzzer so we can avoid a riot." Garrison looked at the crowd and could not believe his eyes.

Some of the people were standing on chairs and twirling shirts, bras and handkerchiefs over their heads. Others had their hands up to their mouths and were making duck calls, turkey calls and other strange whistling sounds. The sounds, however, did not drown out the familiar noise of beer cans popping.

And airplanes!

Several people had made airplanes out of their agendas and were tossing them from one end of the chamber to the other. Some flights launched from the back wall landed between the dais and the front wall, an airborne feat that covered 120 feet.

Mayor Garrison watched as an airplane lost altitude over the council table and nose-dived directly into Hazel Spencer's French Roll. The Kamikaze attack dislodged the giant bobby pin or tall pole that supported the corkscrew-shaped hairdo.

Garrison's lower lip sagged, his eyes widened in disbelief and his brow furrowed as Hazel's scarlet rolls tumbled down like a startled French soufflé.

Even when she turned, Garrison did not know if he was looking at her face or the back of her head.

He had seen and heard enough.

His right hand quivered as he released the gavel. His fingers twitched as he moved his right hand under the table. He trembled impatiently as he felt for and finally found the button. He pushed it three times, long and hard.

The sheriff's department dispatcher sat at her console in the communications room reading the Pensacola Herald when the siren wailed and jolted her into action. It was the first time she had heard the three-loud howl and yowl signals since her training session four years ago. The three long emergency silent alarms from city hall meant there was some serious trouble in Dos Bayou. The dispatcher did what she was trained to do.

She activated the red "SWAT TEAM MOBILIZATION" switch, cut the noise from the siren and began reading the instructions posted under it.

As the noisy demonstration continued, Council members Libby Washington and Carlos Santiago Dominguez looked quizzically at each other and hurriedly thumbed through their agenda supplements. Their search was futile. It did not take them very long to discover that the supplements to items 30 and 31 were not included in their packets.

Carlos Santiago Dominguez turned to page 4 on the agenda and studied item 30. He read the words slowly. "Cost-plus inventory and labor for 24/7-storm damage repair to Elizabeth R. Preston Recreational Park and Nature Trail." Dominguez read the words again. There was a no-cost figure listed, not even an engineer's estimate. Dominguez shook his head. He wondered why the mayor wanted to repair the park on around-the-clock shifts, seven days a week, when so many people were without homes, hundreds of businesses were destroyed, and countless other projects had much higher priorities.

Regardless of the hurricane, Dominguez was also bothered by such a long agenda with cost items dumped in his lap at the last second.

Dominguez raised his head and stared at the people along the back wall. He focused his attention on Duke Hockbarth, a man whose name frequently came up in conversations; a name that belonged to a man who knew a lot about what was going on inside city hall, but did not live or vote in the city.

While Dominguez studied Hockbarth and the way he interacted

with the people around him, Libby Washington shook her head in skepticism as she read the description of item 31 for the second time. "Cost-plus parts, inventory, concrete paving and labor for 24/7-storm damage repair to various streets and boulevards, such as Andalusia, as designated by the Mayor. Cost-plus repair of soil erosion, water main damage and sewer line leakage."

She noted on her copy that no cost estimate was listed, and then scribbled, "agenda distributed too late for research and preparation."

She looked at Dominguez. They stared at each other with blank expressions. Councilmember Curtis Wagner, a pharmacist, watched in disbelief as the crowd changed its refrain and was now chanting in unison, "Duke, Duke, don't puke on Duke."

Council member Kevin Barnett, a liquor distributor, saw nothing unusual about the demonstration except for the timing. He saw the same type of behavior every weekend.

Fury and terror flashed across Mayor Garrison's face. He knew the crowd was uncontrollable, and he forced himself not to speculate on whether or not the cops would arrive in time to stop a riot.

The hoots, shouts and refrains got louder by the second.

"Duke, Duke, don't puke . . . "

A tall man in a three-piece suit at the far left corner of the chamber stood, held his arms skyward, turned and looked at the man who wore the Duke's Independent Plumbing T-shirt.

Duke Hockbarth could not avoid the man's stare. As they eyeballed each other, the suited man lowered his arms to shoulder height, turned his palms toward the floor, spread his fingers, and waved his hands up and down several times.

Duke Hockbarth turned his head slowly from side to side, looked at the angry people, and raised his arms high over his head.

The room became eerily silent.

The man in the suit turned and faced the dais. "Point of personal privilege, Mister Mayor. May I approach?"

The man's mellow, soothing voice was in sharp contrast to what the folks had heard from the mayor.

"You are out of or....."

"I think not, Mister Mayor," the tall man said matter-of-factly as he walked to the front of the chamber, snapped open his briefcase, placed it on the podium, removed a legal tablet, and raised the microphone a couple feet until it was level with his mouth.

He turned, faced the audience and said, "Please be seated, ladies and gentlemen. Your message was heard loud and clear. Thank you."

Mayor Garrison's terror-filled face watched in astonishment as the rowdy people turned from contorted mob activists to subtle restrained believers, and quietly took their seats. As Garrison glared, the people along the back wall suddenly looked like curators at an SRO museum display.

"Mister Mayor and members of the Council," the tall man at the podium said, "I am Jeffery Adam McCormack from the Atlanta, Georgia law firm of McCormack, Hendrix, Barstow, Sheppard, Maxwell, Fulmer and Galloway."

Councilmember Libby Washington had started a notation on her agenda when the sound of McCormack's name turned her casual gaze into a slow-motion sculpture of unadulterated adoration. She had just read a lengthy article on McCormack in the current issue of Chronicle of Higher Education, a nationally distributed news magazine for university officials.

The lanky, extraordinary man at the podium was not only one of the most respected legal minds in the nation, but the sole source of minority scholarships at 78 universities throughout the country, including Libby's alma mater, Howard University.

The memory of how the magazine article had warmed her heart, and the unexpected pleasure of seeing such a dynamic person standing only a few feet away, watered Libby's eyes in homage. She was an outspoken supporter of the NAACP, Howard's policy of admitting poor black students, Nelson Mandela's war against apartheid, the crusade to resurrect black neighborhoods in East St. Louis, and, of course, Dr. King. But she had no white heroes except Lincoln. Now she did.

"To show my support of the mayor's interest in spelling all names accurately," McCormack said, "I shall now give to the clerk my card and the completed forms as the mayor earlier requested.

The forms contain relevant information on each of my eleven senior associates who are here today from my law office in Atlanta. More of my associates will be called down from Atlanta as needed."

Mayor Garrison's big eyes gawked at the man's apparent declaration of war, and his suave act of showmanship.

McCormack stepped around the podium, stopped in front of the acting clerk whose left hand held rolls of hair away from her eyes, dipped his head in polite respect, handed over the pieces of paper, took a step back, and returned to the podium.

Garrison's memory bank was on full-speed rewind and his mind spun in a confused cycle. The name Jeffery Adam McCormack seemed to ring a bell. But why? Where? When? Why was the name familiar? Why did it sound so damn important?

"I appreciate your earlier comments, Mister Mayor," McCormack said with a resounding pronunciation and a slight affected smile, "when you announced that you followed Robert's Rules of Order. That is why I am standing here at the podium and I am not, I repeat, sir, not out of order. I shall now continue to exercise my rights under Robert's Rules. Because of the nature and significance of my presentation, and without objection, and hearing none, the three-minute rule shall be preempted."

A strange glow of respect and enlightenment covered the faces in the audience. To them, the Georgia lawyer looked like the personification of brute force, the toughest of the tough, the fiercest of the fearless, and the bravest beyond the bravado.

"Proceed, sir," the mayor heard himself whisper in a submissive voice.

"Mister Mayor," McCormack said in a melodious tone that sounded like it was dipped in bronze, "I also acknowledge your earlier words when you explained to all these kind people why Greg Robertson, your city manager, is not present at this meeting."

Mayor Garrison's eyes widened and his sore back suddenly became rigid-straight as he sat in his overstuffed executive chair. If there was anything else he needed on this miserable day to awaken his dull faculties, it was for some high-priced lawyer from Georgia to come to Florida and explain why a man from California was absent from the meeting.

"During my presentation to you, I shall explain in detail why Greg, my son-in-law, is not here, and the reasons for my visit with you."

The words hit like a bolt of lightning.

Mayor Garrison's big, fleshy jowls drooped. His rubber-face sagged. A sharp pain entered his head and lodged in the center of his forehead. He ran his tongue over his teeth. Even the molars felt soft and mushy. He shoulders slumped. He put his right elbow on the table and rested his big, hangdog-shaped chin in his hand. His eyes looked dilated.

He could not understand or give credence to any of the wild and lunatic things that had happened since he called the meeting to order nearly an hour ago. He squinted his enlarged eyes, blinked them a few times, and tried to focus on the first page of the agenda. Then he remembered. He had not crossed-off one completed item. So far the whole day had been a total waste of time.

Mayor Garrison looked at the podium and his head snapped.

He remembered!

Facing him with laser-beam, brilliant eyes was Mrs. Brenda Robertson's daddy, the Atlanta icon in the legal profession.

Garrison remembered the stories his old fishing buddy, Chet Andrews, had told him.

According to the news media, big-daddy Jeffery Adam McCormack had declined a shoo-in presidential appointment to the United States Supreme Court because his wife did not want to leave Georgia.

But the story behind the story, like the others, was not true, Garrison was told.

Chester D. Andrews, Presiding Judge of the Second Circuit, heard different accounts from his semi-reliable counterparts in Atlanta. One said that big-britches McCormack turned thumbs down on the position because he did not want to take a $9 million reduction in annual income, or explain to inquiring senators his wife's addiction to scotch during the scrutiny of confirmation hearings.

Another said that Mrs. McCormack told her bridge partners that she would not move to Washington and try to eke by on her husband's hundred and eighty grand salary as a Supreme Court justice.

Mayor Garrison studied the impeccably dressed Jeffery Adam McCormack and wondered what would be novel enough to thrill someone in his late 40s or early 50s, such as McCormack, who could have or do anything he wanted.

Garrison had seen people like McCormack before. The big brash hustler type who strides into town carrying a snake skin briefcase, wearing $2,000 fancy threads, alligator boots, talking loud and sticking his nose into somebody else's business.

Garrison had dealt with hundreds of them.

Mayor Garrison looked at Jeffery Adam McCormack. "Mister McCor . . . "

An explosive jolt slammed into the rear chamber door and smashed it against the inside wall. In the same horrifying instant, a powerful force hit the side doors near the dais and slammed them against the walls with the roar of a thunderclap.

About 30 combat-equipped SWAT team members from the Sheriff's Department ran through the open doors with their faces covered and their weapons drawn.

A short, stocky deputy in a black ski mask ran to the front of the chamber with his M-16 weapon pointed toward the ceiling. He looked at the mayor and council members, turned quickly and faced the startled audience.

"Everyone hit the floor, freeze and keep your mouths shut," the deputy yelled in a high-pitched voice. "I said move, dammit, move."

"Stay put my friends," roared the voice from Duke Hockbarth. "There is no need for such Gestapo tactics while we are here exercising our constitutional rights of assembly. Stay where you are my friends."

Four shotgun armed deputies immediately surrounded Duke. A rifle barrel smashed against Duke's chin and blood splashed on the floor. A rifle butt with an uppercut jab dug deep into his gut.

The two blows were brutal enough to disable any normal man.

Duke Hockbarth was not a normal man. He preplanned everything he did.

He eyed the deputies and stood with his head straight as blood ran from a big gash on his chin. He folded his arms across his chest and moved his feet closer together. He displayed the posture of a submissive noncombatant.

He also looked as solid as the concrete foundation of the Pensacola First Presbyterian Church. He was not moving. Neither was anyone else in the audience.

"I said hit the floor, freeze and keep your mouths shut," the SWAT team leader yelled as he walked toward Duke Hockbarth. "Now. Do it now. There's no need for any more bloodshed."

Libby Washington had seen the same type of police brutality against black students at the University of West Florida. The blacks were not allowed to join white-only fraternities so the black students decided to organize and charter their own fraternity. They purchased a prime piece of land near University Mall, and hired a black architect and a black contractor. Construction was about 75 percent completed when the three-story building mysteriously burned to the ground on the night of Dr. Martin Luther King's birthday.

The next day, a loud argument erupted in the Student Union. The cops were called in. The melee that followed caused fifteen black students to be rushed by ambulance to the emergency department at West Florida Hospital. Two died.

No whites were injured.

Libby Washington, Provost at the University of West Florida – and no stranger to the sight of a bad cop with a heavy badge – had seen enough. As she rose from her chair, she pushed it with the back of her heel and the chair slammed against the hardwood floor. The maneuver worked. Almost. Every head in the room, except two, eyed her as she marched like a 5-star general to the front and center of the council table.

The SWAT team leader stood in front of Duke and their noses were about two inches apart. The lieutenant held his rifle with the left hand around the barrel and the right hand on the stock just above the butt.

A sarcastic grin spread across the lieutenant's face.

Duke knew he was going to get another uppercut in the gut. He flexed his stomach muscles.

"Lieutenant," Libby Washington shouted from the dais. "Look this way."

The lieutenant's right hand had already started its upward motion with the rifle butt.

Duke's spontaneous action was both instinctive and mechanical. His left hand deflected the rifle butt and it harmlessly cleared the space between his head and shoulder. Duke's right hand grabbed the barrel. With brute force, he held the weapon at each end and slammed the center of the gun across his knee.

The rifle fell to the floor in pieces.

The lieutenant jerked his head back and his face quivered in disbelief.

"Lieutenant," Libby Washington said firmly, "you and your officers are not needed here. We will not allow any more acts of excessive force like we have just witnessed. Everything is under control. If you wish to stay lieutenant, clean up the mess you made on the floor, and you and your officers may join the others who are standing in the rear of the room."

Libby Washington pointed her finger at the lieutenant in charge. "Now hear these words," she said in a command voice. "I am quite sure that our distinguished guest, Mister McCormack and his associates, would be delighted to represent anyone who may want to file a class action lawsuit against you and the other officers. Good day."

The lieutenant quickly raised his left wrist to his mouth, said something into a speaker wire, listened for a couple moments, and responded with a meek, submissive "Yes."

He picked up the pieces of his rifle, raised his right hand, made a circling motion with his index finger, gave Duke a hard shoulder bump with a "Kiss my ass," expression, and led his officers out of the chamber.

Councilmember Washington leaned over and whispered to the mayor. He listened attentively like he was receiving an order. When she finished, she walked to her seat, got her purse, and left the dais through the side door that led to the conference room.

"We'll stand in recess for twenty minutes," Mayor Garrison said with a rap on the table.

He hurried off the dais, went into his office, slammed the door and dialed some numbers.

The Honorable Chester Andrews, Presiding Judge of the Second Circuit, answered on the second ring. "Hello."

"We're in deep shit," Garrison shouted. "Guess who's at the council meeting right now?"

Mayor Garrison listened for a few seconds. With an exhausted face he settled into his chair for a long conversation. "How in the hell did you know?" he asked.

Carlos Santiago Dominguez wore a tired, weary brow as he watched the activity in the chamber.

His Pensacola flight out of Miami had landed at 11 last night and it was well after midnight when he got home. While examining spreadsheets and e-mail, he celebrated his most successful trek to Colombia with a hand-rolled Cohibas and the usual number of Coronas.

The celebration ended abruptly, however, when he got to the 37th e-mail message. It was from the nun who had confronted him on the plane.

He memorized her message after three readings. He whispered her words: "Dear Senor Mayor Pro Tempore Don Carlos: My humble appreciation for your professional card and your kind offer to assist for which I am unworthy. I pray to the Holy Father that it is His will that our paths shall cross again soon. But why wait? Please let me know if it is convenient for you to meet me on your next visit to Colombia, or at a site ASAP of your choice. When, where and for how long? Warmest personal regards. SisSheba."

He dug his hand into his coat pocket and withdrew the neatly folded letter. He carefully unfolded it and read the sender's address for about the 10th time: SisSheba@cybertron/world.com. His eyes moved to the bottom of the letter and he mouthed the words, "warmest personal regards."

As he folded the letter, his mind wondered. What organization employs and provides the little toy who calls herself Sis Sheba who wrote the message that starts like it's from Mother Superior, but ends like it's from Madam Singapore? And when did nuns start using ASAP? Or Sis? Or the last two syllables of Bathsheba, the Biblical wife of David and the mother of Solomon?

Carlos wondered. Is she truly a sister, or is she a retainer toy for the FBI, CIA, Interpol or the National Security Agency? He also wondered how she got his e-mail address. It was not on the business card that he gave her.

He returned the letter to his pocket.

Within the hour his sources will know all there is to know about SisSheba@cybertron/world.com.

Carlos Santiago Dominguez forced himself to survey the chamber. The mass of human activity, he thought, was an unusual study in sociology.

Jeffery Adam McCormack had a cell phone to his ear as he huddled on the far left side with his colleagues. Each was scribbling on a legal tablet.

Duke Hockbarth was surrounded by female care givers who fussed over the gash on his chin and his washboard abs.

By now, Dominguez knew, Libby Washington would have the windows open in the conference room, a white-filtered Swisher Sweet between her lips, and a politically incorrect cloud of cigarillo smoke exiting through the window screens.

Dominguez was just a tad wrong.

Councilmember Libby Washington was too preoccupied to open the windows. She sat at the end of the conference table and savored the aroma of the sweet, mild smoke that hung from the ceiling on invisible strings.

Libby was in deep concentration as she took another long drag on the Swisher.

She thought about the article she had read in Chronicle of Higher Education. It was a remarkable story about how Jeffery Adam McCormack, a poor, destitute and homeless young man, climbed from the cotton and watermelon fields of west Georgia to the ownership of Atlanta's tallest skyscraper.

Perhaps no other lawyer remained such a personal mystery

to his country while creating landmarks in jurisprudence than Jeffery Adam McCormack. And, possibly, no other lawyer was so imprisoned by the clash between a public existence and an obsessive desire for privacy.

Libby knew first-hand how accurate the article was in its description of the man.

It said the 52-year-old McCormack is a handsome, hearty man who could be mistaken for Jimmy Stewart without the stop-and-go stutter. He is prematurely white-haired and narrow-faced, with thick, compact eyebrows and blue eyes that often widen with excitement, as if he just witnessed man's first courtroom victory. He is also blessed with a handsome, hearty voice: bass-toned, assuring, and warmly modulated.

Libby agreed with the article's statement that it must be peculiar for a person like McCormack to make his professional mark so young and have to live with that standard ever since.

Athletes expect that, Libby knew, but lawyers don't.

McCormack was less than a year out of the cheapest night law school he could find in Georgia, and was renting desk space in a storefront office on Atlanta's seedy south side, when he struck the mother lode of all lawsuits. A down and out vagabond had staggered into the store one morning, leaned against McCormack's desk, and asked for a quarter. He wanted to buy some coffee "to wet my throat so the sores in my mouth caused by workin' 'round Asbestos don't kill me 'fore my time."

Jeffery Adam McCormack was the lead attorney in a 27-state class action suit that had more than two million clients. At the final settlement hearing, a federal judge cut McCormack's fees for legal services. Although the judge agreed with McCormack's bill for $824 million, out of "judicial restraint" the cash payment was reduced to $412 million.

That was when McCormack very quietly established a large number of scholarships for needy and deserving students.

And he got married to his childhood sweetheart, the former Donna Lynn Aikens whose daddy owned the small watermelon patch in west Georgia where lanky, calm, even-keeled Jeffery got his start in the fields.

Brenda was born the following year.

When she was a junior at Princeton, McCormack concluded the mining of an even larger mother lode: the tobacco settlements.

His portion of the fee was $2.6 billion.

More scholarships were established, and Brenda's trust fund got a hefty deposit.

And McCormack fulfilled his long-held dream.

The tip of Atlanta's tallest building could be seen from the Green Bean, the small burger, hot dog and crawfish diner where McCormack worked six days a week to pay his way through law school.

He now owned that skyscraper.

The diner disappeared. Only a few knew exactly where it was relocated when McCormack purchased it and had it moved to his farm in the rolling hill country east of Atlanta.

Jeffery and Donna loved the relaxed, tranquil pace on the farm, but Donna always got restless after a couple days. She knew there were people in Atlanta who needed her.

At no time did tobacco or alcohol touch Donna's lips. Her small delicate hands never held a deck of cards, tossed a pair of dice or placed a number on a roulette wheel. She never participated in her husband's Shrine "happy hours," or bridge foursomes.

She was, as everyone called her, "just a crew of one."

The crew taught sewing at the shelter for battered women, counseled addicts at the mission, coached girls' basketball at the Y, worked fund drives for the Scouts, served as a Bell Ringer each Christmas for The Salvation Army, and wrote the weekly newsletter for her church.

Donna McCormack was constantly showered with honors, which she politely shunned with simple words which were often the most cryptic. "Give it to someone more deserving." Then she would add her favorite expression that so uncharacteristically linked her to Bob Dylan: "I'm one too many mornings, and a thousand miles behind."

But not anymore.

Tragedy struck in the form of a hit and run drunk driver.

She was a medical miracle after months of surgery and rehab. She was still alive, but an invalid.

Jeffery Adam McCormack's appointment to the United States Supreme Court just came at the wrong time.

He had to build a special home for his "darling Donna."

He wanted one with complete handicap access to every nook and cranny in the house and the outbuildings, as well as the yards, gardens and, of course, the Green Bean that she converted to a Chuck Wagon that served three meals a day to the ranch hands.

Even a justice on the Supreme Court could not find enough available land in Washington, D.C., northern Virginia, southern Maryland or eastern West Virginia to satisfy McCormack's dream for "darling Donna."

Land was not a problem in Atlanta's Fulton County. McCormack just needed some bulldozers and a crack team of architects, interior designers and builders. He gave them maps of the 15,000 acres he owned and told them to get busy. He wanted the project finished before another vacancy occurred on the Supreme Court.

As Libby Washington sat in a cloud of smoke, the warm thoughts of the article caressed her body. She thought of "darling Donna" and how she and Jeffery Adam McCormack had found thoughtfulness, humor and passion in their lives.

Libby remembered the question about McCormack that the magazine writer posed to the President of the United States.

"What makes Jeffery Adam McCormack the best choice to serve as our nation's next Supreme Court Justice or Chief Justice?"

The President: "There are few as charming, as smart, as politically savvy, so learned in each and every aspect of civil, criminal and constitutional law, and so seasoned." The President added, "And there are no others who have that combination."

The magazine article, Councilmember Libby Washington discovered, brought a new meaning, a meaning of solid purpose, to her own existence. Through the McCormacks, Libby filled a void she had for reflection, extension and emotion.

She promised herself that she would bind the meaning, nostalgically, with memories of fine, decent people beyond the animal house antics of those who lived in Dos Bayou.

Libby hummed Dylan's refrain "everybody must get stoned" as a wry smile creased her face. She stood, took the cigar from her lips, held it under her mouth, dripped a stream of saliva, and tossed the wet butt into the trash can.

The council break was over.

Mayor Garrison looked impatient and restless as the council members slowly took their seats around the dais.

Council member Washington looked at Jeffery Adam McCormack as he stood attentively behind the podium. As their eyes met, she dipped her head slightly and smiled without parting her lips. She thought she saw his right eye blink a split second before he turned and focused on the mayor, but she was not sure.

"Mister McCormack," the mayor's voice sounded, "we have a long agenda. Can you conclude your comments in five minutes or so?"

"I shall try, Mister Mayor, to do so without taxing your patience any longer than is absolutely necessary."

"Proceed, sir."

McCormack turned and faced his law firm associates in the audience. The 11 lawyers rose from their seats with their hands full of documents. They walked to the podium, placed bulky files with identifying dividers on the podium, and returned to their seats.

"Thank you, Mister Mayor," McCormack said as he opened the top file.

"For the record, Madam City Clerk, I now announce my firm's civil suit which is number two-five-zero-nine-nine-two-eight. It pertains to the newly purchased white Honda Acura that Dos Bayou Mayor Phillip V. Garrison, and Chester D. Andrews, Presiding Judge of the Second Circuit Court, gave to Mr. and Mrs. Gregory Nathaniel Robertson. Said gift is in violation of the Constitution of the State of Florida.

"In the interest of time, I shall not read the statute citation numbers. They are listed, of course, with the copies I shall leave with the clerk."

Mayor Garrison's elastic face was an angry red and it seemed to stretch all the way to his navel. His eyes were bugged out, his nose itched and his mouth was dry. He scraped his tongue in a big circle to wet his lips.

"You mean, sir, that my courtesy to your daughter is met with a public announcement of a law suit against me?" the mayor asked.

"Mister Mayor," McCormack responded, "said vehicle is parked in the lot behind city hall. The keys are in the file I shall leave with the city clerk, along with all these other files." McCormack lifted the stack of files and dropped them with a loud thud on the podium.

"I won't bother reading the file numbers on our additional law suits. Those suits contain charges of federal civil rights violations, and examples of alleged felonies created by gifts of tax funds. Named are you, Mister Mayor, Judge Andrews, and various third parties. They are Escambia County Sheriff Homer Jedbow Cogburn, Sheriff's Sergeant Billy Ray Lewis, Sheriff's Trooper Timmy Dee Roland, and three Jane Does now known as Wendy Watters, Lolley Freehand and Angela Giuseppi, who is also known as Momma Lou."

City Attorney Victor Maynard hurriedly scribbled a note. He folded the paper, wrote "Mayor" on the cover and passed it along.

Mayor Garrison's face drooped like a Basset's sag as he unfolded the note. With each word he read and mumbled under his breath, his facial features took on the alert peculiarity of a Doberman. Garrison knew that Maynard was one of the dumbest lawyers who ever hung a shingle, but maybe for once in his life, just once, he may have something of merit to contribute.

"Just a minute, sir," the mayor said to McCormack, "City Attorney Victor Maynard has some comments he wants to make."

"Thank you, mayor," the city attorney said glancing over his bifocals that hung on the tip of his nose. Maynard looked at the podium but avoided eye contact with Jeffery Adam McCormack.

"Mister McCormack," the city attorney said in a dawdling voice, "am I to understand that you and your eleven associates who are seated here in the council chamber prepared all the documentation contained in the files now before you, and filed the charges with the appropriate Florida courts? Is that a correct assumption on my part, sir?"

Jeffery Adam McCormack was on familiar ground. He was a master at cat and mouse games, especially when he could be the big, playful long-haired Persian cat who liked hide-and-seek games with stupid, mentally challenged prey.

It was time for the big Persian to be demure, if not just a shade bashful.

"I sincerely trust, counselor, that our efforts were accepted and at least partially recognized by the respective courts as perhaps novice attempts, may I say, at obtaining justice in a venue that has competent jurisdiction."

City Attorney Victor Maynard listened to the explanation with a noticeable smirk on his face. McCormack's response, in Maynard's mind, proved he was on the right track. He now had the out-of-state big-name lawyer right where he wanted him.

Maynard claimed Florida State University as his undergraduate and law school alma mater, but his student years were marked with such low academic standing that the school never had any .reason to claim him. He finally passed the Florida bar on his third attempt, and had practiced law in Dos Bayou for the past seven years, the last two, though default, as city attorney.

No one else expressed any interest for the dead-end job.

As he looked at the nationally renowned Jeffery Adam McCormack, City Attorney Victor Maynard sensed the unsuspecting sitting duck was ready for the kill.

Victor not only knew he was ready for the challenge, but his crosshairs were fixed for the trophy kill.

For the first time in his life, he would accomplish something his VFW bartender mother and municipal meter-reader father would be proud of. They would see their son as a trailblazer, a person who took the lead, a man who stopped a ferocious, mean ogre from running over little people, and a young, fearless city attorney people could look up to.

Never mind that he was the public school pupil the teachers passed to higher grades, even though he got failing grades, because they didn't want to hurt his feelings. He was also the kid whose permissive parents told him to ignore the lines while coloring because the lines got in his way.

Along the way, Victor Maynard was allowed to ignore too many rules, take too many shortcuts, cross too many lines and skip too many grades.

He had just one more question to ask before he placed his adversary, the learned and respected Jeffery Adam McCormack, under arrest – along with the 11 lawyers with him – on first degree felonies. Each of them would face a $50,000 fine and a minimum of six months in state prison.

"Thank you for your honesty, Mister McCormack," the city attorney said in a patronizing voice. "Now in continuance of your honesty, which I deeply appreciate, did you, in fact, file those law suits under your Atlanta law firm address?"

The Persian longhair wanted to take a deep yawn, curl into a ball on a soft chair, close his blue eyes, breathe through his tail, and not be disturbed until dinner was served on his favorite china.

The stupid mouse leaned across the table toward the podium as his mind's eye carefully examined the spelling of his name in the banner headline of tomorrow morning's newspaper. Fame, status and accolades were only a few heartbeats away.

The Persian's interest in playing hide and seek had waned. The mouse was no longer an interesting or intriguing contestant.

"Yes, that is correct," McCormack said. "Do you wish to counsel me?"

Dos Bayou City Attorney Victor Maynard rose slowly from his chair, and like an actor squeezing a scene for maximum dramatic effect, he straightened all five feet six inches of his portly frame to its full vertical height. He raised his right hand and pointed a short, stubby quivering finger at McCormack.

"I charge you with practicing law in the State of Florida without 'of counsel' status or admission to the bar of the State of Florida. Therefore, under the powers granted to me as an officer of the second circuit court, and the powers granted to me as sergeant of arms of this duly incorporated city, I hereby place you and your associate attorneys under arrest. All of you are under my jurisdiction until you are hauled off to jail and bail is posted, if you have the resources to post such bail."

Victor Maynard looked at McCormack who suddenly exhibited

the features of a hungry, sharp-fanged alley cat with long, needle-like claws.

"We don't take kindly to impostors or con men around here," Maynard said. "Do I make myself clear?"

Mayor Garrison's face turned into a huge wrinkled smile. He did not notice the large, expanding wet spot between his legs. But he felt it.

It was time for the mouse to discover that when a Persian cat is not happy, nobody's happy.

"Mister Mayor," McCormack began as he ignored the city attorney, "Mr. Maynard matriculated at Florida State where he was graduated at the very bottom of his law school class. Unfortunately, his stupidity is consistent.

"My law firm associates seated here today are respected members of the Florida bar, and I am associate counsel during these proceedings with my branch firm in Tallahassee, so certified by Chief Justice Muldowney of the Florida Supreme Court.

"Further, we shall increase our law suits and name Mr. Victor Maynard and this city council in a defamation of character and slander suit. We'll add several adjectives to our suit so the court will get a clear picture of the scum-level law Mr. Maynard practices as your legal counsel."

McCormack lifted the stack of documents off the podium, walked to the city clerk and placed the files on the table in front of her. He returned to the podium, closed his briefcase and snapped it shut.

"Oh, by the way, Mr. Mayor," he said matter-of-factly as he pointed to the documents, "those files contain all the cash you delivered to Mr. Robertson's home. There's about sixteen thousand dollars in hundred dollar bills. You may want someone who is bonded to take care of that tax money. Your city manager prefers to be paid with a check and the stub clearly marked with appropriate tax deductions.

"Moreover, your friend and fishing partner, Judge Andrews, has been relieved of his duties, declared persona non grata, and will not participate in any future judicial consideration until Chief

Justice Muldowney conducts and completes a full review of Judge Andrews' actions during the past three years.

"And finally, tomorrow we shall file a class action suit against you, Mr. Mayor, and the sheriff's swat team for the conduct we all saw here today; conduct so wisely termed by Councilmember Libby Washington, as 'excessive.' The suit now has more than three hundred named plaintiffs. Good day."

Mayor Garrison watched as all twelve of the three-piece suits filed out of the chamber.

A strange silence engulfed the room.

"Mr. Mayor," a familiar low-pitched voice sounded from the back wall. The mayor scanned the faces and saw a raised hand. It belonged to Duke Hockbarth.

"Yes, sir," the mayor said reluctantly.

"You would be well advised, mayor, to adjourn this meeting without proceeding on agenda items," Duke said. "That will give the council sufficient time to find a new city attorney, plan for hurricane recovery procedures, and allow the rest of us to conduct a petition campaign to throw your sorry ass out of public office."

Amid snickers, giggles and hog-calling sounds, the gavel pounded hard against the table, the mayor said something as his jowls shook from side to side, and the council disappeared through the side doors.

The city attorney reached over and grabbed the in-basket beside Hazel Spencer. He pulled out all the forms and separated the twelve that were filled-out and handed-in by Jeffery Adam McCormack. Maynard's hands trembled and his face grew puffy as he examined the forms.

Each one contained a license number to practice law in the State of Florida.

Victor Maynard stuffed the forms in his pocket and walked hastily off the dais. As he cleared the side door, he yelled, "Why is there so damn much trouble in Dos Bayou?"

CHAPTER 10

The white Lincoln Navigator's right turn signal blinked as the vehicle veered off Andalusia Street and slowly entered the circular driveway in front of Dos Bayou City Hall. The driver braked to a stop near the front porch, got out, walked briskly around the SUV and opened the door. Powerful hands gently pulled the passenger from his seat, guided him through the door, and balanced him until both feet were firmly planted on terra firma.

"Well, Emil," Greg Robertson said as they reached the top of the stairs and stepped into the foyer, "so far, so good."

"I'll be back in two hours to take you home," Emil said. "I'm going to leave some Percocet with you just in case you need to take one."

"Thanks."

Emil placed a small container in Greg's coat pocket. "Take one only if the pain gets severe," Emil admonished. "Only one," he said shaking his index finger. "They are very potent. Now promise me."

"Oh, Emil, you worry like Brenda. Now go. I'll see you in a couple hours. I'll be okay."

Emil Jura, a gentleman's gentleman, was paid to worry. He had served Jeffery Adam McCormack for the past 24 years. Emil was a multi-talented senior assistant who earned his stripes every day, and the car of his choice every third year.

Emil also selected his boss's attire, watched over lady McCormack's personal staff, organized the spacious household so it functioned in a tidy, smooth manner, supervised the chefs and wait staff so high tea and meals were served on time, and, most importantly, made sure there were no surprises.

But Emil Jura was so much more than a trusted assistant. He was a master black belt in karate, a devotee of Jiu-Jitsu, a disciple of Tae Kwon Do and an explosive kick boxer. The 4-inch barrel hardware clipped to his belt was for backup.

Greg watched as Emil's white SUV moved slowly around the circular driveway, turn on Andalusia and disappear into traffic.

Emil drove two blocks, stopped at the light, turned left, circled back, examined the area, found an unobstructed observation zone between a Dairy Queen and Blockbuster Video, cut the engine, removed the binoculars from the glove box, and settled in with a good view of Dos Bayou City Hall.

Emil was a stickler for following orders.

When the doctor approved Greg Robertson's request to visit city hall for a couple hours, Brenda and her father were very clear in their instructions to Emil: "Make Greg think he's on his own, but don't be too far away in case you're needed."

Greg's feet made scraping sounds as he walked down a long hallway.

"Can I help you?" a high-pitched woman's voice asked from the back of the building.

Greg turned in the direction of the sound. "Yes, ma'am. I'm Greg Robertson. And you?"

A short, slim girlish frisky-cute figure emerged from the dark end of the room.

As she approached, Greg could not avoid noticing her sleeveless red and white striped cotton shirt knotted above the navel, tattooed arms, a bright yellow skin-tight mini-skirt, black eyeliner, heaps of blonde hair in a beehive, and well-worn Nike sneakers. Her flawless, peachy complexion gave the appearance that the sun had seldom hit her, and her flaming-red lips were constantly puckered.

She looked and dressed like she should be tossing a baton at a college football game, or entertaining a john in a back room.

She held a lighter and a pack of Marlboros in her left hand as she smiled broadly and reached out to greet the man she had heard so much about.

"Hi, I'm Tilly Cloud," she said pumping Greg's hand. "I spend most of my day like out on the back porch, you know, with some Cokes and a pack of cigs, okay? Glad to make your acquaintance."

Greg's first impression of Tilly Cloud was the way she enunciated certain words on the first syllable, a sure giveaway that she not only grew up south of the Mason-Dixon line, but south of the Alabama line.

"For me," Tilly said without encouragement, "the best thing about knowing Mayor Garrison is like I get to keep on working. He told me like, I mean, a lot about you, you know. I get bored when I just sit around all day in the trailer park or like at a bowling alley. Know what I mean?"

She did not wait for a response.

"I get bored, sure enough. I was born and raised at Molino just up the road like north of here toward Alabama. All my twenty years on this good earth I've constantly, you know, had to be doing something, well, like something, you know?

"Like I've got to be cleaning, doing this, doing that, dating him, dating them, or dating the whole team. What the hell. I like to party, you know? I have fun. Damn, do I have fun. Especially with Mayor Garrison. It has nothing to do with fame or like being with someone famous, or eating out, you know, in swanky restaurants like Pascali's over at Pensacola.

"Now, Greg, irregardless of how you cut it or like who pays for a fifty-dollar bottle of wine, or my shopping trips to the mall and Dillard's, that's just totally awesome, you know?

"Know, like, where I'm comin' from Greg? Like, I mean, this whole thing is, like, supercalifragilistic."

Her inflection this time – for effect – was on the word, "comin'."

When she talked, Greg noticed, she had a rather gently piercing, softly pouting and eerily empty gaze.

Greg had just heard a great deal more than he ever cared to about Tilly Cloud, a young over-achieving blonde slut puppy who proudly spends her nights dating, dining and wining with the mayor, or anyone else, and her days at $18 per hour downing Cokes and smoking Marlboros on the back porch of city hall.

"I've learned," she continued, "that there is so much like, you know, Greg, that I can't control, whether I'm a blonde, like today, or a brunette like next year with wrinkles, you know, so I control what I can. I mean I know like how to control my abilities.

"I know a lot of people who like just wait for a psychic's promise or some other stuff to happen to them like a great guy like Mayor Garrison to come along and discover them. I'm like, 'Are you bull shitin' this little trailer park gal?' she asked in a Dolly Partonesque accent.

This time her inflection was on the word, "shitin'."

This goofy-meets-gorgeous combination, Greg thought, could be a first-class trouble-maker.

Greg felt a sharp pain flash through his temple. He rubbed his forehead as he fumbled for the Percocet in his coat pocket.

"Now, you make yourself like, you know, like at home, you hear, Greg?" Tilly Cloud said with an inflection on "home."

"I will, thanks," Greg said turning to leave.

"Oh, I just about forgot," she said.

Greg turned and faced her.

" Councilman Carlos Santiago Dominguez arranged a meeting, you know, like with some dude like from a world-wide garbage company who's suppose to be here with Mayor Garrison. They'll probably meet while I'm at lunch."

She stuck out her hand. Tilly pumped even harder than before.

"I'm going back to the porch like to suck down a few," she said. "I'll know when you leave because the chime sounds whenever the front door opens. That's how like, you know, like I know when someone comes in. Come to think of it, go ahead and like turn the knob when you leave. I'm going out for a long lunch. I'm starved, okay?"

She disappeared before Greg could ask for directions to the

water fountain, or fire her for gross negligence, or for just being gross.

Greg walked a few feet and stood in the doorway of an office. A long hallway stretched out in front of him. He was growing weaker and weaker by the moment. It wasn't from the pain, but the weariness that came from listening to Tilly Cloud.

Emil Jura had no trouble with the glasses as he watched a woman walk out onto the back porch of city hall and light a cigarette. He saw her open a can and take a long drink. Emil focused his glasses on the can. It was a Coors. He followed her movement as she stepped off the porch, walked across the side yard and disappeared into a tall hedgerow of camellias.

Emil refocused the glasses as he moved them back and forth from window to window.

Greg had ambled into a long hallway.

Emil wondered how much longer Greg needed to be in city hall. It had been seven weeks since the accident, and the doctors and nurses Jeffery Adam McCormack had retained to watch over Greg had said he was making better than expected recovery.

Emil knew that Greg was still on Cephalexin, Oxycodone, Percocet and Tylenol for various pains, discomforts and torn muscles, and antibiotics to avert the spread of drug-resistant bacteria.

Greg was tired. He leaned hard against a hallway door to rest. As his eyes started to close, he was jarred awake by the sound of a chime.

"Anyone here?" a gravelly voice asked from the foyer.

"Yes, sir," Greg said.

Greg walked slowly toward the front and saw a man standing in the lobby holding a large scratched briefcase in one hand and several rolled sheets of paper, like blueprints, stuck in the crook of his arm. He wore a slate blue shirt, faded denims and a pair of dirty, stained shoes.

"Is your mayor available, young man?" the visitor asked. "I have an appointment."

"Sir, the mayor is not here. I'm the city manager. Greg Robertson's the name. How can I help you, sir?"

"May I sit?" the man asked. "It's been a long day and I have a lot to tell the mayor and even more to show him, Mr. Robertson. I can assure you that it will be worth his while."

The man placed the papers and battered old briefcase on the floor, pulled a card from his sweaty shirt pocket and handed it to Greg.

"Dusty Jason's the name. Trash is the game. You call, we haul."

Greg cracked a smile. "Very well, Mister . . . "

"You'll do me a favor if you call me either Dusty or Jason. Either one is just fine. When you call me Mister, I look around and expect to find my dear father, may God rest his soul."

"Very well, then, Dusty . . . "

The front door opened and Emil Jura entered.

"Emil, this is Dusty Jason. He works for a waste disposal company and he wants to show the mayor something. Why don't you join us? Dusty, I'm pleased to introduce my associate, Emil Jura."

Emil stared at Dusty Jason as their hands clasped. Dusty's features did not register in Emil's computer-bank mind. But his handshake did.

Dusty Jason never rode the back of a garbage truck or held onto the corner handrail with all his strength on sharp turns. He never tossed cans and bags five days a week, cut his palms and fingers on torn, jagged pieces of tin, or change the inside rear tire on a rig that was overdue for emptying at the transfer station.

There was no way, Emil knew, that Dusty could have done any of those jobs. Dusty's hand was soft. His nails were buffed, chalked, neatly filed and squared-off. The rich ointment the manicurist or masseur had used left a delicate, yet familiar, aroma that Emil recognized.

It was the same expensive emollient Jeffery Adam McCormack's manicurist used. Emil had Dusty pegged. Dusty dressed for the role he played, but he didn't look the part. He should have stopped after just the haircut.

To Emil, Dusty was probably a marketing man by nature, but something else by training.

159

He appeared to be an energetic man in his early fifties with tousled, almost wiry, mousse-slicked, salt-and-pepper hair that stood up around the sides of his head. His eyebrows bristled over owlish round spectacles that kept slipping down his nose.

"You'll have to excuse me, Dusty, because I'm new on the job," Greg said. "The secretary just left for lunch. I haven't seen the mayor recently, but I understand he is aware of your appointment that was arranged by Councilman Dominguez. The councilman did arrange the appointment, is that correct?"

"Yes, that's right," Dusty said with an impatient tone.

"You are welcome to wait for the mayor," Greg said, "but if time is a constraint I would be happy to hear what you have to say. I suppose you've traveled some today."

"I sure have, Mr. Robertson. I came here from Seattle by way of Phoenix and will spend tonight on a flight to Newark. I cover all fifty states and territories about every three months. Time is my enterprise. That's why my appointments are scheduled a month in advance and confirmed two weeks later, as was this one. My appointment here in your city hall was for one hour and it started seven minutes ago when I stepped through your door at precisely one o'clock."

Dusty raised his right hand, extended his index finger and moved his glasses back to the bridge of his nose.

Dusty had clearly placed Greg on the defensive.

Emil eyed the punctual visitor who had a tight schedule, and an acidic tongue to match. Greg should give the old fart both barrels, Emil thought. Better yet, with about three Tae Kwon Do maneuvers, Emil could cause Dusty Jason an extensive eye problem, some dislocated teeth, a rearranged larynx and a compound fracture without ever laying a hand on him.

Greg forced himself to flash a broad, congenial smile as he looked squarely at the visitor.

"Dusty, it would be presumptuous if not untoward of me to speak for the mayor or assume his role. However, as city manager, I am at your service as your host to accommodate your desire."

Greg glanced at Dusty's business card. The card was at least twice the size of a normal card and it read like the directory for

Bank of America. It listed Bernard "Dusty" Jason as Senior Vice Chairman of the Venture Capital Division of Forester's of Chicago with branch offices, alphabetically, in each state and territory. The card also contained addresses in North America, South America, Europe, Asia, Australia, and about a dozen different ways to contact Dusty.

Dusty Jason did not show even an iota of surprise at the smooth, diplomatic maneuver so ably spoken by the city manager. Dusty was not one to be defensive when experience clearly proved that profits came from enterprising offensive actions.

Dusty pulled a notebook from his back pocket and thumbed through a few pages. "Ah, ha," he finally said. "You have a woman employed here by the name of Tilly Cloud. I had her called, now, let's see, oh, yes, here it is. I had her called on the sixth of last month. I had her called at the request of the Honorable Carlos Santiago Dominguez, a fine gentleman I met in Buenos Aires."

Greg looked at the visitor and it was obvious that old Dusty would not give an inch. He was also quick to drop names.

"Very well," Greg said, "please accept my profound apology."

Dusty Jason, the kick-ass contract negotiator and financier, had won again. He could now put aside his haughtiness and extend an olive branch of cooperation.

"Well," Dusty said with a slight smirk as he rearranged his glasses, "I sense that I have caught you at an inopportune time. Perhaps I can shorten my presentation to you and your associate. I'm flexible as is my valuable assistant who makes these appointments for me and monitors my trips, bless her heart. For your convenience, should I have you called prior to my next trip this way?"

It was a gamble, but it was never a risky gamble. Dusty never had an appointment postponed by phrasing the words so carefully as he had just done.

Emil quickly raised his cupped hand to his mouth and emitted a slight attention-getting cough. "As only an observer, but a keen and interested associate of the city manager," Emil said with self-confident aplomb, "perhaps we should find a table and proceed to Dusty's items of discussion before our wives beckon us home."

"Well said," Dusty exclaimed with a big smile. He looked around and gestured toward a table in the corner.

As was his custom, even on foreign turf, Dusty Jason led the way.

Greg knew that when circumstances required tact and diplomacy, Emil was a born facilitator. He was also a bachelor. Emil had driven down from Atlanta last week to assist Jeffery Adam McCormack, but soon found full-time activity as Greg's sidekick.

Greg had met Emil during visits to Brenda's parent's house, but family events never allowed Greg to spend much time with Emil. During the past few days, however, their respect for each other grew deep; like a flight leader and a wingman.

By the time Emil and Greg walked to the table and took their seats, Dusty had removed the bonding tape from the rolls of paper, had spread them flat against the center of the table and was anchoring the four sides.

"Perhaps you can see and read for yourselves better than I can explain," Dusty said with a broad smile as he anchored the last corner and pointed at the top paper.

"I trust your interest in saving hard-earned tax money and preserving the fragile and precious environment along the sugar-white sandy beaches of the Florida panhandle are as strong as mine. I will summarize in a few moments."

The words spewed out of Dusty's mouth in a mechanical rhythm.

Greg and Emil leaned over the table and focused their attention on a series of three-color photographs, solid waste compression charts and engineering data that described the front, rear and sides of a factory-delivered, low-cost, high-yield, one-operator, bright yellow, front-end- loader garbage truck with a five-year limited warranty.

The page also displayed hundreds of power and weight grids that depicted the differences in weight distribution of household garbage, yard trash and recyclables.

Some grids showed the annual tonnage of household garbage, yard trash and recyclables from communities of Mobile, Dos Bayou, Pensacola, Fort Walton Beach, Destin and Panama City.

Greg leaned closer to the graphic. Each grid had minuscule – almost microscopic – mathematic formulas listed within green dotted triangles, red dotted squares, orange dotted hexagons, yellow dotted pentagons, and purple dotted octagons.

His fascination with the formulas was quickly extinguished when Dusty lifted two corners of the top paper and hung it over the side of the table.

Greg and Emil found the second display an instant eye catcher.

They looked with amusement at the well-endowed Miss Alabama who was precariously posed atop the hydraulic lift of a five-year-old, front-end-loader that recorded the first 10-ton yard trash compression in the history of Gulf Shores Waste.

"We now record that same tonnage several times each day in the various communities we serve in North America," Dusty said. "We are not only on the cutting edge of new technology, but we are also the pioneer leader in the collection and disposal of household garbage, yard trash and recyclable materials for most of the world."

"I see," Greg said as he tried to display a look of interest in a subject he was not the least bit concerned about.

"Just how large is your company?" Emil asked.

Dusty Jason proudly pointed to the light blue color on the graphic.

"Of the nearly two hundred and sixty nations in the world that have commercial collection and disposal of trash, my company is ranked the largest in annual gross volume."

Emil started to point to a portion of Italy's boot hill when Dusty suddenly pulled two corners of the graphic and hung it over the side of the table.

The third display had bold type under graphs that showed Gulf Shores Waste percentage ratio of complaints during the past year was .0014 of its customer base. Another graph demonstrated how each complaint was resolved to the customer's satisfaction within 30 minutes, but not more than 24 hours, from the time of receipt.

"When a complaint is received, it is given the highest priority by our trained and experienced customer service staff and operations personnel," Dusty boasted.

"How about your technical support staff," Emil asked.

Dusty smiled. He considered the question just another home-run pitch.

"We have the experience, resources and technical support systems to meet or exceed standards established by any governmental agency, business or third-party entity," Dusty explained. "And furthermore, we are proud of our trained, courteous personnel and we will maintain a sufficient work force of competent staff to service the fine city of Dos Bayou starting within sixty days."

Greg and Emil were reading the captions under the customer satisfaction graphs as Dusty talked. It did not take long for Dusty's words about Dos Bayou to sink in.

"Within sixty days?" Greg asked. "Do you have a contract with Dos Bayou?"

"My contract is with the mayor," Dusty said. "I confirmed it with Councilman Dominguez when we met in Ecuador and again in Chile just a few weeks ago. I love South and Central America. Councilman Dominguez is an excellent host. Because of his fine help, I now have every one of the twenty countries down there on a long-term contract."

Emil nudged Greg's arm and pointed to the small type under the bar graph that listed localities where a majority of Forester's Venture Capital Investors lived.

Mafia-infested communities of Newark, Phoenix, Chicago and Fresno were prominent along with investor sources in Eastern Europe, Africa and Central and South America.

Greg looked at Emil. Each was stone-faced.

"And the last chart should be of great interest to you," Dusty Jason said as he pulled away the customer satisfaction page and displayed a graphic of Miss Alabama holding a placard with bold lettering that read, "Profits For Life."

Greg and Emil were immediately suspicious of graphs that showed percentages of profits that were given to city officials or entity leaders who contracted with Gulf Shores Waste for garbage and trash collection.

Greg and Emil could smell bribery and corruption regardless of the terms Dusty and Miss Alabama used.

"We will have a local calling area phone line to receive customers' questions, compliments of admiration, and, in rare instances, complaints," Dusty said. "A manager will be available to personally handle any complaint that may arise, when duly requested, of course."

Greg felt a deep-seated contempt for the conniving, gangster tactics used by slick-tongued Bernard "Dusty" Jason.

Greg tried to ignore Dusty's words, but he couldn't.

"Our fleet of vehicles are state-of-the-art in the industry and were manufactured in either Allentown, Pennsylvania or in Detroit, Michigan. We will use local landfills for household garbage and yard trash, while recyclable commodities will be transported to appropriate processing centers."

Dusty reached down and pulled all the charts up and centered them on the "Profits for Life" graphic. With a seemingly mechanical motion, he rolled each one – as if he had done it a thousand times – bounded it with tape, stuffed it in a tube and carefully placed them on the table.

Greg took a folding chair, turned it around, straddled the seat, and rested his arms on the back. He glared at Dusty Jason, Senior Vice Chairman of the Venture Capital Division of Forester's of Chicago. Greg felt the same hate for old money pockets Dusty Jason as he had felt for Dictator Saddam Hussein and his barbarian rapists in Kuwait.

Screw the first name shit, Greg decided.

"Mr. Jason, if it is your objective to add the city of Dos Bayou to your string of Mafia income producers, I'm afraid you are badly mistaken."

Emil had never heard Greg speak with such a decisive, command tone in his voice.

Dusty looked sheepishly at the rolls of paper on the table. He wiped an imaginary tear from his eye, raised his head, looked at Greg and Emil, and his broad face split into a hearty, boisterous laugh.

If I had a gun, Greg thought to himself, I would kill the son of a bitch right here and now. Then he remembered. Emil carried a gun!

Greg looked at Dusty Jason as he wiped his eyes. The damn loud laughter continued from Dusty's greedy mouth.

The lifetime oath that Greg took when he entered the Air Force Academy flashed through his mind: "I will not lie, cheat or steal nor tolerate those who do."

Greg could not tolerate Dusty Jason or anything he stood for.

"You and your hoodlums may think it's funny to enter into collusion, bribe people and manipulate governmental agencies so you can make more dirty money," Greg yelled over Dusty's boisterous chuckles. "But you'll never get my support or my silence."

Finally, Dusty controlled his outburst, leaned halfway across the table and glared at Greg.

"It's not your support I seek, Mr. Robertson," Dusty said slowly through an ugly, sinister grin.

"It is, rather, your full and complete submissive cooperation that I demand and I expect. You would be well advised to position yourself in a constant state of readiness so you can speedily respond to any of my desires. Your town's residents deserve and need my services. Don't stand in their way, or mine. Am I clear?"

Greg was dumbfounded. Was his medication playing games with his mind? Did he actually hear what he thought he just heard?

He looked at Emil. Emil looked stunned.

Dusty took a long, deep breath and exhaled slowly. He had learned long ago that the art of marketing a product was to believe foremost in honesty, and when one could actually fake honesty – and make it believable – the sky was truly the limit.

Dusty leaned back from the table, straightened himself, propped-up his glasses and displayed his best Jekyll and Hyde forced smile.

"I'm here as your new contractor," he said in a mild, gentle tone. "I was told you would assist me. Your present contractor is on a one-year extension. However, that extension was terminated last month when your mayor gave the contractor a ninety-day notice.

My company takes over the business in sixty days. And that's the way the mop flops, like it or not."

"Perhaps," Greg said.

Dusty's smile vanished.

"We'll have none of that 'perhaps' shit and you had better learn to get my drift the first time I say something," Dusty said with an arrogant smirk. "That word 'perhaps' doesn't fit anywhere in the garbage business."

Greg's expression did not change as he laser-beamed the despicable, self-appointed ass-kicker Dusty Jason.

"And there's something else that doesn't fit," Dusty said as he pushed his glasses back in place, "to reduce our costs, I'm eliminating toters on the back of trucks so there will be only one person on each truck, and that will be the driver. I'll be providing ninety-six-gallon capacity trash carts to each household. Each truck comes equipped with a mechanical lift to hoist carts and empty them. It's up to the occupant of the house to get the cart to the front curb."

"Perhaps," Greg said with a look of defiance. "We'll see."

"What we'll see, Mr. City Manager," Dusty's gravelly voice roared, "is an immediate change in pick-up locations in this city, and you'll be the one explaining the change to angry residents. They'll be angry because we're not having any more side yard or back yard household garbage or yard trash pick-up service.

"That old shit of having a toter get off the truck, walk to a side yard or back yard, carry the can to the truck, empty it, and return to damn can to the side or back of the house is history come sixty days from now."

"You sound pretty sure of yourself," Greg said.

"And here's another thing I'm sure of," Dusty said as he readjusted his glasses and pointed a finger in Greg's face, "we'll see only front curbside pickup of all garbage and trash. If it ain't on the front curb on schedule, it won't be picked-up period, and there won't be any return trips. Is that clear?"

Greg rubbed his chin, narrowed his eyes, shook his head and looked at Dusty with a mischievous smile.

"And here's another thing you'll need to note in all these changes," Dusty said in a dictatorial manner. "My company doesn't provide any complimentary or coupon discounted drop-off bins, roll-off bins, three-yard to forty-yard containers or any other trash or construction debris receptacles in the city of Dos Bayou. You want it, you pay for it. I don't care if it's the Girl Scouts on a cookie drive or the Shriners helping crippled children. You want a bin, you pay for the bin. That's a condition of our exclusive performance-based contract. It's our way or no way. No other garbage company can set foot in Dos Bayou. None."

"Tell me Dusty, in your line of business," Greg asked in a casual and nonchalant voice, "how do you tell the difference?"

"The difference in what?"

"The difference between a big piece of shit like you and a large box of kitty litter."

Dusty reached down, grabbed his huge briefcase, lifted it to the center of the table, placed it on its side and snapped it open.

"I've been called worse," Dusty said. "Besides, I'm not going to fight with you. Two on one ain't fair," he said with a smile.

"But I just have a hunch that each of you would like a piece of my sweet, tender ass. You had better use your time to get ready to defend yourself, because Councilman Dominguez or the mayor are not going to like what I tell them."

Emil looked down and saw a bundle of cashiers' checks in the briefcase.

"As your distinguished Councilman Carlos Santiago Dominguez explained to me, your fine city has been badly damaged by Hurricane Raymond," Dusty said matter-of-factly.

"Per my discussion with Councilman Dominguez, I am prepared to give your mayor a cashier's check for two million dollars. The payee line is blank. The bearer of the note can fill in whoever he wants to be the beneficiary. It's for the mayor or you, Mr. Robertson, to do with as you please. I couldn't care less."

Dusty stuck out an index finger and propped-up his glasses.

"In addition, it is the understanding of my assistant who arranged this meeting with Tilly Cloud that the cashier's check was a condition, or shall I say the desire, of your mayor."

Greg remembered what Brenda had told him about her conversations with teachers at her school; conversations that clearly pointed to Mayor Phillip Garrison being a liar, a crook and a swindler.

"Excuse us for a minute," Greg said as he motioned for Emil to follow.

As they walked away, Greg punched some numbers on his cell phone. He spoke for a few moments, then handed the phone to Emil. Emil went to his SUV and returned a few minutes later with two pieces of paper.

"Very well," Greg said as they approached the table, "Emil, please give Dusty a receipt for his donation. The funds will be deposited for whatever distribution the council desires."

Greg looked at Dusty Jason. "Is that all right with you?"

"Of course it is."

"I will inform the council of your arrangement with the mayor regarding the contract with the city. Emil is preparing your receipt."

"Very well," Dusty said. "I'll be in touch. In the meantime, you know how to reach me."

Emil scribbled something on the two pages and placed them on the table.

"Please sign here for your receipt," Emil said as he held out a pen.

Dusty signed both papers.

Emil folded one and placed it in his pocket.

Dusty took the other one and dropped it unceremoniously into his briefcase and snapped it shut.

"My taxi should be waiting," Dusty said as he gathered his rolls of paper, placed them under his arm and marched toward the front door.

Greg and Emil watched from the front porch as the taxi cleared the circular driveway in front of city hall and disappeared into traffic.

Greg turned the lock on the front door and got into the Lincoln Navigator with some lifting assistance from Emil. Emil casually tossed the $2 million cashier's check in the glove box as if it was something he did every day.

As they waited for a break in traffic, a black Mercedes swerved off Andalusia Avenue, turned onto the circular drive and braked to a stop beside them. The driver's side of each car was about three feet apart.

The man in the Mercedes was dark complexioned and held a long stogie in his mouth.

"Can I help you fellows?" the man asked. "I'm Carlos Dominguez."

Greg leaned over. "Good afternoon, councilman. I'm your new manager, Greg Robertson. I just dropped by to look things over. I'm glad to meet you."

"I heard you were injured," Dominguez said in a concerned tone. "Get well soon. I look forward to working with you."

"Thank you, sir. I will."

Carlos Santiago Dominguez reached into his breast pocket, pulled out two huge cigars and held them in his out-stretched hand.

"Would you fellows like to have a couple Cohibas? They're the finest cigars made in South America."

"Thank you," Emil said as he reached out and accepted the U.S.-banned contraband.

"Well, I've got to get inside," Dominguez said. "The mayor is meeting with someone and I want to sit in on the meeting. Good day."

Greg's forehead furrowed in deep thought as he watched the Mercedes continue down the circular driveway.

"Emil, I think I spent too long in the safe black and white world of the United States Air Force."

"How's that?" Emil asked as he reached over and turned on the CD.

"Well, you could always rely on someone to be honest and aboveboard. But I thought the grass was greener on the other side of the fence. I got out of the service and took a good-paying job in the business world. Then along came a big fish and bought out the company and about three hundred of us were tossed out on our ears."

"So what's new?" Emil asked as a soft vocal played in the background.

"Dusty Jason and Gulf Shores Waste," Greg said.

"He's screwing the little guy and the town residents, and the mayor is supposed to get the payoff," Emil said. "The mayor is going to be pissed, and that's for sure."

"Notice how Councilman Dominguez was such a gentleman?" Greg asked.

"Yes, I sure did. Didn't he vote against you?"

"Yeah, he and Councilwoman Libby Washington. They must be two peas in a pod."

"You want to hear about the fax?"

"Yeah, what did Jeffery send you?"

"Take a look," Emil said. He pulled out the paper and unfolded it.

Greg looked at the bold typed words at the top. PROPOSAL CERTIFICATION.

"Read the second paragraph," Emil said.

Greg read the words slowly: "That the proposer has not divulged, discussed or compared proposals with other proposers, nor colluded with any other proposers, other interested parties, or employees/officials of the City of Dos Bayou."

Greg smiled.

"Well, it looks like Mayor Garrison, big alpha male Dusty Jason, and Councilman Dominguez are grass and Jeffery is a lawn mower," Emil said with a broad grin.

"Damn, I have actually been a working city manager for only about thirty minutes and I already hate the goddamn job," Greg said in a rueful tone.

"You may be in a deep hole, pal," Emil said. "Much deeper than you think. In a way, you're back in the cockpit and I can think of two million reasons why you had better strap yourself in real tight, keep your head down and watch your six."

Greg opened the compartment next to his seat and pulled out a laptop. He typed for a few seconds, read the reply and typed some more.

The familiar sound of a fax machine could be heard under the digital system.

Within a few minutes Greg had a copy of the Articles of

Incorporation filed by Forester's of Chicago, a printout of Forester's Website, the last quarterly financial statement filed by Gulf Shores Waste, this morning's Tokyo, New York, Moscow and London stock market listings for Gulf Shores Waste, and a copy of the City Charter for Dos Bayou.

As the Lincoln Navigator headed east toward Okaloosa Island, Greg put away the laptop, stacked the papers on the console, leaned back into the cushiony headrest and closed his eyes. His self-talk rattled-off all the problems he faced. And there were many.

All of them centered on and around people and events in Dos Bayou. The rapid-fire words spun through his mind.

He had just completed his third visit to Dos Bayou City Hall, and each visit, he knew, had turned into a hellish nightmare.

The first trip to city hall was for a job interview with the mayor. That meeting, or lecture, took only about 20 minutes.

"If I give you the city manager's job," he remembered Mayor Garrison saying, "the way to get along around here is to go along, if you get where I'm comin' from."

When Garrison said that remark with a slight, but all-knowing wink, Greg could smell the distasteful odor of misfeasance in the air. But he needed the job.

The bitter taste of malfeasance occurred on his second visit when the mayor and Judge Andrews handed over the keys and title to a new car that was purchased by tax funds.

The previous rancid smell of misuse and abuse was compounded by actions today that were significantly more grievous than a simple matter of misfeasance, fraud, malfeasance, theft or the stupidity that comes with nonfeasance.

Today's introduction to Bernard "Dusty" Jason, the bullheaded, shameless, scumbag of a trash man, was nothing more than shaking hands with an extension of Councilman Carlos Santiago Dominguez, Mayor Garrison or Judge Andrews.

They were all self-proclaimed warriors with a carefully cultivated reputation of taking a head for an eye and a jaw for a tooth.

Dusty Jason had bribed his way into a lucrative long-term garbage contract that provided fewer services at higher costs than the one Mayor Garrison short-circuited and kicked out of town.

And, Greg knew, the brazen way Dusty Jason did it and boasted about it during their meeting clearly revealed the mysterious, heavy hand of Councilman Dominguez, coupled with the usual corrupt methods of Mayor Garrison.

They were nothing more than common street brawlers, not warriors.

But Greg felt that there was something cartoonish about their characters, and he remembered the report he got about the last council meeting.

Mayor Garrison growled and grunted, and maximized maleness, but when confronted by Libby Washington, he stopped just a dagger away from looking comically grotesque.

Then, there was the biggest, most dangerous bastard of all.

Judge Chester D. Andrews, without his jurist garb, acted like he was the toughest of the tough and the fiercest of the fearless, but Brenda saw right through his yellow spine.

Dusty Jason and his slippery glasses tried to be the personification of brute force, but he could not possibly be taken seriously by any of the nation's Fortune 500, especially without his rolled paper props and his bag full of cashiers' checks that he tosses around like Monopoly money.

It was time, Greg knew, that the Garrisons, Dominguezs, Andrews and Jasons of the world learned that you don't get a Silver Star for target practice.

It was time for combat.

Then there's Tilly Cloud, a young woman whose obsessions with beer-spiked sodas, long filtered Marlboros and old studs trump all other interests, except some form of trailer park comeuppance by dating Mayor Garrison, who had to be the stub of all studs.

Tilly's exposed midriff, suggestive gyrations, frenzied pouts, sassy Southern belle inflections, campy sexuality and plenty of in-your-face-attitude would get her noticed at Pascali's Restaurant, but those little ruses were meaningless at the Early Bird Bar or across the road at the Laundromat.

Tilly had spent too much time borrowing from the MTV book of performing.

Although Greg believed that Tilly was mature beyond her

years, she was not ready or adept at the transformation she would soon have to face with Mayor Garrison: deposition, indictment and prosecution.

Greg rubbed his temples and opened his eyes.

It had already been a long day, but he knew it was far from over.

CHAPTER 11

"**I**'ve heard they're pretty strict around here," Emil said when he saw the El Matador sign, slowed and turned off Santa Rosa Boulevard. The Lincoln Navigator entered a pink and white oleander-lined cobblestone road. "And wealthy too, I might add."

The entry road meandered around huge oak trees on the El Matador resort and ended at a quaint, Spanish-style security post. "Do you think we'll have any problem clearing security?" Emil asked with a chuckle.

"According to the fax, everything is supposed to be arranged," Greg said. "Let's hope it is because it would be a long drive back."

Greg looked at the heavy metal security arm that stretched across the space in front of them. There were uniformed people about every 50 feet and they all looked dreadfully serious and busy. They scurried about their business in gloved hands that held computer chip notepads, and wide black belts that carried pagers, cell phones, mace, handcuffs and flashlights.

"When was the last time you saw so many rent-a-cops mixed in with the real thing?' Greg asked.

"About a year ago," Emil said. "I was in the lobby of the Hyatt Regency in Atlanta waiting for the boss when Britney Spears checked in wearing enough gems to buy Vegas."

"Uh, huh," Greg said, "that's exactly how she looked every time I saw her. It got pretty old after awhile."

Emil tried to hide his smile as he lowered his tinted window and got a close-up view of El Matador's security force on Okaloosa Island.

A no-nonsense looking man in a light green tailored uniform with starched creases and a saucer-hat stepped out of the security post and approached the car. The bill of his hat was pulled down low on his forehead. His Salvador Dali-mustache extended horizontally for a couple inches then climbed skyward until both ends were at eyebrow level. With an ominous glare and a beefy build, the guy was the stereotype of a rental cop with a Walter Mitty-ego problem.

"Can I help you, sir," the guard asked.

"We are with the McCormack party as guests in the plaza three Christina condominiums," Emil said.

"Your names?" the guard asked raising his notepad.

"I am Emil Jura. My passenger is Mister Gregory Robertson."

The guard pressed several keys on the notepad, lifted a small clipboard from his belt, clicked his ballpoint pen and made two check marks on his clipboard roster. "Your vehicle registration please, and some picture IDs."

Emil opened the glove box, looked under the $2 million cashier's check, removed the registration card, pulled his license from his billfold, got Greg's ID, and handed the documents to the guard's outstretched hand.

The guard's examination of the papers became a leisurely respite as he studied and restudied the papers with the same diligence an anxious inheritor would devote to the last will and testament of a favorite uncle.

He finally returned the documents.

"If you have any weapons, gentlemen, now would be the time to declare them and turn them over for the duration of your stay."

Emil looked at Greg with a disconcerted glare. "Looks like we got a John Wayne wannabe," Emil whispered. "Watch this."

Emil faced the guard.

"Mister Robertson is not armed," Emil said. "I have two

concealed weapons' permits issued by the U.S. Marshal's office in Atlanta. They are code one permits that preempt local authority. That includes you. I'm carrying a four-inch, nine-millimeter Beretta. I also have a Smith and Wesson in my toiletry bag. I have now declared my weapons but I will not surrender them to you for any part of my duration. If you need verification of permits, call the Christina condos and ask for Mister McCormack, or, if you have the balls, call the marshal's office in Atlanta."

The guard's expression was half awe and half fear. The vertical ends of his mustache seemed to sag as they tilted toward his nose.

The guard had not heard the last from Emil Jura.

"And do yourself a big favor toward job security," Emil said. "Tell your supervisor that in the future every time this Lincoln Navigator approaches, I want that damn mechanical arm raised and this vehicle waved through. My time is to be spent with Mister McCormack and not with you. Do you have any questions?"

"Sir, no, sir. Sir, yes, sir, a statement please, sir?" the guard asked.

"Go ahead," Emil said, "what it is?"

"An escort, sir," the guard said, "will proudly show you to plaza three. I will arrange a permanent parking space for you near the Christina condos. It's always a pleasure to meet a fellow officer, especially one with the U.S. Marshal's service. Have a nice day, sir."

Emil closed the tinted window just in time to muffle Greg's laughter.

The escort was a pink golf cart that slowly and cautiously moved along well under the 15-MPH posted limit. The slow-paced tour took them near a tree-lined jogging trail, a putting green, an Olympic-size pool, two lap pools, a health club with spa, an aerobics class, tennis courts, shuffleboard and outdoor dining areas. As they reached the top of a small hill, a golf course entwined with the pristine, natural beauty of sugar-white sand that seemed to melt into the deep-blue waters of the Gulf of Mexico.

Greg's eyes widened at the spectacular view.

"The El Matador property is the oldest and most prestigious in the southeast," Emil said.

"I think we just found paradise," Greg said in a low voice, "or at least it's in the same zip code."

"I don't know how the boss does it," Emil said, "but he sure knows how to pick winners."

The pink golf cart came to a stop in front of the parking lot adjacent to plaza three and the Christina condos. A maintenance man stood beside a freshly painted sign on the corner parking spot. The man stepped back, gave Emil a thumbs-up gesture and motioned for him to pull into the spot.

"It's yours, senor, with our compliments," the man said as he tipped the bill of his cap and left.

Emil and Greg got out and gazed at the posted sign.

RESERVED FOR TOP BANANA ONLY.

"How was your day at the office?" Brenda asked as she stepped through the French doors and threw her arms around Greg. Her voice was breathy, barely above a whisper. Her hair was more strawberry than auburn, her eyes were large and the smile larger.

"I think Emil was better suited for it than I was," Greg smiled. "At least he was armed. I was just dangerous."

"Don't you believe him, Brenda," Emil said. "I can vouch for the fact that Greg earned his pay today, all two million dollars."

Brenda's eyes grew into silver dollar-sized circles.

"Hell, I forgot about the check," Greg said. He reached into the SUV, opened the glove box and withdrew the paper. He waved it over his head. "Sweetie, here's a cashier's check for two million. The payee line is blank. Fill in a name, show some ID and the money is yours. No questions asked. Emil and I worked about thirty minutes and we got a check for two mill. Not bad, huh?"

Greg paused and looked at Brenda.

"It's no good," he said shaking his head. "Where I come from, it's called a bribe. Your father already knows about it. The check was meant for the mayor. That SOB. We have a lot of documents to review with your father, and I'm sure he's going to have a lot of questions."

"Well, before you start, let me tell you about a call I just returned," Brenda said.

"Someone called you here?" Emil asked with a quizzical expression.

"No, not here." Brenda said. "It was a message on our machine at home."

"Greg, do you remember when I told you that I was a witness at the swearing-in promotion for First Lieutenant Jefferson Underwood with the county sheriff's office?"

"Yeah, I remember that."

"Well, Eloise, Lieutenant Underwood's wife, called me this morning. She sounded very pleasant. She and some of her friends want to meet me at the Flamingo Café at three. She wouldn't say why. She said they would explain at the meeting. Father said if you approved, Emil would go with me."

"That's fine with me, sweetheart," Greg said, "I have a hunch that I'll be with your father and his people for several hours. We have a lot of ground to cover. But first I'll take some pills and a practice nap."

"Father is in the two connecting corner condos with about a dozen lawyers and that many more support staff," Brenda said. "He had all the furniture removed and the condos are now an office complex. It looks like the war room in a movie. We're at this end of the plaza in condo five. Emil is next door in six. Father rented every Christina condo in plaza three, all eighteen."

Emil checked his watch. "Guess we'll leave in twenty minutes. Okay Brenda?"

"Sure."

"Sweetie," Greg said, "please be very cooperative with the guard at the main gate or he'll confiscate all your guns."

"Huh?" Brenda remarked with an inquisitive look.

Emil tried to hide his snicker.

~ ~ ~ ~ ~ ~

There were five women seated at a large circular booth in the corner of the lounge.

"That must be them," Brenda said. "I hope this won't take too long, whatever it is."

"I'll be over there," Emil said motioning to a table. "Take your time because the meeting must be important to someone."

Emil walked to the bar, ordered a club soda, and took his seat at a table that gave him a clear view of the corner booth. He watched as the women shook hands with Brenda and scooted over to make room.

Emil removed a pen and notepad from his pocket and began his usual disciplined routine of outlining the events of the day, names and titles of people met, and conversations held.

~ ~ ~ ~ ~

The raw wind rattled tree limbs and sent small clouds of red clay dirt swirling across Sheriff Homer Jedbow Cogburn's front porch. The porch resembled many in the timeless back-woods of Florida's panhandle: wicker-back rockers, a bucktoothed rake and withered hanging plants.

But step though the front door and the proud, disheveled 1960s lies before the eyes.

The living rooms walls are adorned with posters for long-ago concerts. Shelves swell with LPs. On table-tops and couches are stacks and stacks of vintage photographs of artists B. B. King, Janis Joplin, Muddy Waters and Howlin' Wolf.

Cogburn's pictures of old bluesmen and women, taken over four decades, included priceless artifacts of the music's glory days.

And mixed in with the artifacts were hundreds upon hundreds of knickknacks, doodads, gewgaws, trinkets, bric-a-brac, trumpery and other collectibles and oddities that would cause a carnival vendor's eyebrows to elevate and quiver at his widow's peak.

Though a relentless advocate of other artists, Cogburn never got around to publishing a lot of his own work, perhaps out of some bone-bred aversion to seeing things through.

He moved the window curtains apart and watched patiently as the sky turned from a purple-pink to a midnight blue. The wind had died down. A low, thick layer of clouds moved in and obscured the stars and moon, and a mild but favorable breeze rustled the leaves in the large oak tree that formed an umbrella over his cabin.

Nights for Homer Jedbow Cogburn were for coon hunting, and tonight his trek would take him northeast of the hollow where he lived near Pace and into a large swampy, wooded area where some of the wiliest raccoons in the entire Florida Panhandle survived by outwitting two-legged creatures.

He looked closely at the leaves as they gently fluttered in the breeze. The wind was a coon hunter's dream. He figured it at about 10 miles an hour out of the northeast. He craned his head and looked out of each side of the window. He nodded, smiled and stuck out his lower lip. The weather and overcast skies, he knew, were perfect.

On a night like this, he figured, if he was just a tad bit lucky, there wasn't a coon alive that could outsmart or outwit old Homer Jedbow Cogburn, especially when he knew the terrain as well as he did, had the wind in his face, and could get his light on the coon's eyes before the coon saw him first.

He released the curtains and looked at his special clothes hanging on the nail by the toilet.

Now came the hard part of going coon hunting.

It was getting more and more difficult for him to squeeze his expanding girth into the camouflaged bushed bib overalls that he had purchased only two years ago at Wal-Mart. The matching ammo vest was no problem to wear because he couldn't button it if he wanted to.

The other problem was the 2-way adjustable strap on his headlamp. The strap was already set in the extra-large extended position, but when he attached it on his baseball cap with the heavy battery pack in back at the base of his skull, the damn front brim squeezed his forehead so hard his eyes sometimes crossed and he had constant headaches.

But no coon hunter worth his salt would go hunting without a headlamp, especially one like the lamp that Homer Jedbow Cogburn customized with a large super bright bulb. With a flip of a finger, he could adjust the focus from spot to flood or flood to spot quicker than a coon could play possum.

The special bulb could throw a spot beam 200 yards and display the separation between a coon's eyes.

And that's when "Big Bubba" came in.

"Big Bubba" was Homer Jedbow Cogburn's 12-gage pump shotgun with an over-bored barrel that could discharge six rounds of high-brass buckshot as fast as the hand could push and yank.

Coon hunting was a wilderness art form that Cogburn ranked just a smidgen below his one and only first love; the mandolin.

To him, coon hunting was unlike any other game sport. It took a special skill to hunt and bag the smartest creature that ever lived in trees but also knew how to forage and survive on the ground.

Homer Jedbow Cogburn never cottoned to deer or turkey hunting. He didn't think they were fair contests.

What was fair, he often argued, about rigging a tree blind with a stool to sit on and then wait for a deer to walk by so you could shoot it in the spine?

That just wasn't fair in Cogburn's book.

The same went for turkey hunts where grown people used mechanical callers that sounded like hens in heat to fool toms into thinking about starting a family and settling down at the very split second their guts were blown away.

No, that wasn't his style.

Homer Jedbow Cogburn's true style could not be fulfilled until he got through another political campaign, another election, and another four years as Sheriff of Escambia County. Only then could he retire and live the good life as a bluegrass tenor with a piercing voice that could break your heart before you've felt the cracks.

He already had his new routine down pat. He and his band, the Cogburn Codgers, had developed a stage and recording style with such unique breakneck tempos that other groups could not even come close to imitating.

And they sure couldn't imitate the voice.

The Cogburn Codgers had evolved into a separate genre.

Their style, like their new recording, "Escape From Milton," was just too unpredictable.

The song soared to the top of the bluegrass charts and became a cult favorite, some DJs said, because the stripped-down, unpretentious arrangement put the emphasis squarely on Cogburn's voice and the hissing sounds from his mandolin.

Homer Jedbow Cogburn's use of acoustic instruments like banjos, fiddles and mandolins created intricate, emotional music that evolved into a subculture with blue-collar folks in the panhandle. They felt a kinship to his music and an allegiance to their redneck traits. And they didn't have to feel stuffy about it.

They also liked his songs because most of them were about a wily cuss and nobody was ever sure of the culprit's motivations until the very end.

Or, as Homer Jedbow Cogburn would proudly say while introducing a new song at a festival, "Here's a little ditty with an ounce of intelligence in the lyrics without a pound of highbrow."

Homer Jedbow Cogburn liked things simple, not that coon hunting was simple, but it sure beat hours after hours of dreadful paper work at the office.

He often thought of his early days in Century when he had a three-man police force and a $70,000 annual budget.

Now, his territory covers 400 times as much land and the population is 2,000 times larger. He has a staff of more than 700 and a budget of $334 million.

In the old days, he drove around Century in a well-used, old Chevrolet sedan and yelled for assistance when he needed help.

And now, to his amazement, he has cruisers, SUVs, dirt bikes, helicopters, an armored car, SWAT teams, bicycles, automatic weapons, computers, radar, hand-held radios and cell phones.

But he doesn't have the slightest idea how all the electronic devices, weaponry, equipment and technical stuff are budgeted or used because he delegated those responsibilities to others.

And, to make matters worse, he couldn't figure out why "Escape From Milton" had suddenly disappeared from country western radio stations, concerts and music stores. One day it was the hottest thing going, and the next day it was dead in the water.

He left the ceiling light on as he slung "Big Bubba" over his shoulder and walked to the door for his last coon hunt this year. He was not looking forward to the next few nightmarish months.

Next week he had to pre-file for reelection. Two weeks later he had to submit his final papers with the filing fee. Then he had to raise about $400,000 in campaign funds. Next came the time-consuming job of selecting an advertising agency to handle his campaign.

And he also had to figure out what happened to "Escape From Milton."

Those were all kind of easy things to do compared to the final decision that officially started the campaign. That was the selection of who would serve as general manager.

His nephew, Sergeant Billy Ray Lewis, had managed the last two campaigns, and would manage another one if asked, but Billy Ray just seemed to go out of his way to annoy as many black and Latino voters that he could.

The ill feeling, Cogburn suspected, might still be lingering in the projects and trailer courts where those people lived.

But there was time to ponder on the coulda, woulda, shoulda stuff later.

The door latch clicked shut and Homer Jedbow Cogburn's mind quickly turned from campaigning to coons.

He headed off in a northeasterly direction and switched-on his headlamp as he disappeared into the woods.

~ ~ ~ ~ ~ ~

"It's fifteen past midnight," Jeffery Adam McCormack said glancing at his watch. "Greg, for the record, we've covered everything you know about alleged criminal activity engaged in or caused by Judge Andrews, Mayor Garrison, Sheriff's Sergeant Billy Ray Lewis, Deputy Timmy Dee Roland, and Tilly Cloud, the secretary."

McCormack turned some pages in his tablet and scanned his notes.

"Brenda has told us about her observations of the chef, Angela Giuseppi, alias Mommy Lou, the maid, Wendy Watters, and the nurse, Lolley Freehand. We have adequately established the fact that those women were employed and sent to your house by Judge Andrews and Mayor Garrison.

"Brenda also told us about the unusual coincidence, if it was, and her suspicions regarding your home repairs following the hurricane, your utility maintenance and car repairs."

McCormack turned some more pages in his tablet.

"And, of course," he said matter-of-factly, "investigators from our firm are checking all of those items. We'll have a full report soon. And Emil has given us the notes he took this afternoon."

McCormack put his hand on Greg's shoulder.

"Do you want to stop, or can you take a few more minutes and tell us about the garbage man you met?"

Greg nodded with a smile. "Let's continue as long as we have coffee."

The 15 lawyers seated along the conference table turned pages in their tablets as one of the staffers walked to a large flip-chart in the corner and printed: Bernard "Dusty" Jason, Senior Vice Chairman, Venture Capital Division, Forester's of Chicago.

Another assistant placed a new tape in the recorder, labeled the old one and settled back for another hour or two of Qs and As.

~ ~ ~ ~ ~ ~

Dos Bayou Mayor Phillip V. Garrison had experienced the most miserable day in his life. It started when $2 million that he was going to split fifty-fifty with Tilly Cloud slipped right through his fingers. Then, like rubbing salt in his wound, his chartered plane had to make an emergency landing at Key Colony Beach, and the only rental car available was a damn Hyundai. He tried to meet the inbound flight at Key West International, but to add insult to injury, he got stuck at Cudjoe Key in a no-passing zone behind a psychedelic Volkswagen pulling a wave runner.

Garrison was late. And he knew there would be hell to pay because she got mad, really mad, when he showed up late. She never was an angry sort when he showed up drunk, but she was like a wild cat if he arrived late and sober. To her that meant there was no excuse.

His mind was racing with all sorts of plausible excuses as he turned onto Roosevelt Boulevard and saw the airport tower in the distance. He glanced at his watch. His hangdog face looked more depressed than ever. "Damn, half past midnight," he said with a disgusted tone.

He drove slowly along the terminal and saw the deserted U.S. Airways Express counter. There wasn't a soul around. He drove forward several yards, parked at the curb, left the motor running, got out and looked through the windows at the Continental Airlines counter. It was vacant.

"You can't park here, mister," a voice commanded.

Mayor Garrison looked behind him and saw a security guard standing at the damn Hyundai.

"I'm not parking," Garrison said. "I'm looking for a passenger that arrived about an hour ago on US Air. But it might have been Continental. After the day I've had, I'm not sure which is which."

"Well, sir, your best bet is Mallory Square," the guard said. "That's where everyone went.

"There was a big, unruly crowd that got off the last two planes. They were drunk, as rude and disorderly as they could get, and they raised hell at the baggage counter when a lot of their bags didn't make it. Yes, sir, if you're looking for someone dead, drunk or getting laid, try Mallory Square."

"Oh, shit," Garrison said as he wiped his brow with the back of his hand. He had a vivid memory of the wild and uninhibited shenanigans that went on at Mallory Square because he initiated most of them during earlier visits.

He got back in the damn Hyundai and drove westward past the Salt Pond toward the city.

As he drove, his mind kept telling him what a complete, sorry-ass bastard he had turned out to be.

The whole damn, rotten day, and now the whole shitty night, was without hesitation or any doubt whatsoever, the costliest and the most miserable 24 hours he had ever spent.

How can one sorry bastard, he asked himself, lose a two million-dollar payoff for rigging a contract by missing an appointment with the top gun from the nation's largest garbage company?

He sadly had to agree with himself that it took some doing to be that stupid.

On second thought, the botched payoff was peanuts compared

to the sheer stupidity of screwing up a weekend shack job in Key West.

All he had to do was arrive in Key West in the chartered plane before his shack-up arrived an hour later on a commercial flight. Now how could that get screwed-up?

The sorry excuse for an airplane, the Lear, had mechanical trouble and had to make an emergency landing at some remote strip, and that's why the sorry bastard of a mayor got stuck behind a Volkswagen pulling a wave runner. That's how!

Garrison had to think. What would he say when he found her?

Oh, shit, he thought as he turned on Duval Street and dodged some chickens on the road, I'll bet she's drunk on her ass by now and she'll believe anything I tell her.

Straight ahead, on the other side of Front Street, he saw the usual huge, raunchy crowd at Mallory Square.

The celebration always started at sunset – every sunset – and ended around midmorning the next day. That gave the revelers time to find their coolers and other belongings, go back to their rooms, clean the chicken shit off their clothes and shoes, change, restock coolers, go back and start the party all over again at sunset.

Mallory Square late at night – any night – made the Vegas Strip look like a Sunday picnic.

Garrison pulled into an alley, parked in the first spot he found, got out of the damn Hyundai, slammed the door and walked toward the familiar mob scene.

He enjoyed visiting here over the years and seeing the old haunts of Ernest Hemingway, James Bond creator Ian Fleming, and Harry Truman's summer White House. But what he hated with a passion were the thousands of wild hens, chicks and roosters that roamed freely around the city and took a shit wherever and whenever they wanted to.

Garrison knew, but hated the fact that the free ranging chickens on the streets and in the trees of the island at the bottom of the Florida Keys had been part of Key West since it was settled in the mid 19th century.

187

That was the only part of Key West that truly disgusted Garrison.

And the chickens seemed to know when he arrived, where he dined and where he slept.

They scratched and clucked all night in the flower beds around his cabana, and the crowing by the largest roosters in existence started exactly at four each morning.

But worst of all, the damn chickens always seem to know where he ate. They would hop on his table, snatch his food, shit on his plate and leave dirty feathers as they fluttered away.

There were several things about chickens that pissed off Garrison, but the crowning blow was when the city closed Higgs Beach, his longtime favorite swimming spot, because piles of chicken shit near storm water drains had contaminated the water.

Garrison has never forgotten the exact date and time his hatred for chickens started. It was 2:37 a.m. on August 6, 1989, when he was in bed at the Cheeca Lodge with a red-headed cocktail waitress. They were both busy and did not notice that a chicken had jumped into the bathroom, went directly to the bed and shit on the woman's red hair.

Garrison, by his own admission, has not tasted a chicken dinner since. Or a chicken salad, which was precisely what the chicken shit looked like when it got smeared in the red hair.

He knew that through the 20th century, while most towns like Dos Bayou removed livestock and other wild animals from their streets, Key West enjoyed leaving local fowl to fend for themselves, a badge of the city's unconventional, idiosyncratic and individualistic view of itself.

But the damn chickens were forcing him to select another site for any future rendezvous.

Chickens, and chicken shit, were everywhere so Garrison watched carefully where he stepped as he crossed Front Street and approached Mallory Square.

Like chickens, coolers were plentiful. Through a long tradition at Mallory Square, cooler contents were considered "help yourself" community property so everyone took what they wanted.

Garrison stopped at a large container, felt through the melted ice, found a Bud, yanked it out and popped it open.

He took a long drink and gazed at the throng.

There were about two dozen or so one-man bands scattered about, but most of the attention was focused on some felines who walked across tightropes and jumped through flaming rings.

A loud roar erupted to his left. Garrison turned and saw a man walk on stage in a long stovepipe hat and a flowing cape.

Oh, shit, he's still here? Garrison asked himself as he looked at The Great Rondigian.

The Great Rondigian strutted to center stage amid enormous fanfare. He gave his hat and cape to a blonde who stood in the front row. The Great Rondigian took a deep bow and blew a kiss to the crowd, and another one to the blonde.

Garrison had lost count of the number of times he had seen the act. But he always applauded with the others when the remarkable feat ended.

The Great Rondigian was noted for his ability to escape from chains and a straitjacket while suspended upside down from a steel tripod while he drank through a long straw from a bottle of Wild Turkey that was held precariously between his knees.

And he did it five times each night or until the bottle was empty!

Garrison was about 100 feet from the stage when the act started. He looked again at the blonde in the front row. Was it her? No, he told himself. How could she know The Great Rondigian?

Garrison inched his way through the crowd toward the blonde.

As he got closer, he could tell the back of her legs were a perfect match. Her small shapely ass was the same, the waist was the identical size, the blonde hair was long and in a ponytail, and her height was the same.

He leaned over, put his mouth close to her ear and said, "Tilly."

She screamed in a high-pitched yelp and jumped straight up just as The Great Rondigian was taking his first long sip through the straw. He overdosed on Wild Turkey, passed out, fell from the tripod and hit the stage floor, head first, with a thud.

"Tilly, it's me," Garrison said.

Tilly turned and looked into a face she suddenly hated.

"You're a miserable like good-for-nothing, you know, son-of-a-bitch," she said with a mean-spirited grimace he had never seen before. "You stood me up like at the airport, okay?"

"Tilly, my plane crashed and . . . "

"Like that's an excuse?" she yelled. "You're a stupid fool, okay?" she screeched. A pout formed on her sensuous lips.

"I thought that maybe like when we hooked up a couple years ago we could just hang out and listen to 'N Sync-like pop tunes or stuff like Reba, Garth or Hank Junior, you know? But no, dude, you like had to go home to your wife. But around me you were always in heat but never in love. You didn't make yourself like fully available, like you promised, okay? I've already made my arrangements for tonight like with The Great Rondigian. He said I could stay with him, okay? Now get lost, man. You can find me around here like somewhere tomorrow. Then we'll talk. I want to know where my million dollars are, okay? I'll settle in two weeks for like half in cash, small bills, or I'll tell your wife and the world all about you and that old bastard, Chester Andrews, and that cunt, Momma Lou, okay?"

Garrison didn't comprehend a word she said. His full attention was on her bare collar-line and gently piercing, softly pouting and eerily empty gaze. She was still, to Garrison, his young, sweet, virginal pop poster girl who had more bedroom stamina than any female sailor he dated at the Navy base.

Garrison's jowls sagged and his eyes looked traumatized as the best piece of ass he ever had climbed onto the stage and knelt beside The Great Rondigian. Tilly lifted his head to her amply proportioned 20-year-old-bosom and cried.

Garrison turned, kicked a pile of chicken shit and walked slowly toward the street.

"That fits," he yelled. "That really fits the whole goddamn, shitty, miserable day I've had."

He stopped and looked at the stage. The Great Rondigian's head looked like it was buried in Tilly's breasts.

"Well, she'll never see the inside of Pascali's again and I'll see to that," Garrison mumbled. He thought for a few seconds and rubbed his chin.

"I'd have to sell everything to come up with a mill that quick. I wonder why she wants it in small bills. Who wants small bills anymore?"

He took the keys out as he entered the alley and approached the damn Hyundai. He thought about how much he hated just about everything, especially Korean products, when something caught his attention. The damn car was tilted. Garrison stepped back and looked at the tires. The two on the driver's side were flat. The car looked like it was in a wreck.

"That really fits everything else that's happened," he yelled. "What a fucked-up miserable day I've had."

He walked about forty-five minutes toward the airport with two heavy suitcases before he found a taxi.

After a two-mile ride, the cab entered the terminal complex and came to a stop behind two police cars that were parked between Continental and U.S. Air. The taxi driver got out, opened the trunk, placed the luggage on the ground and held out his hand. "That'll be thirty-five."

Garrison shoved some bills into the outstretched hand and noticed two officers approaching.

"May I see some ID?" an officer asked as his hand rested on the butt of his pistol.

"You want to see my ID?" Garrison asked in an irritated tone.

"Yes, sir. And I mean right now."

Garrison opened his wallet, pulled out his driver's license, his Pensacola Naval Air Station identification card, his honorary Escambia County Sheriffs card, and his badge that was engraved with his name as Mayor of the Great City of Dos Bayou, Florida.

The officer examined the material and looked at the most pitiful example of manhood he had ever seen.

"Did you rent a Hyundai from the Acme Agency in Key Colony Beach?"

"Yes, I sure did," Garrison said. "And what a piece of crap that turned out to be."

"Well, you're sure right about that," the officer said. "You'll have to come with us. Put your luggage over there by the Skycap's station and we'll leave instructions for them to store it for a few days."

"What do you mean a few days?"

"Well, sir, your rented Hyundai was parked illegally in an alley near Duval and Front Streets close to Mallory Square, and a city garbage truck just ran into it. There was quite a bit of damage that you're liable for."

"Hell, I've got car insurance that will cover anything that happened to that damn Korean piece of shit," Garrison said. "Now if you'll excuse me, I'm going to wait inside for the next plane out of here."

"It's not the Hyundai we're concerned about," the officer said. "It's the garbage truck that was totaled in the collision when it ran over your illegally parked rental car. In fact, both vehicles were totaled. The city sanitation engineer said the garbage truck was a front loader type with a mechanical arm recycling component that just came from the factory two months ago at the tune of hundred forty grand. The engineer said it was the pride of the city. They have pictures."

Garrison looked with benign disinterest at the officer.

Garrison's mouth finally opened and the words spewed out like lava from a volcano.

"This has been without a doubt the most miserable, fucked-up day I have ever experienced in my life. I want you to call Second Circuit Court Presiding Judge Chester D. Andrews. He can explain everything."

"You'll have that chance," the officer said, "right after you're booked. Now just slip into these cuffs, and please watch your head as you get into the back seat of my patrol car. We just started a three-day weekend around here, so you'll be with us at least until Tuesday morning."

CHAPTER 12

Chester D. Andrews seethed with impatience and irritation as he sat slumped over the workbench in his cluttered garage. He held a fishing rod in the crook of his left arm as he tried time and time again to re-string the spool with a new line. He kept dropping the line on the garage floor each time his fingers trembled.

He had rewound spinning reels with spools all of his life. He had a large collection of plain metal, cork, aluminum and platinum spools. It was a simple task, except for this time. Even when he got some of the new line on the spool, the rows would not coil properly.

Nothing, he felt, was done properly anymore.

His mind was over loaded and he had too many things to worry about.

His reputation had gone down the drain, and there was nothing in his career that could be salvaged.

The weather was hot and there was no air circulating in the garage. He wiped his brow with the back of his dirty hand and left streaks of grease on his sweaty face.

He looked at a piece of chrome on the workbench and saw his dirty reflection.

His whole career was ruined, his name was destroyed and now his face was covered with oil from the garage floor.

Could anything else go wrong?

His eyes narrowed as he looked at the old, well-used graphite fishing rod and reel with the empty spool. His face wrinkled in despair as disgust and nausea swelled in his gut.

In exasperation, he lifted the fishing rod over his head with both hands, bent it until it broke, and heaved it with all his strength against the wall. It fell in pieces on a stack of other broken, cut, torn, worn-out or bent fishing gear. He had a vivid memory of how each item earned its keep. There were reels, spools, jigs, lures, hooks, clipper tools, cork-handled casting rods, fishing kits, fly rods, tackle boxes, weights, sinkers, drag-lines, sieves, bait buckets, crawfish traps, hip boots, bait nets, hats, flasks, Coleman coolers, Igloo coolers, lunch pails, rain gear, a bed frame, an air mattress, a dome tent, two rifles and a 22-caliber pistol.

He looked with benign neglect at the collection of trash on the floor. It was an inventory that had taken a lifetime to accumulate. But now it was just good riddance to some useless rubble he had no use for where he was going.

As he looked around the garage that he had dillydallied and tinkered in for more than 40 years, his face swelled with hatred, his eyes blazed with malice and his clenched fists wanted to hit something, anything, anyone.

No three-time loser or hardened, convicted repeat criminal ever received a court order that was so repulsive and so demeaning as the one Chester D. Andrews had received in the morning mail. What made the order even more repugnant and nauseating, Andrews felt, was the way it was so badly handled in Tallahassee, the state capital.

The spineless bastard who signed the order did not have the courtesy to pick up a telephone and call. So much for dear old law school classmate and colleague Waylan Tyler Muldowney, Presiding Judge of the Supreme Court, State of Florida.

During the past year, Andrews had forced himself to believe that his 31-year judicial record was among the premier examples in the field of jurisprudence, a record that he also grew to believe was developed through diligent, judicious and industrious public service.

Chief Justice Muldowney had taken a different view when he read the depositions, interrogatories and briefs filed by Jeffery Adam McCormack's law firm.

Muldowney immediately ordered the State Attorney to conduct his own independent investigation and submit his findings and recommendations forthwith.

During a subsequent meeting in the Chief Justice's chambers, the State Attorney provided an in-depth review of his findings, and concurred with McCormack's recommendations.

With one stroke of a pen, Muldowney dismantled, dismounted, dismembered and dismissed the supreme, sovereign judicial ruler in the Florida Panhandle.

Chester D. Andrews looked at the walls in the garage and studied the hundreds of tools, gadgets and miscellaneous items he had acquired and saved over the years. He looked at the messy floor and could not remember the last time it was cleaned.

His slumped posture slowly straightened as he stood at his workbench. He shoved a hand into his front pocket and pulled out a crumpled piece of paper the mailman made him sign for.

He held the paper close to his sweaty face *as* he again read Muldowney's damnable, outrageous letter.

"You are hereby ordered to cease and desist all civil, criminal and tort judicial and ministerial functions normally, routinely, customarily or summarily performed in the Second Circuit, or in any other court under State Jurisdiction.

"Further, you are hereby ordered to remove your personal property, if any, from the court and chambers, under the supervision of the Chief of Bailiffs, and place yourself forthwith under house arrest at your residence until such time that you are notified of further decisions/actions by this court.

"Furthermore, all of your pending salary payments, compensatory allowances, and pension benefits shall be detained by the finance center until all allegations are litigated and assessments are realized.

"Moreover, you are hereby discharged and relieved of your

position, status, jurisdiction, responsibility and authority within the Second Circuit, and you shall not return to the Second Circuit Court or its environs, effective this date and time certain, without the written authorization, permission and approval of said issuing court."

Andrews crumbled the paper into a small ball and threw it on the pile of trash.

He used the back of his hand to brush away items on the top of his workbench. After he cleared a small area, his shaky hand fumbled in his shirt pocket and withdrew a bullet. He carefully placed the 22-caliber high velocity shell on the bench.

He wiped his brow again and watched as the sweat dripped off his hand.

The Florida panhandle was always hot and humid in August. The summer had been unusually hot, and it was the longest, hottest summer in Andrews' life.

He had never socialized after Alma Beth's death seven years ago, except for occasional brief get-togethers with his only friend, Phil Garrison.

Other than those infrequent visits, Andrews existed in self-imposed solitary confinement under meager, lonely conditions.

Chester D. Andrews had bitterly come to hate his hometown of Milton and everything it stood for. Its hospital had taken Alma Beth from him after a long and costly illness, and the banks had taken everything else he had of value.

Life became unbearably miserable for court clerks who served under Andrews' iron fist. He seemed to revel in making them as miserable as he was. He became, to them, the most forsaken mortal that misery ever held a mortgage on.

His judicious, quick-witted mind with its incomparable built-in wizardry had fascinated people years ago when he was appointed to the bench. But as he developed a stealth-like ability to expand his illegal sources of income, he became a loner, at first more by neglect than by desire. As his loneliness deepened after Alma Beth's death, and he hardened to it, self-inflicted thoughts and deep-seated opinions spread the hatred and hurt throughout his body.

The acid of resentment had altered his personality until self-pity was his only unimpaired faculty.

He grew to accept his disappointments, especially eight years ago when his old law school classmate, Waylan Tyler Muldowney, refused to write a letter of commendation for Andrews' appointment to the Florida Appellate Court.

The letter would have made Andrews the lead contender for advancement to the higher court and only one step away from a seat on the Florida State Supreme Court.

Andrews never left the circuit bench.

If ever a man had an excuse for smoldering resentment about life's close calls, Chester D. Andrews fit the bill.

Another kind of bill came each Sunday night when he finished his weekend gambling on an Internet casino. When he signed off, the "Total Amount Due" flashed on the screen and a copy came through the printer. His long-standing arrangement with the Painted Calico Casino in Minnesota called for a FedEx delivered "Payment in Full" within five days.

In rare instances when a credit balance occurred, the casino electronically transferred payment within an hour to Andrews' credit union account.

Andrews' gambling debts were a constant problem, but somehow the money was always there to feed the Fed Ex envelope.

Bilking developers and fat-cat lawyers with go-for-the-gold-clients had become a common practice for Judge Andrews during discussions in his chambers.

In the beginning, when developers and lawyers ran a little short on their disposable cash, Andrews withdrew funds from his savings account. The withdrawals became a frequent occurrence until the account was closed because withdrawals caused it to fall below the credit union's minimum balance requirement.

Alma Beth's furs and jewelry went to a pawn shop. The proceeds brought relief for three months.

Next came a mortgage on the house. It was no big deal at the time. But a few months later, when disposable cash was short again, Andrews had to refinance his mortgage. This time he had to pay points.

The refinanced mortgage was soon followed by an equity loan, with more points, cash advances on credit cards, and the sale of stocks and mutual funds.

The ultimate high-stakes action occurred last month when he cashed maximum limits on his lines of credit that were originally secured by equity in his residence. He took the action because it carried no further risk to him.

Andrews no longer had any equity in his house. Every asset and ounce of equity he had was maxed-out and some third-party lender held the title.

But Chester D. Andrews, the ultimate, oblique optimist, still had a deep, burning desire to strike it big with the Painted Calico Casino.

He had learned years ago that there was no way a judge could turn a profit and still stay ethical.

He was not known for in-depth cerebral opinions. The only things deep about him were his fleece-lined pockets and his troubles.

Usually, when his computer screen flashed the debit balance due, Andrews would be in the red for an amount that hovered between $8 and $15 thousand.

But last Sunday it flashed $27 thousand. Last Sunday was two days ago. Yesterday was a holiday. Court was not in session.

Muldowney's Certified and Registered letter came this morning, an hour before Judge Andrews' court was scheduled to convene and adjudicate a major land use zoning dispute. The case involved wealthy developers and their congenial lawyers who always carried sealed envelopes in their briefcases when conferences were held in chambers.

At the same time the case was reassigned to another court, First Lieutenant Jefferson Thomas Jake Underwood, Chief of Bailiffs, watched intently as Chester D. Andrews, former Presiding Judge of the Second Circuit Court, dumped his personal property into a large brown paper sack, and handed over his court ID, security card and keys.

Lieutenant Underwood then escorted Andrews home.

After they entered, Underwood locked a detection manacle

around his former boss's ankle, and sternly reminded him of the severe consequences of attempting an escape to avoid prosecution.

"House arrest includes my garage, doesn't it Lieutenant?" Andrews asked in a compliant tone.

"That is correct, sir. Good day."

That was an hour ago.

Chester D. Andrews stood in the garage by his workbench and looked at the pile of trash. As he moved his line of sight, he focused for a moment on the pistol.

Fiery hatred blazed in his eyes.

With a puckish gait he left the debris-strewn garage and headed inside to visit the Painted Calico Casino on the Internet. He had a sudden impulse to play the $25 blackjack table.

He was midway through the kitchen when the wall phone chimed.

"Hello," he said reluctantly.

"This is a long distance call from the Key West Florida police station for Judge Chester D. Andrews. Is the judge available?"

"This is he."

"Hold please for Mayor Phillip Garrison."

"Chet?"

"Phil, what are you doing in a Key West police station?"

"There's been a terrible mistake, Chet. They're holding me until I can post bail and that's why I called you."

"Phil, when did you leave here and go down there?"

"Left last Friday. Today's Tuesday. It's been five of the longest, damndest days of my life. Why?"

"So you haven't seen any news about my situation?"

"Hell, Chet, I didn't arrange this little sortie with Tilly Cloud so I could watch TV! What situation? I'm the guy in a situation who needs help. And I sure the hell can't call my wife. I need twenty-five grand so I can post bail."

"Why that much money? What's the charge?"

"They said I caused the loss of a rental car and a garbage truck. Can you believe that, Chet?"

"Phil, hold on for a minute and let me think."

A deep, frightening scowl spread across Chester D. Andrews' face as he placed the phone on the counter.

In all the years they had known each other, a request for a favor had never been turned down. It was always gladly given. No questions were ever asked.

They both understood and practiced their motto: If you are my enemy, no explanation is accepted. If you are my friend, no explanation is necessary. But friend or no friend, Andrews did not have 25 grand.

Several years ago, he carried a money clip and Grover Cleveland's picture was on all the bills. That was when money was no object, and there always seemed to be enough for whatever the need was at the time. If he wanted a new Buick, he could drive one off the show room floor for about 20 to 25 Grovers. If Alma Beth hinted that a new coat would be nice for Christmas, 10 Grovers paid for the mink that kept her shoulders warm all winter.

But that was then. And this is now.

Right now, he could not borrow, beg or steal 25 Grovers even if his life depended on it. Especially under his present circumstances when everyone knew that he was kicked off the bench, escorted home for house confinement and an ankle manacled so his movements could be easily monitored.

Besides, on Friday – just three days from now – an Indian tribe in Minnesota that owned the Painted Calico Casino would expect a FedEx delivery of 27 Grovers.

But Andrews was not worried about Indians in Minnesota.

Waylan Tyler Muldowney was a bigger and much closer problem.

Andrews' scowl turned into an inquisitive wrinkled frown as he recalled numerous precarious decisions he had handed down just during the past five years; decisions within the statute of limitations that could be reopened and challenged by Muldowney's investigators.

Every reporter and cop in the state knew Waylan Tyler Muldowney was tough. He wielded words with authority, particularly in sentencing announcements, and no other jurist in the state's history had sent more crooks to a life of hard labor, or death row.

Chester D. Andrews knew that Muldowney was so gun-ho on the investigation that he could easily uncover tangled webs of evidence that overlapped into several decisions Andrews had ruled on that benefited commercial and residential developers.

As he stood in the kitchen, Andrews' mind raced through at least three dozen rulings he had made that resulted in substantial favors from grateful developers.

He knew there were a multitude of implications, allegations and speculations about hundreds of his rulings.

He tried not to think about his creative paper shuffling, and his personal checks that were exchanged for cash.

He figured there were about 150 court decisions and about 75 personal actions that would not survive intense scrutiny by Waylan Tyler Muldowney.

For thirty years he had been the face of the second circuit court, and he had come to enjoy being quoted, pictured, cited and courted in all the power centers of the circuit court. But now, in addition to Muldowney, debts had blindsided him with penalties, late charges, interest expenses, posting fees, data entry costs, assessments and fines so egregious a self-inflicted wound was his only way out.

Andrews and his old, dear friend, Phil Garrison, had known each other since they were kids. There was nothing one of them would not do for the other. It had been that way all their lives.

Andrews was too set in his ways to break that special motto he shared with Phil. No, the motto would not be broken without a gutsy, last-minute fight.

There was only one possible outlet available to him that offered a risky but outside chance of obtaining the 25 grand Phil needed.

Chester D. Andrews, the unemployed, bankrupt former judge, would not play the $25 blackjack table.

Andrews, the soon-to-be-indicted embezzler and racketeer artist, would start at the $500 blackjack table. After an hour or so he would switch to the Grover Cleveland table and play for $1,000 a hand.

Andrews was well aware of how fast blackjack hands were dealt on the Internet. He also knew about the rapid computer speed that determined credit balances earned by winners, and debit accounts racked-up by losers.

But he figured that there was a significant factor in his favor. He knew that the pace of the game was entirely up to the player. Slow play would give him the opportunity to count face cards, lower the odds, and increase the chance of winning, but it slowed the flow of income. On the other hand, quick play would not allow him time to count cards, which increased the odds, but with luck he could build a fortune faster if he played the maximum number of hands that he could each minute.

He figured that if he won 70 percent of the hands at the $500 table, his take would be about $3 million for one hour's work.

If he won 60 percent of the hands at the Grover table, his take would be about $7 million for two hours' work.

Within three hours, he pictured his profits at $10 million, minus what the Indians wanted, and Phil needed.

The balance would provide him with enough funds to charter a fast jet and get the hell out of Florida before anyone knew the man with the manacle on his ankle was streaking southeast across the Gulf of Mexico at a high altitude and with a whole new attitude.

Judge Chester D. Andrews carried an IOU in his wallet from an old hometown acquaintance who had apartments all over South and Central America. It was time to call in the chit.

He took the phone off the counter.

"Phil, call me back in three hours. I'll have it for you then."

"I knew I could count on you, Chet. Thanks."

"Say, Phil, remember what we used to talk about when we fished by the old abandoned barn over at Hood Bayou?"

"Hell, how can I forget it?" Garrison asked. "I've often thought of cutting loose of everything and spending the rest of my life down there."

"Keep that in mind, old friend," Andrews said. "Especially the yellow hacienda down the road from the cantina. I'll bet they've got hot chili tonight."

"You can count on it for tonight," Garrison said. "Good bye."

Andrews cracked a smile, put the phone back on the hook,

walked to his study and punched the power key. Within seconds the screen showed the front of the Painted Calico Casino.

Phil Garrison and his burly guard were almost at the bars of the community-shared cell when the front desk officer's voice sounded on the speaker.

"Bring Mister Garrison to the waiting room. He has a visitor."

"Well, now," the guard said with a smirk, "one minute you call a judge, and the next minute you have a visitor. You must be important. Come with me."

They turned around and the guard escorted Garrison to the waiting room.

"Oh, mayor, you really look, I mean, like shitty, okay?"

Phil Garrison had spent four nights and five days on a bottom cot that had a thin lumpy mattress. About 12 other inmates were bunked in the small, crowded room with a concrete floor. Garrison was not allowed to shave, and he absolutely, positively refused to go to the back room, remove his clothes and shower. He still wore what he had on when he left Dos Bayou.

He looked like death warmed over.

So did Tilly. Almost.

Her long blonde hair was dirty, twisted and matted. Her cut off jeans had different colored stains, her halter-top had been cut open in front and was held together by a couple safety pins. Her elbows and knees were bandaged, her purse strap was broken, and her left sandal was missing.

But she was still the sexiest, most interesting creature that Phil Garrison had ever seen.

"I know I look bad, sweetheart, but what happened to you?" he asked with a droopy face.

Tilly opened her purse and took out a pack of Marlboros and lit one.

"When you didn't like show up this morning like we talked about, I mean, when I wanted my share of the money, and I couldn't find you anywhere like where I looked, I mean, you know, there was this cop and I asked him, okay? Hell, it didn't like take him very long at all like to find that you were in jail, okay?"

"I'm glad you did, honey," Garrison said. "I sure do miss you, sweetheart. What have you been doing to get yourself so dirty, bandaged and messed up?"

"Well, thanks to The Great Rondigian, I'm like, you know, the newest member of the Key West Mile High Club, I mean, like that was an hour or so ago, so like now, I mean, you know, I'm probably like one of the older, you know, senior members. There were a lot of people like in line when we landed, you know, and I mean like we had to put our clothes back on real fast like, you know, so we could get out okay? But the sex, like all of it with whoever and whenever, was, I mean, actually like supercalifragilistic, if you know what I mean."

Garrison rolled his eyes. He had just heard more about Tilly's activities than he cared to. The trip was not what he had planned. She was supposed to be with him, he was supposed to be with her, but he's in jail and she's acting like a slut!

Her air fare had cost him a grand, they had not slept together on this trip, and now he's told that she joined the Mile High Club by having sex with a weirdo who drinks Wild Turkey through a straw!

"Well, honey, how did you hurt your elbows and knees that caused all those bandages?" Garrison asked with a quizzical glance.

"Well, it was like a real tiny, small six-seat plane, you know, that was converted, you know, to a two-seater with a lounge area in the back, you know, and like it had a partition like behind the cockpit where the pilot sat to provide, like, you know, some privacy, okay?"

Phil Garrison looked confused.

"Go on, sweetheart, I'm listening," he said.

"Well, just before we took off, here comes another couple who get like on the plane and now, you know, me and The Great Rondigian have to share the little lounge area with this other couple. They are like hornier than rabbits, but I had a hunch that they were not like a couple, okay?"

"So what happened?"

"Like I really don't know, okay?"

She took a long drag, blew the smoke slowly from her mouth

and sucked it into her nostrils. She did that a couple times while she thought.

"I think I had sex like doggy-style with three guys but I'm not sure, you know, who the third guy was because like one guy, you know, had The Great Rondigian tied-up and blindfolded while another guy cut off my top like with his pocket knife, okay?"

Garrison rolled his big brown eyes in disbelief. He wondered why he ever got tangled up with such a dumb blonde.

"So like I joined the Mile High Club three times, I guess," Tilly said. "Ain't that right?"

Garrison didn't say a word. He had never hated a woman so much in his life as he hated Tilly Cloud.

"Well, anyway, you were not around like this morning and like, I mean, a working girl like me has to take care of herself, you know? So, anyway, I called Martha Sue and we had a long talk, okay?"

"Martha Sue!" Garrison yelled.

"You called Martha Sue?"

Phil Garrison flinched like a sledge hammer had just hit him.

"Why did you call my wife?" he shouted.

He wanted to kill the dumb blonde bimbo bitch.

"Well, you never, you know, like gave me my return plane ticket back to Pensacola, so like I thought you probably skipped out on me, okay? So since Martha Sue is suing you for divorce, I made her a deal."

"She what?" Garrison yelled. "What deal, you little bitch?"

"Well, like since a hard-working girl like me can always like use the money, I promised Martha Sue that I would like tell her about all of your secret bank and stock accounts and your monthly retirement income like you told me about one night at Pascali's.

"Anyway, me and Martha Sue like made a deal. I get twenty percent of what Martha Sue gets from you. Martha Sue wants me to be like a witness and I agreed. Like it's nothing personal. You're a good fuck when you get your rest and I'll tell that to the judge. But I need to fuck more often and you're just not around often enough, okay? Maybe, you know, well, like you just might be like a little too old, okay?"

Phil Garrison's ears heard, his mind absorbed but his stomach just could not digest the rotten garbage from Tilly's filthy mouth. The thought of killing her flashed through his mind, but he figured doing it inside a police station was not one of his better ideas.

"You are a detestable little whore and as far as I'm concerned you'll never get a ticket back to Pensacola, and you are fired from Dos Bayou, you little bitch. Now get out of here," Garrison shouted.

"Oh, I have my first class ticket like to get back home," Tilly said. "I called like collect, you know, to the Salvation Army in Miami and offered them five percent of my twenty percent if they bought and delivered to me a first class ticket to Pensacola, plus a lifetime shopping pass with thirty percent off at their thrift stores nationwide, okay?"

Garrison looked at Tilly and wondered if she was as dumb as she appeared. Who would have thought about the Salvation Army? Hell, who would have placed a call to Martha Sue and copped a deal?

Martha Sue! Why is she filing for divorce?

"Oh, and one more thing, okay?" Tilly asked as she opened the door to leave. "You can't fire me because like I work under the city manager. He's the only one who hires and fires employees. That's his authority and not yours, okay? At least I learned that much in two years."

She took another long drag and blew the smoke into Garrison's face.

"Listen to me you sorry, miserable asshole, okay?" she said. "I now own more of your money, property and sorry soul than you do. See you in court you little prick. Bye toots."

The door closed behind her.

The burly guard escorted Garrison back to the cell.

As he stood forlornly beside his bunk, Garrison folded his arms across his chest and thought about his dismal and wasted life. His head and shoulders drooped as his tired, red eyes studied a crack in the concrete floor.

For the first time in his life he was without status or confidence.

Unlike the crack that went under the wall, Garrison knew he wasn't going anywhere.

He thought about years earlier when he had the right stuff to win voter approval in Dos Bayou, and the nod from civil service promotion boards that moved him up the ladder at the Navy base. He viewed the elections and promotions as awards for years of pleasant chitchats with stupid, gullible voters he led around like sheep, and a fiercely competitive spirit that negotiated contracts during luncheons, and cut deals with percentages at dinners.

But now everything he had was gone. Kaput. Lost. Out the window. Window? Hell, he didn't have a pot to piss in or a window to throw it out of. His wife and girlfriend had seen to that.

His head drooped even farther as endless thoughts whirled through his mind. He stretched out on the bunk.

Martha Sue and Tilly, he knew, would end up in a partnership and own everything he had.

A faint smile split his face.

"It sure is a terribly sad day," Garrison said as he thought about the crack in the floor, "when a dumb blonde from a trailer park suddenly becomes smarter than Hillary Clinton."

He closed his eyes and the snoring started.

But not for long.

A baton was raked across the iron bars and the loud noise reverberated off the walls.

"Okay, Garrison," a guard yelled as he shoved a key in the lock, "your boat just came in. Get up. You're out of here."

"What do you mean?" Garrison asked.

"Your bail has been posted," the guard shouted. "They want you over at Western Union. Sign for your personal things at the front desk, and get lost."

~ ~ ~ ~ ~ ~

Tourists in front of Key West International gawked as the stretch limousine came to a smooth stop in front of Continental Airlines. The driver got out, motioned to a Skycap, popped open the trunk, walked around and opened the rear door.

The passenger slowly got out while balancing a large Pineapple

Daiquiri. He took a long drink, handed the glass to the driver and strolled into the terminal.

He was dressed in a prim blue suit with a matching blue and chamois tie centered on an ivory-blue-striped shirt. A bucket hat covered the top half of his head. But when the hat tilted, his face looked as white as a jailhouse inmate.

He walked to the counter reserved for first-class passengers, handed the attendant an envelope, and watched attentively as the Skycap placed two suitcases on the conveyor belt.

"Everything is in order, Senator Garrison," the attendant said through a broad smile.

The Skycap placed two claim tickets on the counter and some bills were stuffed in his hand.

"Your plane departs in fifteen minutes en route to Santiago, Chile by way of your connection in the Bahamas," the attendant said. "You may board now, if you would please, sir. Welcome aboard and here are your tickets with boarding passes for your connection."

The passenger climbed the flight of stairs and handed two tickets to the flight attendant.

"This way, please, sir," she said as she led the way to the two front seats on the left side in first class.

"It will be my pleasure to make sure you have a quiet flight without any disturbances, Senator Garrison."

"Thank you, ma'am, and I'll count on that."

The flight attendant walked away shaking her head. It was the first time she had a first class passenger who traveled alone but purchased two seats so he would not have any company.

Phil Garrison opened the overhead compartment, pulled down two blankets and a pillow and placed them on the window seat. He took some brochures and reading material from his pockets and placed them on top the blankets and pillow. He removed the magazines from his seat pocket and placed them on the window seat.

He then settled into a comfortable position in the aisle seat.

Although he had rested for a few hours, had shaven and taken a leisurely bath before he dressed for the flight, he still felt some discomfort.

It was time to relax.

He raised the armrest and snapped on his seatbelt.

His head drooped like a hangdog, his lower lip sagged, his jowls quivered slightly before they settled down, his brow furrowed briefly before it smoothed, his tongue stretched out of his mouth, curled up, wet the tip of his nose, disappeared back into his mouth, and the snoring started.

Former Dos Bayou Mayor Phillip V. Garrison, who was now a self-appointed Senator, had plenty to dream about.

CHAPTER 13

The front seat passenger held a thick operations manual close to his face and pretended to read as he stole quick glances at the driver's creamy dark legs. As the legs moved and swayed to the rhythm on the CD, the slit in her skirt crawled higher toward her waist.

His glances did not escape her attention. Her alert hazel eyes narrowed into a youthful taunt each time Carpenter Bee strayed from his assignment and ogled at her legs.

He was an intel and munitions tech, or Carpenter Bee, as Yamarie and her senior staff called him, and his bilingual role on the team was vital.

What troubled some of the team members about Carpenter Bee were his strange habits. He showed up each day like a man who had been through hell the night before and made a safe journey back. Everyone suspected he had perverted quirks that someone had satisfied during the night, but no one ever asked.

They never asked because he was not one of them.

Yamarie, the Director of Field Operations for the World Bank, was the only one who knew that Carpenter Bee also played an indispensable role in another field; communicating coded messages to the robots, the Unmanned Aerial Vehicles that were circling the

Andes Mountain range in western Chile at an altitude of 80,000 feet.

If the UAVs were needed for long deployments, they could continue circling their target site for three years without landing. Each solar-powered unmanned plane carried a half-ton payload and consumed five kilowatts of power per week; power that was constantly restored by the sun.

Each day, 24/7, Carpenter Bee dispatched coded messages to the UAVs and they responded by sending hundreds of high-resolution images for each 750-mile-diameter viewing footprint. The images, with coordinates, were flashed to the UAV command center at Edwards Air Force Base, located in the Mojave Desert 70 miles north of Los Angeles.

Intel analysis specialists at Edwards sent their intel updates to Army, Air Force, Navy and Marine Corps task forces who were detailed to the target area.

Carpenter Bee worked for a contractor, so no one on the World Bank Field Operations Team, the team members thought, was accountable for what he did, only for what he didn't do. And so far, he had done everything right.

No one knew of Carpenter Bee ever having a queen Bee, or any female, except probably those in drag. He never took breaks or long lunch hours, and he was always busy on his laptop.

Yamarie looked in the rearview mirror at the men in the back seats. They were still dozing. Their coats were unbuttoned and their shoulder holsters were visible.

She parted her lips to examine her reflection and her perfectly shaped pearl-white teeth glistened in the mirror.

Gloria Estefan's CD vocal jived with a rhythmic beat, and Yamarie's long, tanned legs moved in sync with the vibes.

Carpenter Bee tapped Yamarie's shoulder and pointed ahead to a sign on the road. "Look, Yamarie," he said. "We only have sixty miles to go."

"It will not be long if the road stays this good," Yamarie said with a half smile. "Oh, FYI," Yamarie said, "the Robertson group from Florida has a noon ETA tomorrow."

Carpenter Bee nodded, turned a page in the manual and looked again at the driver.

"Let's hope the Florida people can help. I have about forty more pages to study so I will not tickle your thighs anymore with my eyes," Carpenter Bee said in a nonchalant tone.

"Frankly, Yamarie, your legs are too thin. You should put on some weight."

Yamarie gave him her usual go-to-hell-smirk.

"Now I must finish this manual."

Yamarie Delgado looked in the mirror. The men were still sleeping peacefully. She looked again in the mirror at the Tech-Team leader on the right side. It was his first mission as OIC, logistics, under Yamarie's supervision.

Yamarie thought about how strange it was to be in charge of the most clandestine operation ever attempted in South America, and be the woman responsible for global field operations for the World Bank.

She remembered the training they had recently completed at The School of Americas in Asuncion, Paraguay, and she was impressed with the hard work and dedication of each team member, especially Carpenter Bee who proved to be a fast learner.

She had heard that decision-makers at the World Bank had used Carpenter Bee on other assignments. He must be good, she thought, because they keep renewing and increasing the bottom line of his company's contract.

Instructors were very clear during classroom and field training exercises that the World Bank did not want another Manuel Noriega situation. There would be no press releases or news conferences, and there would be no TV camera recording the strongest nation in the world kidnapping the leader of a sovereign foreign country while he prayed in church!

No, this time decision-makers at the World Bank decided they would use a different approach.

No part of the operation would be discussed with or connected to the FBI, CIA, NATO, the National Security Agency, Defense Investigative Services, or the Pentagon. None of them could be trusted, and not a one of them was qualified to serve on the operations team.

There would not be another stupid mistake such as Ruby Ridge, or one more Waco mass murder in a high profile blunder. The World Bank had a much stronger reason to disassociate itself from the FBI. The decision was an easy one.

Because of how the FBI botched the Timothy McVeigh case, the nation will never know that it was within a razor's edge of having the Oklahoma City bomber back on the streets and in a larger truck.

The unconscionable revelations of misplaced and lost documents, sloppy management and colossal disregard of the nation's security during the entire gut-wrenching McVeigh episode were unscrupulous acts that tore at the very fabric of the nation.

And in the eyes of the World Bank, the CIA, like the FBI, was another agency that required a wide berth.

The Bank decided that there would not be another stupid, clumsy, blind-sided repeat of the CIA's humiliation when Chinese intelligence agents conducted a two-year file raid at New Mexico's Los Alamos National Laboratory, and hauled our most sensitive national defense secrets back to Beijing.

Los Alamos was an inviting super shopping mall for Chinese entrepreneurs.

The shopping included the hauling away of all known data of U.S. nuclear reentry ballistic missile warheads, weaponization features of the neutron bomb which killed by radiation rather than a blast, and millions of lines of computer legacy codes on every nuclear formula known to American and NATO scientists.

Legacy codes, Yamarie knew, were strings of cumulative data that explained and simulated how each nuclear weapon in the U.S. arsenal exploded. The codes were based on 55 years of nuclear research that included more than 1,000 nuke tests.

During their extensive spy mission at Los Alamos, 4,409 espionage agents downloaded more than 84,000 legacy files, and made 12,448 trips home to Beijing.

The CIA never questioned the U.S. issuance of the visas, and not one visa application from the PRC was refused.

Those that got the fast-track CIA stamp of approval included Loo Chin-Wong, an aerospace nuclear engineer, a colonel in the Chinese Army, and her father, General Sin Chang Wong, the PRC's top military commander and a member of the Communist Party's senior leadership.

It was considered only a minor coincidence that Colonel Wong and her father, in their bland civilian attire, were guests at President Bill Clinton's 48th birthday party in the White House.

The World Bank also turned thumbs down on an association with the Pentagon or any other White House tentacle because no one was ever accountable. Recent history clearly showed that when the oval office was involved in an operation, everybody's responsibility was nobody's responsibility and screw-ups were never punished regardless of the number of innocent victims.

So there would be no repeat of Pentagon hodgepodge missions such as the ones to Bosnia, Haiti or Granada where each military branch was involved in decision making, but somehow badly needed tanks and gunships were left behind, and a half dozen Navy Seals forgot how to swim in shallow water and drowned without firing a shot.

No, there would be no kidnapping or screw-ups on this mission.

It was payback time for what terrorists did in New York and Washington. The mission was a simple one.

Yamarie Delgado's Field Operations Team would conduct a swift kill of any and all terrorists – foreign or domestic – suspected of aiding in the disruption of the economic balance of international markets funded by the World Bank.

And there would be no second-guessing of what a kill was, or the tabulation or certification of a body count.

There would be no reading of Miranda Rights, no arrest, no backseat ride to a soft cot and three hots a day, no indictment, no public defender, no jury of peers, no proof of guilt beyond a reasonable doubt, no long suspended sentence by a weak-spined, pencil-neck judge, and no appeal. Period. None of that bullshit.

And there was only one order. It was: Any member of the Field Operations Team will kill any person suspected of aiding and abetting in the disruption of the world's monetary system. It was that simple.

The World Bank was interested in only two things: The maintenance of a strong U.S. dollar compared to the prevailing float rates of the franc, lira, peso, mark, ruble or any other exchange medium based on the gold standard; and, no media coverage.

This mission was also unique for another reason: Yamarie Delgado, under the code name Sister Bathsheba, was also authorized the use nuclear weapons, if the need arose. That was a World Bank condition to the President who reluctantly acquiesced to the condition.

And the Commander-in-chief's approval for nuke bombardment, if requested by Sister Bathsheba, was communicated to the fleet admiral of the U. S. S. Eisenhower Task Force that was on five-minute alert and positioned only 40 miles off the Chilean Coast.

Carpenter Bee's attention was focused on an Appendix in the manual as he studied a series of photographs. Each picture and caption described a different side of the life and times of one Carlos Santiago Dominguez, an American who was born and raised in Argentina.

Some of the material described Dominguez as one who learned his craft at a young age as the only surviving child of a wealthy U.S. Ambassador who was a pioneer profiteer in drug cartels.

Other sections described his mother as the Latino equivalent of San Francisco's infamous brothel madam, Sally Stanford, whose operation eventually expanded north into Marin County.

But Carlos' mother just didn't branch-out to a neighboring community. She, as Senora Dominguez, had a lock on every request phoned-in by any hotel or boarding house in 17 of the 20 Latin American counties.

Carpenter Bee turned another page and read how Carlos Santiago Dominguez was the sole heir to a $350 million tax-free insurance settlement when his parents and siblings were killed in an airplane accident under mysterious circumstances. A case of measles had kept young Carlos at home.

The pilot and body guards were never found.

The next page showed British and Isreali satellite photos of

Carlos Santiago Dominguez meeting with some of the world's most feared terrorists at mountain retreats in Honduras, Colombia, Brazil, Ecuador and Bolivia. A narrative with the photos described how each retreat catered to the world's wealthiest terrorists who observed dry-run and live-fire demonstrations of the latest technology and available inventories of nuclear, biological, radiological and chemical munitions, and gunship firepower exhibitions.

Carpenter Bee was no stranger to the weaponry shown in the photos.

And, since he was schooled in economics, he knew that if the World Bank did not act quickly and decisively to end terrorist-caused fluctuations in world markets, an inflationary spiral would start at any time, cloud the universe in worthless paper, stop all manufacturing and commerce, and sink the human race into a non-reversible depression.

As Carpenter Bee continued to read, he realized the depression could be much sooner than later.

His eyes widened in alarm as the manual described how government offices, banks, businesses and ranches in Argentina were already at severe risk of closing because of mysterious and enormous electronic withdrawals. The average daily withdrawal for the week that just ended exceeded $9 billion, an increase of $3 billion over last week.

The manual reported that if the mass departure of revenue continued at the present rate for another week, Argentina would be nothing more than a memory.

Since withdrawals had already placed liabilities much higher than available assets, banks and other financial institutions were not only canceling loans regardless of the purposes, but were foreclosing on all debit accounts.

The manual explained that Latin American leaders of the Group of Rio had called for a summit conference to assess the crisis, push for efforts to steady turbulent markets battered in neighboring countries, seek funds to replace Argentina's $130 billion bank withdrawal dilemma, and return to sustainable growth.

A Brazilian government official said his government and the

Group of Rio believe the United States should use its decisive influence with the World Bank to ensure the delivery of emergency funds sought by Argentina.

Carpenter Bee clinched his teeth in disbelief when he read that the Brazilian official, who spoke on condition of anonymity, also said the United States should go ahead and pay the $130 billion as a goodwill gesture to battle such scourges in the hemisphere as poverty and unemployment.

The World Bank suspected the mogul orchestrating the disastrous acts was Carlos Santiago Dominguez.

The manual cited letters Dominguez had written years ago when he threatened to initiate a catastrophe on Argentina if its officials did not continue and increase its nationwide search for his family's killers.

"I will not forgive nor forget your decadence, but will rejoice in your decline," he wrote in his last correspondence to the president of Argentina.

Carlos Santiago Dominguez, the manual noted, was masked as a devoted public servant in Dos Bayou, Florida, but was, in fact, a resourceful and vindictive magnate with unlimited access to influence and wealth among the world's most feared terrorists.

Carpenter Bee's eyes widen in disbelief as he closed the manual.

"You now have the crypto-five level intel briefing on our mission," Yamarie said in a business-as-usual tone. "And you now know why Carlos Santiago Dominguez must be killed," she said.

"Yes," he said nodding, "but this certainly is not your typical bank operation. It's such a weirdo trip with so much riding on the outcome."

He padded the manual and turned toward Yamarie. "No one will ever know the outcome unless we fail and a worldwide depression sets in."

"That's why the World Bank got into this business many years ago without any publicity or fanfare," Yamarie said.

"No one, except those with a need to know, are aware of the Field Operations Teams. Some say our teams, such as the one we're on, have not changed very much since Robert McNamara secretly formed them when he was President of the World Bank.

"It is said that he was very pleased when he was President of Ford Motor Company, and ran a professional organization that knew what to do and how to do it. But they say that when he was Secretary of Defense in the Kennedy and Johnson Administrations, he witnessed so many failures and bad decisions by political and military leaders, especially during urban riots, that he formed his own military organization when he was appointed to head the World Bank.

"You, Carpenter Bee, are now a part of that organization."

Yamarie glanced in the rearview mirror. There was no traffic behind her.

"The World Bank has just gone through a tiring and wasteful period, so now we have to get back on track."

"What do you mean?" Carpenter Bee asked.

"Well, we were within five days of killing President Hugo Chavez of Venezuela so we could stabilize our neighbors in Central and South America, and at the same time, stabilize the dollar and secure the future of those twenty countries. Just when we were in the final stage of the assassination, all hell broke loose."

"How?" Carpenter Bee wanted to know.

"We had a new guy come on broad as President of the World Bank and everything was put on hold. No one could talk to him. He was too busy with some romantic involvement that he had no time for us."

"I remember that incident."

"Yeah, the girlfriend left with a big promotion and he was there just long enough to allow that bastard Chavez to cement himself in power with seven rings of bodyguards around him at all times.

"Then the new President quits under intense fire and we get another pinstriped super- wealthy banker from Wall Street running the show. It will take him about a year or two to find all the bathrooms."

Yamarie shook her head and gave Carpenter Bee her patented squint-eyed look of skepticism.

"And in the meantime, while our new boss is trying to find a restroom, Venezuela and Russia are strengthening their strategic alliance with new schemes to control world markets by sharing oil production, masking sole-source contracts on OPEC refineries, acquiring more sophisticated wireless technology and weapons of mass destruction."

Her eyes squinted again.

"Venezuela has also purchased Russian air defense systems, armored vehicles, 100 of the new Su-35 fighter jets, 250,000 Kalashnikov assault rifles and 50 Mi-17 helicopters. And," she said, "if that's not bad enough, Russia is helping Venezuela build factories to make attack submarines, missiles and heavy artillery armament. And further, Russian Blackjack bombers now have landing, flight-line parking and refueling priority at all Venezuelan and Brazilian airports."

Carpenter Bee's facial expression slowly turned from shock to curiosity.

"Tell me, Yamarie," he asked with his familiar sly smile edged with boyish exuberance, "if you ever meet Carlos Santiago Dominguez would you have any hesitation to kill him?"

"Carpenter Bee," Yamarie said with a coy grin, "I have met him, and I have conversed with him, but I could not kill him at that time."

"When and why not?" Carpenter Bee asked with a surprised look.

"By design, I was on the flight he took from Quito International in Ecuador bound for Colombia. I made sure he saw me in the boarding area, and I sat two rows in front of him on the flight. We had a conversation in the aisle when the plane landed. And to answer your second question, there were, how shall I say, too many witnesses."

"Oh. Now how many times have I heard that excuse?" Carpenter Bee said with a glance at her legs.

The deep slit in her skirt displayed more creamy tanned skin than before. Her legs were in sharp contrast to the white carpet interior of the Mercedes.

"For your information, Carpenter Bee," Yamarie said, "I have his business card and I sent him an email."

"What name and address did you use?"

Yamarie smiled. "I was waiting for those questions."

"Well?"

"SisSheba, was the name I used on purpose. And I used our Cybertron address. So far he has not been able to trace it. Too bad."

"Too bad?"

"Yes, had he traced it, I would know his location and could erase him from the earth."

She thought for a moment.

"In my heart of hearts, Carpenter Bee, I know that Carlos Santiago Dominguez will soon be a dead man, and I also know in my heart and in my mind that our mission must succeed for many different reasons."

"Are you referring to Venezuela again?" he asked.

She nodded. "During the past three months, Venezuela has adopted a force structure revitalization program that is expected to be worth more than $150 billion in construction and acquisition in only two years. If fulfilled, this would make the country the leading arms buyer in the continent through the rest of the decade."

"That would make Hugo Chavez a major player among the world's evil empires. Right?" Carpenter Bee asked.

Yamarie nodded.

"The revitalization program is being stoked by strong prices for the country's oil exports, which means that Chavez, a self-proclaimed enemy of America, can finally address pent-up needs to overhaul an aging force structure—in other words, build an offensive military giant with missiles that can hit every state in our nation on the mainland."

They sat in silence for a moment.

"Chavez's Navy has a budget of $43.8 billion to secure 138 vessels of all types, including destroyers and support ships," Yamarie said. "His Air Force is not only buying fighter jets from Russia, but 60 Super Tucano turboprop refueling transports and gunship helicopters from the Chinese.

"And his Army is purchasing 70-plus transport and gunship helos, and light armored vehicles, artillery and various electronics systems. The Army has already purchased JYL-13-D radars from the Chinese at a cost of $750 million."

"Neighboring Colombia must sleep very uneasy at nights," Carpenter Bee said.

Yamarie shook her head in agreement. "Our mission must succeed for if it doesn't, Colombia will be the first to fall," Yamarie said. "Then Honduras, then Brazil, then Argentina and the other sixteen nations in South America will tumble like dominos.

"We are thankful to have Chile with us because Chile is the most active among our few supporters in South America," Yamarie said. "But Chile cannot defend herself against the military giant that Chavez has become.

"Chile is leveraging high copper prices to finish off a major force structure overhaul that includes the purchase of 130 F-15 fighter jets from us and 340 Leopard 4-man battle tanks. With our help, and NATO's help, Chile can defend herself against an invasion from Venezuela, if we have a half-hour's notice."

"Look," Carpenter Bee said as he pointed, "I think we are here."

Yamarie turned on Alameda Boulevard and followed the skyline in Chile's capital, Santiago. The metropolis of soaring modern glass architecture was dwarfed only by the massive mountains that rose in the east.

She knew from previous visits that stretching along the Pacific coast all the way to the tip of South America, and running up the western side of the majestic Andes Mountain chain, Chile's magnificent horizon span from expansive high desert to dramatic icy fjords.

And waiting for discovery in the Torres del Paine National Park were spiky peaks, glaciers, penguins, flamingos, grassy plains, alpine lakes, verdant forests and graceful guanacos grazing in gentle herds.

But this was not the time to explore the meaningful history, rich hospitality and scenic soul of America's southern-most friendly nation.

Because high above the cityscape of Santiago, intelligence photos showed there were hundreds of massive caves in the Andes;

caves connecting to other caves and meandering trails that were camouflaged--sometimes underground--that could hide thousands of terrorists.

The use of conventional weapons only, Yamarie knew, would be risky because hundreds or thousands of the terrorists could escape to their private jets or yachts at nearby airstrips and ports and disappear within minutes.

The use of nuclear force was within her authority, and it weighed heavily on her mind.

Chile, even with the threatening caves, Yamarie thought, was, indeed, an amazing land of contrasts.

Yamarie Delgado pressed her foot lightly against the brake when she saw the traffic officer's white-gloved hands signal for her to turn. Her hazel eyes sparkled as she nodded to the officer. She slowed almost to a standstill as she turned at 136 O'Higgins Avenue and pulled to a stop in front of the hotel.

"Rise and shine you guys," Yamarie said to her back seat passengers. "It's time we went to work."

The cheery face of a bellman peeked through the window.

"Welcome to the Crowne Plaza Santiago," he said. "Is this your first visit to our beautiful country of Chile?"

CHAPTER 14

"Let us pray. Christ Almighty endow with the spirit of wisdom those of whom in thy name we entrust the authority of government in the city of Dos Bayou.

"Bless and watch over us as we replace and repair property that was damaged by a terrible hurricane. We ask that you protect our families and neighbors from any further terrorists' acts, and shine your light for a safe path so our soldiers, sailors and marines in foreign lands may successfully end their mission safely and return home.

"In time of prosperity, fill our hearts with thankfulness; in day of trouble, suffer not our trust in thee to fail. For these things we ask through Jesus Christ, our Lord. Amen."

"The city clerk will call the roll," Councilmember Libby Washington directed as she pounded the gavel.

The Rev. Vernon Addicott stepped from the podium and walked to the rear of the chamber. He paused for a moment, turned, folded his arms around his well-worn Bible, and left the chamber.

Tilly Cloud lifted a pair of bright green, red and orange designer-alternative glasses from the chain around her hickey-bruised neck and adjusted them to her face.

"Councilman Kevin Barnett."

The liquor distributor said, "Yo."

223

"Councilman Curtis Wagner."

"Here," said the pharmacist.

"Councilwoman Libby Washington."

The Provost at the University of West Florida smiled with a nod at Tilly and announced, "Present."

"Mayor Pro Tempore Carlos Santiago Dominguez."

"Hearing no answer," Tilly said, "I now like call, you know, for Mayor Phillip Garrison, okay?

"Not present, either," Tilly said.

She carefully removed the gaudy glasses and rested them in her bountiful cleavage.

"Please let the record show, madam clerk, that both Mayor Pro Tempore Dominguez and Mayor Garrison have resigned from the city council," Council member Washington said.

"So we shall continue with a bare majority of three council members. We have some important items to resolve relating to Hurricane Raymond storm damage recovery, so it will be a long meeting, I'm afraid."

Tilly lifted the glasses back to her face with both hands, balanced the garish spectacles on her nose, and made a couple checkmarks on her agenda.

"Before we proceed any further," Councilman Barnett said, "I want all of you to know that I have to leave in an hour to deliver a large inventory to a customer who's hosting a big party tonight. But I will return as quickly as I can. Now, since we need to appoint a new mayor and new mayor pro tern, I nominate Libby for mayor and Curtis for our new pro tern. I think they'll do just fine."

"Second," came the voice of Councilman Curtis Wagner.

"Well," Libby said, "I guess I'll chair the motion. We have a motion and a second on the floor. Is there any discussion?"

Libby, Curtis, Kevin, Tilly and City Manager Greg Robertson all turned in unison and eyed the folks sitting in the small chamber.

Libby recognized most of the people. There were about 20 who were scattered about and none of them were seated together except three men in the front row who appeared to be acquainted. Greg Robertson gave a modest nod to the two lawyers in pinstripe suits who were seated next to Emil Jura.

Libby's attention was attracted to a man in an aisle seat on the far left. He wore an outfit that glowed with every color in a box of crayons. A stovepipe hat rested on his lap. It was not so much the outfit that got Libby's attention as it was the huge, white neck-brace. But the guy could not be in a lot of pain, Libby thought, and have such a constant, bright smile. Libby stared at the man for a couple moments and noticed that he never moved his smiling face away from the dais.

Libby moved her line of sight and saw a familiar figure standing at attention in his usual spot at the back of the room.

His strong, square-shaped face was as rugged and handsome as ever, and his chin protruded just enough to add a touch of somber determination to his lean tan skin.

Duke Hockbarth held a baseball cap in one hand and an agenda in the other. He wore a pair of clean, ironed faded denims and a spotless new T-shirt that advertised Duke's Independent Plumbing.

"Is there any discussion?" Libby repeated.

"Yes, ma'am," Duke said.

"Duke, do you wish to speak on the motion?" Libby asked.

"No, ma'am."

"Well, Duke, that's the only thing on the floor to discuss at this time."

"Yes, ma'am, but ain't you forgetting something?"

"Would you please enlighten me, Duke, what it is?"

"The flag," Duke said pointing to the Stars and Stripes beside the dais, "don't you think you should lead us in the Pledge of Allegiance before you promote each other into higher salaries?"

Libby Washington did not try to hide her embarrassment as she stood with the audience and led the pledge.

When the recital came to the last three words, Duke's voice was loud and clear above all others as he yelled, "and justice for all."

"Now," Libby said as she took her seat, "all those in favor say yes."

"Yes," said the pharmacist.

"Yo," sounded the liquor distributor.

"I vote yes," Libby said with a smile to Tilly. "Record the vote as unanimous."

"Madam Mayor," Tilly said, "the next item on the agenda is like Public Interest Issues."

The smile quickly disappeared from Libby's face.

Mayor Libby Washington, like everyone else in local government, absolutely hated the law that required cities to place Public Interest Issues on every council agenda.

It was the only thing Lyndon B. Johnson did as President that Libby had grown to regret when she thought about LBJ's War on Poverty.

Libby remembered when the federal government started the War on Poverty in municipalities across the nation the grant money required local governments to prominently list on every agenda "Public Interest Issues" or a "Citizen Participation" section so any person could address the governmental body on any issue.

Sometimes, as Libby knew from experience, angry citizens could line up at the podium and speak all day and well into the night on topics that were not on the agenda, and force the council to adjourn without taking any action on listed items.

Libby thought it unfair, costly and unfortunate that during the latter part of the 1960s and well into the 70s, state legislatures throughout the country enacted laws that required local government agendas to list a section for public comment, but did not require it for themselves.

As much as she disliked the requirement, and felt that Hurricane Raymond recovery items were more important, Libby could not avoid the agenda item.

"Item three is now open for discussion," Libby said looking at the audience. "Since most items usually discussed under Public Interest Issues fall under the purview of the city manager, please be sure you have filled out your speaker's card before stepping to the podium."

A man in the audience held his hand in the air and waved a piece of paper.

"Please step to the podium, sir, and give your completed form to the clerk," Libby said.

A tall man in a plaid shirt, jeans and high heeled boots slowly made his way to the front, handed Tilly a paper, stepped to the podium, looked at the mike and tapped it a few times with his hand.

"Can y'all hear me?" he asked.

"We can hear you just fine," Libby said. "Please proceed."

"Well, first of all, the name's Bartlow and I just want y'all to know that I'm hard to herd and impossible to stampede. Do I make myself clear?"

Libby looked at City Manager Greg Robertson with a wrinkled brow, glanced at her two council colleagues, then glared back at the broncobuster.

"Crystal, sir. Please proceed," Libby said.

"Y'all should know far better than me that we have here in our little part of real estate south of the Mason-Dixon Line, three military bases, and y'all should start passing resolutions, and doing anything it takes to keep these bases here and not allow anyone to close them. Do I make myself clear."

Councilman Curtis Wagner, the pharmacist, was well aware of Stony Bartlow, the opinionated speaker, who had moved into Dos Bayou about two years ago, and was a regular customer at Wagner's Drug Store. About every other week, Bartlow brought in a handful of prescriptions that were written by physicians at Pensacola Naval Air Station, Eglin Air Force Base or Hurlburt Field.

In Curtis Wagner's unique way of figuring how things should be put together in the city of Dos Bayou, he always placed business, his business, before politics. Especially when it came to pacifying an old combat wounded GI who was in and out of veterans' hospitals for treatment of psychotic depression, hallucinations of search and destroy combat missions at the mall, night airborne jumps, anxiety and acute vertigo.

"Madam Mayor," Councilman Wagner said, "Mister Bartlow has called to our attention what may be the most important item we will ever consider. I think it is incumbent upon us to have the city manager prepare a resolution forthwith and send it to the President of the United States. And we should thank Mister

Bartlow for his kind help in calling this important matter to our attention. Thank you so much, Mister Bartlow."

Libby looked quizzically at Curtis Wagner and wondered what he had been drinking all day.

"Agree with me," Wagner whispered. "This guy's crazy."

"So ordered," Libby said as she smiled at Stony Bartlow. "Thank you, so much, sir."

"Now, remember, y'all," Bartlow said as he stepped down, "I'm hard to herd and impossible to stampede."

Curtis Wagner watched closely and breathed a sigh of relief as Bartlow walked down the aisle and left through the back door.

Wagner leaned over to Kevin Barnett. "They should never allow that guy out on the streets," Wagner said.

"Why?" Barnett asked. "Hell, he's just an old man who's hard to herd with time on his hands."

Wagner shook his head. "If he fails to take the medicine in his pocket every four hours, or someone really pisses him off, with or without the medication, do you think it matters to him in the long run if he kills ten, twenty or fifty more people? There's no telling what that old guy with head wounds is carrying in his pocket besides those pills."

"Oh, shit," Barnett said slowly. "I truly do hate citizen participation."

"Yes, ma'am," Libby said to a woman who rose from her seat.

The woman walked to the front, handed Tilly a paper and stepped to the mike.

"I'm a posse member," said the woman as she opened her purse, took out a pistol, held it high in the air for everyone to see, and placed it with a loud thud on the podium.

"Well, hell, Curtis," Barnett said leaning over to Wagner, "how many could she stampede with that thing? Did you see that goddamn pistol?"

"During my twelve years on the posse, I have scolded drunken beach buns, consoled distraught parents of missing children, and kept watch over wild bears that wondered into residential areas. I've also cleaned and bandaged the cut penis of a rapist before I knocked his front teeth out and booked him. And I've patrolled the mall at nights, assisted on search missions for lost hunters, and ticketed speeders at school zones."

This was Greg Robertson's first council meeting as city manager. He turned and looked at Emil Jura with a skeptical frown. Greg wondered how long he could stay with this chicken shit job before he threw-up and resigned.

"I'm like the rest of the posse members," the woman said. "I volunteered to get abused. I drive an old worn-out patrol car that the sheriff's office donated to me, and I'm often mistaken for a deputy.

"I don't have direct arrest power, but like you have seen, I carry a loaded weapon, a badge and fulfill a variety of duties generally reserved for the police.

"I also provide courtroom security, help at drunken driving checkpoints, staff school crossings and assist with beach patrols. During the past year or so, I've been on extra alert for terrorists and anthrax."

The woman paused, put her pistol back in her purse, and looked at the council members as if it was their time to talk.

"What would you like the city to do?" the city manager asked.

"Well, since I'm a resident in Councilman Kevin Barnett's council district, I thought it would generate a lot of favorable publicity for the city of Dos Bayou if you folks passed a resolution or proclamation to honor me and all the other hard workers in the posse who serve without any salary. That's all."

Curtis Wagner bumped Barnett's elbow and said, "Your turn."

"Mayor," Barnett immediately announced, "I can think of no higher priority for this council to engage in than to acknowledge with an official city manager-prepared resolution our heartfelt gratefulness, appreciation and thanks for the fine, no, let's say outstanding, no, I'll say superior accomplishment done day in and day out by our posse members. That's what we should express."

"Well spoken, Councilman Barnett," the posse member said with a nod as she stepped from the podium. "Make sure all those words you spoke are included and some more are written so they fill an entire page. Your clerk has my name and how it is spelled."

She left through the side door.

"Anyone else?" asked Libby as her eyes reluctantly canvassed the audience.

An old man stood, walked with a cane down the row of seats, turned at the aisle, handed Tilly a paper, and stepped to the podium.

"Old Les Arthur, that's me," the man said. "I used to live in the county. Now old Les lives in the city. Old Les hasn't changed his address. The city has.

"Not that many years ago, I could stand on my front porch and make water for the weeds and no one, nary a soul, could see me. I'd spray'em good. Now, who watches old Les every hour of every day? Who?"

Barnett eyed Wagner. "I don't recognize him. Do you?"

"Me neither," Wagner said.

"Old Les Arthur will tell you who," the old timer said.

"People in antique shops, people in spas, people in tanning salons, people in pet stores, people at gas stations, that's who. Businesses and new houses and new places now pepper the landscape like shotgun pellets. There's no organization, no leadership whatsoever. You've allowed all these places including apartment complexes and high-end subdivisions to border run-down flophouses and what us locals call felony flats, the trailer parks.

"You have depreciated property values, allowed condemnation of private property without reasonable, proper and just adjudication, damaged our underground water supply, altered the natural flow and seepage of water to maintain balances in our vital aquifers, and you have undermined the adopted general plan for the area.

"What old Les Arthur sees is a lot of hit and miss."

He pointed to each council member.

"You high and mighty folks sit up there on the podium in your big executive chairs and hand out building permits like a child scribbles outside the lines of a coloring book.

"Your city manager wants to manage, can manage and should be managing, but you keep him busy writing silly, meaningless resolutions and proclamations that are not worth a bucket of warm spit.

"You keep annexing acres after acres of timber land and wetlands so developers can hook up at no extra charge to your city water, sewer and energy lines. Then they sell their little cracker boxes on lots where birds and possums used to play so more kids can crowd our classrooms, more cars can drive on our potholed streets, more hoodlums can roam our playgrounds, and more damage is done to our fragile environment."

Every eye in the place was focused on the old man.

Mayor Libby Washington heard every word. And she knew the old timer was right.

She also knew that over the years too many people had ranted and raved about pet peeves or subjects that were outside the council's purview or authority.

Not so with Les Arthur.

He was on a roll, and no one could stop him.

Barnett leaned over to Wagner. "He's kicking you in the balls, isn't he?"

"What do you mean me?" Curtis asked. "Your balls must be sore too."

"Not me. I wasn't here when you and the others annexed all that property," Barnett said with a mischievous grin. "I'm clean."

Curtis Wagner's chin sagged.

"I liked the old, rutted, dirt road that snaked by my home before you reached out with your long, insidious, lecherous and contemptible tentacles and illegally annexed everything out there in the northeast," Les Arthur continued. "But that wasn't enough.

"Next came developers and their contractors with their big machines and they paved parking lots for strip commercial parcels, and streets for subdivisions and put in concrete sidewalks. But they didn't stop there. They paved private roads, too. Like mine.

"Needless to say, old Les Arthur is mad as a wet hen, and I'm here to find out what you are going to do about it. So I'll stop now for a few minutes so I can hear your response, but I will not yield the floor to anyone in the audience."

"What would you like done?" Barnett asked.

"What I would like to see for starters is a resolution published in the paper."

"What kind of resolution?" Wagner wanted to know.

"Well," Arthur thought for a couple moments and rubbed his nose, "guess it could be a resolution from this city council, signed by the mayor and certified by the clerk, wherein you admit without hesitation, evasion or mental reservation that you illegally annexed the northeast section of inhabited land and did, in fact, spend taxpayers' money to pave private property.

"Yes, like I said, that will do for starters," Arthur said.

Greg Robertson was aghast at the comments.

Greg knew the two lawyers in the pinstripes seated by Emil Jura worked for Jeffery Adam McCormack and were specialists in municipal law. And Greg could tell the two were chomping at the bit to talk.

But first, Greg needed some more information from old Les Arthur. And so did the lawyers.

"Could you please tell us why you believe it was an illegal annexation?" Greg asked.

Les Arthur pulled a folded piece of yellow paper from his shirt pocket. He unfolded it and spread it out on the podium.

"Well, sir," Arthur said as he looked at City Manager Greg Robertson, "I'm not a practicing attorney anymore, and probably never was a good one, so maybe that's why I found more pleasure and satisfaction teaching for twenty years in the graduate school of public administration at Florida State University.

"I'm familiar with our state constitution," Arthur said. "I'll read to you what it says pertaining to my previous comments on annexation.

The old timer held the paper close to his face and started to read.

"Rural or non-incorporated parcels of ten acres or larger with two or more inhabitants dwelling thereon per parcel shall not be annexed to an abutting city without a duly noticed vote by the inhabitants."

"Thank you, Mister Arthur," Curtis Wagner said, "but we are all aware of that provision. I'm sorry, sir, but I do not understand your point."

"Let me explain it this way," Arthur said. "The city knew the people who lived on the land would vote against annexation. The people had already voted against annexation twice in the last six years. So what the city did to get the land annexed and on the city tax rolls was chop the large parcel into small parcels so there were less than two inhabitants per parcel. That's called gerrymandering which in annexation law is also unlawful.

"What you did was take a large parcel of inhabited land, unlawfully gerrymander it into uninhabited land and took it into the city without a vote. That is illegal. It's a felony, sir."

Arthur took out his wallet and withdrew another folded piece of paper.

"I'm going to give this check to the clerk. It's a check to cover the costs for paving the private road in front of my property. In my lawsuit against the city, I fully expect to recover that check, plus a whole lot more."

All eyes watched intently as the old man handed Tilly the check. He turned and walked slowly down the aisle and out of the building.

Libby Washington remembered the annexation. She remembered that Mayor Phillip Garrison had insisted on handling the entire matter himself, which he did. Libby shook her head. Garrison sure did handle it, she thought. He handled it right into another lawsuit against the city.

She looked at the audience. She was confident no one else would want to speak, especially after what they had just heard.

But she had to go through the requirement that LBJ started.

"Is there anyone else who wants to be heard under Public Interest Issues at this time?"

A young black man walked toward the front. He carried several crammed files in his arms. He placed the files on the podium and reached out to give Tilly Cloud his completed form.

Tilly smiled broadly, leaned over, exposed ample cleavage, and took the paper.

The man faced the dais with a somber look.

"Thank you, Madam Mayor, for allowing me to speak."

"You are, indeed, welcome, sir. Proceed."

"The last speaker, Madam Mayor, called to your attention a lot of bad things that have happened in Dos Bayou."

The young man turned and looked at the audience. "Well, ladies and gentlemen, as they say, you ain't heard nothin' yet."

The speaker opened the top file, looked with a sad expression at some pictures, and wiped his face.

"What I have to say, and pictures I will show you, will sadly explain that we have a lot more serious and immediate problems to face than what we just heard from the previous speaker. I hate to be the messenger, but you need to know about some things that point to deep, serious trouble in Dos Bayou."

Curtis, Kevin and Lily edged forward in their seats.

"Oh, shit," Greg Robertson mumbled to himself.

"Dogs look to us for love and protection," the young man said. "What I am going to show you are pictures of dogs, pictures of dogfights and pictures of bloody and dead dogs. Dogs, mostly pit bulls, fight each night here in Dos Bayou. We have here in our city what appears to be the largest dog fighting ring in the Southeast, and, unfortunately, a police cover-up."

The speaker handed the Mayor a file of pictures.

"The sheriff's office won't do anything about what you are now looking at," the speaker said. "You probably recognize the house and backyard on Andalusia Avenue where these fights are held. There is an expensive cover charge to get in, their security is tight, and thousands upon thousands of dollars are won and lost each night."

The Mayor looked with horror at the photos then passed the file to her colleagues.

"I have talked to officers who say there is not enough evidence for them to waste their time," the speaker continued. "I have shown the officers these same photographs you are now looking at. There are deep blood spots on the dogs' bodies, and evidence of heavy scarring around the neck, face, forelegs and shoulders which are consistent with dog fighting.

"I also showed the officers photos that provided substantial, if not absolute proof, that dogfights had taken place at the address noted on the photos. However, I did not show the officers the names of persons who attended those dogfights. Those names were on other photos that showed dogfight scenes."

"Sir," Greg Robertson interrupted, "why didn't you show the officers the names of persons who attended the fights?"

"Because, Mister Robertson, the two officers I talked to, Sergeant Lewis and Deputy Roland, were two of the names on the list. They frequently attended the dogfights, and they were the officers who refused to take any action."

"How did you gather all of this evidence?" Mayor Washington asked with a look of astonishment.

"Ma'am, I'm in the graduate school of criminology at the University of West Florida. I'm writing my master's thesis on how officials in Dos Bayou allow illegal dogfights to occur in their city."

Greg Robertson leaned back in his chair.

"Please tell me again the names of the two officers," Greg said.

"Oh, them? Sergeant Billy Ray Lewis and Deputy Timmy Dee Roland," the man said. "You'll see their names in the files quite often."

He paused and looked at Greg.

Greg looked like he had just seen a ghost.

"Why, do you know them, sir?"

"We've had some contact," Greg said. "Can you leave us a set of these prints along with the files so the council can determine what course of action it wants to take?"

"Sure, I'll be happy to," the man said, "I hope they assist you in taking some action. Call me when you're finished and I'll come over and pick them up. I want to thank you for your time."

"No, sir, we sincerely thank you," Libby said. "And I can assure you that action will be taken."

As the young man departed through the rear door, thunder exploded over the Gulf and rain splashed against the chamber windows.

"Oh, Lord, we don't need another downpour," Libby's voice sounded despondent.

She inhaled with an expression that dared anyone else to

speak, looked around the chamber and slowly let the air out of her lungs.

A strained smile split her face, and with a lot of teeth showing, she asked, "Is there anyone else who would like to address the council?"

No one moved.

Libby waited a couple more seconds. Still no one moved.

"Me," a voice said.

Libby strained her eyes to survey the people in the audience, but nobody stood or motioned.

"I want to like make an announcement, you know, if you don't mind, okay?"

Libby, Curtis Wagner and Kevin Barnett looked at Tilly.

Greg could not believe what he heard. He knew that if Tilly started talking, it would be an all-night session.

Kevin leaned over to Curtis and whispered, "I was going to leave and make that liquor delivery, but now I'm staying to hear this. It's a first."

"Tilly, you wish to address the council?" the mayor asked.

"Oh, no, nothing like that, I mean, what I want to like announce is that I'm engaged to get married, and like I'm the fiancée, you know, to Faldo who performs like, you know, a stuntman actor, okay?"

"Well, now," Libby said with a gentle smile that lifted the edges of her mouth. "That's wonderful, Tilly. When will we meet this young man, Faldo?"

Tilly stood and faced the audience.

"Ladies and gentlemen," she said in a loud, high-pitched voice as she pointed to the left side of the chamber, "please welcome the man I love who like shares my bed, The Great Rondigian, okay?"

Libby Washington watched with inquisitive eyes as the guy in the neck brace slowly got to his feet, held his stovepipe hat high over his head with a bandaged hand, and took a half-bow.

A thunderclap detonated nearby and an eerie light flashed through the rattling windows.

Everyone sat stone-faced as they stared at the handicapped man who was old enough to be Tilly's father.

Finally, Councilman Kevin Barnett tapped Curtis Wagner's arm and leaned over. "Curt, I'll swear on a stack of Bibles that there's no goddamn place on earth that has as many problems as we do right here in Dos Bayou."

Wagner shook his head up and down. "With our luck," he whispered, "in a few months twins or triplets will spring from Tilly's loins and they'll talk just like her, and look just like old fucko Faldo."

Councilman Barnett nodded with a sad expression, but never took his eyes off The Great Rondigian.

Barnett finally stood with slumped shoulders, opened the side door and departed.

CHAPTER 15

The night sky had turned shadowy dark. Rolling thunder roared in from the Gulf of Mexico and sheets of rain hit hard against the Gator Pit Bar's tin roof.

Mary Jean was in her usual denim jumpsuit as she stood at the far end of the bar and cleaned ashtrays. She took quick occasional glimpses at the corner pool table where Red and two customers were talking.

The customers wore soiled fishing garb and were well into their second longneck, but they showed no interest in breaking the balls Red had racked. The voices increased in tempo as the three men carried-on an animated conversation.

Mary Jean busied herself with more ashtrays as the conversation around the pool table faded during crackling sparks of lightening and claps of thunder.

When the noise subsided, her curiosity tweaked, her head turned, and she looked again.

Red had the strangers too engrossed in conversation for them to notice her. Despite the risk, she could not delay the inventory any longer.

Mary Jean pushed the ashtrays away, grabbed a bar towel, folded it in half and placed it on the counter. She stooped, took her heavy purse off the lower shelf, and carefully dumped the contents on the towel.

Both hands moved the items around so everything was clearly visible.

She needed to complete her inventory and be ready when Billy Ray said it was time to go. He wanted her to drive.

Mary Jean and Red were both surprised about Billy Ray's meeting. It was unusual for Billy Ray, the Grand Dragon, to call a special meeting on the spur of the moment, especially in this kind of weather, but it was no big deal to Mary Jean.

She and Red planned to close early anyway and Billy Ray's meeting gave them an excuse to tidy-up the place by cleaning ashtrays, wiping cobwebs off windows, mopping restrooms and spreading a new layer of sawdust on the floor.

Billy Ray and some of the men had been in the back storage room for more than an hour, and Mary Jean knew that no weeknight meeting of the Klan ever lasted much longer than that.

She knew she had to check her inventory, but she had never conducted one when customers were present, and she was not going to start now. It was just too risky, especially since Billy Ray said they were going on an important mission.

"Red, I need you," she yelled. "Tell the fellows we have to close. Now y'all have a good evening, ya hear."

Red followed the men to the door, turned the sign, locked-up and watched as the two strangers got into a battered old Dodge truck and drove away pulling a boat and trailer.

Red finally turned and nodded to Mary Jean.

She looked at all the things that were spread-out on the towel, and quickly started the final phase of the inventory.

The Derringer was a permanent fixture. She put it back in the purse. She gripped the handle of the .45-caliber Glock semiautomatic handgun, counted the rounds in the clip and chamber, and put it in her right front pocket.

The Glock could fire 16 bullets without reloading, and she was prepared to use it to stop anyone who wanted to interfere with her brother's mission.

Mary Jean was an expert at hitting a distant target the size of a man's head with a Derringer, a 22-caliber rifle or pistol, a 45-caliber pistol, a 9mm Walther, or, her favorite, the Glock.

The Derringer was always her backup for one final shot.

Her eyes scanned the other essentials: black Kiwi shoe polish, a wig, blush, lipstick, mascara, eye shadow, eye liner and condoms. Each item was returned to the purse.

She opened her bulky wallet and removed her driver's license, credit cards, fishing and hunting licenses, and photos, and put the wallet back in the purse.

Her sanitized purse no longer carried anything that could be used to run an ID on her. All those items were on the towel.

She carefully lifted each corner of the towel and it sagged in the middle as she carried it past the pine clock and dumped it into the floor vault.

"Will he need any kerosene or C4 explosives?" Red asked.

"He didn't say, but you'd better bring in a five-gallon can and about three or four kilos of plastic just in case," Mary Jean said.

Red took a ring of keys off the wall hook, went out the rear door and headed toward the back shed.

While Red filled a container with kerosene, taped rags, bottles and a box of wooden matches to it, and cut fuses and blocks of C4, two men with camera-mounted night-vision goggles filmed him from their crouched position on the edge of a bayou 100 yards away.

Their old Dodge truck was parked nearby in thick underbrush.

A few minutes later, the two men filmed 12 armed people in battle dress uniforms as they marched military-style in a single-file formation from the Gator Pit Bar toward some vehicles.

The two men in the rear of the formation matched the descriptions of Sergeant Billy Ray Lewis and Deputy Timmy Dee Roland.

Lewis and Roland tossed rifles and bags on the back seat and climbed into a Chevrolet Blazer. A woman got behind the wheel.

Wet red clay flew through the air as she gunned the engine, skidded through a wide 180-turn, and headed west, toward Dos Bayou.

Three armed men followed in a Dodge Ram, and five more were in a Ford Expedition.

They all left in a big hurry.

Except Red. He drove away in the opposite direction, toward Pace, in an old Honda Civic.

"Use the scrambler phone," ordered Jeffery Adam McCormack. "Give descriptions, license numbers and tell them they must cut off the Dodge and the Ford, but let the Chevy Blazer go through. We need to know if there are others in the gang. And follow the Honda."

"Yes, sir," snapped McCormack's investigator. He punched some numbers.

"Dispatcher, U.S. Marshal's office, Pensacola," a voice said.

"This is Choctaw Blue. Are you ready to copy?"

~ ~ ~ ~ ~ ~

Emil Jura heard the subtle, mellow sound on the second chime. He looked down at the small attachment on his belt and read the words that raced across the small screen. They were brief and to the point.

Emil cupped his hand and whispered to his seatmates, "They're twenty-six minutes out. It's still raining, but not as bad."

"Madam Mayor," one of the lawyers said as he rose, "per previous discussion with you and the city manager, we just received notice that the situation is near and preventive action should be taken immediately, ma'am."

The left rear door opened with a thump against the wall and Lieutenant Jake Underwood entered, followed by fifteen deputies. They formed a single file in the rear next to Duke Hockbarth.

More armed men and women in a different kind of uniform entered through the right rear door and formed a line behind Underwood's people.

"Ladies and gentlemen," Mayor Washington said, "This meeting is adjourned. All of us should go directly home. If any of you need a ride, we have plenty of nice folks here to help you. They are Lieutenant Underwood and his deputies along with U.S. Marshals.

They'll make sure you get home safe and sound. Now please leave quickly and quietly. We must vacate this building now. Thank you."

Greg Robertson folded his notebook, left it on the table, and walked over to Underwood with an outstretched hand.

"How did you know about this situation?" Greg asked.

"I don't know anything about a situation," Underwood said shaking his head. "All I know is that your wife called my wife and said I should get some deputies I could trust as fast as I could and hurry over here to help you."

"How did my wife know?"

"Your wife said her father called and told her what to do."

"Welcome aboard," Greg said. "Emil Jura will brief you on what we know."

- - - - - - -

The two old men were in a spirited animated conversation as they played cribbage on the aft deck of their spacious yacht.

The pilot, sitting high above in the captain's seat, reduced the speed and the yacht entered the familiar sights surrounding Puerto Limon harbor on the Caribbean coastline of Costa Rica.

"That's two skunks in two days, and I've had enough of you cutting corners when I'm not looking," one of the men yelled as he slapped his cards down on the table and stood.

A sleek, silver Citation X circled the harbor twice and streaked away into the northern sky.

"Maybe we should get one of those," Chester Andrews said pointing at the sky.

"Hell, this boat cost a couple million," Phil Garrison said. "We only have about eight million left, so let's use it for liquor and women."

"Yeah, and a new deck of cards," the former judge said.

CHAPTER 16

The Chevy Blazer, Dodge Ram and Ford Expedition maintained a constant speed as they headed west on Highway 98. The three-car convoy was midway through the city of Gulf Breeze when Timmy Dee pointed to Sprint Telephone, Cox Cable and Gulf Power workers repairing overhead lines.

"That's one goddamn job I wouldn't have, especially in this weather," Timmy Dee said. "I don't care if they do get double time pay, I still wouldn't have that job."

"Guess we'll have to stop," Mary Jean said. She pointed straight ahead at a flagman. "Look at all those maintenance men. There must be about fifty of them near that flagman and a hundred or more up ahead."

"Yes, sir," Timmy Dee said, "a lot of double time is paid to repair damage around here when we have some bad weather."

He raised up, took off his coat, leaned over and covered the rifles on the back seat.

"We shouldn't have to wait very long because there's only three cars in line and one's already pulling out," Mary Jean said as the flagman approached.

She stopped and lowered the window.

"Ma'am, it'll be just a second," a tall, lanky flagman said as he drooped his head. "We have a line down just ahead of us and we're letting only one vehicle go at a time to keep the risk low. We don't want anyone in harm's way. Appreciate your patience, ma'am. I'll be right back."

Sergeant Billy Ray Lewis yanked a cell phone off his belt and punched some numbers.

"Looks like we'll have to split up for a couple miles because a line's down and they're only lettin' one car through at a time. We'll form together at our preliminary site on the other side of the bridge. If anyone misses that checkpoint, form at our primary site. No one leaves until the target is down. Confirm that he's still there, pass it on and call me back."

The flagman returned, lowered his head and looked through the window.

"Ma'am, you can go now, but please be careful," the flagman warned. "Just do what the flagman up ahead tells you. They'll all have signs."

"I've never seen so many linemen on duty in my whole life," Timmy Dee said as the Chevy Blazer inched its way forward toward the bridge.

"Well, look at that," Mary Jean said with a surprised tone. "Where did that rig come from?"

"Where?" Billy Ray asked as he craned his head from side to side. "I don't see one."

"Behind us," she said. "An eighteen-wheeler is behind us and it's blocked my view of our men."

The driver of the Dodge Ram nodded to the flagman and started forward at a slow pace.

The Chevy Blazer was nowhere in sight and all the Dodge Ram driver could see was a big rig about 50 yards ahead, and, suddenly, in his rearview mirror, the headlights of an 18-wheeler on his tail.

The five Klansmen in the Ford Expedition never had a chance to make a cell call, squeeze a trigger or throw a flaming kerosene Molotov cocktail.

They stopped immediately when a flagman waved his arms, pointed to the ground under their vehicle and yelled, "You've straddled a high voltage line. Wait a sec and we'll have you on your way."

Another Gulf Power man ran toward the truck with an arm load of rubber boots. "Here," the young flagman said, "put these on and step out of the truck so we can move the wire, then you're outta here."

The men looked at each other with quizzical expressions.

"Sorry for the inconvenience," the flagman said, "but it will only take a couple minutes and you'll be on your way."

"Okay," one of the Klansmen finally said, "let's do it."

They hurriedly pulled on the oversized boots and stepped out.

The flagman was almost right.

It took four minutes. During that time the men were searched, cuffed, read their rights, and told that rubber tires were as safe as rubber boots.

Then they were on their way. Downtown. To the third floor of the federal building where the U.S. Marshal's office had public housing with bars on the windows.

The Klansmen had been outsmarted by a gutsy young flagman who was on his first field assignment as a deputy marshal.

The Dodge Ram never made it to the bridge.

It was squeezed between a slow-moving 18-wheeler in front and another one behind.

After a flagman stopped all three vehicles near Dolphin Stadium, swarms of workers in Sprint Telephone gear went about their jobs and were ignored by the men in the Dodge Ram.

When the flagman waved them on, the Dodge lunged forward but its two front tires collapsed with loud swishing sounds.

The workers had placed a spike strip next to the front tires and continued to look busy until the blaring deflation occurred. The workers quickly yanked the doors open, pointed weapons at the noses on surprised faces and jerked the men out.

A call was placed and five more men were on their way downtown to public housing accommodations.

"Where in the hell are they?" yelled Billy Ray Lewis as he stomped around the parking lot and flung his arms in the air.

"Didn't I say the preliminary site? Isn't the preliminary site the tourist center parking lot? Ain't this the tourist center parking lot? Didn't I say that, Timmy Dee?"

"That's what I heard, Billy Ray. As sure as I'm standing here, that's what I heard."

"I've got some ears and a mouthpiece with a phone near the target keeping me informed of his whereabouts, and I'll be goddamned if I don't lose eight of my men, and the goddamn battle hasn't even started yet. Ain't that right, Timmy Dee, or am I dead wrong?"

"You're right," Timmy Dee said, "but don't forget we have the rest of the brothers in the Klan coming in from Pace just as soon as Red can locate'em."

"Well, you can bet that Red will find them," Mary Jean said with her usual tone of spunky, strong-willed stubbornness.

"And if he can't," Billy Ray snapped, "we've got a mission that started out with eleven trained men for sure, possibly twenty, and now we have the same mission with only three of us. Ain't that right, Timmy Dee?"

Mary Jean had never seen her brother so mad. He always had a quick temper, but ever since the Hurricane Raymond incident with the Dos Bayou city manager, Billy Ray had just not been himself.

And, Mary Jean knew, neither had anyone else.

So what, she thought, if the city manager was beaten up a little? He was still alive, but he wouldn't be for long because he signed his own death warrant.

The thing about his hotshot father-in-law coming in and suing everyone was not the straw that broke the camel's back, as far as Billy Ray was concerned.

No, Mary Jean knew that wasn't it.

She also knew for a fact that Sheriff Homer Jedbow Cogburn, the miserable, sweaty bastard of an uncle who raped her every night when she was growing up in Century, should have his reelection campaign all organized, but so far he had not even discussed, much less offered, the job of campaign chairman to Billy Ray.

Yes, Billy Ray was pissed, and Mary Jean knew it.

No, Billy Ray was not pissed because of uncle Homer's silence, but because the city manager should not have allowed his wife, a white blonde woman, to meet with those black women at the Flamingo Café and organize a campaign committee.

Mary Jean knew it was not just a matter of a blonde white woman sitting at a booth in the lounge of a fancy restaurant with a bunch of black women that was the bone in Billy Ray's throat that got him pissed.

No, that wasn't it.

And it wasn't the blonde white woman's damn bodyguard who sat so close to the bar that the bartender, who was paid to have ears, couldn't risk a phone call to Billy Ray and give him a heads up.

No, Mary Jean knew it wasn't any of those things.

But Billy Ray sure did have a mean temper.

Mary Jean felt hopeless as she watched Billy Ray stomp around the parking lot and rave in Timmy Dee's face about the preliminary site.

Mary Jean understood why her brother was so mad.

Billy Ray was pissed because someone had just gotten in the way of something that Billy Ray held dear. Something that Billy Ray had counted on to add a substantial degree of security to his life, a hell of a lot more reason for him to exist, and, most of all, something that just plain made good down-home basic horse sense.

Damned if Billy Ray wasn't pissed.

It just gnawed and gnawed at him for the past few days that the city manager, obviously, his blonde wife, positively, and her daddy, financially, were supporting none other than First Lieutenant Jefferson Thomas Jake Underwood, the black dude, for sheriff.

That's what got Billy Ray pissed.

And Mary Jean was pissed just to think about it.

If she were back in her bar right now, she thought, she would be downing double vodkas like Prohibition might be coming back on the next train.

And the more Billy Ray talked to her about it, the more pissed he got.

But now, the more Mary Jean thought about it, the more she felt that she had a greater cause for being pissed than her brother had.

And that cause, that reason, was none other than miserable old Uncle Homer Jedbow Cogburn.

If he weren't reelected to another four-year term as sheriff, then Billy Ray wouldn't have a job. If Billy Ray didn't have a job, Uncle Homer couldn't hide his sorry ass anywhere without people knowing what he did and the kin he did it to.

Mary Jean remembered word for word what she told Uncle Homer before she ran away from Century with Red: "Keep Billy Ray employed for the rest of your life, never contact me or try to see me again, or I'll tell the world what you did to me and forced me to do to you."

"We've waited long enough," Billy Ray yelled. "We're going to the primary site and take down the target."

~ ~ ~ ~ ~ ~

Emil Jura saw Greg Robertson wave to a group of deputies and walk abruptly back into city hall. Emil could not imagine why Greg needed to go back inside, but Emil had his orders.

Greg's face was a study in concentration as he climbed the stairs, went into the chamber and walked toward the table.

Of all the things he had to worry about, Greg wondered why his mind was so occupied on Duke Hockbarth.

There was something peculiar about Duke Hockbarth that Greg could not put his finger on, and there was also something very strange about the dogfight pictures. Greg needed to look at them again.

At first, when they all left the council chamber and went outside, Greg did not consider it too unusual to see Duke Hockbarth constantly on a cell phone. After all, he was a plumber with a lot of customers. But after several minutes, it seemed as if likable and congenial old Duke Hockbarth had talked to everyone in town. And he always backed away and talked in hushed tones so no one could hear what he said.

That was the curious thing that got Greg's dander up, so he paid close attention to how the calls originated.

What hit Greg between the eyes was the realization that Duke

Hockbarth did not receive any of the calls. He sent every one of them.

Greg had heard from a lot of people, including some councilmembers, that Duke Hockbarth was a troublemaker, and a self-proclaimed activist who liked to rub shoulders with the upper crust one minute, and get down and dirty with other blue collars the next minute. No one, they said, could quite figure out just where old Duke was coming from.

But none of them mentioned anything about what Greg had momentarily viewed, or thought he saw, in the pictures.

He sat down at the table and opened the thick file.

There were about 50 photographs and about 25 typed pages of notes. Each photo had a list attached to it that identified the people and the dogs shown.

Greg started to flip through pictures as he began the search for Duke's face and name.

It did not take long.

Greg's face turned to hate and disgust as he studied the sixth photograph. He held the picture as far away as he could and stared at an unbelievable sight. His stomach became queasy, and for the first time in his life he wanted to kill someone with his bare hands.

His eyes narrowed as they focused on the stout, brawny man in the center, Duke Hockbarth, who stood arm and arm around Billy Ray Lewis and Timmy Dee Roland, and each filthy hand held a wad of money.

Two pit bulls were on the ground. One was dead, and the other was near death but still barely standing.

The dead one had lost a front leg, had numerous open wounds and by the protrusion of ribs that showed through the skin, had also suffered from malnutrition.

The other dog's upper lip was torn oft; a hole on one side of his head was the result of a ripped-off ear, and its body was covered in dark red blood.

Greg wiped his eyes with the back of his hand.

"I'm sorry, but I had to follow."

Greg looked through watery eyes at Emil.

"Take a look at these," Greg said pushing the file toward Emil. "I think I've seen enough."

Emil studied the photo, closed the file and looked at Greg.

"When Jeffery Adam McCormack convinced the attorney general to assign this case to the U.S. Marshal's office instead of the FBI, I frankly didn't think it was such a big deal."

Emil closed his eyes and took a deep breath.

"Then, when the marshal got a court's permission to put phone taps at the Gator Pit Bar, Billy Ray Lewis's trailer, and Mary Jean's and Red's house, the whole thing, I thought, was just another government wild goose chase.

"But I was wrong," Emil said.

"With each call and each subject discussed, the tapes became a prosecutor's dream and a defense attorney's nightmare."

"Yeah, and I got selected by the Klan to die," Greg said. "And the U.S. Marshal, who took an oath to protect American citizens, asked me to hang around out there in the open like live bait in a food chain so Klan sharks can have an easy meal. What's wrong with this picture?

"Shit, I'll tell you what's wrong with this picture," Greg said. "Not too long ago, I was a paid professional killer in a cockpit. I know how to fight, and I'm going to fight those bastards."

"I think I know how you feel," Emil said. "But they've got a ton of marshals out there along with Underwood and his deputies. Let them handle it.

"Everyone from the council meeting has gone home, except your man, bad karma Hockbarth."

"Yeah, now he's my man," Greg said. "Well, at least we know why he's here."

"Hell, all the bases are covered," Emil smiled. "The Klan can't get to you. Marshals are in cars, on bikes and on foot patrols with dogs. Other marshals are up in trees, on cherry pickers, hanging from telephone poles, and on top of every tall building around here. You name the area, except the swamp, and fields of deadly fire overlap like turf at a sod farm. Hell, Greg, they can't get through. Now, how about if we go back outside. Watch me make a deal with the OIC of marshals, and I'll show you a new maneuver when I take out your nemesis, Duke Hockbarth."

"Okay, let's go," Greg said as he started toward the door.

He took a couple steps and froze in his tracks.

"Except the swamp? Why isn't the damn swamp covered?"

"I asked the marshals the same question," Emil said.

"And?" Greg asked impatiently.

"They said the swamp is full of venomous snakes such as water moccasins and rattlers. There are numerous alligators that are never friendly and always hungry, and a whole assortment of ugly alligator snapping turtles with spiked and ridged armor, a sharply hooked beak, and a real nasty bite that can tear off an arm or a leg. Then you've got all that green contaminated water from decayed organisms and animal waste that could easily kill you if it got into a sore or a cut on your skin."

"Is that all?" Greg asked.

"No," Emil shook his head. "They said the bog has floating logs and underwater razor-sharp branches with a swamp bottom so muddy it can easily suck your boots off."

Greg thought about survival school in the air force.

He remembered how he and all the others had to jump from a plane, land on the run and keep running for 20 miles, tie ropes together and rappel off a 90-foot cliff, cross a river on a rope bridge, wade through a chest-deep, snake-infested swamp, and occasionally plunge into deep holes or stumble over submerged needlepoint limbs that ripped the leather on their combat boots.

And, at that point, Greg remembered, they were only halfway through a normal training day.

Greg looked at Emil and thought for a moment.

"When you reviewed Sergeant Billy Ray Lewis's personnel file, do you recall if he was a veteran?" Greg asked.

"Yes. Army," Emil said. "Fort Benning. Squad leader, Ranger platoon, Special Forces."

They looked at each other and said the word at the same time.

"Swamp."

- - - - - - -

Billy Ray Lewis sat stone-faced behind the wheel as the Chevy Blazer bounced down the rutted road. The tops of huge live oak, scrub pine and cedar trees formed a dark, eerie canapé over the road.

They passed a tiny house with raggy curtains that waved through broken windows, a porch with two rickety chairs and a caved-in tin roof. The property still had remnants of hog fencing, wash sheds and an outhouse.

"That was grandpa's house, but now it belongs to the government," Billy Ray said.

"What did our grandparents do way out here?" Mary Jean asked as the small house disappeared when Billy Ray turned at the fork in the road.

"Uncle Homer told me they were homesteaders who owned all this land after seven years. They worked at turpentine stills, like the one you'll see in a minute or two, or in logging, and they raised beans, melons, yams, cows, pigs, chickens and those sort of things."

"That sure sounds like a hard life," Timmy Dee said. "How close are we and tell me once again just what your plan is, Billy Ray?"

"Okay, see that building? We're there," Billy Ray said as he turned the Chevy Blazer off the dirt road and drove past what looked like the front side of an old, deteriorated four-story building.

"What's that?" Mary Jean wanted to know.

"That old building is going to get us safely across the swamp," Billy Ray said. "It's one of the original turpentine stills."

He pointed to a long structure.

"See that ramp?" he asked.

"Yeah, so what?" Timmy Dee responded.

"Well, it's a long concrete incline that starts on the second floor of the building and it keeps going and going until it disappears deep down in the green, filthy water of that enormous swamp over there."

"So what?" Timmy Dee said with a derisive grin.

"Gallons of the most stinky turpentine you could even imagine seep from that old still every day and flow down that ramp into the swamp.

"People think it's too dangerous to wade in the swamp because of snakes, gators and snapping turtles. But those who know about the turpentine seepage keep it to themselves and don't say a word to anyone."

"What is it, about a half-mile or so across that swamp?" Timmy Dee asked.

"You've got it," Billy Ray said. "We'll keep our weapons dry in waterproof bags that we'll strap around our necks. We'll keep a knife in one hand just in case. Even though it's dark and still a little rainy, we'll wade across with a low profile with just our heads out of the water. If we have to talk while we're in the water, we whisper or use hand signals. We'll go ashore at city hall, lock and load, and kill Greg Robertson. And if that black candidate for sheriff is there, well, we'll just rub him out too. Then we wade back, get in the car and we're outta here."

"Hot damn," Timmy Dee said through a broad smile, "I sure do like it when Billy Ray, the Grand Dragon, has a plan that comes together. When do we start?"

"Right now," Billy Ray said.

"How do you know the target is still there?" Mary Jean asked.

"Because Duke said so when he called a couple minutes ago."

"Don't you think you should call him back and verify everything before we get in that swamp?"

"Don't need to, Mary Jean. Besides, I can't. It's too risky. Duke can't take any calls. He has to make all the calls. That's our plan. Take my word for it. I can rely on Duke Hockbarth."

"No need, Mary Jean," Timmy Dee said, "the Grand Dragon has spoken. Let's move out."

"I'll take the point," Billy Ray said. "Mary Jean, you stay between us, and Timmy Dee, you bring up the rear. Make the strap pretty tight around your neck, and keep the knife in your right hand. Now stay close."

The three camouflaged figures walked down the concrete ramp and started wading slowly into the murky, slimy water that smelled like a neglected septic tank with a bad leak.

Timmy Dee kept his eyes focused on the two heads that bobbed up and down in front of him. They had waded chest-deep about

200 yards, and Timmy Dee had no trouble keeping within a few paces of Mary Jean, but it seemed to Timmy Dee that Mary Jean was lagging too far behind Billy Ray.

"Pick up the pace some, Mary Jean, you're falling behind," Timmy Dee said in a voice slightly over a whisper.

"I can't go any faster because the damn mud is almost sucking the boots right off my feet every time I take a step."

"Well, take longer steps," Timmy Dee ordered.

"Shut your face," Mary Jean said in a fit of anger, "you little squirrel-faced asshole."

"Keep the noise down back there," Billy Ray ordered.

Timmy Dee's right foot trudged forward and he stepped on a hard object that moved. Timmy Dee's right foot moved with it.

The giant alligator snapping turtle was one of many that lived in the muck at the bottom of the swamp. During its first 50 years it surfaced only to breathe, breed and get a bite to eat. But when the ugly beast with a sharply hooked beak became a 120-pound, 70-year-old reptile with an attitude, and Timmy Dee's right foot in its mouth, it didn't have to surface to find something to eat.

It kept puffing, tearing and eating on the foot and leg until the entire meal was sprawled on the bottom of the swamp, and Timmy Dee's face was twisted in a grotesque and horrible display of mortal pain.

"I damn near lost it that time," Mary Jean said.

"Lost what," Billy Ray asked.

"The damn boot. They're not tight enough to wade on this muddy bottom. How much longer do we have?"

"We passed the midway point about a hundred yards back."

"Good."

Billy Ray stopped. It wasn't like Timmy Dee to stay quiet when a conversation was going on. Billy Ray turned and stared.

"Where's Timmy Dee?"

"Oh, he's back there complaining . . . "

She turned around. Her wide, glaring eyes glowed with fear and trepidation as she moved her head from side to side and searched the top of the slimy swamp water. A churning, spinning motion about 30 feet behind captured her attention.

Her face revolted in horror as she saw Timmy Dee's arm explode out of the water, the knife fall from his hand, and his arm was violently jerked under the surface.

"Oh, God, Billy Ray . . . "

"Be quiet, hush," he ordered.

Billy Ray's attention was focused on a large, partially submerged log that floated slowly toward them.

"We'll ride that log for a while and get our breath," he said.

The log's speed seemed to increase as it approached them.

Billy Ray's face froze in terror as the log's head suddenly rose out of the water.

The alligator's fang-filled mouth opened wide, the gigantic head turned abruptly toward Mary Jean, and it disappeared.

"Run for your life, Mary Jean," Billy Ray yelled as he desperately waded and paddled with his hands as fast as he could. "We're almost there."

Mary Jean took the longest strides she could through the murky water, but the space between her and Billy Ray grew in distance as her desperation turned to panic.

Her mind screamed at her to go faster. Her body yelled at her to take longer steps. She yanked her right foot out of the thick, muddy bottom and her boot was sucked off her foot.

Billy Ray never looked back when he heard the ferocious impact, the heavy slapping frenzy in the water, and Mary Jean's frantic, pitiful cries for help.

Billy Ray's arms and legs kept spinning in robot sync as the ground under him turned from muddy slim to sand and finally to a firm, rocky shoreline.

He yanked the strap from his neck, threw the waterproof bag on the ground and heaved himself onto the side of a sloping berm and gasped for air.

Deep in the flinty tree line that separated Dos Bayou city hall from the bayou that old-timers called the "the turpentine swamp," Greg Robertson and Emil Jura lurked in the thick brush and peered out through night-vision goggles.

They did not need the element of surprise they had planned.

According to interrogators who questioned the Klan prisoners in the downtown jail, "an invasion force of 20 heavily-armed Klansmen would fight until death, if necessary, to kill Greg Robertson, the money source who could get Jake Underwood elected sheriff."

"Well, let's go see our enemy," Greg said as he waved for the men behind him to move forward.

Lieutenant Jake Underwood rose from his concealed position, checked the line of officers on each flank, and motioned for them to advance.

Underwood was in the middle of the advancing line as 100 armed deputy marshals walked behind Greg and Emil.

A deputy picked up the waterproof bag, opened it, examined the contents and tagged it with an ID.

Sergeant Billy Ray Lewis was a mass of mud and slime as he lay spread-eagled on the berm and panted for air. His boots had numerous jagged cuts, and blood drained through the irregular punctures. His battle dress uniform emitted a putrid stench that filled the air like a low circling hurricane.

TV and newspaper reporters held their breath while they inched closer to hear Underwood read Billy Ray his rights.

Greg watched as two deputies with gloved hands approached Billy Ray and started a search for weapons, explosives and suicide pills. After they completed their squeeze, dig, push, jab, punch, pat and poke routine, they cut off his shirt, removed his boots, stripped off his pants, turned him on his stomach, cuffed his hands, shackled his ankles, turned him over, and put his clothes in a large bag they zipped shut.

With every TV camera in Northwest Florida recording the year's biggest news story, a Deputy U.S. Attorney stepped forward and read the charges. It took eight minutes.

A paddy wagon pulled into the parking lot and slowly made its way toward the berm.

Lieutenant Underwood knelt down and looked Billy Ray Lewis in the face.

"How many others were with you when you started across that swamp?"

"Two," Billy Ray said. "There were two others with me."

"Who were they?"

"One was my sister, Mary Jean. A gator got her."

"Did you see the gator attack her?"

"No, but I heard the whole thing. I can still hear her screaming."

"Did you try to help her?"

"No. I had to save myself."

"Who was the other person with you?"

"I guess you could say it was my significant other."

"What was her name?"

"It was a he."

"It was? What happened to him?"

"Something ate him."

"What was your friend's name."

"Deputy Sheriff Timmy Dee Roland."

"What possessed you to try and wade across that dangerous swamp on a shit night like this?"

"It was supposed to be safe because of the turpentine that seeps from that old still on the other side and runs into the swamp. The turpentine was supposed to kill all the critters."

Jake Underwood shook his head and looked at the most stupid, odorous, wasted specimen of a human being he had ever seen.

"Billy Ray," Underwood said, "that turpentine still went out of business back in the early sixties. There hasn't been any pine tree sap processed at that still for almost fifty years. When will you ever learn that you can't make chicken salad out of chicken shit."

"I don't know," Billy Ray said. "I just remember that I told them it was safe before we started across."

"How could your sister and your friend believe such a stupid lie?" Underwood asked as he stood up.

"Because I'm the Grand Dragon and I told them," Billy Ray said with a sneer.

CHAPTER 17

Homer Jedbow Cogburn sat in his favorite chair with his arms and legs crossed. His face was round and reddish under his trademark salt and pepper cow's lick that formed at his thick widow's peak and sloped all the way back.

He had started reading newspapers again, and stacks of them were at his feet. The morning Herald was on his lap and he planned to read it in a few minutes. But first he had to cogitate. That's why he wore his old orange cardigan sweater and dorky sneakers. They helped him think.

He drank coffee with his hat on and the spoon in, but this morning he felt like having something that had a little kick to it. Two full jiggers were on the table by his right elbow, but he had already forgotten which one was burgundy and which was prune juice.

That was just one of the things he had to ponder as he rested in the quiet comfort of his cabin in the hollow, and waited for the movers and the Mayflower van.

He thought about his life after the goat farm, and the more he mulled over all those years, the luckier he felt.

Homer Jedbow Cogburn, by his very nature, was a betting man.

But what set him apart from the usual self-starting swindlers and suckers was that he always bet with a fervent desire to lose. To him, good things always came in multiples after a substantial loss.

Take the goat farm.

When he wasn't feeding, milking, processing, marketing, delivering or hustling to meet customers' demands for his goat cheese, he was shoveling goat shit. It was not a bad life, but one day greed followed whiskey and he lost the goat farm on what he thought was a sure bet with his neighbor.

That loss resulted in a dynamic transformation in the life of one Homer Jedbow Cogburn.

Bet to lose.

How else can one explain the metamorphosis of a man who spent years eking out a living in dirty clothes by maintaining clean goat pens, and just a few days later, with a badge on his starched shirt, people handed him tax-free money folded around their driver's license?

But the big money came when he was appointed Chief of Police in Century. And even bigger stacks of it showed up in brown paper bags when he became county sheriff.

No, Homer Jedbow Cogburn never had a sense of urgency of ground lost or potential wasted because of bad bets. And he never, ever pushed against the heavy fudge of constituent complacency. Hell, he figured that if they didn't care what went on, he cared even less.

His latest stroke of luck, and the reason for burgundy and prune juice in lieu of coffee, were very large lifetime benefits that came on the heels of another bad venture.

Sheriffing aside, Homer Jedbow Cogburn was known throughout the Florida panhandle as a high tenor bluegrass singer who was long on stamina and finger-quick with the mandolin, banjo, guitar, piano and fiddle.

There were ordinary people in bluegrass who made extraordinary art, and never expected to hit gold. They were the ones contented to just perform.

They were the purists who knew that bluegrass was a combination of many styles, but never country. It took a heavy dose of gospel, a touch of Irish folk music and the wails and whines of Appalachia to form bluegrass.

But Homer Jedbow Cogburn was not contented just to perform. And he didn't stop with the usual run-of-the-mill improvisation.

Homer Jedbow Cogburn and his Cogburn Codgers were a combination of brilliant showmanship and a dream cast of musicians that guaranteed to work magic on highbrow Reba or Martina favorites, or lowbrow Garth and Randy standards with southern-style utterances that soared.

Critics lauded the Cogburn Codgers, and one from Atlanta wrote, "They were a coloratura of amazing agility that imbued their singing with a sense of individuality."

None of the Codgers knew exactly just what that description meant, but they thought it sure sounded good.

Their two-hour concerts, with Cogburn singing half the songs in a sonorous baritone, quavering with a mixture of determination and vulnerability, were about one-third bluegrass and two-thirds everything else.

Through it all, Homer Jedbow Cogburn remained hypnotic and unchanged – his rich and resonant voice, full of ancient hurt when necessary, was coupled with a brooding, hissing mandolin.

And he always changed moods.

One minute a powerful blast, the next something sweet and soaring, then an earthy, sensuous growl.

And each weekend, the festival grounds filled with the faithful, who either stared at Homer Jedbow Cogburn as if transfixed or swayed as if transported.

And "My Way" was always a crowd-pleasing, show stopper during an encore. Homer Jedbow Cogburn didn't just conquer the ridiculously difficult notes of Frank Sinatra's "My Way," he made all the high notes sound easy.

And his voice never thinned where it needed to bloom.

The SRO audiences always went wild.

But the Florida Emerald Coast Bluegrass Music Association in Fort Walton Beach went bananas.

Association directors didn't like it when someone with an attitude got in their face.

Homer Jedbow Cogburn's membership application was rejected.

The association's aristocracy called him in their stinging condemnation letter ". . . a maverick crossover who polluted bluegrass by mixing Bill Monroe's lofty standards with minor league R&R basement players like the Bee Gees, The Beach Boys and The Rolling Stones."

Homer Jedbow Cogburn returned the favor by throwing down the gauntlet in the form of a down-home catchy tune called "Escape From Milton."

The song started out with all the bells and whistles needed to be a chart stopper and a Grand Ole Opry favorite.

Cogburn's stubbornness about artistic freedom and his irreverent diversity with synthesizer noise, hip-hop soul rock, a hissing mandolin and a powerhouse acoustic guitar in "Escape From Milton" were viewed as blasphemy in an era when bluegrass was strictly formatted.

It didn't take long for the nobility in the bluegrass music association to get its message on the streets.

Booking agents, promoters and DJs quickly fell into lockstep. They blackballed "Escape From Milton" from being played on radio stations, and they saw to it that no concerts were booked.

The gauntlet was tossed back in Homer Jedbow Cogburn's face.

He lost a fortune in record sales, and SRO signs at his concerts were no longer needed.

It was just like the damn goat farm all over again.

The stress seemed to cause his voice to be a tab out of sync.

During his two terms as sheriff, Homer Jedbow Cogburn quit reading the newspapers and rarely watched the evening news. But now that he was reading papers and watching TV again, he had a whole new appreciation of just how foolish and manipulative people in the Florida panhandle truly were.

He needed to win his third term so he could qualify for retirement and move to Williston, South Carolina and enjoy his golden years. Retirement meant 60 percent of his $106,000 annual salary.

So with reelection in mind, and Lieutenant Jefferson Thomas Jake Underwood as a strong opponent, Homer Jedbow Cogburn decided to show his stuff.

With the same orchestration he used on the mandolin, Homer Jedbow Cogburn milked the media with an affidavit and warrant for the arrest of Bernard "Dusty" Jason, Vice Chairman of the Venture Capital Division of Forester's of Chicago. The charges were all-inclusive and ranged from bribery to collusion.

Dusty Jason's high-priced Chicago lawyers flew into town with a swarm of thugs. The lead lawyer told the media, "The sheriff doesn't have a case, can't have a case, and won't have a case because Dusty Jason is an honorable man."

Somehow, like the 18-minute gap on a Richard Nixon tape three days after the Watergate break-in, a crevice occurred in the sheriff's department's written, oral, digital and video criminal records department.

Someone broke into the records room over the Labor Day weekend, and everything relating to the Dusty Jason case mysteriously vanished. Evidence, forensic data and fingerprints taken from Dos Bayou City Hall furniture just disappeared.

Everything was gone except the cashier's check for $2 million.

When the state attorney demanded that Jeffery Adam McCormack turn over the check to the county, McCormack announced that the check had been seized by the Dos Bayou city manager, and was deposited in the city's municipal contingency account as forfeitured property.

The state attorney fretted and fumed because the only property he seized were two old pickups and a late model Chevrolet Blazer that were sold at auction. The Blazer brought top dollar but the Ford Expedition and Dodge Ram went for pennies on the dollar.

Homer Jedbow Cogburn remembered the young woman who purchased Mary Jean's Chevy Blazer.

She was the same woman who was featured in last Sunday's Home and Life Section.

The paper had carried a long story with pictures of a beaming Tilly Cloud as she showed off her new five-bedroom, four-bath, two-story home on a four-acre parcel that was the former residence of recently divorced Dos Bayou Mayor Phillip Garrison and Martha Sue Garrison.

The article described how Tilly Cloud and her boyfriend, The Great Faldo Rondigian, were expecting twins, and how pleased they were with their new home.

The paper also carried a story about Greg Robertson, the Dos Bayou city manager. The news article explained that Robertson had resigned from the city to take a job as Chief Executive Officer and Executive Vice President for his father-in-law's nation-wide law firm that was headquartered in Atlanta.

But heaven and the angels also smiled again on Homer Jedbow Cogburn.

After he opened up in front of TV cameras with a three-handkerchief dose of tears over the terrible circumstances of the loss of his only kin, voters were sure that the tragic death of Mary Jean, his dear, sweet niece, caused him the most emotional sorrow, and noticeable fluctuation in his voice.

Some said it just didn't make any sense.

Because on one day, Homer Jedbow Cogburn was agitated over the possibility of losing his bid for reelection, and having to sell his soul to keep Billy Ray employed so Mary Jean would keep her big, fat mouth shut.

And, on the next day, Homer Jedbow Cogburn was declared the conservator of Billy Ray's trailer and assets, and the new owner of Mary Jean's Gator Pit Bar and her bank accounts.

Red, her common-law-husband, never showed up around Pace or anywhere else on the night of the swamp tragedy, and he hadn't been seen since. That was no big deal to anyone including Homer Jedbow Cogburn because Red's name wasn't on any deeds or bank records.

That's why some thought that Homer Jedbow Cogburn's display of emotional grief was worthy of reelection.

"His tone," someone said on a radio talk show, "was reflective, if not solemn or loin-girding."

That was especially true when he went after the people involved in the dogfights.

Duke Hockbarth got both barrels. In addition to bookmaking

and a first-degree charge of conspiracy to commit murder, Hockbarth faced 29 counts of cruelty to animals by aiding and abetting the violation of state law.

Homer Jedbow Cogburn announced the charges in a strong, forceful voice.

He said nothing the next day when a lenient judge suspended jail time on lewd and lascivious act charges against Angela Giuseppi, alias Mommy Lou, Wendy Wafters, the maid, and Lolley Freehand, the nurse.

The judge placed them on probation for three years and ordered them to register as sexual predators in Florida. As such, they would have to notify authorities, who in turn would notify the public, whenever any of the women moved from one address to another.

Two days later, when grand jury indictments were expected against Billy Ray Lewis, a jailer found him on the floor of his cell in the beginning stage of rigor mortis.

The deputy coroner ruled the death was caused from suffocation. A sock had been stuffed into Billy Ray Lewis's mouth, his nose and mouth were taped shut, all of his fingers were cut off, his hands were tied behind him, his feet were wired together, and a white hood covered his head.

The deputy coroner said it took at least three strong persons to carry out the most despicable criminal action he had ever seen. The deputy coroner said there were no suspects, and prisoners in nearly cells said they did not see or hear "any unusual activity."

Billy Ray Lewis' death, the deputy coroner knew, followed the exact pattern that was used in the murder of the coroner the previous day.

The two deaths, the deputy coroner believed, had all the signs of a mafia operation.

After Billy Ray's funeral, Homer Jedbow Cogburn canceled all of his campaign appointments. He had a strong hunch that the recent string of bad luck could be reversed with a miracle if he just gave one the opportunity to rise and shine.

He, and he alone, would determine whether or not his life shrunk or expanded in proportion to his courage. To accomplish what he decided to do would require him to be the Patron Saint of Liars.

Homer Jedbow Cogburn had a plan.

For his next trick, he would take his high-wire act before a court of law.

He needed to develop some easily acquired – and believable – handicaps that would force him to stop singing at bluegrass festivals, and, as a result, cause him to suffer a drastic reduction in income.

It took ten days, and almost that many nights, to rehearse and perfect the disabilities, and make them sound convincing.

He spent the next three days going from one doctor's office to another and from this specialist to that specialist. Finally, when all the tests were completed and the conclusion was unanimous among the learned medical practitioners, Homer Jedbow Cogburn was ready for stage two in his quest for a miracle.

He spent the next day interviewing lawyers.

Then, he spent a half day at the social security office.

It took three days to complete all the claim forms required by two different governmental agencies.

The court hearing took a full week. There were hundreds of exhibits and even more arguments between lawyers who fought over testimony given by medical specialists, economists, legal scholars and professors of bluegrass music. A substantial part of the testimony concerned actuarial studies on projected loss of income due to a stress-caused change in voice, uncontrolled tone fluctuations, memory – or lyrics – loss, and a lisp when certain vowels were vocalized.

Homer Jedbow Cogburn's position was simple. His side argued that bluegrass festivals had increased his income so drastically that he fulfilled his maximum social security deductions by early summer of each year. But now, because of stress, he could no longer perform at festivals as the lead high tenor of the Cogburn Codgers.

He claimed that stress and anxiety from eight tension-filled years of being a dedicated, loyal and conscientious sheriff had changed his voice, caused irrevocable damage to his vocal chords, and he could no longer work as a high tenor vocalist.

His well-paid renowned experts testified that his singing voice was now somewhere between an off key, low tenor with a lyric retention problem, a nondescript, commonplace tenor who lacked timbre, or, possibly, a mediocre low note baritone crooner with a lisp.

His lawyers were quick to point out that mediocre baritone crooners, especially lispers, and dime-a-dozen low tenors with a lyric handicap, were persona non grata at bluegrass festivals, and the Grand Ole Opry.

Homer Jedbow Cogburn struck the mother lode of all veins.

It was a landmark decision.

If Homer Jedbow Cogburn were reelected and served four more years as sheriff his gross taxable retirement income would be $6,360 per month.

By qualifying for workers' comp, he got a tax-free income of 80 percent of $106,000. That's $8,480 each month. Add to that a $1,200 monthly tax-free disability and a tax-free social security check of $1,725. Each source of income included annual increases.

Homer Jedbow Cogburn was a real happy camper. But he was no dummy.

With the court's decision still ringing in his ears, he resigned as sheriff and watched like a proud peacock as Jefferson Thomas Jake Underwood was sworn-in on TV.

That's why the movers and the Mayflower van were coming.

Homer Jedbow Cogburn was 530 miles from paradise. By sunset, he would stroll down the magnolia-lined three-block-long divided main street in beautiful downtown Williston, South Carolina and get to know his new neighbors on the 500 block of Skyland Farm Road.

He looked at the two jiggers on the table. He reached for one and downed the contents in one gulp. It was burgundy.

Damn, he thought, will this lucky streak ever end?

CHAPTER 18

Greg and Brenda Robertson, Emil Jura and Libby Washington were asleep in the comfort of executive leather seats on the port side of the airplane. The hour before takeoff was spent in a perplexed mind-set as they hurried to keep a tight schedule.

First came the call from Jeffery Adam McCormack.

Next were two cars with armed drivers for a code-3 dash to the airport where they were met on the tarmac by several somber looking men who hurried them onto a sleek, silver Citation 10.

Within seconds they were cleared for runway two-niner and were airborne. They leveled at 51,000 feet with an air speed of 600 – a sizzling six seconds per mile – and darted across the Gulf of Mexico on a flight that would take them to the bottom of South America.

Just before he dozed off, Greg heard the pilot announce that they had picked up a tail wind and would land at Benitez International Airport in Santiago, Chile ahead of schedule at 1144 hours, 16 minutes before noon local time.

Brenda was the first one awake. She looked at the arm rests on her spacious seat. Each had the seal of the World Bank.

She turned and looked around the cabin. She saw men who looked like they were on a one-way mission with no return ticket.

Each face was a death mask that stared straight ahead. No one talked. They looked solemn. And very mean.

They were, Brenda thought, the most frightening cast of characters anyone could find this side of roadside lepers. There wasn't a pipe and slippers guy among them. Each one looked like he rode roller-coasters by himself, and had the temper of a cornered Cape buffalo. Time had interred their looks.

The steward was in a pull-down seat at the rear panel. He removed his coat and Brenda knew instantly that he was not a steward. He wore a double-holster shoulder strap and began loading shells into pistol and machine gun clips. He looked to be in his middle 30s, with short whitish hair and a square but handsome face that could serve as a recruiting poster for a patriotic movie.

Brenda's eyes wondered around the stunningly attractive cabin. She saw rich, polished teak cabinets, a computer, telephones, fax, TV, chairs, a private dressing room, a restroom and a galley. She saw custom-tailored amenities, appointments and architectural details that only the deepest pockets could afford. Or petty cash from a World Bank file drawer.

She was impressed.

She wondered, with a faint smile, if her father had one like this.

Her thoughts were interrupted by the pilot's voice.

Greg, Emil and Libby were suddenly wide awake.

"Ladies and gentlemen, the Santiago OIC wants you to be aware of the following situation concerning your mission," the pilot said. "Upon arrival, stay seated. The OIC will board and brief you. All back-up personnel and logistics are positioned. Your schedule will be very busy after the briefing. We land in twenty minutes. Now would be a good time to use the facilities. Good luck."

- - - - - -

The OIC of field operations boarded the aircraft with a large attaché case that hung from her shoulder. She walked directly to the front of the cabin, turned and faced the four people from Florida.

"I am Yamarie Delgado, officer-in-charge," she said. "First," she said with a smile, "who is Brenda?"

Brenda felt apprehensive as she made eye contact and nodded her head.

"I want to thank your father, Brenda, for his kind assistance in getting all of you here so quickly," Yamarie said. "Jeffery Adam McCormack's law firm handles certain matters for the World Bank, and he is aware of the importance of this mission."

"What is the mission?" Greg asked.

"Fair question under the circumstances," Yamarie said with a deep breath.

"In a nutshell, you're here to help us stop another New York and Washington, D.C. tragedy, but in a different form. The al-Qaida organization has a terrorist cell operational here in Chile. The cell has direct connections to lieutenants of Osama bin Laden. Our intel believes this cell has developed a plan to kill or terrify many thousands of citizens, and destroy the Republic of Chile that is the anchor that stabilizes all of South America."

Brenda, whose profession kept her in a classroom, had never seen such a worldly, attractive and sophisticated killer as Yamarie.

Yamarie's eyes were a deep liquid hazel, and her voice was somber and resolute; a voice that matched the "take no prisoners" aura of her uniform. She wore a soft cap with a pointed bill, a light tan special forces-style pantsuit uniform, a brown scarf tucked-in around her neck, a web belt with all the necessary hardware, two extra ammo clips, and combat boots.

And she selected her words like she used ammo; no waste.

"Some of the world's most valuable resources such as cooper, iron ore, precious metals, zinc and multiple mineral mother lodes are here in the Republic of Chile which is our strongest ally in South America," Yamarie said.

"Chile is larger than the state of Montana and is the gate-keeper that protects the United States interest to, from and around both the Pacific and Atlantic Oceans. Its strategic location with sea ports in Valparaiso, Puerto Montt, Puerto Chacabuco and Cape Horn guard the free world.

"To many people," she continued, "bin Laden is a mysterious

figure. He has strong links to the earlier bombing of the World Trade Center, to terrorist attacks on U.S. embassies in East Africa, the attack on the USS Cole in Yemen and the tragedies of 9-11.

"He is even worse, if that is possible, than the late Iraqi President Saddam Hussein."

Yamarie, Brenda noticed, gave the name "Saddam" a snarling, nasal pronunciation.

"Oh, now I understand," Libby Washington said. "We got a bulletin at the university yesterday that ordered all students from Chile to return home immediately. I tried to call the office listed on the fax letterhead, but I got no answer."

"We were aware that he was trying to get all the foreign students to return home so they could be killed," Yamarie said. "It did not surprise us. He is very resourceful in his methods of human destruction."

"What else can you tell us," Libby asked.

"Well," Yamarie said, "let me put it this way. I'm sure you've heard the news about the situation in Argentina. Unfortunately, it's much worse than whatever you've heard. The government is now in rubble, the economy is in bankruptcy and all businesses and agriculture are beyond help. Because of bin Laden and his American associate, Argentina is on the brink of total collapse, and when she falls we fear her weight will carry South and Central America down with her.

"The leaders of bin Laden's cell want to initiate an economic depression that will bankrupt all twenty countries in Latin America, then the United States, and eventually Europe and Asia," Yamarie said.

Brenda looked wide-eyed at Greg, Emil, then Libby.

"You said that bin Laden had an American associate," Greg asked. "Do you know who it is?"

"The mastermind that we are after is a man of many faces, many disguises, a close friend of Osama bin Laden, and a man you, Mr. Robertson, and you, Mayor Washington, know and can identify. I speak of Carlos Santiago Dominguez," Yamarie said.

Libby flinched and stared wide eyed into nowhere.

"When we catch him," Yamarie said matter-of-factly, "we need you to make a positive identification before we kill him. That is why you are here."

"We'll recognize him," Greg said, "We have a lot of his pictures in city hall, and we can get them real fast if we need them."

Yamarie looked at Libby Washington.

"How long have you known him, Mayor Washington?"

"Eight years," Libby said in a murmur. Her face was in shock. "We sat side by side on the council for eight years."

"Is there any unusual mark or characteristic about him?" Yamarie asked.

Libby thought for a moment. "Yes, his left foot and ankle are artificial. He wears a prosthesis."

"Do you know that to be a fact?" Yamarie asked.

"It is a fact."

"How do you know that?"

Libby's embarrassment showed as she glanced at Greg, Brenda and back at Yamarie.

"We have slept together."

She closed her eyes and bit her lower lip.

"I kicked it once by accident and almost broke my toe. I have also removed it and helped him apply it. For some reason, he told me to never say anything about it. Oh, and there's another thing. He's also deaf in his right ear. He wears an invisible signal processing aid in that ear."

"Thank you," Yamarie said. "The information about his appliances is very helpful us, and I assure you," Yamarie said with a look of compassion, "that everything you said, and I mean everything, will stay on this airplane."

The stone-faced agents in the rear of the cabin were not impressed. They had attended hundreds of intelligence briefings in the World Bank on arms-dealer Carlos Santiago Dominguez, his drug-smuggling-father, his whorehouse-madam-mother, and all the others in his family who were killed on orders from the President of Argentina.

As the agents glanced at each other, their eyes shared one opinion: Chaos will soon strike and when it does, the apocalypse will follow. This high-risk mission is no place for Yamarie Delgado, a middle-aged courtesan in mascara, long painted fingernails, and funky, red-rimmed bifocals.

OIC Delgado was known for succinct and compact briefings.

After Libby, Emil, Brenda and Greg had gotten over their initial shock of the situation, Yamarie gave a broad-brush explanation of the intelligence gathered by the World Bank, units assigned to the Santiago mission, their capability, and contingencies for conventional and nuclear terrorist acts from cell members.

Then she dropped rather matter-of-factly the mother of all bombs.

"Carlos Santiago Dominguez has called for a mass meeting in the eastern caves of the Andes. Thousands of terrorists from around the world are now en route to Chile to inspect and purchase the newest and most deadly conventional weapons, chemicals as well as other forms of weapons of mass destruction."

The Florida guests stared into space.

Yamarie opened her attaché case and distributed CIA badge wallets to each person.

"Congress is not aware of this mission, but it provides the money and is aware, of course, that the CIA operates worldwide. Therefore, each of you is now working for the CIA. Are there any questions?"

As usual, at the end of a Yamarie Delgado briefing, there were none.

"Please follow me to the helicopters. We have a thirteen-mile flight to our command post downtown in the Crowne Plaza. It is a safe place because we, that is, the World Bank, owns it."Libby, Brenda, Emil and Greg walked like robots with stunned faces as they held their badges and followed the others toward the helicopters.

They lifted off from Benitez International Airport, banked sharply to the east, and flew at top speed over Highway 5 toward the Crowne Plaza.

Greg, Brenda, Libby and Emil were crowded in the lead helo with Yamarie and six other agents. No one spoke.

Greg leaned over and stared out the window. He shook his head in disbelief.

"What do you see?" Emil asked.

"Look at those thousands and thousands of cars that are all gridlocked," Greg said pointing out the window.

Emil looked for a few moments. "What's so strange about them is that they're all white or light colored. Regardless if it's a car, bus or truck, they're all white or light colored. Look," Emil said.

Greg looked again.

"That's because of the warm weather the year around," Yamarie said. "The owners think the vehicles are more comfortable when the sun is reflected off them by the lighter colors."

Greg looked at Yamarie and jabbed the window several times with his pointed finger. "If I were a terrorist, two or three hundred thousand gridlocked and occupied vehicles that had no exit would be an inviting target. That's a no brainer."

The helo pilot veered ninety degrees south and followed Alameda Boulevard, the main divided highway that led to and from the metropolitan area.

Greg looked out the window and saw the bumper-to-bumper lines that did not move.

"Make that an inviting target of about a half million vehicles, and about a million-plus people," he said.

"Do you have an idea or a suggestion?" Yamarie asked. "I'm all ears."

"If you can get me an airplane, I'll fly surveillance over the commuters. I want all the helos armed so they can fly with me just in case I need them to take out a target."

Greg thought for a moment.

"And get a fast helo, a pilot and a UAV technician for Emil," Greg said.

He looked at his old friend. "Emil, you can get a closer look-see at anything I might find that looks suspicious. What do you think, Emil?"

"Count me in. When do we start?"

"We can start right now," Yamarie said. "As OIC, I own the plane and crew that flew you here. I also have eight helos, a Twin-Otter and crews. All of them are now yours, Greg. They'll be fueled and ready to go in fifteen minutes. And I'll send Carpenter Bee, my top tech with Emil. Carpenter Bee has constant communications with the UAV operators and he has laptop visuals of all current intel photos."

"I'll need commo, too," Greg said.

"You'll have all the communications you need and an ear wire that connects directly to me," Yamarie said. "I'm so happy to have all of you on board."

Greg followed the view of Santiago's skyline and saw the metropolis of soaring modern architecture and the massive mountains that towered in the east. It was an amazing land of contrasts, he thought.

The east side of the Andes looked like the Sierra Mountain range in California. And how many terrorists could hide in the Sierra? Greg asked himself.

The helos passed the familiar landmark of the Hyatt Regency and started their approach to the Crowne Plaza. They landed with the usual hard thuds on the rooftop pads.

Armed personnel ran to the helos and hurriedly escorted the passengers into the building, down a wide well-guarded corridor, through a door that was protected by four sentries, and into a large conference room. About 300 armed agents were studying exhibits.

Brenda and Libby glanced around the room and looked at Greg. They saw maps on walls and easels that showed topography and geography. A poster graphed the population of 15 million people who lived in the metropolitan area of Santiago. Large lettering also showed evacuation routes from an area bounded by Puente Alto, La Calera, San Fernando and Quilpue.

Greg looked at a graphic on an easel. In the center of the poster were two pictures and a red circle. He read the words inside the circle. "Osama bin Laden's al-Qaida Cell No. 17, Santiago, Chile. Recent photos of Co-Leader Suspects Julio Padilla and Manuel Fernando."

Brenda and Emil stepped to an easel that displayed a large picture of a strikingly handsome middle-aged man. Brenda could not hide her coy smile as she leaned over, looked at the debonair gentleman and started to read the caption under his picture.

"Drug kingpin of Latin America. More notorious than the

leader of the Medellin cartel in Colombia. Confidante of Osama bin Laden. Arms dealer for international terrorists. Carlos Santiago Dominguez."

Brenda jerked her head away in angst and felt sick to her stomach.

CHAPTER 19

"There are twenty-five damn nice provinces in Chile," the youngish-looking lieutenant colonel said glancing at his navigator, "and only one real ass-hole of a province that's located way up in the armpit of the Andes Mountains. Now, Bart, tell me once again which province I'm suppose to destroy, and what's my ETA?"

First Lieutenant Bart McKelvey's jaws chewed as fast as they could. He molded a wad of gum with his tongue and blew a large pink bubble that exploded and collapsed on his nose.

"It's the Andes foothills that bleed into the Atacama Desert, sir, in the northeast section of Chile, way down there in the deepest part of South America where they don't have any bagels or pink bubble gum, sir. You're ETA, sir, is 1753 hours."

"Goddamn it," Colonel Sanders yelled, "twenty-five damn nice places for us to sit down and have a cold one, but no, we're sent to the only province in Chile that was made in the spittin' image of Fort Irwin, but with the cliffs, caves and ledges of Afghanistan."

"How's that, colonel?" the navigator asked.

"Well, Fort Irwin on the high Mojave Desert in California, and Afghanistan, are exactly like the cliff section of Atacama because there's no escape on foot, but there are plenty of places to hide. Atacama also has terrain features that are very similar to the massive caves, underground tunnels and ledges in the mountainous cliffs of Afghanistan where bin Laden, the Taliban, and the al-Qaida network used to hide their armor, aircraft, biological weapons and missiles."

Lieutenant McKelvey's jaws were motionless. His computer-mind was absorbed in calculating the likelihood of the plane's onboard heat sensors or overhead intel satellites pinpointing which huge, deep cave, ledge or overhanging cliff contained the human scum that they were ordered to blast to hell. He calculated every way he could, but the odds never got any better than 30 percent.

"I'm going to start the clock on our prelim plan of attack," the pilot said. "Go through your routine and remember we'll approach from the southwest, low and fast off the Pacific Ocean, at an altitude of two thousand. The late afternoon sun will be on our tails and in their eyes."

Lieutenant Bart McKelvey spit the bubble gun onto a piece of paper and wadded it into a ball.

"Sir," Lieutenant McKelvey said as he put the ball of gun on the edge of his navigation board, "with an east heading off the pond, I'll build you a self-contained approach just in case. You can share it with the others. It'll save them time, colonel. Give me a few seconds."

"Go ahead, Bart," the colonel said, "everyone knows you're a good bean counter. That's why you're on board."

Lieutenant McKelvey, a New York Long Island native, smiled as he looked at the drawing pinned to the top of his nav board. It showed five new World Trade Center towers where the two were. The center tower was considerably taller than the two on each side of it. He put his right hand on the drawing and positioned his fingers. It was a perfect fit.

He smiled and read the note someone had scribbled on the edge of the drawing. "Well, you hit the World Trade Center, but you missed America."

He bowed his head and said a quick prayer.

It was time for some fast calculations to build the alternate self-contained approach.

He had majored in math at the Air Force Academy, and was

graduated four years ago at the top of his class. A vision problem put him at the nav board instead of behind the stick.

Since they left Hurlburt Field 18 hours ago, Lieutenant McKelvey had calculated three coordinate options for each new flight pattern they received for their original exercise, and he knew that the combat mission they were diverted to had far greater risks than the one they started on.

The five AC-130 Spectre gunships, four MH-53 Pave Low helos and two C-17s full of Fort Bragg soldiers were originally tasked to play aggressors in a mountain training exercise near Latacunga, Ecuador. But while en route to an intermediate stop, task force commander Lieutenant Colonel Sanders received orders from Special Operations Command, South to disengage from the exercise and proceed to La Calera, Chile where his task force would be mid-aired by refuelers for a combat mission.

There was no time for intel or operational briefings or questions.

Lieutenant McKelvey was in his third year at Hurlburt Field's USAF 16th Special Operations Wing. The unit had 12,200 tactical airborne warriors who had honed their antiterrorist combat skills in nations where they had faced enemies that lived and fought in cities.

The Hurlburt commando veterans were experienced in winning an urban war without destroying a city. Their training ran the gamut from distributing diapers and building wells to chasing loose nukes.

Air Force battle scenarios no longer included laying siege to a city or bombing on the massive level that Berlin or Leningrad experienced, because modern tacticians knew those were no longer realistic choices.

A new strategy was needed after the blatant attacks on New York and Washington, D.C.

Air Force battle planners were now tasked with monitoring and invading 54 al-Qaida terrorist cells that were funded and controlled by Osama bin Laden. Most of the cells had access to nuclear weapons, and the technology to launch them.

Hurlburt Field's Special Operations airmen were the top guns at finding and targeting the terrorists' command and support centers, and rather than attacking those targets with waves of dumb bombs, they used guided bombs and missiles. Or, instead of bombs and missiles, they used nonlethal weapons, or engaged information warfare that targeted the enemy's communications and computer systems.

Hurlburt had more than the crème-de-la-crème of street-smart urban airborne warriors. It had a wing of AC-130U Spectre gunships like the one Lieutenant McKelvey navigated. The Spectre carried a price tag of $42 million and featured a mix of high-tech electronics and old-fashioned firepower.

The heavy-lift Spectre is the largest, most powerful and technologically advanced helicopter in the Air Force inventory. It has radar and terrain-following avoidance systems, night and adverse weather equipment, forward-looking infrared sensors, GPS and onboard computers.

The onboard computers were Lt. McKelvey's toys, especially during search and rescue, direct action and other low-level, long-range missions that featured infiltrating, exfiltrating or resupplying special operations forces in "denied" territory.

Each plane contained more than 609,000 lines of sophisticated onboard computer codes to help the 13-man crew aim surgical firepower at targets. The firepower was provided by a 25- millimeter Galling gun that dispensed 1,800 rounds per minute, a huge 105-mm Howitzer with a recoil of more than four feet, a 40-mm cannon and a 50 caliber machine gun.

The combined firepower was devastatingly accurate on ground targets.

The Spectre gunships were supplemented by two squadrons of Pave Low helicopters that had an air speed of 165 MPH, an unlimited range with aerial refueling, and a takeoff weight of 50,000 pounds.

The Pave Lows were the largest and the most sophisticated and technologically advanced helos in the world. Their bulging noses and sides were filled with electronic gear that allowed the helos to fly low and fast at night. Inside the cargo bays were three posts for 50 caliber machine guns.

Hurlburt's combat aircraft formed a double-threat combination that could get real up close and personal with rooftop snipers, shopping mall terrorists, hijackers or seasoned revolutionaries who were not afraid to meet the devil in a conventional or nuclear blast.

The Fort Bragg soldiers in the two C-17s were a different breed of warriors.

Fort Bragg was the headquarters for 11,000 bilingual airborne-ranger Special Forces who couldn't care less where they were sent. Their training did not emphasize the sophisticated high-tech, cluster-fuck tactics the Air Force used.

Soldiers in Special Forces carried short-barreled M-4 rifles that took 5.56-mm ammo fed through a 30-round clip.

The Fort Bragg soldiers didn't care if they fought on Main Street, in a jungle, on a rugged mountain range, on an arid desert, on a glacier, underwater, or on a beachhead. They didn't care what mode of transportation got them to their mission. They were mean and bad. And they knew how to be mean-spirited and bad-tempered enough to mindfuck terrorists with five different languages until they're totally dysfunctional lunatics.

Special Forces soldiers just lived for the thrill of practicing their fine art of being the hammer in the kisser, kicking ass, cutting throats and opening another case of Bud.

Lieutenant McKelvey kept his eyes and hands moving as he reviewed the different forms of intelligence data that came across his board. He monitored the latest satellite photos on his computer screen, scanned new messages, listened to voice recordings electronically dispatched from Fort Huachuca, and read scrambled codes that selected the coordinates for the ground attack.

He knew the rebuilt self-contained approach had to be absolutely perfect because it would be exactly like a precision approach in a big bird aimed at the beginning of a very small runway. Three yards off in width would put the outboard engines in the jungle; ten yards short in length would put the plane in a 400-yard downward spiral to a rocky grave.

With crew chief Scotty Wilson, Lieutenant McKelvey calculated the maximum landing weight on a 48-foot wide approach. They based the data on maximum aircraft gross weight, pressure altitude and temperature, and allotted 2,400 extra gross for casualty and POW body weight.

McKelvey and Wilson completed the self-contained approach and looked through the window. They recognized the mountain perches in the Andes, and the low-level environment of the Amazon basin.

"Lord, have mercy," Wilson said, "that terrain and those little shacks down there look just like where I grew up."

"Where's that?" McKelvey asked.

"Geneva, Alabama."

- - - - - - -

During the past two months, Santiago cell leader Jose Fernando, a seasoned terrorist and early passionate disciple of Osama bin Laden, had spent most of his time on the terrace of his suite in the Hyatt Regency. After his morning ablutions, he would grab his binoculars and step out onto the terrace to survey the dawn.

Perched on the 15th floor, Fernando would train his field glasses on the four sister towers: the Merced and Cathedral looming off to the right, and the Rosa and Agustnas ahead across the cityscape.

Most of his attention had been directed immediately below him; the two contiguous intersections at Highways 5 and 78.

During Monday through Friday work days, a slow moving bumper-to-bumper stream of vehicles filled each of the eight lanes; four southbound in the mornings; four northbound in the afternoons. The same pattern was also true of the four middle express lanes. Merging traffic from Highway 68 onto 5 was often backed-up for nearly three miles on Avenida Vitacura.

Especially during late afternoons, commuters leaving Santiago were snarled on the concrete ribbons where the two intersections were hated by everyone except tow-truck operators who made 7,600 pesos a haul, and ambulance companies that bilked 8,900 pesos for a six minute horizontal ride to an emergency room.

Fernando's data showed that dangerous stretch of highway

handled more than 425,000 vehicles a day and was the site of more than 5,000 traffic accidents a year.

Fernando also knew it was the perfect place for a major chemical explosion that would tie up thousands of vehicles, bring the afternoon commuters to an absolute standstill, gridlock traffic on the expressways, and test the response time – and the number of personnel – for police and fire agencies to handle such a disaster.

Fernando was also thinking about something else. A successful blockage of Highway 68, timed in conjunction with an emergency shutdown at the international airport, would be a masterful stroke of terrorism that would bring the fear of Allah to the 15 million residents of Santiago.

Eight-hundred trained disciples were at their positions and ready to make the ultimate sacrifice for the hero of Islam, Osama bin Laden, and Almighty Allah.

Successful execution of bin Laden's two-phased plan demanded the assassination of the Chilean President, the closure of all banks and financial institutions, and an incremental escalation of disruptions. Within 10 days, total chaos and complete bankruptcy of the Chilean government would occur, followed by the failure of all businesses, commerce, manufacturing and agriculture within two days.

Osama bin Laden decided that was the price that Chile, her people and her economy must pay for supporting Argentina when it decided to ignore the plea from Carlos Santiago Dominguez to find the killers of his family.

Osama bin Laden and his new friend, Carlos Santiago Dominguez, would soon control the fallen dominoes of what were once ten wealthy South America countries. The next step in their scenario was control of the adjacent ten countries in Central America, one of which, Mexico, abutted the world's biggest Israeli-supporter, the United States.

The U. S. would be pulled into the economic downward spiral until it became just another "undeveloped country."

- - - - - -

From his crouched position on the roof of the Park Plaza, another Santiago cell leader, Manuel Padilla, raised his binoculars and swept them slowly and carefully across the panorama stretched out below.

Years of training and bush jungle combat were now over for Padilla, the first Chilean recruited, trained and blessed by Osama bin Laden.

At night, when he could not sleep, Padilla could still hear the words of his El Salvador amigos: "Manuel, you are the best at killing anyone you want."

But they were so dumb and so easily led, Padilla thought, as he continued his surveillance of the cityscape. He knew Granada should not have fallen. He told Castro about the problem. Castro! He had bastards for his inner-circle advisors. They inflated the ranks in Granada with Walter Mittys who thrilled at the notion that they were inside a world of dramatic adventure, of secret missions and dagger-in-the-teeth commando raids, but they had no battle scars. Their concept of a militarist was one who smoked Turkish cigarettes.

They were a strange army of old soldiers, soldiers of nations that were no more, and, some, soldiers of armies that never were.

Granada fell because too many of Castro's people dressed up in uniforms they bought from dealers or collectors of military paraphernalia, affixed badges and decorations they never earned, and mixed with the real thing from North Korea, Afghanistan, Pakistan and Bulgaria, and acted like they would walk into a history book.

The North Koreans and Bulgarians – like the mujahedeen guerrillas in Afghanistan--were lean and hard and dangerous. Castro's advisors put together people who were long on tooth, thick in the gut and soft in the eye.

Padilla glanced at his watch. Three-thirty. He lifted a mike from his belt and held it close to his mouth. "Timing is bueno," he said. "In thirty or forty minutes, the traffic will be perfect."

"Si, Manuel," responded Jose Fernando. "The mercenarios will pay mucho for this plan of yours. I'm sure you will be proud, as I will."

The words were icy in tone and seeped in sarcasm.

Padilla decided against, as he had done so often during the past two months, of showing his hatred for Fernando. There was time for that later.

Jose Fernando had gotten too close to a new girlfriend, Yamarie Delgado. Padilla suspected that she was just too available, too beautiful, too flirtatious and too brazen in her colorful outfits and vogue-fashion jewelry to work at a small book store on Alameda that she professed to own.

Padilla knew she could be dangerous. How does she support herself? Certainly not from the sale of a few books. Who knows her allegiance?

"Keep a close watch for trouble coming from the south, Jose," Padilla said. "It is my blind side. I must know immediately what you see."

"Si, Manuel."

Fernando was perched on top of a utility pole alongside Highway 68. His clothing and equipment, as well as the repair truck parked on the shoulder, gave him the same appearance as several other utility repairmen the motorists barely noticed every day on the highway.

Fernando's forte was not telephone repair. It was something between a dope pusher, a burglar and a fence for hot goods. He had not killed anyone since he left the Caribbean, and had even voiced reservations about being drafted by bin Laden's people to help Manuel with this mission.

Padilla considered Fernando as nervous scum; a half step above that of a book duster on Yamarie's payroll. Padilla also knew that Yamarie was an alarmingly compatible scourge – a somnambulistic avenger who had left her Derringer calling card in many bedrooms: drilling johns who were double-agents through their crotch as well as their forehead.

Even making generous allowances for the revolutionary fervor that seems to motivate her, Padilla found her tough to warm to; a woman who viewed truth in conversation as only a rumor.

Padilla knew it was a CIA retainer who had introduced him to Yamarie Delgado years ago when she worked as a mole in a bistro in El Salvador. She was the parlor star who attracted SRO crowds during her Friday and Saturday night gigs.

Padilla remembered the Victoria Principal look of innocence in Yamarie's face; a face and figure that was now even more desirable.

Every weekend she acted out her role in the bistro as she developed her own kind of special liaison with the Latin-American intelligence community.

But she always rose early on Sundays for mass. Afterward, she made a series of international calls to God only knows.

Padilla wondered why Yamarie was in Chile. Her bookstore was closed every time he drove by it. Each day brought more questions to his mind about Yamarie. But there was time for that later.

Padilla knew he had to concentrate on fulfilling his personal promise to bin Laden.

Manuel Padilla cherished the weeks he had spent in the Afghanistan mountains where he was trained by the left-handed, soft-spoken bin Laden, an expert with small arms weapons.

Manuel remembered the many private hours he had with the deeply devout follower of Allah.

Hours when bin Laden reminisced nostalgically about his education as an engineer, of being the 11th of 52 children sired by a construction magnate, and how he commanded and financed a unit in the Afghan war against the Soviets.

Manuel Padilla learned quickly during his time with bin Laden that money was never an issue or a hurdle.

With ostrich farms in Kenya, forestry in Turkey, diamond trading in Africa, bridge construction in Sudan and agricultural holdings in Tajikistan, Osama bin Laden was a diversified investor with a $350-plus million portfolio.

"Not bad, my friend," Manuel remembered bin Laden saying, "for an exiled Saudi dissident."

- - - - - - - -

Air Force Special Operations MC-130P crews fly Combat Shadows mostly at night so they can use the darkness to conceal their huge airborne helicopter refuelers. Because the darkness veils their presence, they are the quietest airships in Special Ops, and the crews are the most humble because they don't grab headlines compared to fellow Combat Talon crews who fly deep-penetration, nighttime incursions behind enemy lines to unload or retrieve special forces rangers.

The Shadow's "low technology" is a source of pride for pilots like Major Ted "Jake" Kast, the Combat Shadow aircraft commander and task force leader for aerial helicopter refueling operations during the Chile invasion.

Instead of using terrain following and avoidance features to keep from crashing, Major Kast relies on tweaked navigation and weather radars for ground mapping.

As a geology graduate of California State University, San Jose, Major Kast is well within his comfort zone flying a Shadow because nothing about the old aircraft is very complicated. To him, it's a "flying fossil," and he's comfortable with its sturdiness and simplicity.

Major Kast looked out the window at the desert and mountain range features below. He saw mind pictures of almost identical terrain that he flew over in Iraq and Afghanistan. He also knew from pre-flight briefings that thousands of terrorists were forming in the mountainous caves below, and they were armed with automatic weapons, rocket-propelled grenades and Stingers. And, unlike their Afghani and Iraqi brethren in the Middle East, the ones below were more dangerous with their shoulder-mounted weapons because they had GPS-aided NVGs for pinpoint accuracy.

What Major Kast did not know was during this deployment to South America, he and his aircrews would fly 1,334 hours of combat time, pass more than one million gallons of fuel to helicopters, drop 133,000 pounds of cargo, see hundreds of tracers from automatic weapons float through the sky, and see the well-coordinated killing of about 8,500 terrorists – about double the number of innocent lives that perished in the Twin Towers and the Pentagon.

- - - - - - - - - -

As he completed the last directional turn on the flight to La Calera, Lieutenant Col. Sanders patted his stomach, turned to his copilot and said, "Tell the crew chief it's time to bring'em out. We can't fight a war on an empty stomach."

Crew Chief Scotty Wilson stood near the flight deck and heard his commander's order. Wilson knew what "bring'em out" meant and he started to get sick. He reached in his pocket for the nose clamps.

Wilson began his Air Force career as a security policeman but switched to special operations so he could travel and see some of the hot spots. That was 14 years ago. He was now the crew chief with coveted master sergeant stripes and the "top gun" on the command AC-130U Spectre gunship. As the senior NCO, Scotty Wilson was the glue that held together all the gun-crews on the 11 aircraft formation as they advanced toward their objective.

Chief Wilson was always on the short list for any mission that required low-level, long-range, undetected penetration into denied areas, day or night, in adverse weather, for infiltration or exfiltration. He was known throughout Air Force Special Operations as the only active crew chief who had two Silver Stars, three Bronze Stars, two Purple Hearts, and was just damn smarter than all the Curtis LeMays the Air Force ever had.

But Scotty Wilson had never been on a combat mission where millions of lives depended on precision flying, accurate firepower and beating a ticking time-clock to kill international terrorists before they could cause even more civilian fatalities and property damage than they did in New York and Washington.

Wilson had come a long way from his family's pig farm in Geneva, Alabama.

He and his four brothers and three sisters were raised by hard-shell Baptist parents on grits, roast pork, pork spareribs, smoked pork, hocks, country style ribs, pickled pigs' feet, greens, slaw, corn bread, buttermilk, bacon, and, on holidays, a few slices of pecan pie.

What crew chief Scotty Wilson never had as a kid and never wanted as an adult was what Colonel Sanders, the flight mission commander, just ordered when he said, "bring'em out."

Bagels!

Wilson knew that the colonel and the rest of the crew all loved bagels. They craved bagels. They devoured bagels. They lived for bagels. They were known to extend a training mission by thirty or forty minutes if they had some extra bagels to eat.

They splattered all kinds of terribly smelling spreads like lox, scallion, garlic, olive pimento, sun-dried tomato and cheddar cheese on any bagel they grabbed out of the box and split open.

Scotty Wilson didn't know, and cared less, which spread smelled the worst.

They ate jalapeno cheddar bagels, cinnamon, bran, pumpernickel, whole wheat, spinach, egg, poppy, sesame, onion and garlic. Worse of all, Wilson knew, was a bagel they called "everything."

What really irritated Scotty Wilson the most was when crew members splattered garlic spread on a garlic bagel. And they always seem to do it when they had a radar-evasion mission in bad weather when all the hatches and vents had to be closed.

He often thought about transferring back to security police where the standard menu was chili, pizza, ribs, burgers and doughnuts, but he had a need for speed and loved flying in a Spectre gunship.

He had learned long ago to always carry a set of nose clamps.

"Sir," Lieutenant McKelvey said, "we rendezvous with our combat shadow refuellers in three minutes max."

"Very well," Colonel Sanders said. He flipped a switch on his console. "This is Cajun leader. Spread'em out and prepare for tankers.

"We'll do this one by the book. Every second counts. No short cuts. Top'em off because we'll need every ounce. Over."

"Cajun leader," the voice sounded in Colonel Sander's ear, "this is your Chevron gas passer closing in on you this windy afternoon with two pumps at your five o'clock. You're our first customer and we're heavy. We're two thousand above and one minute to ETA. Please advise, sir. Over."

Colonel Sanders balanced his egg bagel with garlic spread carefully in the palm of his left hand. "Roger, Chevron, this is

Cajun leader. Start with the two rear units and work toward me. I'm the point. Over."

Colonel Sanders had been aerial refueled over land and sea hundreds of times during his career. But he and the other flight crews had never been refueled in a mixed formation of two C-17s that carried airborne rangers, four Pave Low helos, and five Spectre gunships in a shifting, gusting head wind that had increased to 34 knots.

Since they were well past the point of no return, he wanted to be on the safe side and have the two C-17s refueled first. They had 300 troops aboard.

When the MP-130P Combat Shadow lead pilot said he had "two pumps" and was "heavy," Colonel Sanders knew the two refueling aircraft were each maxed-out with 155,000 pounds of JP-8 fuel.

Colonel Sanders envied the 9th Special Operations Squadron at Eglin AFB. Instead of ignored pictures of top brass cluttering hallways, the squadron had walls full of honors for being the best gas passers in the world. The MC-130s were also the only refueling aircraft in Special Operations that had in-flight refueling capability as a receiver.

"Sir, the first two are gassed," Lieutenant McKelvey said.

"Very well."

Colonel Sanders worried about the head wind that was gusting and shifting from east-south-east to east, then northeast, then back to east-south-east.

Aerial refueling, he tried to reassure himself, was a routine part of a pilot's life. But his self-talk was not too encouraging.

He started thinking about the wind shifts, the difficulty in locating the terrorists in the cliffs along the shoreline, and the importance of initiating a surprise attack.

He wondered what would happen if the tanker's hosel drogue unit that transferred the JP-8 fuel got stuck or disengaged prematurely because of a swift downdraft.

How about a sudden lateral change in wind direction?

Or, worst of all, he wondered about an air pocket that could drop them like a ton of bricks several hundred feet, then push them skyward in a violent uncontrollable lunge. He forced himself to forget it.

"Sir, they have two left before they get to us," McKelvey advised.

"Very well."

Earthquakes!

He thought of earthquakes in the Pacific, tidal waves, electrical storms that could destroy their communications, tornadoes, wind funnels, severe turbulence and thunderstorms.

When a thunderstorm cell forms, he remembered from flight school and briefings, warm air at the bottom of the cell is sucked up to the top where it cools and rushes back down again. The upward and downward rushes of air create, as his lecturers said, "extreme vertical updrafts and extreme vertical downdrafts of air. Avoid them at all costs."

Colonel Sanders remembered that the Spectre was designed to withstand a gust load of 30 feet per second. The Pave Low helos were designed to withstand a gust load of 35 feet per second.

Oh, what the hell, he thought, when a plane encounters gust loads exceeding the standards, all bets are off. Forget about it.

He did. But only for a few seconds.

The JP-8 fuel, his self-talk continued, could also be a problem.

The two MC-130s were coming in heavy and we're their first mission. That means they have a combined load of 310,000 pounds of fuel. The Navy uses the lower flash point PJ-5 fuel, but the Air Force uses the higher flash point JP-8.

Flash point!

His concern now turned to a fuel fire.

JP-8 has the highest flash of any fuel! If the hosel becomes disengaged and the smallest amount of that high flash point fuel is sucked into one of the helo's 4,330 shaft horsepower engines, well, it's all over.

Wait just a goddamn minute, he told himself. That can't happen because the special hosel drogue unit that's attached to and trails behind the flying hosel has safety probes.

He tried to convince himself, over and over, that there were safety features, and back-up safety features, in all aerial refuelings, even on this once-in-a-lifetime-mission.

This mission will be successful, he told himself

He started to feel better.

His copilot snapped the intake door and the flying hosel connected.

He remembered the urgency of the message that started the mission, and why there was no time for briefings; briefings that would cover every imaginable contingency, including aerial refueling.

But not even a briefer could speak with experience of leading a U.S. combat force into a foreign country to bomb a meeting of international terrorists.

"Sir," Lieutenant McKelvey said, "we're getting our orders from Special Operations Command, South. They're coming in now, sir."

"It's about time, isn't it?" Colonel Sanders growled as the hosel lifted and disappeared.

"This is Cajun leader, Chevron," Colonel Sanders said to his speaker wire, "thanks for the martini. Catch you later."

Colonel Sanders banked hard and headed west-northwest toward the Pacific Ocean.

He remembered when Special Operations ordered him to disengage from the training exercise they were heading to near Latacunga, Ecuador and proceed immediately to Chile.

His new orders were followed by an intel message relayed from Fort Huachuca's cybernetic voice-match center.

Colonel Sanders remembered the voice-match demonstration he saw at the National War University. In a matter of seconds, the center's sophisticated equipment pulled a specific recorded male voice from the millions of recorded conversations stored in its archives and matched it to a person in Peru who was engaged in a telephone conversation with a drug dealer in Colombia.

The Fort Huachuca voice-match center had picked-up conversations from Osama bin Laden cell leaders and other known international terrorists who were attending a celebration in the cliffs of the Atacama Desert. The conversations identified the host for the celebration as an American cell leader, Carlos Santiago Dominguez, who was born and raised in Argentina, and had strong ties with bin Laden.

According to several conversations recorded and analyzed by the voice-match center during the past few months, Carlos Santiago Dominguez was a master at disguise and deception, but intel was able to determine that he had one unmistakable ID; loss of hearing in his right ear. Newer intel revealed that he wore a prosthesis left foot.

The conversations also sounded like the festivity was mandatory for all Osama bin Laden friends, supporters and new recruits so they could bow and thank the Almighty Allah for the glorious victory in New York and Washington, D.C.

"Sir, we've got a hot one this time," Lieutenant McKelvey said as he handed a message to the pilot.

Colonel Sanders read the message with the same interest and attention that he gave to his last promotion order. He swallowed hard and handed it to his copilot. The copilot read the message in a low, calm voice.

"Destroy all attendees. Team en route to disable nuclear weapons. Reinforcements and missile/warhead transports en route. Carrier USS Eisenhower and Battle Group Task Force offshore to assist with operation. UAV robots and satellite scanning in process to detect movement/heat/sound in Atacama Cliffs of Andes Mountains. Will advise. Keep your commo line open to Special Operations Command, South. Attack at will but ASAP. Advise if conventional arms are not sufficient. Order per Sister Bathsheba."

Colonel Sanders rubbed his chin and thought for a moment. "Lieutenant McKelvey," he said.

"Yes, sir."

"Some yahoo by the name of Carlos Santiago Dominguez is supposed to be the host for the terrorists' celebration at the cliffs. Right."

"Yes, sir, that's affirmative."

"Well, Brad, the only known ID for this yahoo is that he's deaf in his right ear and has a false left foot. Right?"

"Yes, sir, that's affirmative, too, sir."

"Well, work on it."

"Work on what, sir?"

"How are you going to ID him?"

Lieutenant McKelvey thought for a moment and looked at the drawing of the five towers on his nav board.

"That's easy, sir. I'll ID him with the crew chief when we dissect the guy's audio membranes during autopsy. I'll go sharpen my knife right now, sir."

"Sounds reasonable to me," the colonel said.

"Brad, put me on audio with the flight decks of our entire formation," Colonel Sanders ordered. "I had better fill them in on what we know."

"Yes, sir," the lieutenant said. "Standby. Three, two, one. You're on, Sir."

"Okay, listen up people, the colonel began. "Looks like we're in for a real battle when we get to the Andes Mountains north of Santiago, Chile. There are hundreds, maybe thousands, of terrorists up there in the caves meeting with their international leader. Hundreds or thousands of other terrorists are convoying in from the east, north and west to join them.

"Our UAVs are circling over the mountains at 80,000 feet and sending back excellent photos of the bad guys. Intel estimates are coming in every ten minutes from Edwards AFB, which is guiding the UAVs.

"This is going to be one of the bloodiest goat ropes you've ever seen. As you know, we are carrying about 300 Army Special Forces with us. But they can't do their job until we do our job. We've got to precision-dump every piece of ordnance we can so our Army guys will have a level playing field. Any questions?"

"Are we getting any backup or support?"

"Yeah, the Navy has the Eisenhower Battle Group in the area, but we can't count on them. I wouldn't depend on the Marine Corps either. So use the john now and strap yourself in real tight. And, by the way, the OIC for this entire operation is Sister Bathsheba. She has nuke capability if we need it. It's almost show time. Out."

- - - - - - - -

Osama bin Laden's South American cell leader, Manuel Padilla, looked again at the traffic below him. The multicolored metallic ribbons of northbound traffic out of Santiago were four lanes wide and gearing down into its usual slow, miserable pace as it neared the airport intersection on Highway 5.

Manuel knew this dangerous stretch of highway was now backed up all the way to the National Congress Building. He released his right hand from the binoculars, wiped his forehead, and ran his fingers around his neck. His stubble was itching and sweaty, but his eyes remained fixed on the nearly 200,000 slow-moving vehicles below.

Manuel had boastfully projected to bin Laden that a deadly, fast-spreading chemical explosion among the vulnerable slow-moving vehicles could easily double, or increase threefold, the victories in New York and Washington, D.C.

Manuel was proud that his communiqué was answered with a congratulatory message from bin Laden's camp in the Sudan. It mentioned the pleasure that it would bring bin Laden if his holy disciples at Atacama could see the smoke in the skies from such a joyous massacre of innocents on the streets of Santiago.

Because of the honor that would come to his cell, Manuel Padilla knew, the timing had to be perfect. The prevailing southeast wind would help carry the smoke from the carnage toward Atacama, 75 miles away.

The blast and devastation, Manuel knew, would forever disrupt the "regular order" as members of the Chilean congress called the mind-numbing, comforting routine of life that Santiago had enjoyed for hundreds of years.

The destruction, Manuel hoped, would serve as a reminder to Osama bin Laden that Manuel Padilla, unlike Jose Fernando, was a disciple worthy of reward and greater challenges.

A way would be found to let bin Laden know that Jose Fernando was pious, studious and reflective, like an Israeli, but that Padilla was boisterous, rambunctious and impulsive, like an Afghan rebel. Fernando strode warily. Padilla strutted. Fernando was nothing more than a centavo-ante gambler and burglar. Padilla was a leader.

Padilla smiled. He knew the blast, heat and radiation from the massive chemical-aided detonation would serve as his calling card for greater triumphs.

A small black box marked "Transmitter" lay at his feet. Several switches were labeled "Brake On," "Brake Off," "Accel," and "Steer." Under a protective red hood was another switch marked "Detonator."

Beside the transmitter box was a radio receiver that monitored communications traffic. The radio frequency scanner bounced back and forth as it picked up conversations from various law enforcement agencies, fire departments, tow truck firms and ambulance companies. Another machine recorded all the sounds.

Manuel suddenly stopped his slow-moving surveillance and focused his binoculars on a large black truck that approached from the north in the left lane, the one closest to the grid locked northbound traffic.

A moment passed. Then two.

Manuel raised his mike. "Aiee, Jose! Here it comes."

Manuel leaned down and turned up the volume on the radio monitor. His hand moved to the transmitter and pushed the button marked "Power."

A contented grin crossed his face as he again focused his binoculars on the black truck that approached, slowly, from about a mile away.

- - - - - -

Greg Robertson was in the right front seat of the cockpit with his eyes glued to power-enhanced binoculars. The sleek, Twin-Otter aircraft made a wide clockwise circle while Greg and the five agents in the cabin looked searchingly through their windows for any activity below that needed a closer look.

Greg shook his head and pointed north.

The pilot climbed out of the turn in a smooth acceleration that increased their air speed from 100 to 150.

"As soon as we approach Highway Five east of the airport,"

Greg told the pilot, "cut back to the slower speed and let's follow that traffic northward."

The pilot gave a thumbs up.

"Emil," Greg said, "we've covered everything south and west. Nothing. I'm going to head north and we'll make clockwise circles over Highway Five. Try and keep that helo real close. Over."

"As slow as you're flying, staying close is no problem," Emil said. "I don't think we're missing anything. It's just that we're not finding anything out of the ordinary."

"Yes, and I doubt we'll get a second chance," Greg said.

"I know," Emil said. "If there's anything down there worth our attention, we won't miss it."

Greg maintained his vigil as the pilot reduced the air speed back to 100 MPH, banked northeast, and settled into a pattern 1000 feet above the grid-locked traffic.

- - - - - --

"Here's another hot one, sir," Lt McKelvey said handing over a paper. "Very well, Brad, read it."

"Sir, it's from Special Forces Command. FYI Cajun leader, all available overhead focused on site. Start heat/sound seekers. First finder advises."

"Okay, people, saddle up," Colonel Sanders ordered. "Our seekers are on and I'm starting our approach."

The colonel craned his neck and looked at McKelvey. "Brad, if we're the first, be prepared to send if we're too busy up here."

"Yes, sir."

- - - - - -

Vice Admiral Jake Culbertson returned the duty officer's salute, stepped off the bridge, ducked his head to clear the hatch and started toward the pilots' briefing room. At 6-2, his steps were evenly measured at 32 inches.

As he walked, he felt the familiar sway off the ship as it began a starboard turn into the mild wind.

The USS Eisenhower Battle Group, under Admiral Culbertson's flag command, would be positioned in seven minutes at mid-horizon only 43.2 miles off the Chile coastline. When the starboard maneuver was completed, the massive floating armada would be directly south of the Atacama Desert that fed into the Andes mountain range.

Forty F/A-18D Hornets were armed and on "hot" status for takeoff. Twenty-five of the ferocious-looking birds carried a conventional variety of laser guided bombs, Maverick missiles, 2000-pound direct attack munitions, rockets and guns.

Two aircraft carried XWW-6 "Little Dog" nuclear bombs, the smallest in the US Navy's inventory but large enough to level mountains, demolish caves and blanket a twenty square mile mountainous or wilderness area with deadly blast, heat and radiation that would linger for at least seven years.

The planes carrying nukes were positioned near the point so they would be the third element launched.

The second element was the Marine Corps Tiltrotor Squadron of MV-22 Ospreys, the plane that takes off and lands like a helicopter and flies like a propeller aircraft. But the Ospreys are unlike any other flying machine.

The Osprey is comparable to the CH-46 in troop capacity, but exceeds the Sea Knight's airspeed, operating ceiling and maximum range. At a top speed of 275 knots, the Osprey can cruise at an altitude of 26,000 feet with a combat radius of 370 nautical miles. It can carry 32 combat passengers, and their ammo, with a loaded weight of 47,500 pounds. And on this mission, the marines in their Ospreys will fly a 50-mile perimeter pattern of the battle site.

Their orders: Kill anything that moves or they detect with their Mini-QuadEye devices that displays symbology over day or night scenes so the marines can discern the smallest human form.

And they had one other high priority mission: Destroy all private planes at airports, and sink every yacht, barge or private vessel at sea ports in Valparaiso, Puerto Montt and Puerto Chacabuco.

The Osprey air crews knew that they must not let the terrorists escape the same way they arrived, and by now the Chilean government had already confiscated all the ships and planes it could handle and had killed or captured some of the crews.

At the point for first launch were five Sea Cobras with laser-designated target capability. The five aircraft also had intelligence liaison hook up with the Global Hawk Unmanned Aerial Vehicles that were circling the target field at 80,000 feet and sending back photographs. The robots' photos showed a massive buildup of terrorists forming in the caves that dotted the mountain range.

The noise level from the pilots' briefing room was its usual low-key rumble as the Navy and Marine Corps aircrews bantered back and forth in anticipation of another long briefing.

The front side door suddenly opened and the crews snapped to attention.

Tall, Jimmy Stewart look-alike Admiral Culbertson, the Navy's most seasoned combat veteran with 34 years of saltwater in his veins and two Navy Crosses in his desk drawer, walked to front and center and paused.

"Seats," he ordered.

He surveyed the Navy and Marine aircrews slowly from left to right, and then moved his line of sight from right to left to get another look.

"Men, you have been briefed on your mission," the Admiral said in a slow, deliberate delivery. "Normally, we brief the flight and then we fly the briefing."

He shook his head. "Not today."

"We're going to deliver over a thousand tons of precision ordnance on enemy targets not only in the caves forty miles northeast of us, but we are going to destroy every living scumbag in the armored convoys now heading toward those caves. Yes, today we are going to smash about eight thousand terrorists."

He paused, turned and pointed at the photograph on the briefing screen behind him.

"This is Carlos Santiago Dominguez, an American citizen who was born in Argentina. Take a good look at him. You already know his background, his strong ties to terrorists, his inventory of nukes and his desire to rule both North and South America.

"But today," the Admiral said with a creased brow, "this bastard will die a thousand deaths. If there ever was a son-of-a-bitch who should have been a still-birth, it's this fart-face."

The Admiral turned away from the photograph, faced his pilots and wiped his chin with the back of his hand.

"Our intel shows about 14 armored convoys of terrorists are now inbound from east, north and west directions and are heading at top speeds to meet thousands of other terrorists who have already gathered in the caves. Those convoys must be stopped and every living scumbag on them or in the caves must be killed."

Admiral Culbertson removed his glasses and rubbed the bridge of his nose.

"You'll have some help on this mission because Air Force Special Operations and some Army Special Forces have offered to help us. But don't count on them. This is a Navy and Marine Corps air operation.

"After you've dumped everything you have, don't dally around and hover. The OIC of this operation has authority to drop nukes. And we have two of them ready for the order. So get back home fast. If we don't drop nukes, I might have to launch another squadron just to make sure nothing is trying to crawl away.

"Quite frankly, I'm more than just a little pissed off at the pencil-necked do-gooders in Washington and around the world who say we can't do anything that might make us look bad. They say we don't want to upset our close friends in Sweden, France, Germany and Mexico. They say our military can't use its force to fight terrorists until all efforts at diplomacy have failed. They want to appoint some focus groups to see which way the cuckoo's nest is leaning.

"Well, screw those assholes and their focus groups. We finally got a decision that I can live with."

He looked at the men.

"Now, there's one other thing about this mission. The leader of it who has nuke authority is code-named Sister Bathsheba. Yes, Bathsheba, a woman. You can bet she's damn smart or she wouldn't be where she is. She's probably a Navy brat. I'll get my orders from her.

"Good luck and God speed."

- - - - - --

Thousands of years of erosion had bored huge cave-like tunnels through the mountain range on the northeast side of the Atacama Desert.

The 268 disciples of Osama bin Laden gawked in amazement as they walked around the damp, odorous cave illuminated by torches and al-Qaida camera lights. The disciples were boisterous as they gestured and discussed how much wider, higher and deeper the cave was than any they had ever seen in the mountains of Afghanistan.

Their host stood on the ledge in front of the cave. As he turned slowly and faced his guests, his hardened face displayed a forced smile that split the chiseled features of a seasoned, manipulative terrorist. He wore a battle dress uniform, a beret, jungle boots with large metal plates on the inside heels, and a double-holster ammo belt with 9-mm ivory-handled pistols.

He held a bullhorn in his left hand, and his right hand balanced a U.S.-made Stinger that rested on his shoulder.

Carlos Santiago Dominguez, the largest arms dealer in the terrorist world, smiled as he looked at the large gathering of al-Qaida customers assembled before him. He raised the bullhorn to his mouth.

"To you, my brothers from our worldwide network, I thank you for accepting my humble invitation.

"Because of the violence we have created, the American President calls us terrorists. We engage in violence because it is only a reaction against an injustice.

"On behalf of Osama bin Laden and the Taliban Priests, I welcome you to Chile."

Shouts of approval erupted. Arms parted and reached skyward as praise to Allah evolved into a thunderous roar.

"My friends," Carlos Santiago Dominguez said stretching his arms for silence, "before I show you many new products including nuclear warheads, conventional weapons, quality anthrax and hundreds of new Stingers, we must wait seven minutes. Only seven minutes. Watch southeast," he said turning and pointing in the direction of the capital city. "You will soon see a victory far greater than we shared in New York and the Pentagon. Look for the smoke."

He glanced over his left shoulder and a rueful grin flashed across his face. He placed the Stinger on the ground.

He moved his right foot sideways and pulled it back with a quick force and slammed it hard against his left prosthesis.

The throng of guests smiled with amused faces as the loud metallic sound reverberated off the walls of the cave.

"Come, come closer," the host begged, "watch for the smoke."

The honored guests moved eagerly to the forward edge of the massive cave.

– – – – – –

"Colonel, look at the monitor!" McKelvey shouted. "We're locked-on. Our sensors have locked on the target. The coordinates are flashing."

"Let's go," the colonel said. "It's payback time."

The Spectres and Pave Lows came in low off the Pacific and started their counter-clock-wise fire pattern.

The bin Laden disciples looked up and saw gunships directly in front of them, and a sky full of heavily-armed circling Navy F-18 Hornets.

Spectre aircrews opened fire with a cluster-fuck barrage of cannons, Gatling guns, Howitzers, machine guns and rockets.

The twirling rotor blades of Pave Low gunships zoomed-in with 50 caliber machine guns blazing.

Eyes widened in fear as the terrorists focused on the eerie sight of fast-approaching USMC Ospreys as they banked in from the north, changed their helicopter flight mode to turboprops, and unleashed a massive dose of munitions. The caves on each side of the huge mountain range crumbled into millions of pieces of rock and human debris. Thundering cracks of explosives echoed back and forth as thousands of terrorists were trapped in the burning caverns.

And in the mesa below, a long convoy of armored vehicles traveled at high speed toward the caves.

"Here comes our support," a voice yelled. "Allah will not forsake us."

"Look. Look there," another voice commanded as a man pointed toward the western sky.

Three Navy Hornets zoomed down and demolished the head and tail vehicles that caused the entire convoy to brake into a grinding, sandstorm halt.

A USAF Special Operations AC-130 broke out of an overhead hovering pattern and started a low-level length-wise approach. At the convoy's midpoint, the massive attack-cargo gunship dropped an enormous object: the MOAB, the 50,000-pound Mother of All Bombs, courtesy of the Eglin Air Force Base Air Armament Center.

The convoy was history.

Carlos Santiago Dominguez looked in horror at his guests. Most of them were killed or were torn apart with mortal wounds. Those still standing were firing pistols at the airplanes.

Blood and body fragments filled the air.

Dominguez grabbed the Stinger, raised it to his shoulder, pointed it toward a helo, punched the forward button and felt the quiver of the seekerhead. The missile screamed its readiness as the sight was elevated and the trigger engaged.

He growled as the rocket looped slightly as it left the tube and deployed its maneuvering fins.

It never flew any farther than fifty feet until it hit a wall of Stinger flares.

The thunderous explosion decapitated Carlos Santiago Dominguez. Shrapnel tore into his body, and burning fragments lodged in his prosthesis. The wood and metal structure of his left foot smoldered, then burst into flames.

The Air Force Spectre-Pave Low combat rotations were joined by Navy Hornets for six deadly aerial cycles until the airborne rangers were called in, and helos were poised in stationary firing positions at each cave.

Within seconds the sky above the mountain was dotted with

chutes as rangers glided down with their rifles pointed at the caves.

It didn't take long.

"Sir," shouted Lieutenant McKelvey, "the light's flashing on the land frequency line. Must be the Rangers' OIC."

"Go ahead, Brad, take it."

Lieutenant McKelvey listened for a couple minutes with an expression of shock. He finally murmured, "Roger," removed his headset and dropped it on his nav board.

"Sir?"

"Yeah, Brad, what is it?"

"Sir, there are enough nukes, missiles, solid fuel, C-4, uranium, plutonium, boosters, launch pads, anthrax and ordnance of everything you can think of down there. The Rangers OIC on the ground said there was no way the USS Eisenhower could hold all of it. He said the inventory could arm an entire Army battle group and there would still be half of it left over."

"That's good," Colonel Sanders said. "Someone like that yahoo with a bad ear and a false leg had to pay for it, and now we own it."

"And, sir, they're just about finished with all the mug shots," McKelvey said. "It took then a little longer because they had to splash ammonia on hundreds of faces to clean'em so the photos would be clear enough to ID. One guy was decapitated and they think they found a head that fits his torso. The headless man also had part of his leg burned off. The Rangers OIC thinks the guy wore a prosthesis. They took several photos of that poor bastard. I just don't understand those Rangers, sir."

Colonel Sanders turned to his copilot.

"We'll just circle for a while. As soon as the Rangers finish their job, and all the photos are taken, the nuke pukes will go in to haul away the inventory. When that's all done, we'll have the helos fire concussion rockets into the caves. I want each end filled with fifteen to twenty feet of boulders and dirt. The caves will be permanent sealed graveyards."

- - - - - -

"Oh, merda," Manuel said as he watched a white eighteen-wheeler squeeze in front of his large black truck.

As the black truck got closer, Manuel's receiver picked up voices from the driver and helper.

"Look here, Pedro," Manuel heard the helper say, "don't let that hombre cut in front of us like that. We're not going to get nowhere in this traffic. Just 'cause he's got eighteen wheels don't make him no king of the whole mudda fuckin' road."

"Armondo, I was just providin' him the courtesy of the highway, us both being professional truck drivers," Pedro said. "I'm the driver on this trip and you wouldn't know 'bout such things. Besides, there's a cop right over there puttin' the eye on us."

Traffic Officer Jesus Cordova was in the left lane of the gridlocked northbound traffic. He had been on duty five hours and had written only three citations. He was overdue for a break, but was stuck just like all the others. He had no where to go. He looked at the black truck and wondered why the driver was going so slowly in the left lane. The truck was on a wide-open southbound freeway that had no traffic.

"Come on, get off that shit, Pedro. Just 'cause that flashy dude gave you the money for this trip don't make you nothin' but a bigger fool. Thirteen thousand pesos just to take a truck and haul some clothes washers and dryers down to south Santiago? In all this traffic? You're lucky to have me help you with it. Especially with all that noise and traffic in the other lanes."

- - - - - -

"What in the hell is that?" Greg asked as he looked at a huge black truck that crept along like a turtle. "Emil, can you see the southbound traffic?"

"Oh, you mean that truck?" Emil asked. "I sure do"

"Can you come up real low on his rear and check it out?"

"We're on our way. Carpenter Bee is receiving some UAV aerial shots right now."

- - - - - -

Armondo wiped his forehead and shook his head.

"I don't know why we had to do this in the worse part of the day, Pedro. After we unload the stuff, we're gonna be stuck in that northbound traffic all the way to the border. Let's stop for a beer."

"We can't. That dude told me to be in the center of the downtown square where the freeways meet on all four sides at four-thirty-five sharp. We're almost there, Armondo."

- - - - - -

"Greg, it's a four-ton International," Emil said. "It looks like a rental. Wait, Carpenter Bee is trying to read the license plate. Well, I'll be damned."

"What?" Greg asked.

"There's no plate."

"It's a rental truck without a license plate?"

"Yeah, Carpenter Bee and I will climb on board and check it out."

"Be careful and call me as soon as you know something."

- - - - - -

"It won't be long now, Armondo. Wait, what's happenin'?"

Manuel Padilla had his hand on the "Brake On" switch as he looked at the approaching truck.

"How would I know, Pedro. You're the driver. Step on it," Armondo commanded.

- - - - - -

Emil and Carpenter Bee hung from the helo until their feet almost touched the truck. They dropped in unison, worked their way to the rear and slid down the back. Emil pulled a screwdriver out of the ring that held the doors closed, and they climbed in.

The odorous smell of wet C-4 explosives was unmistakable.

They examined the cargo and saw several crates labeled for

Whirlpool washers and dryers. They jerked the tops off two crates and looked in.

"Looks like about two hundred pounds of explosives," Emil said.

"Or more and there's about eight crates," Carpenter Bee said.

Taped to the C-4 was a canister marked CHLORINE GAS. It was wired with sensors that stuck out of the sides of the crate. They yanked the tops off the other crates. Each contained C-4 and attachments of either gas or radiation devices, with sensors sticking from the sides.

They went to the back of the truck to get a bearing on where they were.

Carpenter Bee opened his laptop, glared at the screen and pointed to the skyscrapers as the truck entered the downtown area.

Emil made an exaggerated motion with his hands to wave off the helo.

"Greg," he yelled into the phone, "don't come near this truck. It's full of chemical canisters and explosives. We've got to try and get it away from the downtown area."

"Does it have a timer or a detonator?" Greg asked.

"No, we couldn't find any, but we see a lot of sensors."

"Activation by remote control?" Greg asked.

"Yes, but where? We're going to the cab, yank out the driver, turn this thing around and Carpenter Bee will get us out in the country as fast as we can."

"I've got an idea that might work," Greg said. "I'll get back to you." Greg double-clicked the radio frequency.

"Yes, sir," a voice answered.

"Bring the helos in real close," Greg ordered. "I want a static shield around that black truck. I want each helo spaced around the truck in an overlapping rotor circle. You've got to go almost vertical with your rotors on the outside. Be alert because if we're lucky the truck will speed up real soon."

Emil climbed his way along the driver's side of the truck while

Carpenter Bee took the other side. They reached the doors at the same time and yanked them open.

The startled driver yelled, "Who you?"

"Get out. Vamoose," Emil ordered, and jerked Armondo out of the cab.

Pedro did not need any help from Carpenter Bee. Petro leaped out in one fluid motion.

It took two reverse shifts and three forward shifts by Emil to turn the huge truck and get it heading northbound in the center lane of the southbound highway.

The speedometer was at 65 MPH and climbing when the truck with a circling shield of helos and a trailing Twin Otter, passed Traffic Officer Jesus Cordova.

"Do you have a frequency sensor on this thing?" Greg asked the pilot.

"Hell, yes," the pilot said. "What do you want me to do with it?"

"Fix it on that black truck and calculate an azimuth when it gets a hit," Greg said.

"Holy shit," yelled Carpenter Bee as he looked at the UAV images on his screen.

"Emil, there are thousands of terrorists trying to escape. They're all heading east toward the airports and sea ports."

- - - - - -

Yamarie answered her cell phone on the first ring.

She copied grids and coordinates for a location on Highway 68, and the Park Plaza, six blocks away.

While Yamarie led a combat team to the roof of the Park Plaza, and another team headed to Highway 68, a chemical, biological and radiological hazardous recovery unit was airborne to intercept the black truck.

Emil honked the horn and blinked his headlights as he waved off the helos. He steered the big truck off the highway, through a tunnel and onto the La Calera off ramp that led to a wide range that blended into the foothills.

He looked at the gas gauge. "We're running on empty," he said.

"Go ahead a jump," he told Carpenter Bee. "I'll stay a couple minutes before I jump."

"I'll stay," Carpenter Bee said as he hurriedly keyed in data on his laptop.

He felt under his seat and found a hammer and handed it to Emil.

"Brace it on the accelerator for a constant speed of about thirty and we'll jump," Carpenter Bee said.

They were a second too late.

Greg watched as the huge black truck exploded and burst into a massive fireball. Within seconds, everything within a quarter mile of the truck was engulfed in flames.

- - - - - -

Greg saw different dust trails in the southeast and turned the Twin Otter in that direction and ordered the helos to follow.

There were thousands of terrorists in cars and trucks speeding toward LaPaz and the safety of their private jets. Thousands more were heading toward the Port of Cortez and their yachts.

"Yamarie," he said, "thousands are trying to escape. There is only one way we can stop them. Who's nuke qualified to order a drop?"

"I am, she said. "I'm looking at the images now. You're right. There are thousands of them. Carpenter Bee sent me the data."

"Are all of the good guys out of the target area?" Greg asked.

"That is confirmed," Yamarie said. "All air and ground forces are free and clear."

"Take this down," Greg said as he calculated grid coordinates, "you need to order two Little Dog drops, interdicting and overlapping. Each drop must cover at least fifteen square miles.

The center coordinates for east and south drops are six, four, one, niner, five, two."

"I have it," she said. "Are you safe from drops in twenty seconds?" Yamarie asked.

"We'll be safe in ten seconds."

"Stand by."

"We're out of here," Greg ordered.

They were 94 miles away when the thunderous roar erupted.

Within five minutes the northwest wind blew the radiation south toward the antarctic.

- - - - - -

Yamarie, Brenda and Libby stood with somber faces in front of the hanger and waved as Greg's Twin Otter and the helos landed.

After embraces and tears, Yamarie looked at Greg. She sensed something was wrong. She looked at the helos. "Where's Carpenter Bee and Emil?"

"They died in the explosion when they saved Santiago from being destroyed."

"Oh, my God, I am so sorry."

Brenda's eyes showed their shock as tears fell. She turned to Libby. "Let's wait in the plane."

They turned and walked toward the Citation 10.

"What's the latest on the mission?" Greg asked.

"We killed all of them," Yamarie said. "That was a rather ingenious plan you had in the air, Greg. Thanks for your help. The World Bank owes you one. We also got the cell leaders Manuel Padilla and Jose Fernando."

"What about Carlos Santiago Dominguez?" Greg asked.

"Interpol just faxed me some photos of his decapitated corpse, head and all," she said. "Dominguez and about eight thousand others were killed."

Yamarie took a deep breath and released it slowly.

"I'll have my top forensic team start immediately to work the site where Carpenter Bee and Emil died. After DNA results are in, I'll bring them to the states so we'll have proper funerals."

Greg nodded his head.

"Although we share great losses, all in all, it's been a successful mission," she said.

Yamarie smiled for the first time in days.

"We did what we were trained to do. Your help, Greg, was invaluable."

Yamarie's face turned serious.

"I don't have time for hostages," she said.

CHAPTER 20

The sun was shining on an uncommonly warm November morning as the motorcade departed the United States Marine Corps Barracks at Eighth and I Streets in southeast Washington, D. C., turned onto Pennsylvania Avenue, passed the White House, crossed over Memorial Bridge, entered Arlington National Cemetery and finally came to a stop.

General Douglas W. Bradford, Commandant of the United States Marine Corps, was seated in the lead car with Marylizabeth Stevenson Hussey and her escort, Marine Major Mathew K. Henderson.

Marylizabeth watched in absolute silence as the Marine Corps Honor Guard took the flag draped casket from the hearse and place it on a dais beside the grave.

A Marine Battery approached from the west and marched past the Lee House, maneuvered left oblique around Audie Murphy's grave, moved silently down the gentle slope at the Tomb of the Unknown, and formed squad-files around Master Sergeant Bull Hussey's burial site.

Greg and Brenda Robertson, and Brenda's parents, Jeffery and Donna McCormack, were escorted slowly through the formation and took their place directly behind Marylizabeth Hussey and Major Henderson.

Marylizabeth held in her hands the medals and documents that were presented to her at the Marine Barracks. They were the Medal of Honor, awarded posthumously, letters authorizing enrollment at any U. S. Military Academy for Marylizabeth's twin sons who were due in three months, and a check in the amount of $1.5 million.

The Medal of Honor was the result of a reevaluation of combat actions that led to the award of the Navy Cross—an evaluation that led to up-grading the citation to the Medal of Honor, a unanimous recommendation by the USMC general-officer review board.

Major Henderson, a Clemson University accounting and finance alumnus, had eagerly assisted USMC Vice Commandant General Howard K. Preston carry out their boss's order.

The order was: "Whatever our resources are to right these wrongs, I want them doubled. See to it."

USMC Finance Center bean counters at Quantico used Major Henderson's computer program model to electronically siphon the $1.5 million from the CIA Director's contingency account. The account was dedicated to clandestine operations.

Major Henderson, a self-starter with a fertile and inventive mind, knew the contingency account was the only CIA budget line item that was sacred from audit.

- - - - - - - - -

By late afternoon the sky had turned shadowy dark, thunder roared over the Potomac and rain hit hard against the circular drive of the Washington Hilton on Connecticut Avenue.

Inside the Medallion Restaurant, in a corner booth, Major Henderson and Marylizabeth raised their coffee cups in a toast and started planning for their family's future.

End